# TANGLE OF TRUST

## TANGLE OF MAGIC
### BOOK FIVE

## J.E. NEAL

*To my Dad — The guy who remembers gas station setups in the sixties, knows both electro and thermodynamics, and is always ready to help when I need him*

# CONTENTS

## CHAPTER I
# CHRISTMAS

### GARRETT HAYDENSHIRE

Garrett guided Kaimi past the arched, stained glass windows to the back of the old church. The orphanage was cloaked in peaceful, reticent silence. He knocked on the heavy door.

Sister Mary Benita eased it open a crack. A relieved smile formed on her features. "Garrett, it is always good to have you here with us."

"Thanks, Sister. This is my girlfriend, Kaimi."

"It's so nice to meet you," Kaimi whispered. It seemed everyone was still asleep.

"Would you mind if we set the toys up for the kids in the dining hall?" Garrett asked. He was excited to get to play Santa for so many kids.

"They will love that so." Sister Mary Benita gestured them into the largest room in the tiny orphanage.

Despite the fatigue that weighted their energy bands, Garrett and Kaimi set to work setting up displays of toys, books, board games, stuffed animals, loads of Christmas candy, and new clothes.

After artfully arranging several play kitchens and cookware sets, Kaimi beamed. "This is even more fun than Christmas morning when I was a little girl."

Overwhelming, adoring, all-encompassing love filled Garrett's shield. He brushed a kiss across her cheek. "I love you."

"I love you too. I need dolls to put in the high chairs."

"In the big boxes over there." He directed her to the bags and boxes of yet to be unloaded toys.


**Dan Vindico**


Both Dan and Fionna's parents were still irritated about their upcoming move to Hawaii, so Christmas dinner was sure to be fraught with snipes from Dan's mother and glares from Fionna's dad.

Dan lifted a screaming Halia from Fionna's arms as she tried to console her.

"What's wrong, baby girl?" Dan soothed.

Fionna let her eyes close in exhaustion. "She's just frustrated. I don't know why. Just having big feelings this afternoon, I guess."

Dan eased Halia's hand near her mouth, hoping she might soothe herself with her fingers which usually worked. But her mouth turned downward in a pitiful frown, and she sobbed harder.

"Maybe she's a little tired of the hustle and bustle of all of this." Fionna gestured to the Christmas tree, gifts, food, and decorations in general. "Plus the back and forth from Kauai to here. She's off her routine."

Dan swayed his little girl back and forth, trying to soothe her. Fionna laid one of Halia's muslin blankets on Dan's shoulder. Halia grasped it in her fist. Dan formed his shield around his little girl and filled it with calming energy. A few minutes later, she wore herself out and fell asleep in his arms.

Just before Dan was going to try to ease Halia into her crib so he could help Fionna finish getting the food ready, a Taylor Swift song boomed from Aida's room via her brand-new karaoke machine. Halia tensed and then wailed out her displeasure, while Aida serenaded her family at the top of her lungs. Both Dan and Fionna whimpered. Apparently, deafen was one of the volume settings on the karaoke machine they'd purchased.

"Aida, baby, that's too loud. Turn down the volume, please," Fionna called up the stairs.

"What?" Aida shouted from her room.

Fionna rubbed her temples but then summoned and lowered the volume of noise energy in the air around them before she headed up the stairs to rectify the situation.

Dan went back to trying to calm Halia. "I think maybe we'll put the karaoke machine out on the deck at the new house," he explained to Halia who was still highly perturbed about her nap being interrupted. "Shh, shh, it's okay," he tried to reassure her.

He reformed his shield around her and then summoned from the sound waves floating around the living room. He pressed them outside of his shield to create a sound vacuum around them so she couldn't hear anything that was outside his shield.

**Garrett Haydenshire**

"Like this?" A little girl named Eliana moved closer to Kaimi and desperately tried to demonstrate first position which Kaimi had been teaching them for the last ten minutes.

"That's really good!" Kaimi nodded. Eliana beamed as she threw her arms around Kaimi. Her eyes rose to meet Garrett's as she hugged the little girl fiercely.

Garrett had been playing hide and seek with some of the kids, while Kaimi gave a rudimentary dance class to the others. They'd begged her to teach them as soon as Garrett told them that she was a dancer.

"I think you're a princess," Eliana exclaimed as she finally released Kaimi.

"Me too," Garrett agreed as he put his arm around her.

"They're so sweet. I want to move down here and take care of them all." Kaimi grinned as she watched the children explore their new Christmas toys.

"I just signed a contract to become the deputy commander of Hawaiian Iodex, sweetheart, but if you ever decided that you wanted to have kids, there are so many here that could use a mom like I know you would be."

Kaimi stared up at him like somehow he wasn't a complete disappointment, like somehow he was the thing she'd been praying for. Garrett couldn't fathom that.

"Would you really want to do that? I've never even thought about being a mom before I was here. But I could see it with you and with them," she whispered as they gazed out at the little ones in the playroom.

"I'd never thought about adopting any of them except Aida, and I never thought I wanted to be a dad until I met you."

"Okay, but let's get married first. But I really want to keep coming back here with you all the time. This is just amazing. I want to help them as much as we can."

Garrett never thought the orphans would mean so much to anyone but himself and the nuns that cared for them, but he could see the love in Kaimi's eyes. She'd fallen in love with the kids just like he'd fallen head over heels for her.

"We can, but I'll have to fly straight from here to meet Rainer and Dan in London. Fi could get you in DC if you want to go back there, or you could fly from here to Lihue."

"I need to go back home. I'll work on the apartment while you're in London, and I'll come back to DC after you get back."

"If that's what you want."

"I love it here. I feel close to Nana here."

Garrett understood that as well. He nodded his agreement as one of the little boys took off in a headlong sprint toward him. He picked him up and spun him in the air as he laughed delightedly.

# CHAPTER 2

# ROOKIE MISTAKE

## ~DAN VINDICO~

Dan carried a screaming baby Halia to the door to let Meredith and her family in. Aida was still singing random parts of Taylor Swift's greatest hits in succession. Halia was still not a fan of her sister's chosen Christmas afternoon activity.

Olivia raced around Dan's legs and headed up the stairs to Aida's room.

"Santa brought a karaoke machine," Dan explained the onslaught of noise.

Meredith's brow furrowed. "You got her something with a microphone?"

Tim cringed and slapped Dan on the shoulder. "Rookie mistake."

All too soon, Aida and Olivia were belting out duets with the doorbell as their accompaniment. Dan opened the door, desperate to end at least one source of noise. His parents stepped inside followed by Kara and Zach and little Aiden. He didn't seem to care for the noise either and immediately joined Halia's sobbing baby band.

Oliver had been clinging to Meredith's hand, but he seemed to decide it was time to add his own voice to the mix and began shouting, "I sing!" at the top of his lungs.

Fionna's eyes closed in defeat. "Okay, I think we're going to have to put the karaoke machine away for today." She headed up the stairs.

Governor Vindico stared at Dan like he'd lost all of his God-given sense. "You got her something with a microphone?" He shook his head. "Rookie mistake, son."

"I know, I know. She loves to sing," he explained.

"Yes, but children don't really need help with volume amplification." Kara began walking with Aiden trying to soothe him.

Mrs. Vindico's lips were already pursed in annoyance as she balanced a large pot in her hands. The governor was carrying a cake plate. Dan knew whatever was about to be revealed would not improve anyone's mood.

Fionna returned down the stairs with the girls. "Why don't we start getting everything ready to eat. Aida, you and Olivia set the table for me. When Aunt Lindley and Pops and Abuelita get here then we'll eat."

"And then we can put on a show for everyone!" Olivia was ecstatic. Aida's eyes lit in excitement as she nodded.

"And then you can put on a show for everyone." Fionna did a decent job of sounding thrilled about the idea.

"Yes, I need to reheat this Dr Pepper." Mrs. Vindico headed into the kitchen. Dan and Fionna shared a horrified glance.

"Dr Pepper?" Fionna mouthed. Dan squeezed his eyes shut and willed the day to be over with quickly.

"I found this recipe in an older copy of *Women of the Realm*. Fionna, do you have any lemons?" Mrs. Vindico asked as she set the pot on the stove and summoned it on.

"Uh…yes, ma'am." Fionna seemed almost frightened to admit that, but she went to the refrigerator and offered her mother-in-law two lemons.

She didn't take them and looked offended that she was being given them. "I'll need them sliced thinly and put into mugs."

Dan rolled his eyes. "I'll slice them."

"No, you keep holding her," Fionna commanded. Since Halia did seem to be calming down, Dan nodded.

As Fionna pulled out a cutting board, the governor revealed the cake.

Kara scowled as she heated a bottle for Aiden in her hand. "Mom, is that salami on the cake?" she gasped.

"Yes, you just mix a box of white cake mix in with pistachio pudding mix, a few eggs, and heavy cream. Then a container of white icing that you press coconut flakes into. Then you cut salami slices to look like poinsettia leaves and gumdrops for the center of the flowers. *Women of the Realm* says it's the perfect Christmas dessert."

"Yet another thing they are wrong about," Dan spoke through his teeth.

"It took quite a bit of time," Mrs. Vindico huffed as she began stirring the pot of Dr Pepper. "I used half Dr Pepper and half Diet Dr Pepper. That'll save us some calories."

Fionna and Dan both tried not to gag. The syrup appeared to be sticking to the bottom, and the entire kitchen now smelled of burnt sugar and aspartame.

Fionna finished slicing the lemons and added them to a few mugs. She pulled the lasagnas out of the oven and set them on the island. At least something would be delicious.

"Why is that not ham?" Mrs. Vindico demanded as the doorbell rang, and Halia fussed again.

"I told you I was making lasagna. You were supposed to bring a salad. Not…that." Fionna gestured to the Dr Pepper.

"I don't recall you ever saying anything about lasagna. It's Christmas."

"There is not a law that states that you must have ham on Christmas," Dan bellowed as he headed to the door yet again.

"The Dr Pepper goes with ham," Mrs. Vindico shrieked.

"Great. We won't serve that either," Dan came right back. Kara and Meredith bit back laughter.

This time Fionna's parents, Samuel and Gretta, entered. Gretta gave Dan an adoring grin. Unlike Dan's parents, they were both carrying trays and a cake plate, and it all smelled delicious.

"Where would you like the appetizers, Dan, because I need to hold the baby," Gretta informed him.

"She's not in a very good mood," Dan warned as he exchanged Halia for the tray in Gretta's arms.

"That's because you are moving her away," Samuel sneered.

"Not today," Gretta snapped as she swayed Halia back and forth.

Ignoring the quip, Dan set the platter of sweet tamales on the coffee table.

"I know Maylea made lasagna, but she loves sweet tamales so we made her some," Gretta explained. "We can celebrate Christmas from around the world."

"They smell great." Dan helped himself to one.

Samuel headed into the kitchen and set a tray of focaccia and a tres leches cake on the table. Dan's mouth watered.

Fionna grinned. "Thanks, Daddy."

He stared at her, and tears imminently threatened his eyes. Dan tried to think of some way to get her father to admit that Fionna would be better off in Kauai, and that if he'd man up just a little, he could come visit whenever he wanted.

Her dad seemed to forcibly remove all emotion from his features. He stalked to the oven. Dan followed after him to see how this was going to play out.

Mrs. Vindico was ladling burnt Dr Pepper into mugs preprepared with lemon slices.

Samuel's brow furrowed.

"It's uh…"—Fionna grimaced—"warm Dr Pepper."

"Why?"

"I don't really know, Daddy."

"The syrup will separate from the water. This is not to be cooked."

"I know," Fionna whimpered.

The doorbell rang one final time. "Great, Ryan and Lindley are here," Dan huffed as he passed by Kara.

She offered him a sympathetic smile. "Just don't give *her* a microphone."

Dan had to laugh as he opened the door. Ryan fell back into Dan who caught him instinctively. "What the hell?!"

Lindley lifted her lips from Ryan's. She'd apparently had him leaned up against the door. Ryan straightened himself up and gave Dan a nod. "Merry Christmas."

"Okay."

While having his mouth attacked by Dan's sister, Ryan was carrying four small, rectangular wrapped packages. They were all identical. Dan couldn't recall another time in his life when Lindley had gotten anyone anything for Christmas, and the look on Tuttle and Lindley's faces said nothing good was going to come in those packages.

# CHAPTER 3

# TIED UP WITH BOWS

Ryan set the packages under the tree. He wrapped his arm around Lindley's shoulders, and Dan saw something glint in the lights of the tree. He narrowed his eyes.

*Oh fuck.* There on Tuttle's left ring finger was a gold band. Dan studied Lindley's left hand. Her overtly phallic engagement ring was now surrounded by two other diamond bands. Dan's eyes closed in defeat. His mother was going to lose all of her shit and several other people's as well when she realized that Lindley and Ryan were already married. She'd been planning a full Senate affair wedding. It was to be sometime in February. Dan knew she'd already spent a bundle on caterers, dressmakers, flowers, and the venue.

Of course, his mother also had not consulted either Ryan or Lindley on her plans, so unlike Christmases in the past, the inevitable blowup really wasn't going to be Lindley's fault. But Dan had no doubt that she'd revel in their mother's fury.

Kara got Aiden calm, and Zach held him on his shoulder as everyone took a seat at the dining room table. Aida and Olivia were regaling each other with their Christmas morning toy hauls.

Gretta had managed to get Halia to sleep in the relative absence of noise.

"Here, I'll put her in her cradle." Fionna eased Halia from her grandmother. Dan wondered how long that would last. As soon as his mother began shouting, his baby girl wasn't likely to remain asleep.

He followed his wife up the stairs and into the nursery.

"Ryan and Lindley are married," he whispered. He had no idea what Fionna could do about that fact, but he wanted to warn her that the emotions of the afternoon were about to get even worse.

She gently laid a blanket over Halia's legs, nodded, and headed out of the nursery. They stopped in the hallway. "That's why Lindley feels so gleeful, and Ryan feels so nervous."

"They're both wearing rings, so Mom's going to notice soon. My only hope is that she won't make too big of an ass of herself in front of your parents."

Fionna gave him a speculative look. "Between her and my father's anger, this is going to be a long, long day."

"I'm sorry, baby doll." He drew her into his chest and held her tight.

"Let's just go get it over with."

They headed downstairs in time to hear Mrs. Vindico demand that everyone try the Dr Pepper.

Lindley narrowed her eyes defiantly, stood from her chair, went to the kitchen, and made a cold casted cup of ice. Dan knew what was coming. She added some of the Dr Pepper abomination to the iced glass, and took a minute sip. "This tastes like burnt ass."

It was one of the first times in Dan's life that he'd ever wholeheartedly agreed with Lindley. Ryan chuckled, and everyone else braced for impact.

"Aunt Lindley, you're not supposed to say that word," Aida informed her.

Oliver exuberantly exclaimed, "Burnt ass!"

Meredith shot an infuriated glare at Lindley who found the entire thing hysterical.

"Burnt ass!" Oliver continued.

"No sir," Meredith scolded.

"Why?"

"Because that's not a nice word."

"Burnt ass!"

Eventually the lasagna and focaccia bread was served. Since his mother had failed to bring the salad she'd been instructed to bring, the plates did seem a little light.

"I really find it rude to serve a meal with no side dishes," his mother sniped.

Fionna ground her teeth.

"You were supposed to bring the salad, Mom," Meredith reminded her.

"I was never told about a salad, and I was certainly never told we'd be having lasagna."

"It's not that you weren't told. It's that you don't listen," Dan informed his mother.

And of course she ignored him. But in that moment, the governor's eyes narrowed, not on Dan but on Tuttle. He had to have seen the rings. He shot Dan a withering look. Dan nodded his unspoken understanding.

Dinner dragged on with most of the table raving about the lasagna amid his mother's bitching about it not being Christmas dinner and how rude it was not to have a vegetable and fruit with a meal. She was so busy being a pain in the ass she hadn't noticed the rings.

Dan allowed himself to feel a moment of hopefulness. His mother typically only thought of herself. Maybe she wouldn't notice the rings and Lindley would keep her mouth shut. That seemed highly unlikely, but hope was a stubborn thing.

Dan helped Fionna with the dishes and rescued Halia from her cradle. He changed her diaper. She still seemed every bit as frustrated that there were so many people in her house as Dan felt.

Fionna joined him in the nursery. "It's weird Lindley hasn't just gone ahead and thrown this in your mom's face. What is she waiting on?"

"I have no idea, but it can't be good."

They returned downstairs, and Fionna fixed Halia a bottle, while Aida and Olivia handed out gifts.

"There's not a name on this." Aida held up one of the packages that Ryan had carried in.

He smiled at her. "They're all the same. Just give one to each family."

Aida's brow furrowed.

Dan stepped in. "One to Aunt Meredith, one to Aunt Kara, one to me and Mommy, and one to Grandpa and Grandma."

She nodded and completed the task.

"I don't need anymore presents. I already got so many," she explained quietly to Dan as she climbed in his lap.

"I know, sweetheart, but it's okay for people who love you to get you gifts. If you don't want to open them right now, you don't have to though."

Aida considered that while Mrs. Vindico looked set to maim. "She is opening the gifts. Despite whatever dinner that was, it is Christmas."

Aida tucked back into Dan's chest. He went ahead and set his shield over her and shot his mother a warning glare.

When Fionna settled on the couch with Halia, his mother began ordering everyone around. "Now, I read an article in *Women of the Realm* on how to have a meaningful Christmas celebration. So, I decided that this year we'll each go around the room and open gifts one at a time. You should start with ours."

Kara and Fionna shared an eye roll.

"Kara you can go first," Mrs. Vindico encouraged.

With an audible sigh, Kara picked one of the gifts from her parents and pulled off the paper. Zach grimaced, and fury tinged Kara's energy bands red. She flung two books onto the carpet.

"*Women of the Realm* has launched its own publishing imprint, so I took the liberty of getting all of you girls books from them," Mrs. Vindico declared like this was a great gift to humanity.

The books she'd chosen to give Kara included—*Walk Off the Weight: Drop Thirteen Pounds in One Week* and *Save On Groceries*.

Dan shuddered to think what his mother might've chosen for Fionna. Zach put his arm around Kara and began whispering in her ear, but Dan knew that was going to take quite a bit to undo.

Kara was an Occamist and an outstanding cook. It annoyed Mrs. Vindico that people vastly preferred Kara's meals to her own.

"Lindley, why don't you go next." Mrs. Vindico was preening. The rest of the room stared longingly at Dan's shield still pulsing around Aida.

Lindley spared her mother an eye roll, but, to Dan's shock, she did grab the present that matched the one Kara had opened. She pulled the paper off and scowled. "What the fuck is this supposed to mean?" she snarled as she held up two books. One was titled—*Busy Business Boutiques: An Appropriate Woman's Guide to Making Money.* The other was, *Proper Weddings Done Right.*

"Aunt Lindley, you're not supposed—" Aida started, but Dan gently cupped his hand over her mouth and shook his head.

Ryan eased the books from Lindley's grip and laced his fingers through hers.

"Fionna, your turn," Mrs. Vindico commanded.

With a concerned glance to Dan, Fionna stared at her packages. There was one that matched the approximate shape of the ones Kara and Lindley had opened, but there was a smaller box taped to it.

Mrs. Vindico announced, "I decided those went together."

Fionna gave her a begrudged nod. She started with the larger of the two boxes.

Dan clenched his jaw to keep from whimpering aloud.

"It's okay, Daddy," Aida reassured him quietly.

The book Fionna opened had her normally soothing rhythms jagged in an instant. She lifted the book to show Dan. *Ways to Spend Less of Your Husband's Hard-Earned Money.*

"Mother!" Dan roared. "My God. What is wrong with you?"

The governor looked appalled. "Marion, she made at minimum ten times what Dan makes now for almost a decade. Why would you get her that?"

"It goes with the other gift," Mrs. Vindico insisted.

Fionna's eyes were already narrowed into dagger slits. She tore into the other package, but her brow furrowed. "What is this?"

"It's a rechargeable epilator, of course." Mrs. Vindico stared at Fionna like she was obviously the most unintelligent woman in the room.

"What the hell is an epilator?" Dan demanded.

"Daddy…" Aida sighed.

"I think we're going to have to let that rule go for today, Aida," Fionna urged.

Aida shrugged and fell back against Dan in exasperation.

"It's a far more appropriate way to permanently remove hair."

Dan fought the abject desire to throw everyone out of his house. "If it's permanent, why the hell would it need to be rechargeable?"

"We found them at the hardware store, so I took the liberty of getting you one. That will be good for your budget and reputation."

"You got me a hair removal *thing* at a hardware store?" Fionna shook her head.

"They were buy one, get one sixty percent off, so I got all of you girls one."

Kara shook her head. "How good for us all."

Meredith took the box from Fionna's hands and studied it. "Wait a second. I've heard of this company." Her brow knitted for a minute, but then realization lit her eyes. "I supplied the financial documents to the Senate when this company was sued for leaving keloid scars that required a trip to the medio to be healed. The company didn't disclose the information to consumers, and the Auxiliary Department got involved. Do not use this," she commanded her sisters and Fionna.

"Which would explain why they're on sale," Kara sighed.

"I'm certain those people weren't using them properly," Mrs. Vindico scoffed. "They're a much more appropriate way to"—she bristled—"do that kind of grooming."

The Stylers were visibly uncomfortable but didn't seem to know what to say.

Gretta encouraged everyone to open the gifts from them. They were beautiful baskets filled with treats from the Stylers' bakery along with candles.

Eventually the gifts were all opened save the ones from Tuttle and Lindley. Everyone but Mrs. Vindico had noticed the rings. No one had said a word.

"It was so thoughtful of you to bring gifts, Lindley," Mrs. Vindico praised the effort, which was certainly out of the ordinary.

"You should all open them together," Tuttle encouraged with a genuine smile. He looked thrilled.

The governor drew a deep, audible breath and popped the corner of the paper on their gift. Dan followed suit. Aida and Fionna looked on. Slowly, every couple began opening the presents.

Dan decided to get it over with quickly. That way he could assess the incoming damage. But as he ripped the paper away from the framed photograph, he sincerely regretted his decision. He scowled. Fionna's mouth dropped open.

Meredith had gotten the paper off their photo right after Dan.

Olivia giggled. "Why is Aunt Lindley naked?"

Dan handed the photo to Fionna and willed away the desire to vomit.

"Lindley, what is the meaning of this?" Governor Vindico demanded while he turned the frame glass side down on the table near him.

Lindley leapt up out of the armchair. "We're married!"

"You are not married," Mrs. Vindico shrieked. She lifted the photo the governor had tried to hide to reveal Ryan and Lindley posed almost completely bare. Lindley was wearing what appeared to be a very skimpy bikini that was covered in green leaves. Ryan was wearing a leaf-covered Speedo.

Mrs. Vindico spluttered out, "You will not be married until February eighteenth at the Beaumont. Seven p.m. Black-tie. Custom monogrammed napkins. A fourteen-piece orchestra. Bespoke bone china with the Vindico crest. I've hired a local artist to hand paint the ceremony on linen."

"You did what?" the governor roared. "How much did all of that cost?"

Both Halia and Aiden started to cry. Fionna looked like she might join in.

Dan turned to Ryan and Lindley, certain his sister was going to have plenty to say to that, but to his shock they both looked completely stunned.

Ryan shook his head. "What are you talking about, Mama V?"

"Do not call me that!"

Lindley huffed, "Better than what I'd like to call you. What do you mean we're not married?" She pointed to her ring. "We told you we were going to Jamaica last weekend. That's our wedding picture thing."

"You did not tell me you were going anywhere! You are not married."

"Yes, I am!" Lindley defied.

"I'm thinking Lindley *didn't* tell her about Jamaica the same way I *didn't* tell her about the lasagna," Fionna spoke under her breath. Dan was certain she was correct.

"Mrs. Vindico, why would you plan a wedding we didn't know anything about?" Ryan demanded.

"I told you all about it!" she insisted. "The night you got engaged." She gestured to the dining room where the engagement had occurred.

"No, you didn't."

"You are not married. You cannot wear,"—Mrs. Vindico shook her head—"landscaping to a wedding!"

"I can wear whatever I want to *my* wedding," Lindley snarled. She narrowed her eyes. "A bush for my bush."

The entire room cringed, and the babies continued to sob.

"You are getting married February eighteenth at the Beaumont! You are not married!"

Before Lindley could choke her mother, Ryan took her hand, pulled her back down beside him, and then stood. "Mrs. Vindico, just because we wanted our wedding to be fun and not some stiff affair where everyone's in tuxes and uncomfortable doesn't mean that I take my vows to her any less seriously than you take yours to the governor. It was the happiest day of my life. There's nothing wrong with us having a little fun on our terms. You had no right to plan a wedding without even mentioning it to us. I love your daughter, but I love her for who she is. I'm not so sure you do."

Stunned disbelief rocked Dan to the core. He was speechless, and it appeared his father was as well.

Tears were often his mother's weapon of choice when she got called on the carpet, and she employed them readily. "How dare you speak to me that way?"

"Because it was high time somebody said it. We're not like you, and hey, I'm good as long as what you have going on works for you. But Lindley and I work. We're better together than apart. Why can't you just be happy for us?"

The governor drew a deep, steadying breath. "You're right, Ryan, and I'm very happy that you and Lindley found each other. We just weren't aware that you were having the ceremony without her family."

"I get that, but it's our marriage and this is how we wanted to start it."

"I do most certainly love my daughter," Mrs. Vindico huffed.

"Actions speak louder than words, Mom," Dan reminded her before he turned to Ryan. "Congratulations, man. Just take care of her."

"Always. She's my girl," Ryan vowed.

# CHAPTER 4

# SHIELDS AND STORIES

Garrett stood in Galeão Airport with Kaimi pinned between his body and a concrete block pillar, devouring her mouth. She wouldn't relent and go back to DC without him. She'd promised to fly out when he returned home from London, but Garrett just couldn't let her go. He clung to her and kept up his constant kisses and vows of his eternal love.

"God, I just don't want you to go," he grunted as he pulled away for a split second and then leaned back in, hungry for more.

Final boarding call for the Senate flight to Lihue rang from the nearby speaker in Portuguese and then in English.

"I'll come back as soon as you get home," Kaimi breathed the words as she buried her head in his massive shoulder and let him cradle her in his arms.

"I just won't go," he decided instantly. "Dan and Rainer can figure this guy, and Fitz will be there. I'm going home with you."

"No." Kaimi shook her head. "They need your help. You're the shit, remember?" She grinned through her tears.

Garrett laughed and shook his head. "Call me when you get there so I know you're safe, please."

"I will." Kaimi planted another kiss on his lips.

"I love you," he whispered as she pulled away and hoisted her bags on her shoulder.

"I love you too." She waved and raced onto the plane just before they sealed the doors shut.

Garrett watched the plane taxi down the runway. *I'm going to London. I'm finding this fucking moron. I'm talking to Chloe. I'm breaking my lease, and then I'm moving to Kauai. I've been miserable for fucking long enough.*

With that, he slung his bag on his shoulder and stomped to the jetway where his father's jet awaited him.

Eight hours later he awoke covered in salty sweat. His muscles ached from fighting the demons in his sleep. He heard the landing gear descend, and he rubbed his face with his hands. He grabbed his phone and texted her.

You okay, baby?

I miss you

I miss you too. We're landing. Call me when you touch down. I love you.

I love you too.

Garrett's chest was hollow. His heartbeat was distant and faint. It couldn't seem to locate a constant beat. The steadying rhythms his body required were just too far away. His shield was weighted with leaded grief.

He managed to thank Pete for the flight and then traipse dejectedly to the pub just outside of Heathrow where he was to meet Dan and Rainer. It was bustling with Boxing Day revelers.

"Damn, look at that scowl. He's got it bad." Rainer chuckled as he shook his head. "I'll refrain from reminding you how you acted when I looked just like that when Em had to go to Brazil."

"I know, I know. I'm sorry." Garrett sighed.

"I had a feeling this might be the Garrett we got for our little mission." Dan ordered Garrett a beer. "Being a Shield is tough on the best days. Being one without the object of your shield is hell." He shook his head. "Fitz'll be landing in just a minute. Then we can go to the hotel and go over everything."

"Let's just get this done tonight. I've got things I need to do," Garrett spat just before he drew a long sip of the beer that had been sloshed in front of him.

"Yeah, well, I hope one of those things is talking to Chloe. She's been lighting up Fi's phone for the past week wanting to know where you are."

Garrett nodded. He already knew that. He'd blocked her calls and texts from his cell, terrified that Kaimi might see something that would have her freaking and running. The number of times his screen warned him of a blocked incoming call kept him on a razor's edge of terror.

"Yeah, she's my first call when we get back, then I'm heading to Kauai."

"She didn't want to move to DC?" Dan lamented.

"I don't think she knows what she wants. Her grandmother just died. She feels like she has to be there to deal with all of that, and her job is there. I'll just go there and help her get everything settled. I'll go back and forth until we get this shit cleaned up, but if we could speed it up, that'd be fucking awesome."

Dan and Rainer shared a concerned glance as Dan nodded what Garrett supposed was his acceptance of the plans.

After another beer, he loosened up a little, and by the time they'd checked into four hotel rooms at the London Holiday Inn Express, he was even smiling. Kaimi called, and he talked to her as Malie picked her up from the airport and drove her home.

"Okay, I'm gonna get tons of stuff done here, and you go catch a bad guy, and then I'm coming to DC, and I'm meeting you in your bed," she'd informed him with a great deal of sass. Garrett gave her a shuddering growl that had her laughing.

A half hour later, he joined everyone in Dan's room to begin going over the case.

Fitzroy smirked. "I hear you've been caught, my friend. Don't worry. It happens to the best of us, and if you've been caught by a good one, the process is damn near enjoyable."

"Yeah, what was it you said about Fi last Valentine's? Something about her having 'a nut crackin' man catcher' in the, and I quote, 'sweet snatch between her thighs,'" Dan sneered.

Garrett let his head fall in his own defeat.

Rainer laughed. "Oh no, no. I've got one *way* better than that. When Logan and I turned fourteen, and Governor Haydenshire and my dad gave us the, 'Now, boys, I know you have urges' speech, and all the stuff about it being better if you find the one girl you want to spend the rest of your life with, Garrett followed that up with his own informative lecture. It was something along the lines of, if you only have sex with one girl in your life, your dick will shrivel up and fall off because it gets sad."

Dan and Fitz guffawed as Garrett cringed.

"Okay, okay, I was an ass. I admit it. I will give you each a hundred dollars if you promise never ever to tell Kaimi those stories." Garrett brought on more raucous laughter from his friends.

"I think my story is worth more than that, personally," Rainer continued to taunt.

"Could we get on with this, Commander?" Garrett gestured to the files on the bed in front of them.

Dan shot him another goading smirk. "Fine. Here is Mentor Chase Salzman's ID photo from several years ago when he was an employee of Venton Academy. His address here in London is only a few blocks from Oxford Street. Trust me, Venton does not pay well enough for him to live there, so I'm not certain what he's doing now, but he's making good money."

Everyone shared a knowing glance. An entire unearned yearly income of a mentor would certainly give you a nice life if you added it to the income of another profession.

Rainer shook his head. "I'm telling you, though, from what I remember, the guy was kind of nuts. He didn't seem like the embezzling type. He was more cardigan sweaters and standing on a mountainside reading poetry to the wildflowers kind of guy."

"Guy's got no record or anything?" Garrett picked up one of the folders and began flipping through it.

"Nothing, but a lead mentor paycheck is going to an account registered to his name, so he's the next step in figuring out where all of the money is going. Then we figure out the drug tests and the thumb drives, and you're getting lucky with your very own nut-cracking equipped snatch each night, my friend," Dan harassed and rolled his eyes but couldn't quite halt his own laughter.

Fitz slapped Garrett on the back. "According to Dan, the Hawaiian issued models of those are especially difficult to get your rod back out of." He feigned sorrow.

"Believe me, I'm not trying to get it out. She really likes it in there," Garrett assured him, bringing on more groans and eye rolls. "Let's get this done. We're not on anybody's watch, so let's just go in big. Get out of here by tomorrow." Garrett knew the challenge was intriguing. He *was* a cop.

"All right, but nothing any of us are going to be written up about later. Play it cool," Dan warned as they headed out into the foggy streets of London.

The bitter cold seeped into their bones as they sloshed through the waterlogged streets and headed for the Tube station. They shivered slightly as they entered the train headed toward Oxford Station.

"If Logan were here, he'd say we need a theme song." Rainer lamented the absence of his Iodex partner and best friend.

Garrett and Dan leapt. They seemed to both have the very same childhood memory at the same moment.

"Not Trivette," they both chanted as they stared one another down.

"Dude, I am so Chuck Norris it's not even funny," Garrett sneered.

"Whatever, Deputy," Dan teased.

Rainer rolled his eyes. "All right now, boys, maybe you can take turns."

"You're just pissed 'cause you know you're Francis," Garrett harassed.

"I am so not Francis."

"Hey, I'm good, as long as none of you pulls out a pair of sunglasses and starts setting shit on fire for effect," Fitz vowed. He cleared his throat, and in his best David Caruso impersonation from twenty years before, he said, "The question is…deputy…was the mob of marshmallow gun wielding fiends sent as a sticky distraction…or to sweeten the deal?"

Garrett stepped in to provide the guitar peal effect.

Everyone cracked up as Fitzroy then pointed to Dan and Garrett, and in a dramatic change of coastline, hummed out the theme song for *Hawaii Five-0*, complete with air drum accompaniment.

# CHAPTER 5
# IDENTITIES

They quieted down as they exited the Tube and trudged through the crowds of people heading out to pubs for more Boxing Day festivities. The gray mist clung to the darkening skies that faded into the blacktop.

Dan pointed to the street that was lined with mansions. A shrug moved through the ensembled law enforcement officers. If this was where Chase Satzman resided, he was doing rather well for himself.

Dan's brow furrowed as he led the group of men discreetly to 12 Pelham Square. They certainly didn't have a warrant, so winging it was their only option.

They stood on the concrete sidewalk and stared up at a five-story manor home that all of their current abodes would have fit inside of.

"Damn," Garrett gasped.

"Yeah, you still thinking this isn't the guy?" Dan challenged.

"Let's go see." Fitz proceeded to the opulent front door.

With their badges on full display, Fitz raised his fist to knock, but the door flung open before he got the chance. Garrett's arm shot out to knock Rainer away as they all turned in a well-rehearsed move and ducked. Two marble bookends were hurled onto the front steps.

Shields went up instantly as they ducked their heads.

"You're under arrest for attempting to assault International Iodex officers," Fitzroy shouted as they raced into the home.

Suddenly, two badly damaged flannel suitcases were hurled down the stairs in the entryway.

"What the fuck?" Garrett demanded.

A pile of clothes, mostly men's cardigans and wool slacks, landed on top of the suitcases.

Fury lit through Dan as he stared up the marble staircase in rapt disbelief.

He tore upward in a sprint with Garrett on his heels. Rainer and Fitz were right behind them with guns drawn.

Dan grabbed the woman who was set to hurl a stack of well-worn hardback novels out one of the bedroom doors and spun her against the wall.

"You're under arrest." Fitz cuffed her.

"What in the ruddy hell do you suppose you're doing to me?" the woman spat angrily.

"Where is Chase Satzman?" Dan growled.

"How would I know? The useless tosser spends his squid getting bladdered and paying rent boys and hasn't paid me board in months."

"Care to translate that?" Garrett demanded of Fitzroy.

Fitz nodded. "That would be something along the lines of the useless guy spends what little money he has getting drunk and on male prostitutes and hasn't paid rent in months." He turned back to the woman. "I assume this is Mr. Satzman's room, ma'am?"

"Are you thick?" The woman stared at Fitzroy like he didn't have enough sense to come in out of the rain. "Not any longer!" She gestured around the room with her head. All of the belongings were being dispensed with.

Fitz unlocked the cuffs, and Dan backed away from the woman.

"Do you have any idea where Mr. Satzman might be? We need to speak with him." Dan sighed as he glanced around the rather barren room.

"His bum's usually on a stool at O'Dooley's, just down the road, innit? If you sees him, tell him he can take his rubbish and go."

"Thank you, ma'am." They bid their farewells and headed back down the flight of stairs.

A long string of expletives exited Dan's mouth as he looked up O'Dooley's pub on his phone and pointed back to the Tube station.

They entered the pub several minutes later.

"That'd be him." Rainer made the ID instantly. Dan and Garrett shared a dejected expression as they took in a man well in his sixties dressed in woolen slacks and a red cardigan. He had approximately four strands of hair that stretched across his balding head, and he was humming loudly into his beer mug.

"Dude, this never happened to Cordell Walker." Garrett feigned heartbreak and achieved laughter from his cohorts as he took a stool beside Satzman.

"Evening." Garrett nodded to him.

Satzman's eyes were spinning. He braced himself on Garrett's shoulder as he sloshed beer on his jeans.

"*Lo! Where the moon along the sky Sails with her happy destiny,*" Satzman bellowed stupidly. Garrett turned to Dan in utter astonishment.

Dan moved in front of Satzman's face. "Mr. Satzman, sir, could we ask you a few questions?"

"*What is it women do in men require? The lineaments of Gratified Desire.*" Satzman sighed dramatically and then began to weep.

"I told you," Rainer huffed.

Rainer moved to Satzman's other side and tried to lift the man's head from the bar. "Mentor Satzman, do you remember me? I'm Rainer Lawson. I was in your Gifted literature class several years ago. My father was Joseph Lawson."

"*O dearest, dearest boy! my heart For better lore would seldom yearn, Could I but teach, the hundredth part, Of what from thee I learn,*" Satzman cried out as he brought his hand to admire Rainer's face.

The bartender stepped in. "He comes in every night spouting off like that. He arrives off his trolley. Has a tab he'll never pay," the man lamented as he shook his head at Satzman.

"What's he drinking?" Dan asked.

"He can't afford anything but bottom shelf water."

"Does he have a job?" Garrett quizzed.

"Bin dumper at the kipper plant, ain't he?" The man shuddered slightly as Garrett nodded his understanding.

"Shall we." Garrett gestured to a booth in the pub as everyone nodded their agreement. "I will never let Will live this down."

"Who's getting those paychecks, though?" Rainer asked.

"That's what we have to figure out quickly," Dan sighed.

"I'm telling you it's Wilshire. He had to have some way to keep his side piece happy, especially since he got her fired temporarily," Garrett vowed.

"It's not Wilshire. Will chased that lead forever. He checked everything."

The barman moved to their table to take their orders. Everyone but Dan ordered a pint.

"Can I get a decent Scotch? Do not bring me a Johnny Walker, and don't fuck with it," Dan commanded.

"You got it, mate." The bartender seemed to agree with Dan's assessment.

Their drinks arrived and they all ordered standard British fare burgers and fish and chips, which Garrett had to admit were delicious.

They turned back and tried not to laugh as Satzman fell off his stool while heralding, *"Taken from life when life and love were new, The youngest of the martyrs here is lain."* He lay on the floor of the pub. Dan helped him back onto the bar stool.

He returned to the booth and to his Scotch. "I cannot believe I am sitting here when I could be lying in my bed with my wife."

"Aww, I'll snuggle with you, Danny," Fitzroy harassed.

Garrett's phone chirped, and he smiled automatically as he lifted it from his pocket. He'd already texted Kaimi to tell her that they hadn't gotten very far in London and were heading home the next day, but she hadn't responded.

Garrett smiled at her plans.







He positioned himself to the side so that Rainer couldn't see his phone. He certainly wasn't being nosy, but he was seated right beside Garrett.

A minute later, a shot of Kaimi topless with her head turned to the side revealed two surface piercings with tiny, turquoise stones each positioned at the very top of the swells of her breasts. Garrett couldn't halt the shuddering growl that echoed from his lungs as he tried not to drool.

Fitz, Dan, and Rainer all doubled over laughing.

"Haydenshire just got himself the illustrated edition of the story," Fitz teased.

"Try not to lick your phone, man," Rainer harassed.

"Seriously, she is so fucking gorgeous I almost want to show you this," Garrett explained.

"Uh, we're good, thanks." Dan rolled his eyes.



Garrett typed as soon as he remembered how to breathe and formulate sentences.

> :) I will definitely let you finish healing it for me since I can't mess with it other than to put salt water in it for the next twenty-four hours. And I'm glad you like it. Can't wait to see how much!

Garrett's entire body ached for her. His shield throbbed disconcertingly. His lungs begged to breathe in her sweet scent. His hands longed for her silky, olive skin. His blood thirsted for her rhythms. The extreme tightening of his jeans let him know just how badly he needed to bury himself inside of the tight wet perfection of her. That beast in his mind snarled at the cage he'd been trapped in.

> I want you, sweetheart. So damn bad.

He no longer cared about anyone else seated at the table. He just wanted her back in his arms and in his bed.

She texted him another picture of her blowing him a kiss from her bedroom.

> I'm gonna start going through Nana's stuff to see what I can donate. I might go to the beach for a little while with Starren and Trisha but then I'm gonna curl up with Ringo and dream about you.

> I've never wanted to be a stuffed frog so badly in my life.

If he allowed himself a moment to drown out the clinks of the beer mugs, the sliding of stools against the stone floor, and the bellowing laughter of the pub goers, Garrett could hear her adorable giggle in the recesses of his soul.

He and Dan helped Satzman back to their hotel, and Rainer put him up for two weeks before they all retired to their rooms well after midnight in London. Fitzroy canceled his room and took a late flight home.

# CHAPTER 6
# LOST

Garrett was utterly exhausted by the time he fell into his apartment the next day. It was just before lunch. He tossed his bags on his bed and ordered a pizza. He grabbed a beer from the fridge and rubbed his hands over his face, trying to force his mind and body back into the appropriate time zone.

Kaimi had texted him that morning before he'd left London that she was about to go to sleep. Garrett glanced at his watch and mentally counted the hours until she arrived the next day. In a moment that he would never admit having to anyone, he flung the zipper of his suitcase open and grabbed the T-shirt he'd been wearing the last day they'd been in Brazil. It still smelled like her. He inhaled deeply. It was all there. The plumeria peach scent of her mixed with the musk of his cologne. The combination that only came from being together in positions so intimate the memories had Garrett swallowing down his desperate need as his muscles clenched and ached.

A knock sounded on his door, and he grunted as he stood. *'Bout time Louis got a delivery guy with some pep.* He pulled two twenties out of his wallet.

"Oh." His face fell as soon as he opened the door. "Chloe," he sighed. Her eyes were furious and narrowed in hatefully on him.

"Come on in. We need to talk." Garrett supposed now was as good a time as any. He'd been planning on calling her later on and giving her the whole "This time, I'm serious, it's over. Stop calling me" speech over the phone.

"Where the fuck have you been?" she demanded.

"Nice to see you too." Garrett slammed the door behind her. "Listen, I'm serious this time. I'm moving, and there's someone else. We need to end this." He hammered out the first three lines of his speech before she rolled her eyes.

"Whatever. You know there will always be us. And you know you'll be back in town all the time."

"Chloe, listen to me. This time there's somebody else. We're really over."

"Would you just shut up, and let's go have some fun. Talking is not what I want you doing with your lips." She headed toward the bedroom and began unbuttoning her blouse.

Garrett panicked.

"No!" He rushed to her in an effort to prevent her progress.

"We are not having fun anymore. My God, stop undressing," he ordered.

Another knock sounded on the door, and Garrett fought the whimper that threatened to erupt from his lungs.

"Look, you stay dressed, and we'll have pizza. But I am serious. I'm moving soon, and I'm planning on proposing to Kaimi." He grabbed the twenties from the nearby table and flung open the door.

His heart stopped as he stared down at none other than Kaimi.

"Surprise!" She gave him a broad, delighted grin.

"Uh…hey, baby," he managed in a choked whisper. Dread slithered through him just a moment before absolute panic took grip. His shield tried to set within his own muscles. He forced it away. "What are you doing here?" Kaimi looked crestfallen as the words left his lips. "I mean…I'm thrilled you're here. I'm just surprised." He tried desperately to cover his gaffe.

He stepped back to allow her in as his stomach churned violently. His shield vibrated against his skin. He broke out in a cold sweat as he watched Kaimi and Chloe stare each other down. Chloe's blouse was still half unbuttoned.

"This is what you're planning on proposing to?" Chloe spat viciously. "Are you kidding me? Honey, listen." She turned and narrowed her eyes in on Kaimi. "He's been fucking me for the past fifteen years. Me." She gestured to her own very nicely defined curves. "Garrett Haydenshire doesn't settle down for anyone, so I don't know what he's been telling you, but don't believe it." She flung her huge designer handbag back over her shoulder and shoved past Kaimi and Garrett.

Kaimi stared up at Garrett for one endless, heartbreaking moment before tears began flowing down her beautiful face. She shook her head and ran out the door.

"Kaimi!" Garrett shouted as he raced after her. She flew to the stairs, and he almost reached her but she slammed the door in his face. He flung it back open. "I swear we weren't doing anything."

She raced out into a crowd of people. He shoved two guys out of his way trying to get to her. To his horror, she leapt on a bus that was picking up in front of his building at that moment, and she was gone.

"Dammit," he spat as he grabbed his phone and called her cell.

"Kaimi, please," he begged her voicemail. "I'm sorry about her. I was going to tell you. She never meant anything to me. We just…" The call ended on that note. Garrett began running after the bus. If he went to the parking deck and got out his bike or car, he'd never be able to find her. But it turned down the next road and joined a dozen other buses that looked just like it that were heading out of the city. He called her cell constantly for the next hour but had no idea how to find her. He paced and let his shield abuse him. He deserved the burning ache it wielded.

He'd debated calling Portwood and having her cell traced. He tried to decide if that would only scare her more and if he even deserved her in the first place. He hated himself for never having her share her location. Of course, he'd never planned on being anywhere she wasn't.

His cell rang and he answered without checking the ID.

"Kaimi, I'm sorry. I swear we were not doing anything. She never meant anything to me…" erupted from his mouth without thought.

"It's Dan," Dan soothed. "I'm on my way to your apartment. Kaimi called Fi. She tried to change buses in Baltimore, but she's out of money. I told her to wait at the station and that I'd come get her. She asked me not to call you so I'm breaking my word, but you better not have been doing what she told Fionna you were doing." His voice was calm but fury perforated his tone.

"I swear, Chloe showed up at my apartment. She was mad. I told her it was over. She started taking off her clothes. That's when Kaimi showed up." Garrett's voice was hollow and broken. He'd never imagined that the life he'd lived for so long could somehow decimate the one he'd so desperately wanted but that had always been just out of his reach.

"She tried to tell me which station she's at, but she's not all that good with directions, so we're going to have to find her."

"Fine, I'll find her." Garrett choked as he tried to steel his body against tears that threatened imminently. His baby was out in the middle of Maryland, having no idea where she was or how to get back to him or even to get home.

"I didn't tell her that any bus in Baltimore would take her to the airport, so you better hope she doesn't figure that out and find a little money before we get there. I'm in front of your building. Get your ass out here," he ordered.

Fionna was in the passenger seat so Garrett leapt in the middle. Her arms were crossed over her chest, and she was simultaneously scowling and crying.

"You better make this right with both of them," she demanded furiously.

"I can't make it right with Chloe. That's what I was trying to do, and she won't take the end for an answer. But I swear to you I will make this right with Kaimi and then I'm never going to speak to Chloe again. I should have done that a long time ago."

CHAPTER 7

# BROKEN

Dan casted and floored the SUV, and they were in Shipley Hill in under fifteen minutes. Garrett tore through the station, shoving people out of his way, but she wasn't there. He shook his head as he leapt back in, and Dan took off again. They repeated this process to every address Garrett could locate on his phone until they pulled up to a busy station in Glen Burnie.

Garrett frantically sprinted inside and searched face after face as they moved through the blur of his tears.

"Kaimi," he shouted and reached to grasp her shoulder, but the woman that spun to shoot him a scowl wasn't her. He searched on, staring at every person at the expansive ticket counter and at the pay phone booths that were no longer hooked up. Then he saw her, and his heart shattered. She was hunched over, sitting in the corner, staring out a dirty window with tears still pouring down her face.

"Kaimi." He flew to her side. "Baby, please just let me explain. I'm so sorry," he begged. "Please," he couldn't halt the plea.

Fury lit through her like flame through gasoline. Her rhythms tensed violent red, but she shook her head again and turned to stare out the window, refusing to look at him. "You're not even worth it."

"Fine, don't look at me, but please, please just listen to me," he choked out. "Chloe and I were nothing more than cheap momentary thrills that meant nothing more than that one of us was bored for the last fifteen years. There were long periods of time when we didn't see each other at all, but lately we'd been hooking up. I haven't talked to her, seen her, or been with her, since I started talking to you the day I texted you accidentally."

Kaimi's head shot back to his, and she narrowed her eyes hatefully. "Fifteen years never meant anything to you?!" she shrieked out her disbelief.

"I am telling you the absolute truth. I never called her my girlfriend, asked her to be my girlfriend, asked her to be anything more than a girl that is much more interested in what's in my pants that she ever was in me. And yes, that's exactly how I felt about her as well. I told you that I'd had a lot of sex. I never meant to hide anything from you. She showed up at my apartment when I got back from London this morning. I was in the process of telling her never to call me again, that I was moving, and asking you to marry me, when she started undressing."

Kaimi swallowed down her furious emotion the best that she was able.

"I really think I let you play me long enough. I don't believe you. I will find some way out of here, but I don't ever want to see you again. Just leave," she ordered. Garrett's eyes closed for a split second, but he wasn't giving up.

"No," he defied. "No, I will not leave here when the one woman who means more to me than anything in the whole world is sitting here." She stood, and he stood with her. She shoved him with all of her might, but he caught her hands.

"You can hit me, and scream at me, and cuss me out. I don't care. I deserve it all. But I'm not leaving," he vowed again.

"Kaimi." Fionna raced toward them with Dan on her heels.

"I asked you not to bring him," Kaimi shrieked at Dan, and the entire train station was shocked into silence.

"I'm sorry, but I think you need to talk," Dan explained.

"I never told her…" Garrett began again, well aware that an entire station full of people were now listening to his adamant pleas. "I never told her about Cal, or what I did in Brazil, or what happened to me. I never told her anything at all. I never told her that I loved her. I never loved her," he corrected. "I've never told anyone any of that except for you. I never, ever put her in my shield. I couldn't because I can't change what's in my energy, and she would have felt how little I cared. You are the only woman that I have ever held in my shield like that, ever."

"Is that true?" she turned on Fionna.

"Yes." Fionna nodded as she wiped away tears. "He never told her any of that. He really, really loves you. Please believe him," she begged on Garrett's behalf. Dan stepped up next.

"I've been friends with Garrett since we were toddlers. I've seen him go through women for the last twenty years, and I swear to you, I have never seen him really be in love until he met you."

"I've held you in my shield. If I hadn't known that you would feel my love when you were inside of my rhythms, I would never have done that, but I wanted you to feel that because I do love you," Garrett reiterated.

"That's true. He can't hide anything once you're inside of him like that. A Shield's energy is so fierce in keeping everything else out that if you're inside of it, it's like reading their minds," Fionna explained urgently.

"If you'll just please let me try to show you what you mean to me, I swear I will never speak to Chloe Sawyer again because she was such a bitch to you and because I only want you. You and no one else. I'd already blocked her calls as soon as I got to Kauai to take care of you. That's why she just showed up today, because I wouldn't answer her calls or texts. I swear, I had been home less than five minutes when she knocked on my door. Look at my call list. Look at anything at all. I have not spoken to her in weeks." Garrett fished around for his phone to prove his point. "I quit my job for you. I would do anything for you, just please, please give me a chance."

"He didn't call her, Kaimi. I let it slip that they were in London when she called me last night and that they'd be home this afternoon. She was waiting on his car to pull in, I think. Chloe gets like that. She doesn't really want him for herself, but she liked the idea that he was available if she did want him." Fionna explained the parameters of Garrett and Chloe's relationship for as long as he could remember.

"He talked about you all night long last night and then went to his hotel room alone," Dan vowed. "He checked his watch and phone constantly on the flight home this morning. I've never seen him so eager to get home so he could start packing to move to Kauai early to be with you. He was going to try to help me as much as he could this week while you were here and then move with you whenever you wanted to go back home."

Kaimi grabbed Garrett's phone in a moment of spite and read down the list of recent calls. Garrett waited patiently.

"Who's Emily?" she spat viciously.

"My sister," Garrett replied.

"She's with the girls," Fionna added.

"Oh, right." Kaimi seemed to recall meeting Emily and she lost a little of her wrath-fueled fire.

"I never took anyone to Brazil to the orphanage with just me. The Angels have been there to work, and Chloe hated every minute of it. I have never shared my life with anyone but you."

Fi's mouth opened again, but Garrett shook his head. "Just give us a minute," he demanded.

Dan led Fionna to a bench several yards away.

"But she's beautiful." Kaimi's fury dissolved into terror-filled sobs.

"No, sweetheart. She's a bitch with a pretty face. You are beautiful inside and out. Beautiful smile, beautiful eyes, gorgeous body, brilliant mind, and most important, a beautiful soul. And you are all I will ever want or ever need." Garrett took a chance. With a quick prayer, he wrapped his arms around her, and she broke down on his chest.

"Just come to the apartment with me. I'll pack my bags. I'll fly back with you tonight. And I will stay right beside you for the rest of my life for as long as you'll have me. I will be faithful and true to only you, just please. Please don't let my past ruin this. Please, I will do anything." He continued his terrified pleas as he whispered in her ear and swayed her gently in the train station. As a last-ditch effort, Garrett's shield bled from his pores and surrounded her completely. "I am not lying to you."

40

Kaimi lifted her head from Garrett's chest and stared up into his eyes. He never dropped her gaze. "And I will *never* lie to you."

"Is there anyone else that you've been sleeping with for half of your life?" she huffed.

"No, and I don't ever want to sleep with anyone ever again except for you." He kept his shield firmly locked over her. She knew he wasn't lying.

"I'm not marrying you until I can trust you again, and that's really hard for me so it'll be a long time."

"Okay." Garrett couldn't allow the hope he wanted so desperately to feel to flood his rhythms yet. He would do anything to earn back her trust. "I will spend every single day of the rest of my life trying to prove to you that I belong only to you, and you don't ever have to marry me. But that's what I'm going to do from now on no matter what you decide. Please come home with me. I won't touch you or do anything at all that you don't want. I just want to know that you're safe, and I want to prove myself to you."

Kaimi glanced back out the plate glass windows for a long moment. Garrett's heart seized as it refused him the next beat.

"Okay." She broke down in sobs again. Garrett's heart flooded his body with his own life's blood. He was fevered and faint as he clung to her. His shield finally eased and stopped abusing his muscles in punishment for hurting her—the one his shield had sought endlessly, the one he would stop at nothing to protect.

# CHAPTER 8
# FAMILY

"I left after I talked to you this morning," Kaimi explained as she lay on top of Garrett's chest in his bed, wrapped up in one of his T-shirts.

"I was going to call Chloe after I took a nap. I was exhausted. I didn't think she'd just show up here. I wasn't even going to meet with her. I was going to tell her never to call me again. I always knew she wouldn't really go away that quietly, so I was going to tell her and then get a new phone," Garrett tried to reassure her.

"If I wanted to go to your dad and get married right now, would you go?" Kaimi demanded suddenly.

"Yes, right now, let's go." He prayed she wasn't testing him, that she actually wanted to marry him right then, but he knew she didn't.

She did seem somewhat shocked by his vehemence.

"I kind of wanted to get married on Kauai where we met, and I do *not* trust you."

"We could have a ceremony there too. We'll just have the marriage here. I'll call Dad right now. I've never been more serious about anything in my entire life."

"What if I did come live here while you're here and then sign a new contract when Maylea and Dan move?" She continued her test.

"Then I would be so freaking happy I can't even tell you. You could help us with the stuff at Venton, and we could be together all the time. We can figure out how to make this relationship everything we want it to be, and then we could move and work out our life there."

"Garrett." She allowed herself to cling to him for just a moment. The feeling was exquisite.

He cradled her to him, making certain every part of her body touched some part of his. "What, sweetheart?"

"Miss Leialanie is going to close the studio Friday. Her son wants her to move now. He's worried about her health. I'm out of a job." Her body trembled against his.

The sheer toll her life had taken on her broke him thoroughly. He hated that one of the reasons she'd come with him was because she had nowhere else to go. He had to build her a foundation, and he'd done a piss-poor job of that so far.

"It's okay," Garrett whispered. "We'll do whatever you want to do. I'll move and we can live on the farm. I can run Iodex until Dan gets out there, or you can stay here and move in with me. We'll talk about what we want out of the rest of this life and the next one because only one with you isn't enough for me."

She began crying in earnest, and he held her tightly.

"My chest hurts really, really bad," she finally admitted through her tears. Garrett kissed her forehead. She was so pitiful it broke his heart.

"Can I see them, sweetheart, just so I can heal them up for you? I swear I won't touch anything else. Just let me make it stop hurting you. I can't let anything hurt you ever. That would kill me."

In that moment, Kaimi seemed to decide to trust him with this one thing. The weight of the burdens were too much for her to bear alone. She needed him, and Garrett took the opportunity to prove his undying love and faithfulness to her.

She sat up and hesitantly pulled off the T-shirt she was wearing. He'd left the room earlier when she'd changed to try to give her a little space and time to heal.

"Baby," he gasped. The dermal piercings on her chest were enflamed. They practically glowed a bright purple and pink.

"I think they're infected." She started crying again.

"They are. I'm going to heal them up the best I can, and then we're going to call Adeline. We may have to go back to the farm so she can look at them, but she'll call you in some antibiotics." Garrett grimaced. "Shh, it's okay. Come here." He laid her head on his shoulder and his hand just above her right breast to begin healing the piercings around the hole that was supposed to remain. She shivered against him as he began to draw the infection out of her and fill her with soothing calm and his steadfast love. He moved to the left until the fever was gone from it as well.

"Does that feel better?" he whispered. Relief flooded through him when she nodded, and her entire body relaxed in his arms. Adeline was at Georgetown when Garrett called Logan. He phoned Adeline there and explained the problem. She immediately called Kaimi in a prescription and told Garrett that she would come by his apartment in a few minutes since she was taking a late lunch.

She brought by the prescription along with several samples of an ointment and saline that she instructed Kaimi to wash the piercings with morning and night.

"Do you want me to go, sweetheart?" Garrett soothed when Adeline asked to see the piercings to make certain that he'd removed all of the infection.

"No, stay with me, please," Kaimi begged.

Garrett felt rather odd as he watched his sister-in-law examine and touch his girlfriend's breasts. He was so worried about Kaimi he didn't think much beyond the fact that it was odd.

Adeline nodded several times as she studied the piercings.

"Garrett did excellent work," she assured.

Kaimi sighed. "He thinks he's awesome."

"Logan and I were just saying this morning how we'd never seen Garrett in love before. He's kind of like a whole new person. He reminds me of Logan," Adeline stated thoughtfully.

Garrett was honored at the comparison. His brother was a tremendous Shield and an outstanding human being. Kaimi glanced from Adeline to Garrett. He shrugged as he begged her with his eyes to believe what Adeline was saying. "I think if you'd stayed on Kauai, you would have kept healing, but your rhythms are a little fragmented. Do you have other health problems?"

"I was born at twenty-five weeks, so I have problems with my digestive system, my immune system, my lungs, and my reproductive organs," Kaimi supplied dejectedly. "I get sick a lot."

Adeline offered a reassuring smile. "Your rhythms are definitely Kauaian. I know because I worked on Fionna so much, so I think that's probably where you'll always be strongest and healthiest. You broke the connection when you left to come here, and your body stopped healing. Infection probably set in on the plane. The Kauaian rhythms are very healing for Gifted people because of the way the islands were formed. Have you lived there your whole life?"

"No, I grew up on Oahu. I've lived there almost two years now. But I did used to get sick a lot more when I lived in Honolulu, and I got really sick when I lived in New York."

"I'm sure." Adeline didn't sound like she thought that was odd. "I'm going to cast them and heal what I can. If I can't get rid of the infection, we might have to remove them."

"Do we need to go back to Kauai now?" Garrett stepped in.

"I'm hoping she'll be all right as long she takes the antibiotic and uses the ointment. I'd be very gentle around there for the next few days. The infection and all of the traveling you've been doing have worn you out. You could use a good bit of sleep, and if Garrett calls Mrs. Haydenshire, I know she'd make you some of her chicken soup. I swear it can cure anything."

"Done." Garrett decided he would call as soon as Adeline was finished.

"Rest," Adeline urged again, and Kaimi nodded. "Keep it clean, and use the medications. If it doesn't hurt for Garrett to touch there, keep a cool hand on them off and on for a few minutes at a time. That would keep the swelling down until the antibiotics can kill off the infection." She handed Kaimi the shirt of Garrett's she'd been wearing. "Call me if anything gets worse."

"Thank you." Kaimi gave her a weak smile.

"No problem. That's what family is for," Adeline reassured.

# CHAPTER 9

# PRIOR ENGAGEMENTS

Garrett scrubbed his hands and tenderly applied the ointment around the piercings. She was completely exhausted although she had engaged him in several kisses over the last few minutes. He was thrilled but wasn't doing anything with her until she'd slept and had several doses of the penicillin.

He handed her a large glass of water and one of the pills. She swallowed it down, and he cradled her on his chest.

"Go to sleep, baby. I'm right here, and I will *always* be right here." He filled his shield with cooling calm.

"Thank you for taking such good care of me," she whispered.

"I love you, and I love taking care of you."

He settled Kaimi back on his chest, careful not to bump the new piercings.

"I love you too, and my heart wants to trust you. I know you didn't lie to me, but my brain is kind of stubborn."

Garrett chuckled as he kissed the top of her head. "I'll take your heart for now, and I'll just keep working on your brain because I want all of you. I'm the one that screwed up. I should have told you all of the shit with Chloe, and I should have told you I was going to call her and end it for good. Probably should've done that while I was with you last week." He laid out all of the things he wished he could change. They joined the life-long list that tallied in his mind.

"Let's maybe not say her name," Kaimi ordered.

His chest jostled slightly as he laughed again. "Deal. Whatever it takes for you to know that you're it for me."

A deep yawn overtook her, and he brushed his hand tenderly over her face.

"Go to sleep, baby. I'll stay right here with you all afternoon if that's what you want."

"I love you." She seemed to force the words from her lips, but Garrett's entire body flooded with elation. She felt that as well, and it strengthened her plea. "It's kind of like I can't not. It's like I don't have a choice. I don't like that. That's why I kept crying so hard at the bus station because I knew I couldn't stop it, and I was so scared." She finally seemed to puncture the tightly knitted cover she'd tried so hard to keep over her emotions.

"I know. I love you too, sweetheart, so, so much. I don't have a choice either, but I don't need one. You are my choice. I know that I will never deserve your love, but my God, baby, I will spend the rest of my life trying to earn it." Emotion strangled his vow.

"I know you will," she admitted as she clung to him tighter. "I'm sorry I'm so tired."

"We found each other, traveled from Kauai, to DC, to Rio, to London, back to Kauai, back here, then almost lost each other. I'd say exhaustion is probably to be expected at this point."

It was almost five the next time Garrett woke up. Kaimi was shivering with fever again.

"Shh, baby." Garrett wet a washcloth and ran it tenderly over her face. "I think we need to go to Georgetown and let Adeline check you again." He tried not to panic. She was pale and shaking convulsively. Garrett set his shield over her and began lowering her temperature with his rhythms. "Can you draw from me, sweetheart? That will help me get it down faster."

Kaimi gave a weak nod and drew from Garrett's hand. He dropped his shield. Her rhythms were weaker than he'd ever felt them before.

"Adeline Haydenshire, please. It's an emergency," he commanded into his phone as he stood and helped Kaimi dress in sweats and one of his T-shirts.

Adeline was summoned to the phone. "This is Medio Haydenshire."

"It's Garrett. Kaimi's worse, much much worse," he explained frantically.

"Okay, bring her in. I'll meet you in the emergency room."

Kaimi could barely stand on her own. She was dizzy as the fever continued to climb. Garrett half walked her and half carried her into the Highlander and then flew to Georgetown that was only a few miles away. He lifted her into his arms with ease and raced into the emergency room. Adeline was waiting and directed him to a gurney.

"Just take them out," Kaimi urged, but her voice was ragged and weak.

"I don't think we have any choice at this point. Her body can't seem to heal around them." Adeline jerked the curtains shut and had an IV started at a moment's notice. Two nurses began casting Kaimi, drawing the infection out. "Unfortunately, dermal piercings on the chest are notorious for holding infection. I'm going to remove them. We have to make certain this infection doesn't make you septic." Adeline began her work delicately. She lifted her eyes to Garrett. "Logan called me right after you called. I told him what happened. Your dad's on his way from the Senate. Dan and Fionna are heading up as well. Logan and Rainer are coming with the governor, I think."

Kaimi looked completely stunned, but Garrett wasn't. He'd pushed his family away for so long, but he'd always known they would be there when and if he wanted to return.

"I think I'm going to go ahead and admit her on my floor. That way I can make sure that this round of IV antibiotics does the trick. Can Garrett sign the papers for you?" Adeline asked as she made her way out of the curtained-off room and returned with a clipboard loaded down with hospital paperwork.

"Yes." Kaimi's voice sounded slightly stronger, and Garrett allowed himself to breathe as he watched over her obsessively.

"You fill those out while we walk her upstairs," Adeline directed Garrett.

The nurses who'd been casting Kaimi pushed the gurney onto the elevator. Garrett gave her sorrowful glances as he tried to sign his name and fill in Kaimi's birthday while he walked beside her.

"Those are high-powered antibiotics. We're going to leave them in throughout the night. I don't want to mess around with this and have it affecting your mammary glands. That could get very serious very quickly." Adeline pointed to the large bags hanging off the IV pole. She turned to the nurse. "Add a bag of antifungals as well." Then she turned back to Kaimi. "Have you had anything to eat?" she asked, and Garrett felt horrible. He should have fixed her something to eat before their nap. He lambasted himself. Kaimi shook her head, and her hand sought Garrett's.

"I ate on the flight this morning but I haven't had anything else." Kaimi's voice gained fervor the longer the IV dripped and the nurses worked.

"I'm going to go get you something to eat. That will hopefully regulate your rhythms, and I'm going to add a fluid bag because you're dehydrated."

"Are you feeling any better?" Garrett soothed as soon as Adeline went to bring Kaimi some food. "I'm sorry. I should've gotten you to eat." He eased beside her legs on the bed and let the sheer amount of love he had for the woman before him wash through his weary veins.

"I'm okay." Her skin was pale, and her cheeks blazed from the fever. "Do you think your dad will yell at me? I did this to myself."

"Sweetheart, no. Dad is not in the habit of yelling at anyone while they're sick, and he would never yell at you for anything. Me, on the other hand...if he finds out I didn't make you eat, I'll get my ass chewed but not you."

A knock sounded on the already opened door, and Governor Haydenshire poked his head in. "May I come in?"

"Yes, sir." Kaimi tried to sit up in the bed and smooth her rumpled hair from her long slumber.

"Son, are we going to be okay?" Governor Haydenshire offered Kaimi his kind fatherly smile as he patted her shin.

"I think so. Ad's taking care of her."

"Then she's in excellent hands," the governor vowed. "Kaimi, I wanted to ask you first, but I'd really like to give you Crown Governor's privileges while you're in the hospital to make absolutely certain you get Adeline's full attention until we get you well. But in order to do that…"

"We either have to be engaged or married," Garrett concluded for him.

"I'm certainly not suggesting we perform a marriage right here. The papers lack but one of my signatures. I wanted to make sure both of you would be okay with that if it should get out in the press that Garrett is engaged. I hope I'm not making either of you want to run away."

Garrett rarely saw his father so unnerved. He glanced constantly between Garrett and Kaimi.

Adeline joined them. "If I could just add in here that I'm worried your other health concerns could make this more difficult to heal. Sepsis is still a very real possibility at this point. I would really like to be your sole medio just so I can make certain this doesn't get spread and get worse." Adeline slid a tray of chicken tenders and a baked potato under Kaimi's nose.

The governor scowled at the morosely beige tray of food. "Lillian's home making you soup, sweetheart. She'll be up here as soon as it's finished. Tad and Nathan are going to keep the little ones, but I suspect they'll be up here later this evening," he assured Kaimi as if all of Garrett's family coming to check on her would have been expected. "Will's coming by as soon as he gets off work."

"That's so nice. They don't have to do that," Kaimi stammered as she regained enough strength to draw timidly from Garrett's hand. His eyes closed and his breaths quickened as he tried to supply her with his healing strength.

"Let us talk for a minute, okay, Dad?" Garrett urged when she eased the draw.

The governor smiled and nodded. "Of course, and please

understand I'm not trying to push anything on you two. The hospital has a strict policy on that kind of care."

"I understand." Kaimi gave him a weak smile.

"Lillian assured me I wouldn't scare you if I asked. I usually just go with what she says." He chuckled. "Just let me know. And Logan and Rainer are here. Portwood said he'd be up in a little while. If you want one of them to go to your apartment and bring you anything, they can. I expect you'll be staying with her tonight." The governor's assumption was an order, but certainly not one that Garrett needed.

"Nowhere else I'd ever be, Dad. I love her."

Kaimi's beautiful grin spread rapidly across her sallow skin.

"I know, son, and you have no idea how much that means to me and to your mother." He gave Kaimi a kind smile as he patted her hand and then made his exit.

"Please, baby. We don't have to really be engaged, but I need to know you're okay. Adeline is the best damn medio in the whole hospital." Garrett began begging as soon as his father and Adeline left the room.

"Is it bad that the first thing I thought was that I really wanted the press to know and for Chloe to read that we were engaged in the papers?" she admitted sheepishly.

Garrett laughed and brushed a kiss on her forehead. "I can have Fi call her now if you want, and I will get you a ring. But if this makes you uncomfortable and you're not ready for engagement, we can just pull a little white lie until you are ready." He tried to read the emotions in her rhythm streams, but they were still too weak.

"I guess being engaged to one of the Crown Governor's sons is a huge deal."

Garrett nodded. He knew perfectly well the papers would eat it up. His rather wanton ways and the press's obsession with his family had named him the family playboy for years. Him settling down would probably make the front page.

"I think being engaged is always a huge deal and not something we should take lightly, but nothing about being engaged to you scares me. Believe me, with every other woman, the thought of that would've had me bolting."

"This isn't really how I imagined being proposed to. You know, when I was a little girl and imagined stuff like that." She wrinkled her nose and began to pick at the greasy chicken.

"How did you imagine it?" Garrett wanted to make all of her dreams come true.

"I don't know. It's been a long time since I thought about it, but when you were leaned over my car that day and you were so sweet and so freaking good-looking,"—she giggled as Garrett smirked—"I thought about those guys who put the ring in a glass of champagne, and how I would probably choke on it and that I would hate it if a guy did that, but you didn't seem like the champagne sort of guy."

"No champagne glass. I got it. You know Dan and Fionna did actually get engaged here in one of the trauma rooms." He'd watched the entire process, but the tenderness of the moment always made him feel like he shouldn't have been witness to it. The love between them flooded the room, and at the time, it made Garrett uncomfortable.

"I know, but all of that horrible stuff had just happened to them. I would want it to be somewhere that meant something to us. Somewhere we knew we wanted to really be together forever." Garrett nodded as an idea began to take shape.

"Okay, so for now, can we be engaged long enough to get you well? Then when you decide you're ready, I'll take you to the place where I knew beyond a shadow of a doubt that you were all I would ever want."

"I don't know," she fussed with more exuberance this time. "I'm so confused. I don't want to get engaged in a hospital room, but I really don't want your family to lie for me. I've never had so many people willing to take care of me, and I don't want any part of us to be a lie." She spelled out all of her concerns. "Maybe we could really be engaged but not en-ringed or something?" Garrett chuckled at her terminology.

He decided to go on with it. "Kaimi, I love you, and I know this has been crazy fast. But when I see you, my heart damn near breaks out of my rib cage. When you walk in a room, I can't even see anything else. When I touch you, I never want to let you go. When I kiss you, I just never want to stop, and when we make love, my God, baby, you have no idea what that does to me. It's the most astounding thing I've ever felt. For so long, it was like I couldn't breathe. I couldn't think. I was completely consumed by this thing that had me in a chokehold. It wouldn't let me go. And you, I don't know how, but you make me able to breathe again. You made it let go of me. So, will you please, please marry me if I promise never to lie to you, or let you down, and to try to earn your love each and every day for the rest of our lives?"

"Wow." Kaimi's breath panted slightly. "Do you promise, promise, you weren't messing around with her yesterday?" she demanded suddenly.

"I swear to you. I would never lie to you." Garrett held her eyes with his own and then let his shield spin over her again. "Please."

"Okay," she managed before tears flowed and beaded rapidly down her face. "Okay." She nodded again as Garrett's entire life drew taut into that perfect moment. "But we still have a lot of work to do."

Garrett wiped away her tears as he nodded. "I know. I swear I will be the husband you need and deserve. I have several really good examples."

"You better."

# CHAPTER 10

# TENDER LOVING CARE

Garrett informed his father that he could sign the papers and then returned to Kaimi's side. He'd urged the governor to try to be discreet but assumed that would be a fruitless effort. The fact that the Crown Governor was at Georgetown already had the press thirsty for more.

Adeline checked on Kaimi constantly. Garrett gave a list to Logan and Rainer of things to bring from his apartment. Fionna and Emily sat in the room with Kaimi and tried to keep her mind off the pain in her hand from the IV and in her chest from the removed piercings.

There were several discussions Garrett wished he didn't have to hear about what the women had named their tits or their *girls* as they referred to them. Kaimi blushed and never admitted her names though Emily and Fionna did readily. Adeline giggled and after a little coaxing admitted that Logan had named hers though she wouldn't tell either. Garrett shook his head and finally stepped in.

"Why don't you talk about anything else, and then later I'll make Kaimi's feel better, not that you want to hear about that any more than I want to hear this conversation."

Kaimi cracked up and beamed at him as she reached his hand.

Mrs. Haydenshire rushed into the room a little while later with the old red and white flip-top cooler that would forever be an indelible mark on Garrett's mind from his childhood. It served them on every camping trip, every vacation, and every picnic. Ever since his mother had discovered that her chilling casts held longer in that particular insulated container, it had been readily employed.

"Are you feeling any better, sweetheart?" Mrs. Haydenshire was blinking back tears. Garrett couldn't quite hide his grin. His mom already thought of Kaimi as one of her own, and it physically wounded her for one of her children to be hurt. *Everyone should have a mom like that.* He tried and failed to swallow back the guilt that flooded his rhythms when he thought of the pain his previous life had caused the woman who'd given him birth.

"I feel a little better, but I hate that you went to all of this trouble." Kaimi shuddered slightly, not certain how to accept the sudden onslaught of love.

"If you make one of my children smile the way I saw my son smiling the other night at dinner, when I haven't seen him look that happy in years, you get extra special treatment." Mrs. Haydenshire pulled out one of the many Styrofoam bowls she packed, poured a bowl of soup, heated it with her hand, and then handed it to Garrett. "I made you grilled ham and cheese, Garrett, and Kaimi I did you a few with just cheese whenever you're ready for that."

His mom's grilled ham and cheese sandwiches were one of his favorites.

Garrett placed the bowl on the table in front of Kaimi and took the plastic spoon his mother offered him. Then he pulled his mom into his embrace. "Thank you."

She squeezed him tight. "That's what moms are for."

"Yeah, but you're the best."

She chuckled and directed Garrett to the bowl of soup for Kaimi.

Garrett picked up the spoon to feed her. "I can do it," Kaimi fussed.

"Let him feed you, and Fi and I will tell you all about what being the object of a Shield's occasionally obsessive love means for you," Emily teased. Kaimi settled back as Garrett fed her the soup.

"Which is wonderful," Fionna vowed. "But it can get a little intense on occasion."

"It *is* wonderful," Emily assured her. "But I just thought you might

56

want a crash course in how my big brother, who has finally fallen in love, is going to act for the next two weeks after he gets you home from here. He'll check on you constantly."

"He won't even sleep," Fionna joined in as Garrett brought the spoon to Kaimi's mouth.

"I will sleep as long as she's on me, and I can check on her constantly," Garrett mocked. Kaimi looked very pleased with the thought, and Garrett winked at her.

"Oh, and if you get up to pee, he will follow after you," Fionna added with a slight chuckle that said she adored her occasionally overbearing husband.

"Do you know what kinds of things could happen while you stumble to the bathroom in the dark?" Garrett scoffed. "You could trip. You could fall. You could walk into something. You could stub your toe. There might be some masked gunman just waiting on my baby to have to pee," Garrett continued to harass as Kaimi was giggling and eating with vigor.

Fionna beamed. "He'll try to carry you pretty much everywhere because once a Shield senses that you're hurt, they'll worry that walking is too much for you."

Emily nodded. "But it's because he loves you so much."

"That is definitely it," Garrett agreed as Kaimi took a sip of water from a massive water bottle Adeline had supplied her with.

Adeline returned to check on Kaimi, and Emily explained, "We were just trying to help prepare Kaimi for life with an Ioses Shield."

Adeline grinned. "It still dumbfounds me how much Logan loves me, and how he's always so worried about me. Sometimes he comes and picks me up from work and then drives me back the next day because he doesn't want me driving while I'm tired. Nobody has ever taken care of me the way he does."

"Did you pay them for all of this publicity?" Kaimi laughed as Garrett handed her a napkin.

"No, but maybe I should."

Logan knocked on the door just then and carried in a very misshapen gym bag.

"Dude, tell me you did not pack our stuff in that," Garrett pled.

"It was all I could find."

"Her luggage is lying on the floor, and that's my gym bag." Garrett began unpacking the items he'd asked Logan and Rainer to pick up from the apartment. He stacked T-shirts for both him and Kaimi along with a pair of Kaimi's jeans and the pillow she'd been sleeping on in his bed. He pulled Ringo out and handed it to her.

"Hopefully he doesn't smell like my gym shorts." Garrett rolled his eyes at his little brother.

"You're welcome, by the way," Logan huffed.

"Aww, you told him to bring me Ringo." Kaimi looked like she might cry as she took Ringo tenderly into her hands.

"See, this is why Shields are the best, best, best, *best* guys," Fionna vowed.

"I take great offense to that, Mrs. Vindico," Governor Haydenshire teased as he joined the crowd in Kaimi's large hospital room.

Everyone laughed as Mrs. Haydenshire shook her head.

"The press has arrived in droves, eager to know the girl who stole your heart, son, and they'd love to know why she's a patient." The governor sighed. "I'm sorry the leak at Georgetown continues, it seems."

Garrett didn't comment on Kaimi's excited grin that she was trying desperately to hide. He found her failure of the task adorable.

"We're going to let the soup settle for several minutes, and then we need to bathe the area and let me examine it again." Adeline urged everyone politely to leave. Garrett's friends and family got the message and headed to the waiting room.

"Garrett can do the saline bath, or I can have a nurse do it," Adeline offered.

Garrett raised his eyebrows. He wasn't pushing anything on her. He would take everything else at her pace.

"You do it, please."

"Just tell me what needs to be done." He was thrilled to be able to show her that he would always take care of her.

Adeline provided him with a plastic wash basin, Epsom salt tablets, bottled water, and several washcloths.

"Clean the holes with salt water and then put this on them." She handed Garrett another tube of ointment. "I'll check them in a half hour. Logan and I are going to go eat, but then I'll be right back.

"I'll take care of her."

"Yeah, I know." Adeline's brief statement showed the depth and clarity of her soul and reflected the changes in Garrett's. She moved to the large picture windows and lowered the shades with a sigh. "Guess we'll be playing dodge the reporter." Garrett and Kaimi chuckled at Emily's coined phrase for the many ways the Haydenshire children had come up with to avoid the press.

"You can tell them we're engaged. I want it to be real," Kaimi whispered as she kept her eyes locked on Garrett's.

"Me too." His muscles vibrated in his elated need to tell the world she was his.

Adeline closed the door and lowered the blaring fluorescent lights in the room.

"Okay, sweetheart, how do you want to do this?" Garrett rolled the table with all of the bathing items to the bed and seated himself beside her.

"Mrs. Kaimi Haydenshire." She grinned. "Garrett and Kaimi Haydenshire."

"That sounds really good to me."

"You'll never cheat on me?" Fear and panic crept back in.

"Never, ever, and if it helps, if I did, trust me, my father, Dan, and all seven of my brothers would beat the shit out of me. I don't even want to think about what Emily and Fionna would do, but there would be fire and explosives involved, and no one would ever find my body."

"I do kind of like that," she admitted with another laugh.

Garrett shook his head at her. He poured the water in the basin and dropped in the salt tablets. "Would you come here?" He eased her forward and carefully untied the hospital gown.

"Warm water or cool water?" he asked but wasn't quite able to look her in the eye with her breasts on full display. Her nipples were pulled taut from being exposed, and Garrett longed to suck them and bring her relief.

"Warm," Kaimi insisted with a slight shiver. "Cold nips make me want to cry."

Garrett warmed the water in the basin with his hand. "I'll warm them up for you, sweetheart. I can't let my baby cry." He winked at her again, mostly because her energy trilled in delight every time he did it. He dipped one of the washcloths in the salty water and wrung it out.

"Tell me if anything hurts."

Kaimi positioned a towel at her waist to keep her lap dry. Her muscles tensed as Garrett tenderly patted around the holes.

"That feels good," she whispered, and Garrett fought the hardening in his jeans over which he seemed to have no control. Her eyes were locked on his with that deliciously curious, hungry stare.

"God, baby, don't look at me like that. It's taking everything I have to keep my hands off of you." The water beaded and trickled over her nipples, and Garrett moaned. Kaimi, however, looked completely delighted as she began to really understand the power she held over him.

"I want to kiss you." The voracious storm in her eyes began its luscious churns. Unable to tell her no, Garrett simply nodded as his strength and stubbornness washed from his body. He set the cloth back in the basin and edged closer. His shield sought her in earnest.

"I love you and I cannot wait to make you my wife," he whispered as their breaths mingled in the moment between them. She nodded as she stared up at him. Their energy danced in heated desperation to be joined. His shield seemed to believe it could heal her far better than anything else.

Her tender, wild spirit urged him on. He brushed her cheek with his thumb, as her fingers laced through his hair. Garrett growled just before he parted her lips with his tongue and crushed her mouth to his. He tried to be gentle, but the only thing that made sense to him in that moment was to consume more of her. He'd never get enough. His hand lightly caressed the swollen bottom curve of her left breast, and she drew a quick breath.

"I'm sorry." He jerked his hand away as he began lambasting himself again.

"No, it felt amazing. Please." She lifted his hand back to her breast, and a thundering groan seared through him as he touched her so gently their skin barely connected, but their energy was so frantic to be joined it danced between his finger and her breast.

She panted as he turned his head to the other side and flooded his energy through her mouth until she was inhaling it, letting it reassure her and make her well. Garrett pulled away after a long moment and forced himself to breathe.

"I need to finish your bath," he gently reminded her.

Kaimi sighed out her disappointment. "Tutu says I need to take baths every day, and that if I put the stuff in there she gives me that it will help me to heal. But you know I can't be healed…right?" Deep concern was evident in her tone.

"Sweetheart, I love you just the way you are. I wouldn't change anything about you, and believe me, I do understand the medios looking at you with that canned devastation and telling you nothing can be done." He despised the pity the medios at the aid center and the one he'd visited in New York had offered him.

"Yeah, I really hate that too." She nodded as their understanding of each other deepened even more. "They used to talk to my nana about me like I wasn't even in the room." She seemed to revel in the sensations from Garrett's tender care of her piercings.

He was relieved they were no longer red and swollen and that he no longer felt infection in them. The holes looked like they were healing up. "I wanted to scream. I just wanted them to stop talking about everything that was wrong with me and all of the stuff that could happen to me later because of it. They'd say things like, 'She'll never be right, and it could get worse as she ages.' I wanted to scream, 'I'm right here and I'm fine.'" Her irritation grew the longer she talked. "But Adeline is really nice, and she doesn't make me feel like I'm defective, you know?" She urged out the heartfelt desperation for Garrett to understand her.

"I think you're absolutely incredible, and I'd say I know a hell of a lot more about what you can do with that phenomenal body than any medio. And Adeline is awesome. My little brother did a hell of a job. No one else would even talk to her, but Lo saw her, and he was done for. Turns out much to the fury of all of his moronic classmates at the academy that treated her like shit, my baby brother was marrying a princess."

"I know. That news made it all the way to Kauai. They kept saying things like your dad was trying to gain favor with the Australian Royal Family, and I was like it says right here Logan didn't know she was a princess until after he'd been dating her forever and had married her."

"So, you know what kind of shit you could be getting yourself into when we get married then."

"I'm definitely not a princess, so they couldn't possibly be all that interested in me."

Garrett finished washing Kaimi's wounds and shook his head. "You're my princess, and just wait 'til you see the papers tomorrow." He dried his hands and then squirted the ointment on his fingers. "You ready?"

Kaimi nodded though she was trying not to pout. The ointment stung, and Garrett hated that he had to put it on her at all, but her fever and misery had to be vanquished. He gently rubbed his index finger around each of the holes.

Kaimi tensed but then relaxed as soon as Garrett began sending soothing rhythms through her chest. She sighed contentedly.

"Thank you for taking care of me." She grinned up at him.

"I told you that's my job." He kissed her forehead. She pulled the gown back up and he tied it for her.

# OUTRANKED OMISSIONS

A timid knock sounded on the door, and Garrett pulled the covers higher over Kaimi's stomach before he answered.

"Hi," Aida whispered as she hugged Garrett. "Mommy and Daddy said I could come check on Kaimi. We brought her some flowers like Papa grows, and I drew her a picture."

Dan and Fionna were standing behind Aida, grinning at their little girl. Dan was holding a babbling Halia, and Fionna was holding a huge bouquet of Hawaiian blooms.

"You can come in. She's not sleeping." Garrett guided Aida forward. Kaimi smiled as she made her approach.

"I drew you a picture to make you feel better."

"Thank you. That's so sweet. This is beautiful. Is this your Tutu's farm?"

Aida gave a delighted nod. "Daddy said you're going to marry Uncle Garrett, and I said I already knew that because when he sees you he feels happy and you feel happy. And 'cause Tutu told me after Daddy and Uncle Garrett came back here."

"Your Tutu told you that?" Shock lifted in Kaimi's rhythms. Garrett's shield followed suit.

"Yes." Aida seemed confused by their surprise.

"You get used to that too," Dan assured them.

"Still improving?" Fionna asked.

"I think so. Seeing as how I did this to myself, and have had this horrible day, and then got engaged, and now, I'm really just confused."

"Been there," Fionna sighed. Dan nodded as he kissed Halia's cheek. She nuzzled her head on her daddy's shoulder and took firm hold of his chin. "I brought you a few things I had from the farm. They'll help you heal if you want to use them."

Kaimi considered. "The 'Ōhi'a lehua works really well, and Tutu helped Nana so much."

"She healed Aida's ear infection over the summer without us ever having to see a medio, and when I...got hurt back in the spring, she made me able to carry our little coconut." Fionna tried to refer to being shot without telling Aida what had actually happened to her.

"What do I do?" Kaimi seemed willing to leave her skepticism behind and go with what felt right to her.

Fionna was visibly elated that Kaimi was going to try her grandmother's remedies. "I brought you some salt from the Kauaian shoreline, so it's kind of like a little piece of home. There are a few oils that will help draw out any infection that might resurface. If you just soak in a tub with the salt and then follow the instructions on the bottles, I think it will really help. Dan and I take a bath almost every night," she added hopefully.

Garrett shot Dan a look that said he highly doubted the healing benefits of salt water were what had him climbing in the tub with his wife every night.

Dan smirked. "Don't knock it 'til you've tried it."

Kaimi and Fionna continued an in-depth conversation about Tutu's beliefs when suddenly, a rather loud argument bellowed from the hallway. Dan handed Halia to Fionna as he and Garrett moved into the corridor.

Garrett was furious. How was anyone supposed to get well if people were shouting at each other in front of the rooms? He'd planned on telling off the participants for disturbing Kaimi, but he stopped short as he took in Governor Sapman shouting at none other than Hospital Chief of Staff Harrison Sawyer—Chloe's father.

"I'm sorry, Governor Sapman," Medio Sawyer huffed. "Medio

Haydenshire is having dinner. She's been working since this morning and is going to stay all night, but she has also already been assigned exclusively to another patient."

"You are aware of who I am?" Governor Sapman demanded.

"Yes, we all are, but there are a few people who outrank even you."

"So, one of Stephen's kids is here?" Governor Sapman challenged the obvious conclusion.

Medio Sawyer discreetly glanced Garrett's way. "Yes." Garrett saw the resentment color his features. "I will be happy to attend Becca. You know, I have been doing this several decades longer than Medio Haydenshire, not that she isn't extremely talented."

Dan began methodically searching the open corridor, with a large nurses' station in its center. They both saw Jeff Strenton in a room on the opposite side of Kaimi's.

"I'll be right back." Dan walked away from Garrett and the governor.

"Becca prefers Adeline," Governor Sapman defied.

"Your daughter's husband just informed me that he doesn't care who does the operation as long as someone stops the excessive bleeding and tries to keep her from losing their child. Now, that sounds like a very logical statement. So, if it's all right with you, I'll go attend Becca. It appears she has full-blown placenta previa, just like Sarah had. Remember, I delivered Becca. I would like to see if perhaps we can lock on to the placenta and move it to a different position around the baby. That is an extremely complicated procedure, one Medio Haydenshire has never performed alone at this stage of pregnancy, but one that I have done more times than I care to remember."

"Fine, yes, please." Governor Sapman seemed to come to his senses as he followed Medio Sawyer toward Becca.

Garrett returned to Kaimi's room and wondered how he might explain to Kaimi that Chloe's father was the hospital chief of staff, a fact he hadn't even considered until that moment.

"Is everything okay?" Kaimi asked.

"Another one of the governors' kids is here—Becca Sapman."

"Oh no," Fionna gasped.

"They were arguing over Adeline."

Kaimi glanced from Garrett to Fionna. "If she needs her, I don't want to keep her with me. I feel a lot better."

"It sounded to me like she needs Medio Sawyer. He's Chloe's dad… and the chief of staff here."

"Would you mind watching the girls for just a minute?" Fionna hoisted Halia into Garrett's arms.

"Sure," Kaimi replied though she was studying Garrett like she couldn't quite believe what he'd just said.

Fionna offered Garrett her customary good luck smile. She told Aida she'd be right back and raced from the room.

"So, your ex-girlfriend's father is the head of the hospital where I am currently a patient because of body piercings?" Kaimi shuddered.

"Never my girlfriend, and…yes."

"I want Nana." She closed her eyes in defeat.

"It's okay." Aida crawled up onto the bed and looked deeply concerned as she took Kaimi's hands in her own. "We could talk about your nana if you want. Whenever I miss my mamãe and pai, then Mommy and Daddy and I talk about them, and then I can feel them in my heart again. And your nana is in your heart too, and she loves you so much just like Uncle Garrett loves you so much. Can't you feel it? Close your eyes and do like this." Aida's little face contorted in deep concentration as she squeezed her eyes shut. "And then you can feel it," she said as if such a thing wouldn't require much effort. Garrett supposed it wouldn't if you were a Receiver. "Then, when you feel it, you can have the sunshine back in your tummy that you feel when Uncle Garrett hugs you. Do you want to tell me about your nana? Mommy and Mrs. Powell say I'm a very good listener."

Steady tears were leaking down Kaimi's face as she gazed adoringly at Aida.

"Yeah, remember she's part of the package," Garrett urged hopefully. Kaimi smiled through her tears. "I swear, I just never thought to tell you. I wasn't trying to keep anything from you. I never thought you'd end up in the hospital, and then when you did, all I was worried about was getting you well."

"I know," she begrudgingly agreed.

Aida was waiting expectantly for Kaimi to begin discussing her grandmother.

"My nana was really good friends with your Tutu."

"I love all of Tutu's friends. They come to the shop on Fridays, and I get to help them, and they say, 'Aloha, Aida. She's her Papa's makamae keiki.' Do you know what that means?"

Kaimi nodded. "Precious child."

"And when we move to the farm and not live here anymore, then you can help in the shop too if you want. It's very fun, and we can play with my new doll," Aida reminded Kaimi.

"Oh, Aida, baby, I still have your Christmas and birthday presents at my apartment." Garrett felt terrible he'd forgotten.

Kaimi wrinkled her nose. "Uncle Garrett has been a little forgetful lately, huh?"

Aida nodded sheepishly. "But it's okay, because he's been gone for a while because he took the presents to the orphanage, and I think because he wants to kiss you a lot."

"That is definitely it," Garrett agreed mostly to make both of his girls giggle.

"My mommy and daddy kiss a lot."

"They do?" Kaimi feigned surprise.

"Yes, all the time, and when Alex was at my house, I said he could kiss me like Daddy kisses Mommy, and he said that was gross, but that he wanted to kiss me right here." She pointed to the apple of her right cheek, and Garrett's mind fought the anger that flooded through him. His shield pulsed in fury, and Kaimi bit her lips together to keep from laughing at him outright. "So, I said yes, and then he did." Aida lit in delight, and Kaimi began laughing at Garrett.

Her entire spirit seemed to lift in Aida's presence. "You should only let boys kiss you if you want them to though."

"I wanted him to, and I told Mommy that he did, and she said maybe to let her tell my daddy, so I don't know if he knows yet." Aida shrugged.

Since Alexander Fitzroy was still walking around uninjured and unafraid, Garrett doubted Dan knew about Aida's kiss.

"Does it make you feel like sparkly stars are in your tummy when

Uncle Garrett kisses you?" Aida gazed at Kaimi like she'd made a cherished new friend. Garrett was reeling from her question, but realized in that moment that Aida already saw Kaimi as her aunt.

Kaimi glanced at Garrett and grinned. "I do feel like that."

"And it made my cheek feel hot." Aida gingerly touched the approximate location of Alex's kiss. "I really liked it!" she whispered excitedly.

Garrett's head sank as he cradled Halia closer and willed her not to grow up.

"Just don't grow up too fast, okay," Kaimi encouraged her sweetly. She might not have thought she was good with kids, but Garrett thought differently.

Dan and Fionna returned just then. They both looked devastated.

"She'll be all right, baby," Dan soothed.

"I'm more worried about Jeff." Fionna smiled at Aida and Kaimi. "What are you two talking about?" She looked very pleased that Aida was so taken with Kaimi.

"I told Aunt Kaimi about when Alex kissed me!"

"What!?" Dan's eyes goggled in fury.

"I thought you might have told Daddy?"

"Fionna," Dan shouted.

Fionna rolled her eyes slightly. "Daddy," she drawled out in several consolatory syllables, "it's no big deal." Dan had his cell phone out in a half of a second. Fionna grasped his hand and shook her head. "You are not calling Fitz. Aida and Alex are friends."

Aida nodded and then bit her lip. "And maybe my boyfriend," she announced hopefully.

Dan was set to detonate, and Garrett had to agree with his acrimony.

Adeline knocked on the door and let herself in.

"Such a crazy night," she lamented. "They've taken Becca into surgery, and I tried to read your urine analysis results, but the lab tablets aren't working. For some reason, I can only see the digital readouts of the recent Venton drug tests. I'm going to have to go down to the lab and rerun the sample myself, but it will be a few minutes," she explained to Kaimi. "I'm just making certain that your kidneys and liver aren't housing the infection."

"Oh, okay." Kaimi nodded concernedly. Her distress penetrated Garrett's irritation that Alex Fitzroy had kissed his goddaughter. He handed Halia off to Dan in an effort to calm him down and moved to Kaimi. He kissed her forehead as he laced his fingers through hers.

Adeline approached the bed and smiled at Garrett. "I need to read her rhythms without yours." He stepped back begrudgingly, and she casted Kaimi.

"Much stronger." She sounded relieved. "We'll leave the IV in overnight, but if you keep improving, Garrett can take you back home tomorrow."

Kaimi's relief was evident though Garrett was several feet away.

"Adeline, what was that you said about the Venton drug tests?" Fionna asked as soon as Adeline released the cast on Kaimi.

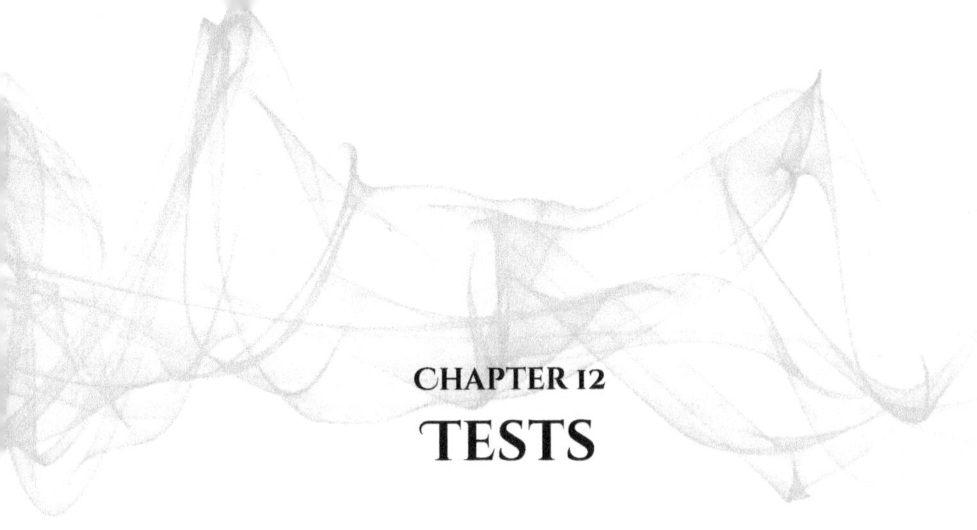

CHAPTER 12

# TESTS

"I was going to tell Dan about it, but I wanted to see what I find once I'm down in the lab. Logan already knows. He's waiting on Dan in the waiting room, since he knew Garrett was giving Kaimi a bath."

"That's one of the things you have to figure out before we can move, right?" Kaimi asked. Garrett felt a sting of regret as he began to realize how badly she wanted to go back to Kauai. He was simultaneously pleased that she'd said we.

"Yeah." He nodded as he and Dan shared a cautiously hopeful glance.

"So, go talk to Logan," she commanded.

"You sure you're all right for me to go for a few minutes?" He politely ignored the adoring swoon Fionna gave Dan over him actually taking care of his girl.

"Aida and Maylea will take care of me," she assured him as Aida nodded. Garrett winked at her as he and Dan made their way out to talk to Logan.

Adeline joined them. "I'm going to go down to the lab and run Kaimi's urine sample. That will only take a few minutes, but I can snoop around a little while I'm down there."

"Okay," Logan acquiesced. "Be careful, please. I don't want anyone to know something is weird with those iPads, and I sure as hell don't want anyone to know that you're helping us and deciding they might like to put a stop to that." Logan was on the verge of panic. His shield gave several rapid pulses.

Garrett instinctively reached and squeezed his little brother's shoulder and smiled. Logan had clearly been working out. He'd bulked up quite a bit from the gangly kid he'd been a few years before.

"She'll be all right, man," Garrett reassured.

"Yeah, well, seeing as how you're new to this whole being someone's Shield, I think I'll just stick to my low level panic," Logan offered him wryly. Dan couldn't quite halt his chuckle. Garrett rolled his eyes as Adeline beamed and gave Logan a quick kiss on the cheek.

"Adeline, could some kind of glitch or alteration of the Venton tests have caused them to be the only thing you're seeing?" Dan asked.

"Jeff would probably be the person to ask that, but if the testing was performed and then the results were changed, I would think that could throw off the entire system."

Dan, Garrett, and Logan all nodded their agreement.

"Please be careful," Logan begged again.

"I'll be right back, and I'll be fine." With that, she headed toward the elevator and checked her hospital iPad on her way.

"So, Garrett Haydenshire, the man who prosed the famous speech, 'Getting married is for dumb fucks'...at my wedding...is engaged," Logan drawled just before he cracked himself up. Dan nodded as he joined in the laughter.

"Are you about done with that?" Garrett rolled his eyes. Truthfully, he didn't mind the teasing. He certainly deserved it.

"I'm definitely not. I'm writing my own speech for your wedding."

"Who says we'd invite you?"

"That would be our parental figures." He had Garrett there.

"Is Kaimi okay, son? Why are you all standing out here?" Governor Haydenshire broached as he returned to the hospital to check on Kaimi.

"Actually, we are waiting on my phenomenally beautiful and talented wife to not only bring back lab results on Kaimi but probably to solve all of the additional cases we've been working on." Logan raised his eyebrows to indicate which cases.

"Is Adeline upset with you?" the governor huffed. Dan and Garrett laughed.

"No."

"Adeline is certainly all of those things you just mentioned. I just wasn't sure why you felt the need to brag so suddenly." Governor Haydenshire took Logan down a notch or two just as he had all of his sons. Logan rolled his eyes but gave no verbal response.

"Kaimi's much better," Garrett supplied. "Adeline wants to keep her on the IV overnight to make sure all of the infection is killed, but the piercings are healing, and the fever is gone."

The governor nodded his relief.

"They just took Becca into surgery," Logan added.

"I heard, son. If she carries that little boy full term, it will be a miracle. I'll say that."

Adeline returned a few minutes later. The men crowded around her. Dan summoned a sound cast that created a vacuum around them so that no one else could hear them talking.

"Okay." Adeline drew a deep breath. "A bunch of the tests in the paper files are different from what's showing on everyone's iPads." Her whisper bordered on panic.

"Okay." Logan took Adeline's hand. She drew from him, but everyone else politely ignored them, as was customary whenever a Gifted person witnessed such a thing.

"Don't you see? This is the test that was performed the last day of school before Christmas break. The Valeduto students who work in the lab haven't been here. They're off for break. That's why Governor Vindico wanted the additional test run. That means that someone who is employed by the hospital is changing the tests. It's the only thing that makes any sense, but who would do that?" She glanced around up the corridors at the medios, doctors, nurses, and orderlies methodically moving around the hospital.

"We'll figure that out," Dan assured her. "Does the lab have a staff or do the medios all do their own lab work? And I need a list of the students whose results were changed."

"The lab has its own staff. There are quite a few people who only work in the lab. There were several other medios in the lab when I was down there, so I was thinking I could go back and see if I could discreetly sort of clear it out and then write the names down. But, Dan, it was at least thirty students. Venton has never had more than five in a test."

"We don't know if those tests were legal either," Garrett added as the governor gave a weary nod.

"I'll start with those thirty students and go from there," Dan explained. Two medios exited the nearby elevator.

"They're on the lab staff, but there are probably thirty medios who only work in the lab. Other medios go down there to perform tests they don't want queued because if one of us does it then we don't have to wait, just like I did with Kaimi's. The Non-Gifted doctors don't go down there. They can't alter the energy of what's being tested, so they have to wait. I'd say it's either a lab employee or one of the medios or Gifted nurses."

Adeline's nerves were palpable in her rhythms.

"Can I go back down there with you?" Logan soothed.

"No, you're not allowed down there. Then I might be the one in big trouble."

The medios who'd exited the elevator walked past them. "That's Medio Borrey and Medio Reinas," she whispered. "They're leaving the lab. I'm going to go back down there. Oh, Garrett, tell Kaimi her tests were good. Her organs are fine." Relief washed through Garrett's shield.

"I'll tell her, and thank you."

"Go on and tell her, son," the governor ordered. "She's probably worried."

# CHAPTER 13

# UNDER THE COVERS

Fionna and Kaimi's heads shot up as soon as Garrett entered the room.

"What did Adeline find out?" Fionna asked.

"We're not sure yet. She's going back down there to look around some more, but she says your tests were good, baby. You can come home tomorrow." Garrett phrased his label of their home very carefully.

"You're sure you want me to live in your apartment until you move? I should go back to Kauai and find something to do, but all I really know how to do is dance," she fretted. "There aren't any strip clubs in Kauai, but I could move back to Honolulu temporarily and do the pole and stuff there? I'd make good tips, then I could pay off my credit cards."

"Aida." Fionna tugged Aida toward the door while balancing Halia on her shoulder. "Uncle Garrett is about to lose his temper, so we're going outside with Daddy," she explained as she closed the door.

Fury and jealousy did indeed explode through Garrett's veins. His shield lit in outrage. It took him a moment to regulate his voice so he wasn't shouting. "Clearly the fever is making you insane!"

A deep flush moved up her neck and settled in her cheeks. "It is not." She giggled.

"As we just found out yesterday, life doesn't work so well when we're apart. In fact, it tends to go to hell. So, no more of that. We can stay here, or we can go back to Kauai, but together is the way it works. And in what universe did you imagine that I would let you work in a strip club?" he huffed indignantly. "I'm a Shield." He shook his head and corrected. "I'm *your* Shield."

"I don't really want to, but the money would be good. I could probably get hired quick. I just feel weird letting you take care of me. I've always taken care of myself."

Garrett settled himself beside her. "You'll help take care of both of us once you become the lead instructor at the hula studio after we move, but for now, I'd really like you to stay here. Let's do a little living on love and on my savings. I'll help you pay down your credit card debt. Let's build the foundation of this relationship, so there's never any room for doubt again, okay?"

A broad grin spread across Kaimi's face as she gave a hesitant nod.

"Plus, if we run out of food, Mom's the best cook in the Realm," Garrett teased just to hear her sweet giggle again.

A fierce knock sounded on the door, and Garrett assumed it was Dan.

Garrett kissed Kaimi's forehead. He couldn't recall a time before that moment when he was annoyed with a case that needed to be worked. He loved being a detective, but right now, he wanted everyone else to go away and let him take care of his baby.

He knew how to take care of her. He knew she would never have really wanted all of this attention. She just needed to be reassured that she could depend on him, and that he would never try to stifle her independence or tie her down. Watching her fly was the most enchanting thing he'd ever seen. He wanted her out of the hospital bed and in his arms, so he could lift her higher and show her that he would always help her soar. He would never weigh her down.

"Let me get this taken care of and then how about if I kick everybody out, and we get a little sleep," Garrett offered before he answered the door. That beautiful light swam in her eyes, the one he knew how to stir and ignite so that it would turn into his stunning wildfire. She nodded.

Kaimi leaned back against the pillows. She tried not to let anyone else hear her slightly impatient moan, but it made Garrett chuckle as he winked at her.

He stepped back as Dan, Logan, Governor Haydenshire, Adeline, and Jeff Strenton entered.

The governor offered Kaimi his kind smile. "Sweetheart, I'm sorry we're using your hospital room as some kind of command base. I'm certain you'd like us all to leave you and Garrett be. I imagine a few hours of peace in my son's arms might not be unwelcome."

"It's okay. I know you need to figure this out, but that other part sounds good too," she admitted sheepishly. Adeline chuckled as she checked the machine monitoring Kaimi's vital signs and temperature. The governor looked very pleased, and Dan gave her a deeply apologetic gaze.

"I'm sorry. When Fi was here, I finally just kicked everyone out. It was ridiculous."

"Finally?" Garrett smirked. "Man, you kicked everyone out before anyone even visited her."

"That...wasn't entirely me."

Garrett understood that it had been Fionna who hadn't wanted to be bombarded with visitors when she'd been in the hospital, and that Dan had seen to her requests. He was her Shield.

"Is Becca okay?" Garrett asked Jeff. He was shocked Jeff wasn't with his wife. He gave an exhausted nod.

"Yeah, Medio Sawyer moved the placenta, and she's still asleep. I'm gonna tell you what I know, but then I'm going back. She's probably going to have to stay up here for several weeks," he explained in a pain-filled choke.

Dan slapped him on the back. "She'll be all right. Sawyer said the surgery went well, better than he'd hoped. Just a few more months."

Jeff drew a deep breath and rubbed his eyes.

"Hi, I'm Kaimi," she offered sweetly from her bed.

"Oh, I'm sorry. Jeff, this is my fiancée, Kaimi Walyuo. Kaimi, this is Jeff Strenton. He's the newest hire on Elite Iodex and a good friend of Dan and Fi's."

"Nice to meet you," Jeff managed as he stifled a yawn.

"What'd we find?" Garrett directed his question to Adeline in an effort to move everything along before he shut the door on visitors for the evening.

"I pulled up the list of medios and staff members who used their cards to get into the lab since the last drug test was run, but of course that's hundreds and hundreds of names. I have no idea how to email that out or anything. I couldn't spend any real time studying the paper copies of the Venton tests, and I also don't know how to get the information off of the iPads," Adeline lamented dejectedly. "So, basically I was no help at all."

"That's not true. You figured out they were different. You just broke the case," Logan scoffed.

Dan looked at Garrett. "Jeff's going to tell you and me how to copy the files we need and get them onto my laptop, and I'm going to photograph the paper documents downstairs. Since we're not currently employed by Elite Iodex or Georgetown Hospital, I was hoping you might want to go undercover with me as a medio for a few minutes. Then I promise we'll leave you and Kaimi alone."

"I can get you the scrubs." Adeline looked intrigued, like Dan and Garrett were stepping into a Nancy Drew novel or something. "I just can't get you entry key cards, and the magnetic pulse locks change every time they're used. It would be really hard to break in."

Dan and Garrett nodded. Neither of them were terribly concerned about breaking into the magnetically locked doors to the hospital lab.

"I was also thinking if you and I get caught, Sawyer might not get too up in arms if it was us," Dan eased hesitantly.

Garrett cringed. "I'm not sure about that. If Chloe's already called him, he's probably out for my blood, but it doesn't sound like we have a choice."

"I could get Fi to tell him what we're doing. Do we want to ask forgiveness or permission?"

"He won't tell Fionna no," Garrett stated confidently.

"I know."

"I much prefer you asking for permission." Governor Haydenshire concluded the debate.

"Go tell Fionna to talk to Sawyer, and get us some scrubs." Garrett gave his orders to Dan and Adeline. He turned to Jeff. "Tell us what we need to do. I know in here is not where you really want to be."

He nodded appreciatively. "Okay." He accepted the iPad Adeline handed him as she left. He explained what would need to happen to get the information off the hospital mainframes and onto Dan's enhanced laptop quickly and without anyone knowing.

Adeline returned with the appropriately sized scrubs. She provided a few other tools—a stethoscope, otoscope, blood pressure monitor, and a few other things neither Garrett nor Dan recognized. Kaimi's hand went to her mouth. Adeline and Kaimi began giggling. Logan turned from checking a text and began laughing as well.

"Okay, what are those?" Dan took the bait.

"Dude, obviously they're duck quackers used to treat a squeaky throat," Logan harassed as he grabbed the instrument and began making it open and close repeatedly in what did look like a duck beak. Kaimi began laughing harder as Garrett rolled his eyes.

"I believe those would be speculums that my sister-in-law has provided us," Garrett huffed. Dan shuddered visibly.

"Vaginal speculums." Adeline nodded. "Because OBs are in the lab a lot because of all of the urine samples we run. I thought it might make you seem more credible."

"No." Garrett shook his head as he backed away from the small rolling tray where Adeline had dumped the load of instruments. "Nope. They can just arrest me. I'm not carrying those."

The governor found this all hilarious, but Dan nodded his agreement with Garrett.

"Okay, but if you're down there and someone asks who you are or where you work, say that you're a visiting obstetrics medio from Cedars-Sinai. We've had a bunch of them in lately. That way they won't ask you about any patients because you won't have any. You're just observing me, and I sent you to the lab to bring back results from Miss Walyuo's urine culture." Adeline provided their cover story along with hospital credentials.

"Okay." Dan and Garrett gave their customary single nod before they slipped into the large bathroom in Kaimi's room to change into the scrubs.

Nervous tension spun constantly in Adeline's rhythms. "Don't leave here at the same time, and just try to blend in, I guess. I wish you two weren't so well-known."

"We've done this before," Garrett assured her. "Well, not this exactly, but we can handle it."

"Good luck," Kaimi offered.

Garrett saw the desolation she was trying to hide. He kissed her forehead once again. "I'll be right back," he assured her in a barely audible whisper. She nodded and discreetly drew from his hand as he placed it on hers just under her sheets and blankets. "Better?"

Dan made his exit as Kaimi gave a slight nod and then pulled just a little more of Garrett's energy into her body. Garrett sank his teeth into his tongue to keep from ordering everyone from the room so he could be with her alone. He wanted to hold her against him to give her his energy in every possible way.

"I love you, and when I get back, it'll just be you and me."

"Promise?" she whispered as the day seemed to finally get the better of her.

"Promise."

"Okay, you go," Adeline urged. With a nod, Garrett slung a stethoscope over his neck, tightened a scrub hat over his hair, and walked out of the room like he owned the place.

# CHAPTER 14
# TAB A, SLOT B

Confidence would get you everywhere. Garrett and Dan both knew that. If you seemed like you should be wherever you were, ninety-five percent chance no one would think you shouldn't be there. But Adeline had rushed Garrett's exit, and he ended up on the same elevator with Dan. They were recognizable enough in DC alone, but together was going to be disastrous. As several nurses and medios joined them, Dan exited two floors down, keeping his head down without ever giving Garrett a second glance. Garrett checked his watch and then proceeded on to the lab in the basement.

Two nurses glanced Garrett's way. "Are you the new intern visiting from Spain? You don't look Spanish? You look familiar though," one of them quizzed. When people that felt they should know everyone around them locked onto someone they didn't recognize, they would often make up their own version of a plausible story. It was always best to go with whatever they'd assumed.

"Uh, lo siento, no hablo mucho Ingles," Garrett apologized in his virtually perfected Spanish accent. The nurses giggled. Having possible witnesses think that you didn't speak or understand English was ideal. They would often talk like you weren't even there.

"Fat lot of good he's gonna do. What's he supposed to learn if he can't even understand us?" the plump brunette with a southern accent quipped. Her friend, a dyed redhead with something smeared all over her blue scrubs, nodded.

"Who knows what this hospital is thinking half the time? The OBs can't even figure out how to work their freaking iPads, and they're the ones that make all the money." The elevator opened on the pediatric floor and they exited.

Garrett let the air he'd pent up in his lungs escape but went back to ducking in the corner and pretending to study his own iPad as other hospital visitors entered the elevator.

It's only the obstetrics medios' iPads that are displaying the Venton drug tests.

Garrett typed in his phone and sent the text to Dan. Everyone exited on the ground floor, and Garrett casted the elevator and sent it to the basement quickly.

Dan was pretending to talk on his phone outside the lab door as Garrett approached. His toe was holding the door open rather discreetly. He must've pretended to talk while another medio had exited and then stopped the door before it latched, which was a huge break. Now, they wouldn't have to try and decipher a magnetic code that would work on the door.


### Fionna Vindico


*Sorrow, frustration* and *fear* fought for dominance in Medio Sawyer's rhythms as he stared at Fionna from across his desk.

"Sir, I just wanted to tell you what Dan and Garrett need to do." *Are doing,* she mentally corrected her lie.

"I'd rather you tell me what happened between Garrett and Chloe? Kaimi isn't pregnant. I assumed that was why Garrett suddenly had a fiancée, but I looked over Medio Haydenshire's tests. A pregnancy test was run and she isn't."

"No, sir, she isn't," Fionna agreed softly.

Truthfully, as much as she and Chloe had hung out when Fionna had challenged for the Angels, they'd grown apart since Fionna had quit the team, gotten married, and had children. Chloe resented both Dan and Aida. Fionna could always feel that whenever she was near. It seemed most of the time they lived in two different worlds.

"Chloe and Sasha Cohen and a couple of the girls have gone off to Vegas. She's devastated. I just don't understand how Garrett could have done this."

"Sir, I really don't think he meant to hurt Chloe. They were never exclusive. He met someone else and fell in love," Fionna eased. She hated the customary *confusion* and *heartbreak* that always pulsed in Medio Sawyer's rhythms whenever he thought of Chloe.

"Yes, I know," he sighed. "I just always hoped they would settle down and marry. Start a life together."

Fionna knew what he'd hoped, and that Kaimi had dashed all of his aspirations for his one and only daughter to become the wife of one of the Crown Governor's sons.

"I really just wanted to tell you that Iodex suspects that one of your employees might have switched the drug test results for Venton. Dan wanted me to assure you that they would come to you with the findings first." Fionna drew a deep breath.

"I think Chloe was at a point where she might've been willing to consider marriage and now this." He gestured his hand toward Kaimi's room though it was several floors below them.

*Defeated sadness* clouded Medio Sawyer's rhythms, and Fionna felt her rhythms tense to try and help him.

"Chloe has always had a lot of uh…male interest, and I don't think she ever wants to get married. I'm sure in a few weeks Garrett won't cross her mind much anymore."

Chloe would always be angry that Garrett wasn't available to mess around with anymore. Chloe's emotions always ran in a confusing jumble. Once Fionna learned to accept them as a package, Chloe was easy to be around. Her chaos usually brought Fionna calm. Her emotional streams ran in highs and lows, and usually she didn't feel that much at all. She was tougher to penetrate, and as long as Fionna taught herself not to try to decipher Chloe's rhythms, they were happy together.

"I caught them in her bed when they were sixteen. How long would they have let this go on with no commitment?" Medio Sawyer shook Fionna from her reverie again.

*Forever.*

"I don't know, sir," Fionna lied. "Like I said, they were never exclusive, and sometimes you just discover the person you were meant to be with. Look at Dan and me."

Medio Sawyer gave a dramatic eye roll. "I've told you for years now, love doesn't exist. It's a science just like anything else. Tab A slot B. I've made it my career, and that's all there is to it. You find someone you basically get along with, you marry, and if it doesn't work out, screw the next girl and move on." Medio Sawyer spat out the very speech that had made his daughter into the woman she'd become. It had also lost him three wives that currently took a large portion of his vast wealth.

"Sir, did you hear what I said about Dan and Garrett?"

# CHAPTER 15

# SEMINAL WORK
## ~GARRETT HAYDENSHIRE~

A lab tech exited, and Dan continued his fake conversation. Garrett stepped away from the door and made a second approach. As the tech exited, he entered. Dan followed and shoved the phone in his pocket as soon as they were in the large room alone.

"Block the door," Dan commanded. Like the well-oiled machine they were, they lifted one of the lab tables and slid it in front of the door. That was the part of the procedure they hadn't told Adeline they'd be doing.

They were both just a little too recognizable to pull off visiting medios from Cedars-Sinai. Plus, that cover would've required more research than either of them had done. Carrying on an intelligent medical conversation wasn't in their skill set.

"Go," was the next command. Dan raced to the filing cabinet Adeline had instructed him to go to, entered the opening code using a plastic glove he grabbed from a box on the counter, and smiled as he located the file Adeline had discreetly tagged.

He began photographing records page after page while Garrett set to work on the lock key codes recorded on one of the older computers. Adeline had left the window minimized, and Garrett hoped no one else had noticed that. He followed Jeff's instructions and prayed he was getting the information to Dan's laptop which he'd pulled from the briefcase he'd carried it in and set beside the computer in question. Garrett stopped to check his progress and smiled as he saw the files uploading on Dan's hard drive.

Suddenly, the door shook.

"Shit, I'm not half done," Dan whispered. Garrett nodded and moved near the door.

"This is hazmat," he called in a low Southern drawl. "Got a spill in here. Be just a minute."

"You have to put the cones and signs out for that," the woman on the other side of the door fumed.

"Dammit, Smith, you forget them cones again?" Garrett called from slightly farther away.

"Sorry, sir," Dan answered readily in a nasal squeak without ever stopping his work.

"What spilled?" The woman sighed.

"Oh, uh…fluids." Garrett shrugged. Dan laughed silently.

"Yes, I assumed, but what kind of fluids?" She sounded antsy. Garrett tried to think of something that came in ready supply and wouldn't be that hard to replace therefore wouldn't cause a panic. Blood seemed like a bad plan, and apparently, urine was used to make sure women's whole bodies were working correctly, as he'd learned from his time in the room with his newly minted fiancée. So, he went with the next thing he thought of.

"Uh, sperm samples. Just a few," he added hopefully. Dan shook with laughter as he continued to snap pictures.

"Oh, good grief," the woman huffed. "I hope whoever spilled it plans on letting the donors know. You know, sometimes it's cancer treatment patients and they could sue if the chemo leaves them impotent."

Garrett and Dan both shuddered from the word. It was one Garrett had heard far too many times in his life. He cringed. He hadn't known that about cancer patients, and now felt badly he'd said it. "We'll have it cleaned up in a minute."

They heard the squeak of her shoes as she moved back down the hallway, and Garrett made certain the files were still copying onto Dan's computer.

They finished five minutes later and returned everything to its previous state. Garrett exited first this time and moved to the elevator quickly. When he entered the sliding doors, a medio whisked past him.

She stopped Dan as he left the lab. "Was there a seminal fluid spill?"

"Not that I heard." Dan shrugged as he headed to the elevator.

Garrett rushed to the third floor men's room that was relatively out of the way. He found his and Dan's clothes where Logan had left them per Adeline's instructions and changed out of the scrubs.

Dan entered several minutes later. "Sperm," he chanted over the bathroom divider.

Garrett laughed. "I tried to think of something that would have her running."

Dan shook his head as they left the bathroom together and moved back to the elevators.

"Do you have the whole ring thing down because the press is out there desperate for a picture of her and the ring?"

"She won't have it tomorrow so they'll have to get over it, but I've definitely got a plan. I have to call a few friends of mine at the precinct, but I think she'll like it."

"Please tell me you're not having her arrested and then giving her the key to your heart or some dumbass thing like that."

Garrett laughed as they exited on the obstetrics floor again. "I'm not a fifteen-year-old douche canoe with a missing paddle, man. Give me a little credit."

Kaimi's eyes lit as soon as Garrett entered the room. His heart beat disjointedly as he stared at her, and everything else faded in the background.

"Did you talk to Sawyer, baby?" Dan asked Fionna who was seated in a rocker feeding Halia a bottle.

"Kind of," she sighed. "We need to get the girls to bed. I'll tell you about it on the way home." She stood as soon as the bottle was empty. She shifted her expertly to her shoulder to burp her while she guided

Aida to clean up her coloring books and to tell Kaimi and Garrett goodbye.

"I'm just happy that's done. We've got to get this mess cleaned up, or your father is going to take the fall for this. It's coming closer every day. The parents are getting restless," Governor Haydenshire lamented.

"I know, sir. We're going to figure this out. Between this,"—he pointed to his laptop bag—"and the thumb drives, I'm making progress," Dan assured Garrett's father.

Governor Haydenshire nodded. "I can't think of two finer officers to figure this out, even if your methods occasionally concern me."

"But we *do* figure it out," Dan and Garrett pointed out at the same moment.

Everyone wished Kaimi well and told her they would check on her the next day. Adeline made one last check of Kaimi's chest and seemed pleased with her healing.

"You need a good night's sleep, which really doesn't happen in the hospital. So, here's what I usually tell my patients who have a really great guy with them that I know will be with them all night. If Garrett promises to come and get me immediately if your fever goes back up or if you start to feel nauseated, I won't bother you until about five tomorrow morning. Hopefully, if no one is in and out of your room all night and you sleep, you'll be healed and ready to head out for your news debut."

Kaimi's brow furrowed. "My debut?"

"We haven't turned on the television. We'll see what they're doing before I get her to sleep. And you know I'll watch her all night," Garrett vowed.

Adeline nodded and offered Kaimi a sweet smile. "If you need anything at all, press this button." She pointed to a button near Kaimi's fingers. "I'm going to leave your heart and rhythm monitor on all night. I can check them remotely without having to disturb you. Also, I'll know if you do anything more than sleep, so please don't."

Garrett laughed while Kaimi's eyes goggled.

"In a hospital!?" She gasped.

"Oh, you'd be surprised."

"We'll be good," Garrett pledged as he laced his fingers through Kaimi's.

"Thank you." Adeline summoned and lowered the lights in the room to a gentle glow and then gave a slight wave as she closed the door.

# CHAPTER 16

# CONFIRMATIONS

"**B**etter?" Garrett assumed.

Kaimi gave a sheepish grin as she nodded. "That was so sweet of everyone. I'm overwhelmed."

"Time's been running pretty fast for the last few weeks. I wouldn't mind slowing it down just a little."

"Will you sit here with me?" Kaimi scooted over in the bed to try and make room for Garrett.

"Nothing," he drawled as he edged beside her and carefully settled her body on his chest, "would make me happier." Her rhythms eased as soon as Garrett's arms were around her. That's where she belonged. "Would you like to see what an overnight celebrity you've become?" He prayed that the press in Hawaii would keep its policy of respecting everyone that came to the islands, celebrity or not.

"I guess."

Garrett summoned and turned on the television in Kaimi's room. He casted it and tuned in one of the local Gifted news stations.

"We are still here reporting outside Georgetown Hospital where we've learned that the Crown Governor's son Garrett, confirmed bachelor playboy of the lead governing family, is engaged. His fiancée, a Miss Kaimi Walyuo, is a patient here. We've been given very little information on Miss Walyuo's condition or why she was admitted to

Georgetown this afternoon. They have Garrett's fiancée listed as stable, and we have confirmed that Garrett has been by her side the entire stay. The Crown Governor and Mrs. Haydenshire were both in several times today to see Miss Walyuo along with Emily and Rainer Lawson.

"Several of the Haydenshire brothers have also made appearances, though they all declined comment as they came and went. Logan Haydenshire and his wife, Princess of the Australian Realm Her Royal Highness Mrs. Adeline Haydenshire, who is an obstetrics medio here at Georgetown, did confirm the engagement though not much else was mentioned. But we will stay here until we find out what the Realm wants to know."

They cut to a shot of Dan and Fionna blocking the girls' faces from the cameras as they rushed out of the hospital.

"Here!" The reporter started to sprint. "We have former Elite Iodex Chief Daniel Vindico with his wife and daughters. Dan, were you here visiting Miss Walyuo? What can you tell us about Garrett's engagement?" The reporter thrust the mic in Dan's face. Garrett chuckled as he noted the look in Dan's eyes that said the guy should be careful, or he'd find his mic shoved up his ass.

"No comment. Get the cameras away from my daughters," Dan barked as he checked to make certain that Halia's entire little body was covered in several blankets.

With that, Garrett switched off the TV and turned to Kaimi. Panic began to pulse in his rhythms.

"Wow." Kaimi continued to stare at the blank screen in abject disbelief.

"Are you okay with all of that? It'll be better in Kauai." He assured her what he hoped was the truth. She cuddled farther into his embrace. He was pleased that her chest being next to his didn't seem to hurt her.

"But I'm just a regular person who fell in love with a guy and then got taken to the hospital because of an infection. Why is that news?"

"All of us Haydenshires, and most especially Emily and Rainer, have been asking that all of our lives. We have no freaking clue.

They're going to be all over you tomorrow. I'll do my best to keep them away. Dad can call in Iodex, but it'll be a madhouse."

"It's okay. I still want to marry you, and what you said about building our foundation, that sounds really, really perfect. I don't want you to pay my bills though, but I'd really like to spend some more time with your mom. She's like what a mom is supposed to be, you know? I never had that."

Garrett's heart pricked as he nodded. "Believe me, sweetheart, you do now." In that moment, he knew he wanted and needed his family back in his life because she needed them. He wanted her to have each and every single thing she ever needed. Anything that would make her whole, he would give her. He'd cut his family out so many years ago, but they'd never shut the door on him. Now, he wanted to go back home.

"Would you do the shield thing again for just a few minutes?" Kaimi whispered.

"Yeah, baby, of course." Garrett set his shield firmly over her. Her rhythms trilled inside of his as her entire body relaxed against him. He flooded it with his adoring love and protection. Then he eased her chin upward and traced her lips with his thumb as he cradled her face. "I love you," he whispered.

"I love you too."

He leaned in and let their breaths mingle in the moment between them. She closed the distance. She brushed her lips against his. His needy groan of relent filled her mouth just before his tongue moved with hers.

She drew from the energy in his mouth. Her hand traced down his pecs. He turned his head, gripped her ass, and moved her closer. He couldn't get enough. "You're so fucking sweet," he grunted when he allowed her breath and then moved back in to stake another needy claim. He kept her enveloped inside of his barrier from the corrosive world.

Eventually, she settled back against the pillows and grinned. "I bet Adeline saw that."

"Don't really give a damn," Garrett assured her. "Go to sleep, sweetheart. I've got you."

She nodded against him, and a few minutes later, she was out. Garrett kept his shield in place. He wanted to know she was safe and secure. He wanted her in his arms. He dozed off a half hour later but then jerked awake almost instantly.

He eased away from Kaimi. He was certain she would sleep better alone in the small hospital bed though he longed to hold her all night. He watched the machine attached to her until it flashed her temperature. All looked normal.

After pulling his phone from his pocket, Garrett settled in the reclining leatherette chair in the room and decided it was good he wouldn't be comfortable That way he could keep constant watch on Kaimi.

"Hey Wexler, it's Garrett Haydenshire. How are you?" He spoke as quietly as he was able.

"Man, you're all over the news again. Mandy said you're engaged. I told her she was crazy," Officer Wexler harassed.

Garrett chuckled. "All true, man, and I was kind of hoping you could do me a favor about that."

"Oh, yeah? What do you need?"

Garrett explained his plan. A minute later, he was grinning excitedly. "Yeah, send me the pics and stats. I'll let you know tonight. They're Pasha's, right?"

"Yeah, of course."

"That's perfect. That's what I wanted. Thanks, and I'll get you a check as soon as I get out of Georgetown."

Next, Garrett phoned his Uncle Tad. They talked for almost fifteen minutes and then Garrett checked Kaimi's monitors again before he sank back into his plastic bed for the evening. He opened the texts from Wexler and carefully studied each picture. With a delighted grin of his own, he sent Wexler his choice, set the alarm on his phone to vibrate every half hour, and then tried to get a little sleep.

# CHAPTER 17

# COMFORTS OF HOME

"I feel much better. Just a little tired still," Kaimi confirmed as Adeline was signing her release papers.

"It's going to take a few days after an infection like that to have your Gifted energies back fully. Keep taking the antibiotic I'm sending home with you, and I'll check you again in a day or two."

Garrett glanced out the large windows to the gathering press. The crowds had swelled with news that his fiancée was being discharged.

"I'd go get you coffee, but I don't think I'd make it back before dinner." He continued to gather Ringo, Kaimi's dirty clothes, and the few items he had, and stuff them back into his gym bag.

Kaimi smiled and reached for his hand.

"Right here," he soothed as he kissed her head and supplied his strength.

"Try to sleep twelve to sixteen hours today if you can, then you should be feeling almost back to normal. Try to eat six small meals today and drink as much water as you're able. Celebrate your engagement carefully." Adeline shot a quick warning glance at Garrett before she returned her attention to her iPad.

He sincerely hoped that his forced chuckle covered his desperate need. Carefully was perfectly fine. Any way at all was perfectly fine, but he needed to be with her again. Needed to join their energy together with the thrust of his body up into hers. Needed to feel her envelop him in the warm, wet perfection between her legs. Needed her to know that he adored her and loved her and that he was all hers and no one else's ever again. He longed to have her under him as he stared down into the copper pools of her needy eyes, so ready for him to guide her into the depths of ecstasy as he drowned himself in all of her.

Kaimi was a nervous wreck. The press coupled with several of her friends calling from Kauai and Honolulu as news of their engagement reached the extreme West Coast, not to congratulate her, but to ask if she was insane, had her fettered and bound. She needed to come undone in his arms to be set free inside of his all-consuming love for her.

Logan knocked on the door.

The governor followed him in, shaking his head. "We pulled the Highlander up to the side entrance, but they're everywhere, so you may have to answer a few questions."

"It's fine, Dad. I'll handle everything. I just want her home."

The governor looked startled momentarily but then grinned as he nodded his agreement.

"Are you ready?" Garrett kept Kaimi's hand laced in his with the duffle bag thrown over his shoulder. She nodded though it appeared that might've been the biggest lie she'd ever told.

"We're out there. The blockade is set up, so just try to be quick." Logan pointed to the Iodex blockade the governor had called for. Garrett noted Tuttle and Portwood along the line holding back the press.

"Let's just get out of here." Garrett tried not to sound as annoyed as he felt. He knew his father blamed himself, but irritation perforated his tone.

"Okay, you're all ready. Call me if you need anything at all." Adeline gave the go, and Kaimi sat down in the provided wheelchair. Garrett guided her onto the elevator with Logan as their provided Iodex security guide.

When he rolled the wheelchair out of the hospital, Kaimi seemed to decide she was done with the chair. She stood, and Garrett braced as she shrunk into his side. They stepped out into the throngs of press.

"Is she pregnant? Are you expecting?" It was relentless. Every reporter from every news organization in the entire Realm had jumped to the same conclusion. The bitter disappointment that immediately etched Kaimi's face cut Garrett like a dagger.

"No!" Garrett wrapped his arm around her and rushed her to the car.

"When's the wedding, Garrett?" Natalie Sarenmoor, a reporter from one of the local news stations, chanted just as they reached the Highlander.

"As soon as possible." He closed Kaimi in while the cameras caught her from every available angle.

To his relief, Kaimi was smiling as he entered the driver's side and threw the SUV into drive.

"Wow," she gasped as they pulled away with Iodex blocking the press from following after them.

"I guess the Realm was surprised as well."

"Will they be at your apartment?" Disappointment colored her tone.

"No, they won't be at *our* apartment. They may camp out across the street, but it's private property. I provide a fair amount of security to the tenants, so the landlord has been really good about keeping the press out."

"Good. I kind of want to just be alone with you. It's so intimidating." She tried to explain the unexplainable. Having your life dissected and interfered with was bizarre. It was infuriating and occasionally terrifying.

"Alone with me sounds perfect. If I know my mother, the apartment will be stocked with groceries."

"But we can still go to the farm soon, right?" she quizzed hopefully. Garrett grinned as he doubled around his building to make certain no one was following them.

"Yeah, I was hoping you might want to go over there tomorrow evening. Adeline could check your chest, and we could have dinner."

Kaimi grinned. The relief that she could visit the farm again the next day seemed to bring her a great deal of peace.

Garrett pulled into the parking garage and helped her out of the car. She was moving with ease now that the infection seemed to be at bay. After a quick, casted elevator ride, Garrett unlocked the door. He made a mental note to give Kaimi his other key. A plate of his mother's gooey chocolate chip cookies was on the kitchen counter with a note about what she'd put in the fridge and pantry.

"Try one of these." Garrett pulled the plastic wrap back and supplied a cookie to Kaimi. Her eyes were sparkling again as she settled in.

"Oh my gosh! Yum!" she groaned as Garrett laughed and took one for himself. He poured her a cup of milk and then led her back to the sofa in the living room. She crawled against his chest and curled herself tightly into his arms.

"I'm so glad you're here and you're better. You scared me." Garrett brushed the cookie crumbs off his jeans and then wrapped both of his arms around her.

"Thank you for taking such good care of me and for asking me to marry you."

"Thank you for saying yes."

"Tell me what happened when you and Dan went to the lab?" Her natural curiosity seemed to be making its comeback.

Garrett joined in her laughter as he concluded the story of his going from a Spanish intern to a hazmat cleanup crew from Eastern Alabama in about a ten-minute span. She was laughing, and Garrett had never heard anything sweeter.

"Okay, you really are the shit." She shook her head at him.

Garrett gave her a mock bow. "Well, thank you, little lady," he provided in his best Southern accent which truthfully needed some work.

She stopped laughing and gazed up at Garrett sweetly. He grinned and brushed the hair away from her face as she settled her head under his chin.

"I love you," she whispered, and his heart pounded in his chest.

"I love you too, baby. I can't wait to marry you." The words still shocked him each and every time he voiced the truth.

He saw the curiosity and the hunger make their customary return to her eyes. His wildfire began its needy glow. His breath panted as her eyes begged him.

"Do you want a kiss, sweet girl?" He angled his head downward and cradled her face in his hands. She gave a slight nod. With a voracious moan, he devoured her beautiful lips.

He forced himself to remember not to touch near her piercings as he slid his hands down her neck and then scooped her right breast upward. She shuddered, and a furtive moan spilled into his mouth. He swelled fiercely, and she felt him prod and beg for her attention through his jeans.

Another low moan echoed from her as she rubbed him, and he slid farther down the sofa. He guided her on top of him as she massaged. She popped the snap on his jeans, and a greed-filled growl thundered from his lungs.

He grabbed her hand. "We don't have to do this, sweetheart, but if you want to, after everything that happened, after you said you'd marry me, it's not gonna be on my couch. When you're ready, I'll take you to bed. We're going to make love. I'm going to make you mine." He was somewhat shocked at his own insistence.

Kaimi looked overwhelmed as she nodded.

"Please," she pled tenderly. "Please, now."

# CHAPTER 18

# SECRETS AND REVELATIONS

Garrett lifted her into his arms. He carried her carefully to their bedroom and laid her in the fresh flannel sheets. His mother had changed his linens as well. He gently eased the sweatshirt from her delicate curves. She wasn't wearing a bra, afraid that it might irritate the piercings, and a low, shuddering groan spilled from Garrett's mouth as he took her in.

"I need the stuff, but I want you so bad. I want to be yours," she continued to beg.

"I'll get the stuff, but right now I want to see you." He grunted as he took in the heavenly sight before him as he lifted the weight of her breasts tenderly with his hands. "You are so damn beautiful." He pulled off her jeans and panties and reclined her in his bed. He stripped quickly, grabbed the lube from her suitcase, and joined her. He cradled her body to his as he pulled her close.

He leaned and kissed her hungrily, allowing no space between her body and his. Garrett inhaled deeply as the heady scent of lush peach plumeria blooms and of Kaimi filled his nostrils. The tender heat she created began to restore and soothe him as the scent of sex flooded the air around them. His entire world narrowed to the feeling of her energy pulling toward his.

Her fingers traced down the trail of hair that led her to the base of his cock. He grunted in desperation.

She gave him a coy grin that did things to him he couldn't begin to understand. Garrett's head fell back as she traced his thickened veins and rubbed him. He grabbed her hand with his own and wrapped it tightly around his strain.

"Don't fucking tease, sweet girl. I can't take it. Pull from me. I want everything I am inside of you."

A voracious moan echoed all around him as she made heavenly draws of his erotic energy. Garrett reveled in the sensation and then dipped his fingers in the lube as he began to trace over her lips. She used the lack of space between them to grind her mound against his strain. Her warm, wet little pussy had him desperate and aching.

"Is that what you need, sweet girl? Do you need my cock to make it feel better?"

"God yes," she panted.

Garrett pressed his fingers inside of her and set to give her relief. He continued to stroke her tenderly and then pull away to use more lube as her body began to pitch and toss beside him.

"Can I suck you, baby?" he begged. "God, I need you in my mouth."

"Please, please." Her back arched as she moved her breasts toward his mouth. Garrett forced himself to work slowly. He kissed around the heavenly swells and licked the dew from between them. He drew her energy out and into his mouth in heavy doses. Her body writhed and rolled under his so he continued. He pulled her right breast in his mouth, swirling his tongue around her nipple as her moans grew fierce in their intensity. Her nipples throbbed rhythmically, matching the arc of her energy as it pulsed and thrummed around his hand.

"Feel it, baby. Relax and let me have you. I want to watch you come undone in my hand." Garrett urged her onward. He went back for more lube and on his re-entry she lost it all. Her body spasmed out of control as she convulsed from the sensation he hadn't brought her in far too many days.

"Just been too long, hasn't it," Garrett moaned. "Not anymore, honey. I'm gonna take good care of you." He pulled her body under his and braced himself on the mattress.

She continued to writhe underneath him. Her insatiable anticipation drove him wild. His mouth watered as fire exploded from his groin. He needed to drown himself in her. She held the only antidote to his exquisite pain

"You are so damn beautiful, so needy for me." Her body glowed from the heat they created together. That wildfire raged in her eyes. Her hands were wrapped around his cock, desperate for him to stake his claim and make every inch of her belong to him. Garrett had never seen anything more stunningly gorgeous. He let the potent energy of her desire fill him and the friction of their bodies moving together consume him.

He prodded at her lips with his length then guided his strain over her clit until her moans were unending.

"I need you. I need to be inside of you," he pled. With that, he pinned her arms over her head and sank low. He eased himself inside of her delicate little pussy. Her body inhaled his as he began to thrust gently trying to prepare her for more force.

With virtually no effort, his shield spilled from his pores, encapsulating them in his adoring love and complete devotion to her.

"Garrett," panted from her as her eyes closed in their ecstasy.

"That's right, sweet girl. Tell everyone who makes it feel better. Tell them who you belong to."

She swelled, and he transitioned until he was burying himself deeply within her—a place made all for him. He wanted only to exist in the ecstasy of her, to fill her so full she was complete only in him. He pounded into her, watching her tits dance to the rhythm of his force.

"Look at me, sweet girl," he urged.

Her eyes flashed open and they locked their eyes on one another as Garrett continued to make them one. Their energy was frantic in its elation to be rolling as one strain. It shimmered and danced inside of his shield with the heat rolling off of their bodies.

"You're so fucking perfect. I want to fill you so fucking full," he gasped as he lost his rhythm and took her hard and fast, and she spiraled over. The quivering pulse of her orgasm drove his, and he throbbed inside of her as he spilled everything he was deep inside of the woman that he was going to make his wife.

He collapsed on top of her, gasping for breath as he tensed through the end of his orgasm. Garrett eased from her and pulled her onto his chest as he covered them in the sheets and blankets. He kept her cradled to him. He never wanted her to move from right there.

"That was wow," she gasped when she could draw full breaths. He chuckled as he began rubbing more of the healing salve back over her lips and her slit. A harsh swallow tensed her neck, and she moved closer still. Garrett strengthened his hold on her.

"It was incredible. Being with you is always incredible."

"I love being inside of your shield. I feel so safe and loved. I mean, you must know what it feels like, but it's so amazing. I've never really felt safe before you put me in your shield. My life took its toll, I guess."

Garrett instantly spun his rhythms over her again. They were more languid now after his release but always held his love and his fierce protection for her.

"I love having you in here. It's where you should always be."

"Can we talk for a few minutes, even if I'm really, really tired?"

"Of course, but then you need to sleep. I'm beat too."

"You woke yourself up every half hour last night to check on me. That's why you're so tired." She shook her head at him.

"Someday you're going to understand that taking care of you is why I'm here on this earth. Fionna and Emily weren't exaggerating. Every cell of my body is intent on keeping you safe at all times. Shields are intense. We don't know how to be any other way."

"It's okay. I don't want you to be any other way. But do you remember yesterday when Adeline said that my rhythms were Kauaian?" He nodded as he recalled Adeline saying that she'd known because Kaimi's rhythms were similar to Fionna's. "But you don't know what that means so I want to tell you, but then I don't want to tell anyone else."

Garrett was deeply touched. "That's the way this is supposed to work, isn't it? We tell each other everything. I'll always keep your secrets, sweetheart." He was overwhelmed and so thankful that he'd been given the opportunity to rebuild their beginning with nothing between them ever again.

"I know you will," she whispered, and Garrett's heart soared. She brushed a kiss across his chest, making him smile.

"Tell me what it means."

"To have Kauaian rhythms means that one of your parents has those same island rhythms and that you were conceived on Kauai. Nana told me that she got pregnant with my mom on their honeymoon in California, and Nana was from Honolulu. So," Kaimi drew a deep breath.

"Your dad is from Kauai," Garrett finished for her. "And you were conceived there."

Relief poured from Kaimi as she nodded.

"Do you want to look for him, sweetheart? Maybe he still lives there."

"No!" Panic replaced her relief.

"Okay." Garrett backed off immediately.

"But that means I'll probably always be healthiest there because those are my rhythms."

Garrett lowered his shield. He was exhausted and needed to concentrate to talk to her. "I'm getting you back there as fast as I can."

"Oh, I know. I just thought it was kind of cool. I've never really known all of that before. The medios might have told Nana when I was little and sick all the time, but she never thought the island rhythms were that different. But I think they are."

"Near the end of Fionna's pregnancy, she was having all kinds of problems because of the gunshot wound. Dan took her to Kauai for two weeks because it made her better. It made her able to carry Halia as long as she could. So, from here to there makes a huge difference. Maybe your grandmother just had you as close as she could get you."

Kaimi seemed to revel in the fact that Garrett understood that her life hadn't been easy and that she had to make do with what they had quite often.

"I'm just excited to get to go back there and have you. I'm actually going to marry this amazing guy, and you really, really love me."

Garrett was elated she seemed to allow herself to believe that, but he was still hesitant. "Yeah, well, yesterday you weren't thinking I was too amazing, so I still have a lot to make up for."

Kaimi eased her head away from Garrett's chest to stare up into his eyes.

"Yesterday, after Maylea went to talk to *her* dad."

"Medio Sawyer," he provided.

"Right. Your dad had the girls, so she came back in the room. We talked about all of that. Maylea is amazing. She knows stuff about me I don't even know. How does she do that?"

Garrett grinned over just how adorable Kaimi was, especially when she was free of infection and letting him see into her capricious, wild soul.

Her rhythms had begun rolling in their customary, fluctuating pulses while she'd slept last night. Garrett had picked up on them in one of the many reads he'd drawn from her in the early morning hours. He'd made certain her fever never returned, and when her rhythms began to feel like her again, he'd been so relieved he'd almost cried.

She was his constant erratic and unpredictable baby. His wild girl that would love him for all eternity as long as he did the same, but that might, at a moment's notice, decide to streak her hair any number of colors, go get a body piercing or tat, or fly across the country to see him completely unannounced, and Garrett could never love anything more. She was incapable of staying on any one topic for any length of time. She was absolute perfection. He shook himself from his reverie to answer her question.

"Maylea is the most Gifted Receiver of our generation. She can even feel emotions from Non-Gifted people. Somehow, when she and Dan met and then refused to ever be apart, she got even stronger. She can feel stuff from both of us whenever we're near her. That's why she's so certain I've never been in love before and that you're all I'll ever want," Garrett explained softly.

"She gets that from Tutu. And she got stronger because Dan accepted her for who she is. He believes in her. When she tells him something, he never doubts her. He never tried to change her. He's in awe of her. You can tell by the way he looks at her. Anyway," Kaimi continued as they lay there in the soft serenity of their bed. The last of their erotic rhythms dissipated in the air around them as their whispers warmed them and their bodies continued to seek one another in the tranquil space of their love. "We talked about you and a little about her, and I believe you. I was just so scared."

He swallowed down the deep regret for what felt like the hundredth time. "I know, sweetheart. But the fact that I did something that scared you like that fucking destroys me. I love you too much for that." He tried to explain that she wasn't the only one that had been deeply affected by everything that had happened.

"Maylea said that too," she whispered. Clearly, Garrett had a lot of appreciation to give Fionna. He hadn't been sure she would come so readily to his defense. She and Chloe had been good friends at the academy and then through the Angels, but in that moment, he knew that his and Fionna's relationship had always been so much deeper than hers and Chloe's.

Garrett knew and loved Fionna for who she was, exactly the way she was. Chloe only wanted her as a cohort to go along with whatever Chloe wanted.

"I'm just really happy," Kaimi finally decided.

"Me too," Garrett agreed. They talked in whispers until they both fell asleep wrapped up in one another.

# CHAPTER 19

# PLANS AND SURPRISES

Late the next morning, Garrett awoke and smiled as Kaimi crawled back onto his chest. It had been an odd evening. They'd slept most of the afternoon, and then gotten up around eight and scoped out the news vans camped out in front of his apartment. They'd watched the Non-Gifted police run off the Gifted media for blocking traffic.

They'd watched television, eaten more of Mrs. Haydenshire's chicken soup, and then fell back asleep on the couch still curled up around each other. In the middle of the night, they'd woken back up, and Kaimi had been overjoyed with the fact that in downtown DC, you could have pizza delivered at three in the morning. Garrett had never had a pizza without pepperoni or ham, but the veggie pizza had been outstanding.

They'd gone back to bed after inhaling pizza and talking endlessly about their lives before and what the future might hold. After Garrett had pinned her to his bed and tickled her to get her to reveal the thing that he did when they made love that made her see stars, they'd engaged in another round of lovemaking. This one much more carnal and quick, which, much to his chagrin, had ended in her being sore. He'd lambasted himself until she'd pointed out that since it was her who had crawled over him and given herself a ride, she'd been the one who had gotten overzealous.

But at nine the next morning as she wiggled back into bed beside him, she seemed to be feeling better. Garrett had methodically rubbed her down with the lube as soon as she'd confessed her tenderness, and it appeared to have helped.

"It's so cold here when you get out of bed to pee. I forgot about that from when I lived in New York." She shivered, and Garrett spun heat out of his pores as he wrapped his arms around her and then swathed them in the flannel sheets and blankets of their bed.

"I'll keep my baby warm. Believe me, every winter day here I want to go back to Kauai probably worse than you."

"My tushy's cold," she whimpered with an adorable giggle.

"Can't have that." Garrett laughed as he moved his hands to her cheeks and pushed heat through them as he massaged. "Better?" He patted her backside then moved his hands up her back to cuddle her closer.

"Yes, but you don't have to move your hands," she informed him mischievously. Garrett continued to laugh as he kissed her and relocated his hands once again.

"We should get up. My body is confused about the time, and we have to figure out what life is going to be like until we move back."

Garrett understood her need for a little routine that would allow her to feel more free. "I've been really good with the whole sex, sleep, eat thing we've had going on. Pretty much a guy's dream come true."

"Aren't you supposed to be helping Dan with Venton, and Maylea and I are going to work on the new studio schedules and changes and the classes and routines with Malani remotely." She was thrilled with the latitude that Fionna was giving her with the new studio. "I'll be over at their house a lot."

"I have a Harley that I hardly ever get to drive. If you need to be over there and I need to be somewhere else, you can take the Highlander."

"It's winter and you'll freeze, and how did I not know you liked motorcycles?"

"I got it several years ago. I was into it then, but like I said, I hardly ever ride it anymore. Lost interest, I guess. I've been meaning to sell it."

"Can I ride on it first?" She sounded thrilled.

"Sure, sweetheart. I don't have to sell it. I could move it, but I could also get another once we move if you want." If it was something they could do together that she enjoyed, he certainly didn't mind, but he'd purchased it at a time when escape was all that sounded desirable to him. The faster the better. He knew Dan planned to bring his Agusta with him to Kauai.

"It's okay. I've just never ridden one. Nana would have croaked, well, earlier than she just did." She grimaced over her own expression.

"I will be happy to take you for a ride, baby. Anytime, anywhere—you just say when."

"Can we ride it over to the farm in a little while?"

"No," he lamented though he wasn't actually sorry at all. She tried not to act disappointed, but they'd been way too intimately bonded in the last twenty hours for him not to know that she was. "I have a surprise for you at the farm tonight, and all of my grandparents are coming over to meet you. Dan and Maylea and the girls are coming as well. Mom's throwing us an engagement dinner. So, I'm going to take you over there and hang until you're comfortable, then Logan and Dan are going with me to go get the surprise, and then we'll be back."

He'd planned his trip very carefully in the hospital the night before. Him leaving her at the farm and going off alone would only have bred more insecurity about Chloe and his past. But she seemed to adore Adeline and had extended her trust of Adeline onto Logan. She was growing to trust Dan more and more each day, so taking them with him assured her that Garrett wasn't going anywhere he shouldn't have been. He hated that he'd had to go to such lengths to earn back her trust, but he would do anything it took.

"I don't need a surprise. What if I get in your parents' way?"

"Sweetheart, my parents adore you. They'll be thrilled you're there, and hell, there are like two hundred acres out there. If they all start driving you nuts, you can escape. Just don't go too far 'cause I'll miss you."

"But…" she started to fuss again.

"Please let me do this. It's kind of a surprise for me too. I just need a few hours." He supposed he could take her with him out to the Wexlers' small farm in Maryland, but he really wanted to surprise her. "My mom wanted you to help her with dinner. She wants to get to know you. You know, some girl time. And Maylea and Adeline will be there."

Kaimi seemed to understand his desperation, so she gave a hesitant nod. "You're not going…" She wanted so badly to ask but decided she shouldn't.

"Never. I will never see her or talk to her again. I do keep my promises. This is for you and for me. Remember, I'm taking Logan and Dan with me. I'll take Dad too if that would make you feel better."

"No, it's okay. I'm going to marry you, so I have to be with your family. I love your family. I just want them to love me too. I don't want to get in their way."

"They already do love you, sweetheart."

"Okay, let's get ready to go over there. 'Cause now I kinda want my surprise."

Garrett chuckled. "There's one other stop I want to make first. There's someone I need to introduce you to. But before that, how about a nice hot shower with your own personal shampoo and lather guy?"

"Oh, is that what you're calling yourself now?" She feigned confusion.

"I'm out of work, so I figured I could try out a few new titles." He stood, grabbed her knees, and slid her to the end of the bed. He took her hands and hoisted her upward then threw her over his shoulder, thoroughly delighting the love of his life.

# CHAPTER 20

# THINGS THAT MATTER

After a long shower where Garrett had used every ounce of strength in his rather well-built body to repeatedly turn down Kaimi's offers of shower sex, since he was certain what happened in the middle of the night hadn't healed, he was smiling in the Highlander as he recalled their compromise.

"Seriously, that was awesome," she announced again.

Garrett had been grinning for almost a full hour about the way he'd pushed her over the edge without ever entering her. She'd returned the favor using her breasts, and her hands, and then her thighs, and that had been exquisite as well.

"We can learn all kinds of new ways to drive each other wild, and we have the rest of our life to discover all of them."

"Where are we going?" she finally asked as he turned down a two-lane road deep in Alexandria.

"There's someone who means a lot to me, a lot to my whole family, that I want you to meet. Plus, I owe him an apology."

Her brow furrowed. "An apology for what?"

"Not listening to him when I sure as hell should've." He turned into the gravel lot and smiled. Sam was in his customary coveralls and was hunched over a classic Oldsmobile Cutlass convertible. When Garrett threw the Highlander into park, Sam stood and smiled. The smell of gasoline and oil mixed with the scent of Old Spice aftershave, and Garrett's entire body eased.

Sam grabbed a rag and wiped his hands while Garrett helped Kaimi out of the car.

"Don't tell him I said this, but she's a whole lot prettier than Big Man." Sam offered Garrett his hand.

He chuckled. "I won't tell him. This is Kaimi Walyuo, my fiancée."

Sam's smirk turned into a broad grin. "Miss Walyuo, I'm Sam, and you can call me Sam."

"He's been taking care of the Haydenshire cars and all of the Haydenshires for as long as I can remember," Garrett explained.

"It's so nice to meet you." Kaimi gave Sam one of her beautiful smiles.

Sam turned his kind eyes on Garrett. "Yeah, I read in the papers this morning that congratulations were in order. Funny thing when you finally meet the one your mama's been praying for and you've been refusing to believe in, isn't it?"

"Yeah, kind of like meeting an angel."

"Believe I told you she was out there. You weren't ever much on listening to anything that wasn't your own voice though."

Garrett nodded. He stared Sam down. "I'm sorry about that. I should've listened."

Kaimi swooned and stood on her tiptoes to brush a kiss on his cheek.

Sam chuckled. "How 'bout a Coke for old times' sake."

"That'd be good." Garrett nodded. He gestured to the Olds Sam had been working on. "Is that a '65?"

Sam casted the ancient Coke machine in the back of the shop and forced it to give him three Cokes in glass bottles. He handed one to Garrett and one to Kaimi. "Got a bad fuel pump and 'bout every hose that can have a leak is leaking, so it's either a '65 or Oldsmobile hadn't learned much in the last few decades."

"Did you buy it or are you fixing it for someone?" Garrett helped Kaimi up onto the bed of a truck parked in the lot.

"I seem to have inherited it." Sam didn't look too thrilled with that information.

"From who?"

"My brother-in-law."

Shock washed through Garrett. "I didn't know either you or Dolores had any siblings."

"I never did. Don't s'pose she really did either. Seems to me you shouldn't be qualified as a brother if you never did much caring, but blood's blood. Dolores's brother passed a few weeks ago. Probate court let me know I was willed this." He gestured to the car.

"I'm…sorry," Garrett offered.

"Me too."

"Do you not think you can fix it?" Garrett couldn't fathom a car that Sam couldn't fix. The same went for life problems. Confusion furrowed his brow.

"It's not that I can't. It's that I don't want to."

"Why?" Kaimi asked and then cringed like she hadn't meant to speak. Garrett laced her fingers through his.

Sam gave her another kind smile. He stared at the Olds but seemed to be seeing through it. "First time I ever seen that car, I'd say I was about twelve or thirteen years old. I spent every summer all summer working at my uncle's filling station. Wasn't too far from here. Only day we weren't open was Sunday, which meant that was my least favorite day of the whole week. I used to sit in Sunday services and listen to the preacher talk about heaven. I'd tug at the collar of my starched shirt and sweat in that wool suit my mama forced me into, and I'd try to envision it. I couldn't reckon what anybody would want with streets of gold. Didn't seem to me that cars would get any kind of good traction on that. I couldn't see the point. What good's a road without a car?

"'Sides, I was pretty sure my uncle's filling station was better than heaven anyway. It was a big deal station with three pumps and an old Coke machine that was brand new back then." He gestured to the Coke machine in his own shop. "Sold S&H Green Stamps, Atlas Plycron tires, and Cherry Bomb mufflers so every mama, daddy, and hotrodder for miles 'round DC knew our name. I got to work on 'em all.

"I spent my days pumping gas, checking batteries, and filling up radiators. If I was real lucky, one of the hotrodders might let me kick the whitewalls with him for a few. One of 'em had a '64 Chevelle. Used to let me drive it around the back lot as long as my uncle didn't notice.

"Every now and then, some white lady'd pull up in her car, and I'd come out when the bell rang. She'd decide she didn't want me working on her car. Didn't even want me near her. I never understood that. I'd try to tell 'em that I was better at pumping gas and putting air in tires than anybody else. Uncle Roy'd always shake his head and tell me it didn't matter how good I was. They couldn't see outside their own fancy hats. I never did care for that excuse. Seemed to me, if they couldn't see outside of their hats, maybe they should take 'em off. Used to make me so mad. Made me mad 'cause it made me doubt that Uncle Roy's shop was heaven, and I didn't care for that thought." He shook his head and drew a long sip of his Coke.

"But when I got to worrying about all that's wrong in this world, Uncle Roy'd pull me a pack of bubblegum that he sold near the register, feel around in it real good, tell me that he was certain the baseball card in it was Willie Mays, and he'd hand it over." Sam's smile touched the deepest wells of Garrett's heart.

Kaimi blinked back tears. "Did you get Willie Mays?" she asked. "Please say you did."

Sam patted her leg and shook his head. "Nah, I didn't ever get Willie Mays, but tell you the truth, that wasn't who I wanted anyway."

"Who'd you want?" Garrett asked.

"Ernie Banks. Five grand slams in one season and more home runs than any shortstop I'd ever heard of. Used to wonder if the white ladies ever told him that he wasn't good enough to run the infield. Made me kind of feel better to think they did, and then he showed them."

Garrett gave him a solemn nod. "Banks was the best damn shortstop there's ever been, and you're an even better mechanic than he was a shortstop. Did you ever get his card?"

"I did. Had to chew a whole lot of gum, but the day I finally got Banks's card in a pack of bubble gum was the first day I ever saw that car." He pointed back to the Olds. "I figured it was a red-letter day.

The Coke man had come up from Atlanta the day before. He'd filled the machine so the bottles were nice and cold by the time I got to work. I put my shiny new Banks card in my front pocket, got me a Coke, and got to work. I was putting oil in a Bel Air, when I seen this fancy Olds convertible pull in. I hadn't gotten to work on a 4-4-2 yet. I'd only been under the hood of a F-85.

"I rushed to finish up the Bel Air and went to see what the Olds needed. I just knew he was gonna let me install a Cherry Bomb in that Cutlass. I couldn't wait. Big guy who looked a lot like me rolled the window down and asked to see somebody who knew what they was doing." Sam shook his head. Disbelief still wounded his tone. "I told him I knew what I was doing. I was happy to help. Said I'd just fixed that Bel Air up. Olds were easier to work on than Chevys.

"He climbed out of the car. I looked up at him and figured he had to be six foot six at the least. I figured he was a big time basketball player maybe, and he just thought a little too much of himself. He waltzed into the shop, and I figured my uncle'd tell him I was plenty good enough to work on his Olds.

"While he was gone, I looked over in the passenger seat and saw this girl who was about my age. Prettiest thing I'd ever laid eyes on. She waved at me and smiled. Said she was real sorry her brother was such a drag. I waltzed over to her side of the car. She rolled the window down and smiled. It was right then and there that I learned that heaven wasn't at the gas station. Heaven was when she smiled.

"Being a boy of about thirteen, I figured I knew just the way to impress her. I pulled out my brand new Ernie Banks card and showed it to her. She didn't tell me 'til after we married that she was a Mets fan." He shook his head. "I think I still woulda gone on with the marriage, even if I'd known beforehand."

Garrett and Kaimi laughed.

"She told me her name was Dolores and her family was new in DC. That she didn't know nobody. Her brother had just been hired on as a preacher at a church downtown. I told her I'd show her around, that I knew just about everybody worth knowing and lots of folks who weren't. She laughed, and I fell in love right then and there, standing on an old oil stain on the concrete in dirty coveralls with her holding my Banks card.

"Right about then, her brother came back outta the shop. He already didn't much like me, and my uncle hadn't improved things. Told him he was a showoff. Made him even madder than he was normally. He got to the car and saw me talking with his little sister. He yanked my card out of her hands and tore it up. It was in almost as many pieces as my heart. He told me I was a disappointment to my kind, that I'd never be any good to anyone, and to stay away from his sister. Got in his car and left."

"Sam," Garrett choked out as he shook his head in devastation. "My god."

Kaimi was crying in earnest. "I'm so sorry people are so mean."

Sam nodded. "I'd never had anybody but them ladies think that I wasn't good for anything. I learned that there will always be people who decide that you should be something different to suit them. In my experience, they're the ones who dislike themselves the most and tend to want you to feel that way too so they can feel better.

"But a few years later, I started at Venton and ran into the girl who'd been sitting in that car. I hadn't seen her since that day. Turns out she was even prettier at sixteen than she was at thirteen and that's saying something. Honest to goodness, it didn't occur to me when I asked her to go with me to the drive-in that Friday night that I'd have to see her brother when I picked her up.

"It hit me when I pulled in her driveway and saw that Olds though. I decided I didn't care what he thought. I was gonna take her out and show her a good time. I'd prove myself. But that's the thing. You can't prove anything to anyone who can't see outside of their own hat. I marched up to the door and rang the bell. He answered. He didn't seem to remember me at all. I'd never forget his face. I told him I was there to pick up Dolores. He asked what I did for a living. I puffed up as tall as I could get myself and told him I was a mechanic at Roy's Texaco. Before he could say too much, Dolores was heading my way.

"He spent his whole life and our whole marriage telling us that we were disappointments. One day Dolores finally asked him what it was that made us so bad. All he could really tell her is that we weren't the way he wanted us to be. Weren't educated enough, smart enough, wealthy enough, godly enough. That did it. She told him she was tired of his kind of ugly, and she wasn't having it no more. That God had made us just the way we were and if he couldn't see that maybe he shouldn't be preaching the word. We never saw him again. He didn't come to her funeral. I didn't go to his."

Garrett considered the entire story. "So, you don't know if him willing you that car is supposed to be some kind of amends or if he's getting in one last dig."

Sam nodded. "That's the thing people don't seem to understand. Once you go on, all that vengeance and miserable you carried around with you, it dies too. I wonder now if it's still worth it to him. He missed a whole lot of good times trying to turn us into something we weren't ever gonna be."

Garrett slapped him on the back and squeezed his shoulder. "You know what I think you should do with that Olds?"

"What's that?" Sam grinned like he already knew what Garrett was going to say.

"I think you oughta fix it up, sell it, and get yourself an Ernie Banks card, just to show him."

Kaimi nodded her adamant agreement.

Sam laughed but then he shook his head. "I've no need to show anybody anything. But I did marry his sister, and we had a good life. When I found the one my mama had been praying for me to find, and I made her mine, that card just didn't mean much anymore. There are a lot of things people want in this life, but there aren't that many things they really need." He nodded to Kaimi. "If you've got what you need, ain't no use to anyone chasing something you just want to spite someone else. You keep holding on to your angel, and let 'em have their miserable. I promise when the time comes that you and I are figuring out how to get traction on those roads of gold, that'll be the only thing that really mattered. So get that in your head right now, boy, before you get her down an aisle. There are things that matter, and there're things that don't."

Just then an M-Class pulled onto the lot, and Sam beamed.

Garrett and Kaimi hopped off the tail of the truck.

Sam's daughter, Deidre, climbed out of the car, and his granddaughter, Amena, raced into her granddaddy's arms.

Sam looked up at Garrett as he scooped her up. "It's all that'll ever matter."

Garrett hugged Deidre and introduced her to Kaimi. She told him her daddy had always told her that Garrett would settle down someday, but she hadn't believed it.

Garrett nodded. "He was right. He always is."

"Don't tell him that," she teased.

CHAPTER 21

# PRIDE OF THE LION

"Will you give me a hint about my surprise?" Kaimi tried again as they turned down the two-lane road that led to Haydenshire Farm. Garrett considered, but he didn't want to give anything away.

"I think I'll just keep you guessing."

"Ugh," she huffed.

As he helped her out of the Highlander, Garrett moved his back in front of Kaimi. He stooped down, reached back, and grasped her backside.

"What are you doing?" She giggled.

"Jump," he urged.

She leapt up on his back, and he looped his hands under her thighs to keep her steady.

"I told you I like to give you rides." He was so thrilled she felt better he wanted to revel in her for the next few minutes before he had to leave to go get her surprise. She wrapped her arms around his neck.

Garrett bound up the steps, making her shriek as he exploded through the kitchen door. Mrs. Haydenshire shook her head from her almost permanent location behind the island cutting up vegetables.

"Garrett, son, she just got out of the hospital. Please don't break your fiancée," the governor scolded. He was seated at the kitchen table where he was spooning applesauce up for Abigail who was licking the spoon delightedly.

Kaimi giggled. "I'm much better."

"Dan and Fionna are on their way. They would have already been here, but Halia apparently felt that her outfit and car seat lacked what was supposed to remain inside of her diaper and decided to rectify that situation on their way," Mrs. Haydenshire explained.

Kaimi and Garrett both cringed as the governor chuckled his understanding.

"Not sorry I missed that," Garrett said.

Haydenshires began arriving and meandering in and out of the house.

"Is Grandpa coming tonight?" Garrett handed Kaimi a Dr Pepper from the fridge and then got one for himself.

"Yes, and you might want to give Kaimi a little warning about him before you go on your errands," Mrs. Haydenshire suggested.

"Aww, he's not that bad." Garrett had never understood his family's inability to ignore ninety-nine percent of what came out of Grandpa Haydenshire's mouth. He just wanted to rile them up. Getting a reaction was always his goal though he'd never admit that.

Grandpa Haydenshire's rude thoughts on Adeline's parentage had been thrown in his face when she proved to be a princess, and he'd even apologized. Grandpa lived his life in a battle zone. When he'd retired from the Gifted branch of the army, the entire world had become his frontline. If you gave him a little argument, he was happy.

"Yes, well, he can be a little hard to take if you're unprepared," Garrett's mother reminded him.

Garrett turned to Kaimi. "Then allow me to prepare you, my love. My grandpa is full of one hundred proof, Grade A bullshit. He loves to argue. Don't listen to most of what he says. If he gets out of line, ignore him. If he bothers you, I'll take care of it."

"Uh, okay." Kaimi's brow furrowed.

Logan and Adeline arrived. Adeline guided Kaimi and Garrett up to Emily's old bedroom to check her chest.

"You look much happier than you did in the hospital," she commented with a knowing grin as she examined Kaimi's breasts.

"I am," Kaimi assured her as she and Garrett were absorbed in simply staring into the depths of one another's eyes. Adeline chuckled at them as she lowered the sweatshirt back down.

"I'd say another few days without a bra, or at least maybe go get a few that are low cups so they don't irritate. They're almost healed up and look much better."

"I don't have any bras with low cups. I need to go get some new clothes and stuff if we're going to live here for a while. All of my stuff is island weather rated not Virginia winter ready."

"You can borrow some of my stuff if you want," Adeline offered excitedly. "I wear scrubs most of the time anyway." Garrett doubted that would work. Kaimi was several inches shorter and had more muscular curves than Adeline who was tall and willowy.

"Oh, it's okay. Thank you though. I'll just get a few things. Maylea probably knows where I could get some good deals."

Adeline laughed. "Fionna probably knows what's on sale, what's coming in for the next three seasons, and what you'll be able to wear to be in high fashion for the next two years in every store in the city."

Garrett chuckled at the girls' awe of Fionna. Neither he nor Logan would ever have cared what either of their wives or soon-to-be wives wore as long as they were comfortable. Garrett enjoyed a skimpy bikini or a low-cut dress as much as the next guy, but neither he nor his little brother would ever want Kaimi or Adeline to be more like Fionna.

"I'll take her with me maybe."

"Oh, I would. Shopping with Fionna is so much fun, and she can seriously take rags and make them look good."

"If you look like her, everything looks good."

"Okay, would you both stop?" Garrett wasn't certain how much more female self deprecation and admiration he could withstand. "It's getting deep in here."

Kaimi stood up from Emily's old bed, and Adeline blushed slightly.

"You're fine—just keep taking the antibiotics and you'll be good." Adeline assured her.

A few minutes later, Garrett left Kaimi on the couch with Fionna, Adeline, and Emily all discussing places to acquire Kaimi a small winter wardrobe for as little money as possible since neither she nor Garrett were employed.

"Fi and I are happy to pay her for her preliminary work on the studio," Dan commented as he followed Garrett and Logan out to the Highlander. "Fionna is in awe of her ideas and the classes she wants to teach. We don't mind."

"I'll talk to her, but I doubt she'll let you. She wants the studio to be bringing in money first. If we get Venton cleaned up, then we can all move and make that happen, right?" Garrett headed toward the Wexlers' acreage outside of Lanham.

"You seem a little excited about all of this, bro," Logan called Garrett on his enthusiasm. He and Logan's rhythms had always run similarly. Keeping his promise to Cal, Garrett had spent a lot of time with Logan in the last several years. He could read Logan just as easily as Logan could read him.

"I am. She'll love it. I've thought about doing this a million times, but I never had enough time. So, now I do, and she'll be there when I'm not." Garrett pushed the pedal faster and pulled into the parking lot of their first stop.

Two hours later, Garrett took his surprise from Dan's arms and leapt out of the Highlander.

"She and Fionna took Aida out to the lake." Tad met him at his car and handed him the ring which he quickly attached.

"Perfect. Thank you." Garrett was thrilled. His entire family discreetly slipped out the side kitchen door as Garrett rushed toward the backyard.

He set his surprise on the ground with an urged, "Go get her, boy." He gestured to the lake, and the golden retriever puppy took off toward Kaimi and Aida.

"Hey, baby," Garrett called as Kaimi turned, and her eyes goggled.

124

Her mouth fell open in a delighted grin as she scooped up the bounding puppy.

"Oh my gosh!" Garrett raced toward them. "Is this for us? We get to keep him?" she gasped. "How did you do this?" She hadn't seen the ring. "I love him so much. I always wanted a dog, but I could never have one in any of our apartments."

"He's ours and he has a surprise for you too."

Her brow furrowed as Garrett proceeded to scratch under the dog's chin, making him rear his head back and reveal the tiny band of intricate diamonds with one larger swirled in the center that Tad had made to match the tattoo wedding bands Kaimi had designed.

She almost dropped their new puppy. Tears sprung to her eyes.

"Oh my gosh. It's perfect. How did you do this?" She began crying in earnest.

Garrett unhooked the collar and took the ring before reclasping it. He got down on one knee. There, on his parents' dock by the lake, on the farm that had raised him, with his family surrounding him, he gazed up into her tear-filled eyes and watched his entire life finally fall into perfect accord. He had what he'd so desperately needed, the woman his mama had been praying for.

"Will you please, please marry me, Kaimi?" he asked with urgency and a fervency like he'd never felt.

"Yes," she managed as she cried on the dog while she tried to cradle him and let Garrett put the ring on her finger.

Garrett's heart flew. His entire body rang with love and fulfilled completion. He pulled the puppy from her grasp so he could kiss her.

When they finally broke apart, he made introductions. "This is Duke. His mama was a drug dog down at the main precinct. Pasha saved my life once. They've bred her a few times since she retired. I always wanted one of her pups, but I felt bad having to lock it up in my apartment all day every day. So, now we can take care of him while we figure out how our life together is going to be."

"This is perfect. I love him so much, and I love you so much," she gasped through her tears. Duke leaned and licked the tears from her face, making them laugh.

Fionna was sobbing as well, and Aida was jumping up and down and clapping. Dan and Fionna joined them on the dock.

Suddenly, Keaton took off in a headlong sprint toward the water.

"Keaton!" the governor shouted, "Do not get in the water! It's freezing."

But Keaton only laughed as he raced down the dock. "I swim!"

"No, sir," Mrs. Haydenshire called.

"Yes!" He shot a defiant glare at his mother.

Garrett shook his head, leaned back, and scooped Keaton into his arms just before he dove into the water.

Kaimi bit her lips together to keep from laughing as Keaton wriggled and tried to get away.

"You are in trouble, little man," Garrett warned.

"Yes, you are," Governor Haydenshire informed him as he lifted him from Garrett's arms and carried him back inside. He wriggled constantly in an effort to get out of his father's arms.

Mrs. Haydenshire shook her head but then pulled Kaimi in for a tight hug. She winced slightly.

"Careful, Mom." Garrett tapped his own pecs, and Mrs. Haydenshire backed away.

"Oh, I'm sorry, sweetheart. I forgot. I'm just so happy for you and proud of you. We're so happy to have you in the family."

"Thank you. I've never had a family before." She petted Duke's face. He licked her hand excitedly. As they were hugged repeatedly and slapped on the back, they meandered back into the farmhouse.

"Wexler said Duke was a natural-born protector just like his mama. They were going to send him into training until Garrett called," Dan explained to Fionna. "He'll be great to have on the farm." He scratched behind Duke's ears, thoroughly delighting the dog.

"I'm so excited. This was the best surprise ever," Kaimi continued to gush as she cradled Duke in her arms.

"Just so long as I get to be your favorite guy," Garrett harassed her.

"Maybe like a really close second."

"Oh, she's going to fit in just fine." Mrs. Haydenshire chuckled.

Garrett and Kaimi stayed outside with Duke until they were relatively certain the farmhouse floors wouldn't suffer his visit.

"You know when I said that I thought about being proposed to when I was Aida's age?" Kaimi reminded Garrett as she laid her head on his chest.

"Yeah." He kissed the top of her head.

"I never ever came up with anything as good as that." She wrapped her arms around him. Garrett beamed as he squeezed her to him. "How did you know I wanted a puppy?" Duke left the bushes he'd been investigating and bound in an odd sideways gallop back to Garrett.

"It was an educated guess, and I really wanted one. Now, we can both be home with him, and soon he'll have a massive farm to roam around, so it seemed like the perfect time. I was hoping that if you weren't sure about the little guy that the ring would win you over, but as you seem more taken with the pup than the ring, then I'm good with that as well." Garrett chuckled.

"Oh my gosh, no!" Kaimi shot her left hand out to admire the ring. "It's beautiful and perfect, and the whole entire thing is the most perfect day ever!!" She bounced against him.

CHAPTER 22

# SPARKS

A little while later, Garrett set Duke back in the crate he'd purchased on the way to the Wexlers' and joined everyone at the dining room table. The entire family was inundated with Keaton's infuriated shouts from the bottom step where he'd been seated to calm down.

"Da-yee is mean!" screeched from him constantly as he wriggled and stomped his feet.

Garrett shook his head, and everyone tried not to laugh.

"When you can take deep breaths and use your kind voice again, you can come tell everyone you're sorry and have dinner with your brothers and sisters," Governor Haydenshire informed him.

He burst from the step and stomped to his booster seat. Mrs. Haydenshire discreetly rolled her eyes, but then she cleared her throat. "What do you say, Keaton?"

"Not sorry!" he defied.

She directed him back to the step.

He glared at her. "Sorry," he huffed.

Will lifted him up into the booster seat and strapped him in. "Use your big boy manners, Keat," he directed. Since pleasing his older siblings was still something he was interested in, Keaton gave him a sincere nod. Everyone dug in to the delectable meal.

"Got yourself a nice hunting dog there, Garrett. Now, what I want to know is what you're gonna do with her?" Grandpa Haydenshire pointed his index finger in Kaimi's face. Garrett chuckled under his breath as he lowered his grandfather's hand and wrapped his arm over Kaimi's shoulders.

"You've got to have somebody to come home to, right, Grandpa? Keep your bed warm, all that, otherwise what's the three-day pass for?"

Grandpa chuckled as he gave Kaimi an approving nod and continued to eat.

The dumbfounded expressions on his brothers' faces had Kaimi beaming up at Garrett as she leaned and kissed his cheek. He winked at her before returning to the chicken parmesan his mother had created.

"When Aunt Kaimi comes to my house to play and to help Mommy dance, can Duke come too?" Aida asked Dan.

"Sure, baby, and soon we'll all live on the same farm so you'll be able to see Duke every day," Dan assured her. She beamed at Garrett.

"Commander Vindico, I heard you came back to your senses and are gonna lay siege to the great state of Hawaii. Japan tried that, boy. Didn't work too well for them," Grandpa Haydenshire challenged.

Dan chuckled. He had Grandpa's number as well. "Yes, sir. I'm looking forward to getting back into law enforcement. Been way too long. We move out as soon as I take care of the conflicts at Venton. It's a mess, sir." He said *all* of the right things.

"I tell you what was a mess, Daniel…" Grandpa began.

"Korea," Garrett, Rainer, Logan, Dan, Will, Patrick, Connor, and Levi all mouthed the word as it fell from Grandpa Haydenshire's mouth. He talked for fifteen minutes while everyone else ate in relative peace.

"That's a great base out there in Oahu. Met quite a girl out there once. Hawaiian girls, they're something else, aren't they, boys?" Grandpa Haydenshire waggled his eyebrows at Dan and Garrett.

"None like 'em anywhere else, sir." Dan kissed Fionna's cheek. She and Kaimi were laughing.

"Amen," Garrett chimed.

After dessert, Kaimi and Garrett helped with the dishes. Kaimi would occasionally pause to stare at her ring in disbelief.

"You're engaged. Do you want us to jump up and down with you?" Emily offered as Fionna nodded her agreement.

"Maybe." Kaimi giggled.

"I just got Abby to bed, girls, but you're welcome to jump outside," the governor directed them to the back deck, bringing on more laughter.

~

"All right, Duke, welcome home." Garrett set him on the hardwood floor of the apartment. He and Kaimi watched him explore with his nose and then his tongue. He moved toward the couch and immediately sank his teeth into the soft leather end. Garrett pulled him away making him whine.

"Aww, did Daddy make you cry?" Kaimi scooped him up as Garrett shook his head at her.

"Uh-huh, I see where this is going fast."

She settled on the couch with Duke in her lap, and Garrett joined them. Duke crawled between their thighs and fell asleep a moment later.

"Thank you so much. He's so sweet, and I'm just so happy. After everything, I just wish I could show you how much I love you." Kaimi leaned over their puppy to lay her head on Garrett's shoulder.

"I could think of a few ways, baby. Don't worry." Garrett chuckled as he wrapped his arm around her.

She smirked. "Can you?"

"Come here to me. I'll show you." Garrett engaged her in several long, drawn-out kisses.

Duke leapt up suddenly and decided to join in the kissing.

"Hey, only I get to lick her, man," Garrett harassed as he and Duke began playing with one of the toys Garrett had purchased for him.

"How did his mama save your life?" Kaimi whispered as she joined Garrett and Duke on the floor for tug-of-war.

"Pasha worked with the Non-Gifted drug enforcement unit. I went out with them one night. I always volunteered for those because they can get ugly quick, and I loved working with Pasha. She was incredible. We were in the cars watching a house before we went in. I was in a squad car alone with Pash. She started barking to raise the roof and jumped in my lap about two seconds before a carbine round from a sub-machine bounced off the shield I'd just thrown. It would have come through the window and hit my face and her. I never saw the gunman. She somehow knew they were going to fire." Garrett shuddered slightly.

"Oh my gosh." Kaimi hugged Duke fiercely. "I'm really, really glad you're coming home with me. Being a cop here is too dangerous."

Duke bolted back to the door, slipping and sliding most of the way as his paws were still too big for the rest of his body. He barked and then turned his head expectantly back to Garrett.

"He's already house-trained?" Kaimi looked stunned as Garrett quickly harnessed Duke and grabbed his Iodex heat-synced jacket.

"Wexler trains the drug dogs. He's the best trainer I've ever seen. He started training Duke as soon as he was weaned, so he's mostly trained. He will be fiercely defensive of me and you just like his mama. So, when I'm not there, he'll keep you safe, which is another reason I wanted to get him for you." He was surprised that Kaimi grabbed another of his Iodex coats. He stopped her and used his hand to fill the heat syncs before he allowed her to join them for their chilly evening stroll.

"Do you think his bed will be warm enough?" Kaimi worried as she clung to Garrett's arm as he held the leash.

"We can put it in our bedroom in the corner. I bought him some blankets too. He'll be all right. I'd say he could sleep at the end of our bed, but I have plans for you this evening, Miss Walyuo, and Duke seems to be getting all of my kisses."

She giggled and gave him his favorite curious, mischievous grin. "What kinds of plans?"

Garrett inhaled deeply. He caught the slight scent of her in the thin, icy air. "The kind that end up with me deep inside of you, sweetheart. We're going to celebrate this roller-coaster ride we're on that I don't ever want to stop."

She beamed and watched as Duke picked out a bush to make use of. "Hurry up, Duke. I'm cold, and Garrett has really good plans for the evening."

Garrett laughed at her outright as he kissed her forehead. His visible breath caressed her face, and she shivered deliciously.

Kaimi examined her ring again. She was still grinning broadly every time she looked at her hand.

"Do you still want to do the tattoo bands?" she asked suddenly.

"I'm good with whatever means I'm married to you and that you're mine forever, but if you want traditional bands, I'll never take that off either."

"My mom's been married seven times," she confessed in a disappointed whisper. Garrett had never thought to ask.

"Wow."

"I like the idea that the tat is on there, you know. It's permanent. I want that. Going back isn't an option."

"Done." Garrett certainly understood her reasoning.

"Is your whole ginormous family going to come out for the wedding?" The hope in her eye pricked Garrett's heart.

"I can't see why not. I can't guarantee everyone, but Mom and Dad definitely, and as many of the others as can possibly be there."

She grinned and nodded as Duke finished up and galloped back to Garrett.

"Who will you choose to be your best man? You have to have one for the exchanging of leis." Kaimi seemed thrilled to be thinking about their wedding.

"Will," Garrett answered without thought. Kaimi nodded, and another beautiful smile lit her face that was pink from the cold.

"That's what I thought. I was trying to guess, and I had it narrowed down to Will or Dan but I couldn't decide."

"Both excellent choices, but Will and I have been partners in crime for far too long for me not to have him there."

"Did you ever tell Will?" she whispered as Duke began sniffing the concrete sidewalk with a great deal of interest.

"No, baby. I told Dan and Fi just a few weeks before I met you. They're the only ones that know besides you." He tried to make her understand the depth of his devotion to her. Kaimi nodded as she leaned up on her tiptoes and kissed his jawline.

"All right, boy, let's go get you to bed. I have plans for Mommy," Garrett urged Duke just to hear Kaimi giggle again.

The sound warmed places of his soul that he hardly recognized. They'd been buried for too damn long, and with that luscious grin and sweet laugh, with every draw of her energy, every spark between them when their lips met and their tongues danced together, every time he felt her body make his whole, he knew she was the only thing he could never live without. He couldn't fathom how he'd gone on for so long without her already.

# CHAPTER 23
# FLAMES

They walked hand in hand back through the parking deck and removed the rest of the supplies for Duke from the back of the Highlander. Suddenly, Duke jerked at the leash on Garrett's wrist. He began barking and growling, trying desperately to be ferocious.

Garrett spun and threw his shield instantly over Kaimi and Duke. His mouth hung open in shock as he took in Chloe standing before them, scowling viciously beside some guy Garrett had never seen before.

He started to demand to know why she was in his parking deck and how she'd gotten in, but then he recalled his promise that he'd never speak to her again.

"You know, I think before you go off and get married, I deserved at least a conversation," Chloe spat viciously.

The guy with her looked utterly bewildered, but Chloe Sawyer had a way of getting men to do whatever she wanted, so Garrett wasn't surprised he'd agreed to come along.

He remained silent. He wasn't breaking his promise to Kaimi. He kept her hand locked in his own, and his shield in place over her. Kaimi stared up at him with shock etched on her beautiful face.

"Answer her," she urged in a pleading whisper.

"Are you sure?"

She nodded as she clung more forcefully to Garrett's hand and forearm.

Garrett moved his shield off his own body, but kept it wrapped around Kaimi.

Chloe rolled her eyes.

"I don't know what the hell you've come to do, so don't roll your eyes at me for trying to keep my fiancée safe. And you're absolutely right. You did deserve a conversation, which I tried to have with you right up until the moment you started taking your clothes off and then acted like a fucking bitch. So, no, we're done. This is it." He pointed to Kaimi's hand to display the engagement ring. "I have nothing else to say to you." He turned to the guy standing steadfast by Chloe's side. "Did she bring you to fight her battles for her? Because take it from me, run now. We're through, Chloe, so however the hell you got in here, turn around and go back."

"Uh…you didn't say he was an Iodex officer." The guy cringed and gestured to Garrett's jacket.

"Yeah, I was second in command of the Elite squadron and am set to help run Iodex in Hawaii soon. So, how about I don't smash your face in because of how she's looking at my fiancée, and you take her home?" Garrett offered the bargain. The guy gave a slight nod and stepped back. Kaimi leaned down, and Garrett released her hand long enough for her to scoop up Duke who was still growling ferociously at Chloe.

"Shh, it's okay." Kaimi comforted the puppy. He turned to lick her face, showing his loyalty, before he whipped his head back and bared his teeth at Chloe.

"So that's it. You're just gonna go off to Hawaii and get married. You're engaged, and we slept together a few weeks ago."

Kaimi tried to hide her disgust and hurt, but Garrett felt it instantly.

"I fail to see your point. I didn't see you again or even talk to you after I started talking to Kaimi. I never cheated on her, and I will never cheat on her. I don't want whatever it was we had anymore. I'm sorry if that's hard for you to hear, but this is all I want. Somehow, I got it, so please just go. You've said your piece, so for once, just leave and don't come back," Garrett commanded. "Do not ever call me again."

Kaimi stared up at him. She seemed somewhat shocked by his vehemence. He had to have her trust. It was the only way a marriage was going to work. He would crawl to the ends of the earth to earn it back if he had to.

"Chloe, baby, come on. This guy's obviously over it, but I'm all about it. Let's go have some fun," the guy urged.

"You know what, *honey*," Chloe jeered as close to Kaimi as she could get without intercepting Garrett's shield. "You can have him and go play house until he gets bored. The one guy, with the house, and kids, and his mistress on the side, never really did it for me."

Kaimi drew deeply from Garrett's hand. Resolve and determination formulated in her features. "I do understand that this is all kind of a surprise. We're surprised as well. But what you just described isn't what we have. I'm tired of you just showing up here and treating me like I'm some kind of brainless slut. I feel sorry for you." Kaimi's fervor erupted in her vow. "Believe me, I know it isn't easy to find the right guy for you, and I know Garrett has a past, but I don't care. I love him and that's my decision no matter what you think. Maybe if you stop convincing yourself you don't want the right guy, you'd stop finding the wrong ones." She huffed with a slight nod at her own accomplishment.

Garrett couldn't help the broad, beaming grin that spread across his face as he gazed at her, certain he would never love anything more.

"Whatever," Chloe spat. "You can both go to hell for your honeymoon. Let's go, Greg."

Relief flooded Greg's demeanor as he grabbed Chloe's hand and pulled her out of the parking garage.

Garrett released his shield as he kept his eyes locked on Kaimi.

"Wow." He wrapped his long, muscled arms around her, and they kept Duke cradled between them. "That was quite a speech, the future Mrs. Kaimi Haydenshire." The pride and self-worth that seemed to bloom within her at that moment delighted Garrett. She nodded and then a grin spread across her face.

"You're mine," she vowed.

"Yes, I am, and thank you for letting me be yours."

"I'm tired of doubting you because of her. I don't like that. Sometimes you have to just make the jump because that's the dance and,"—she paused and stared up at Garrett expectantly—"I have to let you catch me. I have to believe that you will."

Garrett swallowed down the onslaught of emotion that flooded his rhythms.

"I will. I swear to you. Don't be afraid, sweetheart. I'll always be there to catch you, always." He knew those words spoken in the parking deck of their temporary home were probably just as important as the ones he would make in front of a Hawaiian holy man on a beach somewhere in Kauai.

"Okay." She nodded determinedly. "I'm going to believe you."

"Come on." Garrett carried all of Duke's things onto the elevator. "I want you to fly for me tonight, sweetheart. And when you finally come back down, I want you to land in my arms because that's where you belong." The elevator doors closed on the two of them lip-locked in a fiery kiss that could've lit the entire building ablaze.

## CHAPTER 24
# UNITED

They fell into the apartment, still lip-locked and trying to manage dog toys, a bed, and blankets between them. Garrett unhooked Duke's leash and rushed to lay the large flannel dog bed in the corner of their bedroom.

"I want you, right now, in my bed, under me. I want to open you up for me." He grabbed Kaimi's waist and dragged her back to him. He crushed her mouth to his own. Garrett tried desperately to remember to be gentle with her chest and with the paradise between her legs, but he wanted her so badly he ached. Every breath, every nerve ending, every rhythm of his shield, every cell in his body quaked and begged to move her body with his own.

Duke seemed far more interested in barking by the door as he paced in an effort to make certain Chloe didn't return than in what Garrett and Kaimi were doing.

"Now," Kaimi commanded as she closed the bedroom door and shoved Garrett down on the bed. She was on fire. It lit from her eyes and blazed in her cheeks flushed from her desire. Her lips were already kiss swollen and glistened the color of strawberry wine. Her lush olive skin glowed enticingly. She stood before him so eager and ready to be taken it drove Garrett wild. She dispensed with the shirt she was wearing and stepped between his legs from his seated position on the bed.

Garrett wrapped his hands around her luscious backside and brought her breasts to his mouth. His hands slid up her slender waist, and he lifted her breasts as he began to consume them with his mouth. His tongue bathed her nipples as he sucked.

"I know what my sweet girl likes," he assured her as her moans began to pant and gasp from her body. "And I know how to get my baby wet and ready for me." He growled as he slid his teeth over her nipples, moving back and forth between them then sucking the nip he'd left, bringing her exquisite relief.

"You're all mine, sweetheart. All mine. I know it aches, doesn't it. That needy little ache deep in that sweet pussy needs to be filled, doesn't it? It's throbbing for me, isn't it? You feel it when I suck you. Only I can make it better, baby. My sweet girl needs to be filled full of me," he commanded, and she ignited in a blaze so fierce Garrett wasn't certain he was going to be able to contain her.

"Oh god, yes, please!" She clawed at his chest in desperation. She had her jeans off in a second flat, and Garrett pulled her back. He traced his fingers over the crotch of the cotton panties she was wearing. The sensations had her eyes rolling back as she trembled, hardly able to remain on her feet.

"You're swollen so nice and tight, sweet girl. I'm gonna drink you, and then I'm gonna open you up. And then when you're ready, baby, I'll fill you so full I make everything feel better."

She cried out for him in unending moans of ecstasy.

Garrett stood, tore his shirt from his chest, and dropped trou as he scooped Kaimi off the floor and laid her on the bed. He dragged her panties down her legs.

"You got these wet, baby. Such a sweet girl. You didn't mean to, did you? Just couldn't help it. It felt too good, didn't it? It's all right. I'm gonna drink it all. I want to taste that sweet honey." He eased her legs apart and stared down into the pulsing pink heart of her. Her body bucked, so desperate for him to begin.

"So fucking beautiful. My god, I'll never get enough."

He swirled his tongue just outside of her opening, and her body bucked off the bed forcefully. Her moans were unending as he licked below her, and she screamed out for him and for more. He lapped his tongue back up her slit, not giving in. Her fingers laced through his hair as she pulled him in, desperate for more.

He sucked her lips near her opening, driving her wild, and then swirled his tongue up over her clit before he returned just below her, giving her what she wanted but would never have asked for. He dragged his tongue upward and dipped it between her folds, and she lost it instantly. Her energy spilled in his mouth, and he sucked her dry.

"That's my sweet girl," he moaned as he delved back for more. Her rhythms exploded in intoxicating waves of erotic need. Garrett had never felt anything so astounding. It seared through him, lighting a fire that surged straight to his groin.

Her temperature spiked constantly as her body craved the unending, rolling orgasms he was set to make certain she had. Her hands clawed the sheets under her as her body arched back off the bed from the powerful orgasm.

Garrett grabbed the lube and dipped his fingers inside. He spread it over her opening and then pushed his fingers deep inside of her.

"Listen to me, sweetheart," he soothed. "I want you to come for me again like my sweet girl. I want you to feel me touching all of those places that are all for me. They ache to be full, don't they? I know, baby. Be a sweet girl and come for me, and I'll make it feel so much better. I know what you need. I'll fill that tight pussy so full, but not until you give me another one. You let go for me like my sweet girl, and then I'll bury it in so I can feel it with you."

Keeping his strokes deep and rhythmic as she shuddered and pitched under his hand, Garrett grabbed her right hand. He wrapped it around his strain.

"Feel how fucking hard you make me. You're gonna take it all. I know you want it. My sweet girl loves to be full of me." He had her. She convulsed and her entire body writhed against his. Her screaming moans reverberated in their rhythms spinning wildly around them, so desperate to be joined they glowed red in their heated need. The air they breathed swam thickly with the fiery passion of their consuming love.

Just as he'd promised, Garrett moved over her as the climax began to pulse around him. He pulled his hand away, moved on top of her, and thrust hard up inside her.

"Take it. Take what you need." He assured her as he began to open her. When she finally relaxed enough that he sank to his hilt, he groaned. "That's my sweet, sweet girl. Opens up wide for me."

He transitioned until he was pounding into her and pulling away in rhythms that had her begging for him never to stop as her orgasms continued to quake around him. "Take it all. You take everything I give you." He kept up his erotic commands. They had her going like nothing he'd ever seen before. "That's it. My sweet girl takes all of me and just keeps begging for more. You know you need it, don't you, baby?"

She was absolute perfection. She inhaled him in an exquisite blaze that lit from their souls as Garrett made them one.

"You feel so damn good. It's incredible," he growled as his body waged war against his mind. He fought his own release, but she was so tight and her orgasms rolled in unending perfection. They kept her trembling and tensing around him.

He pulled out to give himself a moment. She whimpered and writhed. "You put your ass up in the air and keep your head down, sweet girl. You fucking turn me into an animal, so you're gonna take it for me."

Her eyes flashed in raw, unadulterated ecstasy.

"Now," he commanded.

With an urgent, needy moan, she flipped onto all fours and shook her luscious ass for him. Unable to wait even a second more, Garrett grasped her hips and hammered her depths.

"Yes, yes," she gasped and clawed at the sheets.

Her warm, wet pussy clenched tight around him, and another feral growl poured from his lungs.

"Take every drop, baby. I'm about to fucking lose it all," was his last deep guttural command as his cock gave one last fierce throb and then erupted inside of her. He buried himself in deep and then collapsed on top of her.

As the erotic stupor began to dissipate, Garrett eased from her and prayed he hadn't gotten carried away. She'd loved every second of it, but she might not enjoy it so much in the morning.

Kaimi fell onto his chest, still gasping for breath.

"Are you okay, baby?" He hesitated. "I'm sorry that was too much." He went on with what he was certain would be a night full of apologies.

"Are you kidding me? That was the most amazing sex I have ever had and that includes all of the times I've been with you, which I was fairly certain couldn't be topped, but I was so, so wrong," she vowed with a delighted grin. "That kind of dirty talk…wow. Keep doing that."

Garrett smirked as he leaned and grabbed the lube again to try to ward off any potential pain. "I had a feeling you might like that."

She'd been told her entire life that desire was wrong, that sex wasn't something she should like or should want. When he had the opportunity to stand in slight authority over her and assure her that what she wanted was pure unadulterated perfection, he unlocked the very heart of her and slayed every doubt she'd been force-fed.

"I do now completely understand Chloe's devastation that somehow I got you, however." She giggled and let her eyes close as Garrett tenderly soothed her lips with his own calming energies and the lube.

He couldn't halt the chuckle that spilled from his mouth. "I'm not touching that with a fifty-foot pole."

He wiped his hands on a towel they'd used earlier in the day and then wrapped his arms around her tightly. Suddenly, they heard the frightened whines of Duke as he pawed at the door.

"Oh, my poor baby." Kaimi tried to stand but wasn't quite able to walk just yet.

Garrett tried to hide his smirk as he ran his hand over his mouth and raced to the door. "You sit. I'll get him."

Duke was pouting as his paws clicked on the hardwood floor as he raced to Kaimi in the bed.

"Mama's loud when Daddy gets her going, isn't she, buddy?"

Garrett lifted Duke up on the bed, and he immediately began licking Kaimi's face and crawling in her lap.

Kaimi giggled as she cradled Duke. He settled down immediately.

"I didn't mean to scare you." She apologized to Duke.

"He'll get used to it." Garrett waggled his eyebrows, effectively cracking her up.

The phone beside the bed rang.

"Whoops," Garrett grimaced. "Hello," he begrudged. "Yeah, sorry about that, Ms. Bakston."

Kaimi's eyes goggled as she turned back into Garrett's peach, her face streaked with red and pink in her deep embarrassment.

"Uh, no, you are allowed to have dogs here, but we'll try to keep him quiet." Garrett tried to pacify his elderly next-door neighbor who frequently used her hearing aid to listen in on all of the people in the building and then phoned them to complain. "Yes, I know, ma'am. Police officers should keep the peace. You're right." He rolled his eyes as Kaimi began giggling again.

"I don't actually think I'll tell my fiancée that, but we will try to keep it down."

# CHAPTER 25

# GROWING UP

Kaimi and Duke were both under the covers, one laughing, the other sighing contentedly.

"Bye." Garrett shook his head as he dropped the phone back in the charger on the bedside table.

"Oh my gosh, I can never leave your apartment." Kaimi refused to unearth herself from the sheets and blankets.

With a shrug, Garrett pulled on a pair of underwear and decided to join her, since it didn't appear that she was willing to resurface anytime soon. She laughed as he summoned a slight light cast and lit her crimson face.

"She does that to everyone, and she, the precinct, and my parents are the only people who have the phone number here, so I always know it's her. I have to have the stupid landline because of the precinct."

Garrett chuckled as Duke grabbed the sheets between his teeth and dragged them back down the bed.

Kaimi leaned and reached for the T-shirt Garrett had been wearing. She slid it over her head before she started petting Duke's ears.

"What did she want you to tell me?" She was still glowing crimson.

Garrett rolled his eyes again and shook his head.

"Tell me..." she urged. "Please...." She poked her lip out in a delicious pout that had Garrett chuckling.

"That will only get you so far, sweetheart." With a sigh, he began scratching Duke's side, until he rolled over for a belly rub. "Something about proper girls and decorum in the bedroom." He chuckled as Kaimi covered her face with her hands this time. "And by the way, it's *our* apartment."

"Oh, so now I have a crazy nosy neighbor too?" She giggled.

"I believe the saying goes for better or for worse."

The next morning, Garrett's stomach tensed, and his breath caught sharply as Duke's front paws hit his gut. He licked Garrett's chin.

"Glad you didn't land those a little lower." Garrett yawned as he shifted to pet Duke's head. Duke gave an urgent bark.

"Okay, okay, let Mama sleep." He eased from the bed as Kaimi grinned but didn't open her eyes.

"I see that." He kissed her cheek as he pulled on a pair of sweatpants.

"Shh, I'm sleeping." She giggled, still refusing to open her beautiful copper eyes.

"I'll just point out that you gave me the face last night, and now, our golden retriever thinks he gets to sleep at the end of our bed. Yet, I am the one taking him out at five thirty in the morning."

"I love you, and Duke loves you," Kaimi vowed as she tucked farther down in the bed, pulled Garrett's pillow into her chest, and squeezed it tightly.

"Uh-huh, well, I love you too." Garrett's shield lit as he let her vow wash over him.

Several minutes later, he and Duke raced back into the apartment.

"Okay, we have to get you and Mommy back to Kauai. She needs to be there, and I do not want to keep going out with you in twenty-degree weather." He scratched behind his ears and under his chin. He chuckled as Duke reveled in the sensation.

Garrett poured a bowl of puppy chow and wet it down per

Wexler's instructions. He set the food in front of Duke on the tile kitchen floor before refilling the water bowl. Duke leapt to the food and water as Garrett washed his hands and returned to Kaimi.

He grinned as he slid back in the soft flannel sheets and discovered that she'd heated them for him. Kaimi slipped onto his chest and formed herself against him.

"Mm," he sighed. "This is pretty much perfection."

"That's just what I was thinking," she informed him. "What time are we supposed to be at Dan and Maylea's?" She yawned as she began tracing her index finger over him through his sweats. Garrett shuddered as his cock began its rise to the occasion.

"Where?" Garrett feigned confusion as she continued to play. She giggled mischievously.

She continued to engage him in a playful make-out session that he suspected she would've liked to have gone further but was a little concerned after their intense lovemaking the night before that it might be more than her delicate body could handle.

Garrett's cell chirped from the bedside table, and he slid upright while keeping Kaimi tucked to his chest. He read Dan's text.

Chloe is asleep in our guest bedroom. Figured you might want to delay your arrival until Fi can get her up and out.

Garrett rolled his eyes. He tried to be patient. He knew Chloe Sawyer could be a genuinely kind person. She'd grown up with her father cheating on every relationship he'd ever committed to and then buying her love. But, all Garrett could think in that moment was how incredibly selfish it was that she'd gone to Dan and Fionna's when they had an infant and an eight-year-old who didn't need to be exposed to her drama.


**Dan Vindico**


"Did he reply?" Fionna sighed as she slid back onto Dan's chest.

"They may not be up yet, baby." Dan tried not to be annoyed that Chloe Sawyer was at their house. She'd shown up at eleven thirty the night before just as Dan was trying to sweet-talk his way into his wife.

Dan kept the mantra running in his head that Chloe and Fionna had been friends for years and that Chloe had always been there for Fionna. But after listening to Fionna talk her through Garrett's rather abrupt engagement and move, Dan didn't like Chloe any more than he had when he'd first started dating Fionna.

She'd finally gotten Chloe to admit that even if Garrett had professed unending love and had proposed to her, she wouldn't have accepted. She didn't want to get married or even be in a monogamous relationship with anyone. Basically, from what Dan discerned, she wanted Garrett to be available when she wanted to make use of his package, and there wasn't much more to it.

Dan reminded himself that those had been Garrett Haydenshire's precise requirements for the relationship as well. He refused to cast judgment on either one. But Garrett had done a great deal of changing in the past few weeks, and guys just didn't change that rapidly unless they'd buried their actual selves so deep they became dormant. It took the right person with the right heart and soul to awaken the man to the way he was meant to be.

Dan knew that from personal experience. He cradled his own personal saving grace naked in his arms in their bed that morning. But Chloe wasn't Kaimi. She couldn't see the changes in Garrett because Kaimi *was* the change in Garrett. Fionna had worked through the logic with Chloe and tried to direct her hatred away from Kaimi.

"He's moving thousands of miles away, and their jobs in Hawaii will take up a lot of time," she pointed out gently. This, however, had only brought on more tears as Fionna had been effectively confessing the fact that she wouldn't be back in Arlington too often either.

"I cannot believe she went over there last night. Poor Kaimi." Fionna's dejection pulled Dan from his reverie.

"Yeah, I'd love to know how Garrett talked his way out of that. I hope he didn't end up sleeping on the couch the night he gave her a ring."

"From what I could tell, Kaimi is the one that did the talking. I know Chloe was a total bitch to her. I just know she was. But whatever Kaimi said, it got to her."

Dan nodded. "I can't believe she gave the parking deck security a twenty, and he let her in." Halia's timid grunts of hunger came through the monitor.

Fionna sat up and grabbed her robe from the end of the bed. "Chloe is going to have to go home. As hard as I know this is for her, and as bad as I feel for her, I'm married and have children. I just can't live in her world anymore. I...don't want to," Fionna vowed as she let the final fragmented piece of her life before Dan and their daughters drift away from her soul. The papers had been reporting for months on her retirement from the Angels, but Dan knew it wasn't until that moment that she really let go.

He pulled her into his chest. "I love every version of you, past, present, and future. I'll get the little coconut. You go talk to Chloe. Growing up and moving on are tough even if you and I waited a little late to do that."

"Thank you." She leaned and kissed his jawline.

# CHAPTER 26

# PREFERENCE AND DEFERENCE

## ~GARRETT HAYDENSHIRE~

> Let me know when she goes home.

G arrett begrudgingly replied to Dan's text.

With an irritated sigh, he slid back down and wrapped his arms over Kaimi again. "Apparently, Chloe stayed over with Fionna last night. I think it's probably best if we just hang here until she's long gone," he replied to her question of when they needed to be at Dan and Fionna's.

"Seems like she's taking this really hard to have never been your girlfriend."

Garrett knew her faith and determination from the evening before had abated some in the morning light. He had to be patient. He'd lived the life that had earned her distrust.

"Let's talk about Chloe for a minute, okay?"

"Do we have to?"

"Yes." Garrett lifted Duke back up into the bed before he attempted to make the jump up himself. He gave up on trying to formulate what to say and decided to just speak. "Chloe doesn't really want me," he began but was met with an eye roll. "Listen to me, please. Chloe wants me to be available when she wants to have sex, and on some level, whether she'd ever admit this out loud or not, she knows that when I say I'm committed to someone, I'm engaged, and getting married, that I would never cheat on the person I'd made that commitment to. Chloe is just as incapable of having what we have as I am of having this with anyone else but you." That did it. Kaimi's entire body melted into a heartfelt swoon.

"Why did she say that last night? You know about you having a mistress and everything?" The very thought seemed to rob her of the will or ability to breathe. The thought made Garrett sick, so he understood.

"That's all she's ever known. Her parents divorced when she was six. Medio Sawyer is a hell of a medio, but when he wasn't in surgery, he and one of the nurses at the hospital had a thing going on. Chloe's mom found out and that was that. Chloe bounced back and forth from a mom who hated men and a dad who never told her no and just paid for whatever she wanted because he felt guilty for what he'd done.

"He remarried when Chloe was ten. That lasted about three years before he got caught pulling the same stunt with one of the surgeons. It happened again when she was fifteen. I think that time it was one of the department admins. He's got a girlfriend who lives with him now and two on the side last time Chloe said anything about it. So, to Chloe, that's how marriage works. She adores her father, but his life makes her believe all men are incapable of not cheating, so she's never given one the chance to hurt her like that."

"Wow," Kaimi whispered in begrudged acceptance that perhaps Chloe wasn't all bad. She turned introspective as she shifted so Duke could snuggle himself between them. "But I mean, of the four or five guys I've been in a relationship with, they all cheated on me. I still think you have to take a chance. I know she'd probably tell me I'm stupid, but what if you could get married and actually work on that relationship? You know, like Dan and Maylea do. What if you could do stuff that cements you as a couple? I think people can do that if they want to. I know it's hard though."

"They have to *want* to. Chloe's not willing to put in that effort. I wasn't willing to put in that effort until I met you. Now, that's all I think about—how to make you happy and keep us going strong. So, maybe the right guy is out there, and he'll do that for her, but it sure as hell isn't me. She's terrified of getting hurt, and honestly, she has a right to that fear."

Kaimi gave him a nod. "I'm gonna ask Maylea about being married. I'll be working with her every day, and I want her to tell me. She and Dan are so happy, and so close, and Aida said they kiss all the time. They both light up when the other one comes in the room. I want that."

"Yeah, Dan and Fi definitely have it going on. They work on it. They're not afraid to let people take the girls so they can have a little fun. I can also tell you that Aida walked in on them once with Fi in a corset and heels, leaned up against the wall, getting a spanking, so...." He chuckled.

Kaimi's mouth dropped open in shock. "They told you that?" She laughed.

"Fi told me. Dan would never tell anyone that."

~

At ten, Garrett knocked on the door to Dan and Fionna's home and was greeted exuberantly by Aida who leapt into his arms.

"Hey, baby girl." Garrett handed her the Christmas and birthday gifts that had been in his apartment.

"Thank you!"

Dan sauntered to the door carrying Halia and grinning.

"She's been talking about Duke all morning," he explained.

Duke was on his leash and sniffing around the Vindicos' front porch.

"Thank you for letting us bring him." Kaimi unclasped the leash as Duke followed Aida inside.

"No problem. I always thought about getting one of Pasha's pups, but I was never home and then we had these fairly quickly." Dan gestured to the girls.

"Hi, Duke, remember, I'm Aida." Aida leaned to pat Duke's head. He sprung up and licked her face delightedly. She giggled as she sat down, and he crawled in her lap. Eventually she opened her gifts from Garrett and thanked him profusely.

Fionna rushed down from upstairs looking flustered.

"Sorry, I was in the shower," she apologized.

Kaimi grinned as Fionna entered. She seemed relieved to have her there instead of just Dan.

"Can I ask you something?" Kaimi whispered.

"Of course." Fionna seemed happy to do just about anything for Kaimi. "I'm so relieved to see you smiling. I'd been worried all morning that you might be upset."

"Oh, about last night?" Kaimi sighed. Fionna gave a hesitant nod. "I'm trying to not think about her, but then she keeps showing up," she confessed, and Dan gave Garrett a sympathetic glance.

"I talked to her for a long time last night. I think she's going to back off. What did you want to ask me?"

Kaimi blushed. Her face gave its customary streaks of olive and peach. Garrett grinned and kissed her cheek, unable to help himself. She whispered something in Fionna's ear.

Fionna's entire body lit. She grabbed Kaimi's forearm and dragged her toward her purse, hanging on the coat rack near the door. Kaimi's bewildered expression had Garrett stepping in.

"Where are you going with my fiancée?" He grabbed Kaimi's other hand in a mock tug-of-war.

"I need to go too. We'll be back," she informed Dan who appeared to be just as confused as Garrett. Fionna leaned up on her tiptoes and kissed Dan's jawline though she never released Kaimi's arm.

Kaimi grinned. "Apparently we'll be back in a little while."

"We'll go get you some clothes too." Fionna was nearly jumping up and down.

"Uh," Kaimi panicked.

"Here." Garrett reached in his back pocket and handed her two credit cards, which did nothing to lessen her embarrassment. He wasn't certain any other way to go about it though. He prayed Fionna didn't plan on taking Kaimi to the stores she normally preferred. The price tags would make Kaimi uncomfortable.

"Stop. This is how I'm going to pay you for all the work I'm about to get you to do. I need major hula review and then we have tons of work on the studio. I know you aren't going to let me actually pay you, so I'm taking you out for a few hours of fun. Plus, you have to have warm clothes or you'll end up back in the hospital. And Tutu sent you a kit to my house for you to use."

"Still." Garrett slid the cards in Kaimi's purse. Duke seemed to realize his mommy was leaving, and he bolted from Aida's lap to her side. He began whining and nudging her calf with his nose.

"Oh." Kaimi swooned. Fionna released her, and she knelt down to love Duke.

"If I whine like that, will you stay with me?" Garrett teased. She giggled as she stood back up and planted a kiss on Garrett's lips.

"You'll probably be glad I did this, and even if you aren't, I will be glad I did this." She wrinkled her nose. "And I am a little tired of wearing your sweatshirts. And you know…we could talk." She subtly reminded Garrett that she'd wanted to talk to Fionna about being happily married.

Garrett nodded. "Love you."

"I love you too." Kaimi beamed. Fionna was overjoyed as she tugged Kaimi out to Dan's Ferrari.

"Do you have any idea where they're going? I'm still new to all this." Garrett tried not to sound as irritable as he felt. It unnerved him not to know where she was going. Her safety brought on worry like he'd never experienced before. Suddenly, all of Dan and Logan's freaking out about Fionna and Adeline made sense to him. He'd never understood it before. He'd harassed them about it regularly.

Dan chuckled as he glanced Aida's way. Duke had returned to her, and she was trying to cheer him up about Kaimi leaving. As she seemed thoroughly distracted, Dan cleared his throat. "I'm going to go with the wax salon."

Garrett tried to hide his delighted grin as he nodded his understanding. Dan laughed at him outright as he gestured to his dining room table where his own personal laptop was set beside his Venton laptop along with a pile of thumb drives and file folders.

"How the hell did you talk your way out of that shit last night?" Dan asked as Garrett fell into a chair and started flipping through the files of evidence. "Will's on his way over here to help us figure out the extra teacher thing," he added with a frustrated sigh.

"I still don't know how the hell Chloe got in there, but I told her off. I made sure I said that she was taking her clothes off when she came to my apartment the other day when Kaimi showed up. I knew she wouldn't argue, and I wanted Kaimi to know I was telling her the truth.

"By the grace of God, it somehow worked out so that I didn't end up getting arrested for beating the shit out of the guy she convinced to come take a swing at me for whatever it is she told him I did. And then Kaimi started talking, and I stood there like a moron. But Chloe left, which was all that mattered to me." Garrett shrugged as he left out how exactly Kaimi hadn't been furious with him for Chloe's showing up yet again. Kaimi was just a phenomenal woman, and somehow she loved Garrett for the person he'd been before her, even though he was so much better now.

"Chloe gave the parking security detail a twenty, and he agreed to walk away," Dan informed him readily.

"Are you shitting me?" Fury seared through Garrett's shield. Dan shook his head and seemed to share in his disdain. "Give me about two minutes, and he'll no longer be employed." Garrett whipped his cell from his pocket and had his building landlord on the phone a moment later. As he began going over all of the things that Matt could be sued for when his tenants paid to live in a building with a staffed parking deck in the city if something were to happen while the guard was taking a twenty-dollar walk, Matt agreed to rectify the situation.

A knock sounded on the door, and Dan stood to let Will inside.

"You talk. I've done a ton of research for both of you, but I've haven't seen or heard from you in three weeks. You show up at Mom and Dad's with the woman you're now engaged to, and I want to know what the hell happened?" Will didn't appear to be joking.

Garrett grimaced. "I'm sorry. I know I should've called you. I met her when we went out to sign the new contracts. We talked day in, day out for weeks. I'm serious when I say that I've never talked to anyone as much as I talked to her. She called me when her grandmother went in the hospital, and I headed out there. I don't really know what happened. I just know this feels really right, and I can't imagine not marrying her. All that shit I used to harass both of you about with Fi and Brooke, I get it now. You can throw it all back in my face, but she's all I want." He explained everything for his big brother, not certain what else to say.

The signature Haydenshire smirk formed on Will's face. "Nah, I mean, I'm thrilled for you. Shocked but thrilled, and Brooke's dying to get to know Kaimi better. She says any girl who locked you down willingly should be given a crown and we should all bow at her feet. Honest, when Dad called and told me you were bringing a girl home, calling her your girlfriend, and wanted her to meet everyone, I was sure she was pregnant."

"Nope." Garrett shook his head. He tried to ignore the split second of pained mourning that crossed Dan's face and then was gone.

"So, you're really going to marry her, kids, the whole bit?" Will probed again.

"I'm going to marry her. We'll see what happens after that. I'm good with just her. Like I said, she's all I want." At that moment, a dejected Duke moped into the dining room and put his paws in Garrett's lap hopefully. "I want you too, buddy." Garrett lifted Duke up into his lap and accepted his licks on his cheeks and chin. Duke settled down and kept a watch on the door as the men started to work.

When Dan left to give Halia a bottle, Will and Garrett helped themselves to Dr Peppers from the fridge and settled on the couch. Duke moved to Garrett again. He kept constant watch on the door to the garage where Kaimi had disappeared.

"I miss her too, buddy. She'll be back soon." Garrett slid to the floor to pet Duke and try to console him. Duke had apparently fallen in love with Kaimi just as quickly as Garrett.

"Where'd they go?" Will quizzed as Dan sat down with a screaming Halia. She quieted as soon as her daddy got the bottle to her lips.

Aida had gone upstairs to play with her new doll, now that she had the play shop that Garrett had given her for Christmas. Dan's niece, Olivia, had come over to join her.

"Fi took her shopping, and apparently, to do other girlie grooming things we all like, but I will not discuss as that would embarrass my future bride," Garrett explained.

Will laughed as he stared at Garrett in shock. "You're going to have to give me some time to get to know my new little brother. You not saying things because you're trying to be sensitive and respectful is almost as shocking as, 'hey, I'm getting hitched.' And what is this that we all like? Don't make assumptions, man."

Dan's head shot up from gazing down at Halia. Neither he nor Garrett could believe Will had begun a conversation of that nature. He usually kept his relationship with Brooke very close to his vest.

Garrett also couldn't believe he didn't like what was being discussed. "Dude, your wife is Brazilian. That's just…oddly ironic."

Will shrugged with another wry grin. Garrett wondered if Brooke had given Will the freeze, and he was horny and therefore willing to talk about his sex life. What he actually suspected was that Will had been waiting, hoping, maybe even praying, that at some point Garrett would fall in love and that they could actually talk about love and life, something Garrett had no real experience with before now.

"I don't like that. She's not a six-year-old." Will gagged reflexively just as Dan and Garrett did the same thing. "I never liked it. After we started living together, I asked her if she'd mind stopping, and we reached a compromise."

Garrett caught the advice thinly veiled in a topic Will hoped Garrett might discuss.

"Yeah, well, my fiancée just said she didn't really care if I liked it, which by the way I do and I think you're insane, but she did like it, so she was going."

"I'm not commenting on my likes or dislikes, but I do *not* like the implication that if I prefer my wife like that it would be relating her to a little girl. That is sick and disgusting, and I kind of want to hit you right now," Dan allowed in an oddly confused stammer. It was not something anyone but the men currently in the room had ever heard from Dan Vindico. His ever overconfident manner always came down just a little when he was with Will and Garrett. He may call Fitz his best friend, but Garrett knew better.

Will chuckled with another shrug. "Okay, I'm sorry. It's a hang-up I have, I guess. I like it short but there."

"I cannot believe you just told us that." Garrett shook his head. He was stunned.

"Yeah, welcome to my world." Will threw his hand out to Garrett.

In the gesture, Garrett understood. Will was not only shocked by his sudden life turnaround. He felt left out. They'd functioned as a solid team their entire life. Will was no longer certain where he stood. Garrett had not only announced his engagement to his family without letting Will know first, but he'd up and decided he was moving to Hawaii without a discussion as well. Guilt filled Garrett's shield.

"Hey, you and Brooke and Lily Ana will come to Kauai for the wedding, right? I want you to be my best man, and it's a bigger deal there than here in the Senate deals." Garrett tried to bridge the gap he'd created.

Will chuckled as he nodded and relaxed before Dan and Garrett's very eyes.

"Yeah, of course. Are you kidding me? I'm not missing that. Somebody's got to throw your bachelor party."

"That's fine, but the only girl that I want dancing naked in my lap is Kaimi, so keep that in mind."

"It's like we're in some kind of parallel universe," Will huffed.

"I'm speechless," Dan agreed.

"We should check and make sure he isn't a pod."

"If either of you come anywhere near me, I'll hurt both of you. Aida and Duke will help me."

# CHAPTER 27

# SUSPICIONS SURPRISES

Dan laid Halia on a baby mat and summoned to turn on the overhead fan. He set it to barely spin. Halia gasped her approval as she stared hypnotically at the fan above her.

"Is that how Fionna entertains you as well?" Will harassed.

"Nah, she makes other things spin for me," Dan came right back with a cocky smirk. Will and Garrett laughed as they settled back at the dining room table to continue their work.

"Like I was saying, I'd bet my next two paychecks you've got yourself a dirty accountant. I may not dismantle criminal organizations, but this is my forte. However, every lead we have takes me right back to Katherine Bryant. Pretty bold to be walking away with that much cash, so it's not uncatchable, but I can't figure out exactly who is doing this," Will concluded.

"Every time I think I'm getting somewhere, another huge pit of crap opens up below me. Is there anyone working at that school who isn't corrupt?" Dan spat. "Sullivan said Bryant had something brewing."

"He may be right, but we're going to have to trace the extra paycheck very discreetly."

"Yeah, but we can figure this out. It sounds like we need school to start back so we can set a few traps and see who we pull up out of the weeds," Garrett assured them. "Let's stop shitting around. I'm coming up there with you. We'll blow the whole thing out as an investigation. These are kids. You never know who might start talking if they get scared."

Dan nodded his begrudged agreement. "I'm trying to keep the press from jumping all over my dad."

"Then hire me. You don't have to pay me, but I'll come in as some kind of guest mentor, or some shit, or your assistant. I don't care, but let's get this show on the road. I could talk about being a liaison."

Dan and Will both looked impressed.

"That's a good idea. I'll call Dad." Dan pulled his phone from his pocket. After he talked to his father, he ordered pizzas for Will, Garrett, himself, and the girls. Aida regaled them with everything she and Olivia had been playing with their new dolls. Dan's shield had tensed as he'd narrowed his eyes when Aida explained that she thought the doll she'd gotten for Christmas had a boyfriend that lived in Paris and was named Alex.

By two o'clock, Dan had explained that he couldn't load the information on the drug tests onto his Venton computer because he suspected the casted thumb drives were sending back all of the information on the mentors' laptops to whomever was stealing the tests. Garrett listened, but he was getting antsy. He missed Kaimi. He needed her beside him.

He needed to feel her intoxicating energy near his. He let their session the evening before run through his mind in slow, precise detail. The way she tasted formed the customary thirst on his tongue —so damn sweet and so hungry for him always.

She was so willing to let him introduce her to a few new things he knew would drive her wild. He loved that she never tried to hide her ardent craving of him. That voracious curiosity that swirled in her eyes whenever she wanted him to bring her sweet relief had him shifting uncomfortably at the table. *"More, please, please Garrett more."*

Her panted cry of timid need when he was building her, and she was so desperate for his pleasure.

She begged every time they were together, and he would never hear it enough. He stifled a moan. Will was talking, something about Katherine Bryant, but Garrett just couldn't quite hear him over his recollections of her sweet moans of ecstasy and her begging him to penetrate her fully.

His cell chirped, and he nearly fell out of the chair pulling it from his pocket.

"Anxious?" Will sneered.

"Have you been looking at him? He hasn't heard a damn thing you've said," Dan huffed. Garrett rolled his eyes as he flipped Dan off and read Kaimi's text.



Garrett grinned and scolded himself for wishing she would come back.



Garrett added his customary name for Kaimi when he had her in his arms, inside of his tempting shelter, inside the heat they created together. She was the sweetest damn thing he'd ever seen, tasted, or felt, so the name was perfect. He wanted her to know what he was thinking about and that this time it was him who was starving for her.

Garrett smirked over her response. She texted again immediately.



Garrett laughed as he read the text. Dan and Will both rolled their eyes and shook their heads at him.

~

The ladies returned an hour later, both giggling and looking thick as thieves.

"Mommy!" Aida bound down the stairs and into Fionna's arms.

"Hey, baby, did you have fun?" Fionna soothed. She grimaced as she checked her watch. It appeared time had gotten away from her.

"Yes, and Daddy said I could spend the night with Olivia tonight if it was okay with you, and I want to," Aida urged.

Dan and Fionna shared a quick, concerned expression and a silent conversation.

"I think Tim and Meredith have come around." Dan seemed to know what Fionna was worried about.

"Okay," Fionna agreed.

Duke barked as he raced toward Kaimi, almost bowling her over.

"Hey there, boy." Kaimi set down the bags she was carrying and loved on Duke.

She stood and wound her arms around Garrett's neck.

"I missed you," she confessed in a giggled whisper that let Garrett know she didn't want anyone else to hear her. She turned her head away from everyone else in the room and laid it against his chest. He wrapped his arms around her tightly.

"I missed you too." He kissed the top of her head. "Did you get clothes?" He wondered what kinds of things she might've purchased. This, however, brought on hysterical giggles from both Fionna and Kaimi. Dan chuckled as he stared at Fionna and shook his head.

"She got cute jeans that show off her tushy, and then we went to

Target and found these adorable long-sleeved shirts and sweaters, really inexpensively, so now she will be warm and cute while we have to live off of our island where we can wear bikinis and sundresses every day." Fionna sighed with more than a hint of longing.

"We're working on it, sweetheart," Dan vowed.

Fionna grimaced. "Oh, I know. I was just kidding." Garrett knew she hadn't meant to add to their burdens, but the pressure was mounting.

"We went to see Lindley at work," she announced with a mischievous gleam in her eye. Kaimi began laughing hysterically against Garrett's chest.

Dan's little sister had settled down some since she'd started dating Ryan Tuttle. She was currently employed at one of the larger sex shops in downtown DC. He wondered what kinds of things Fionna might've learned about Kaimi and if she'd purchased anything.

"Did you now?" Dan chuckled.

"Yes, and I've decided to host one of those Thrilling Romance parties in a few months. I've been wanting to have a girls' night going-away kind of party before we move, and that will be perfect. Kaimi's going to help me, so she can have all the party prize things. I already have a drawer full."

"I was aware," Dan teased her.

Fionna giggled as she continued. "Emily and Adeline will help too and Kara and Brooke. Oh, I wonder if your mom would like to come?" Fionna asked Will.

"Please, please, please do not make me think about that." Will shuddered convulsively. Fionna and Kaimi both laughed at him outright.

"I'm going to invite her, but you don't have to think about it. You just have to keep Lily Ana so Brooke can come and have a good time."

"Done, but why aren't you inviting Dan's mom? That seems rude," Will harassed Fionna with a derisive chuckle. Dan and Fionna both cracked up as Kaimi's brow furrowed.

"You'll have to meet Mrs. Vindico," Garrett tried to explain.

"It's something everyone should do...once." Dan chuckled.

"...a few Angels and some of the girls from my class." Fionna continued to spew forth information.

Kaimi was still cradled in Garrett's arms. He could feel the heat from her cheeks through his shirt.

"How much coffee did you have, baby doll?" Dan asked.

"Too much, obviously. I'm hyper. I had so much fun. I think I kind of needed a fun day out. You love me," Fionna commanded. "I wish Becca could come." She continued her rapid-fire train of thoughts.

"Wouldn't the Sapmans love that."

Fionna's expression changed in a heartbeat. "Becca's going to have to stay at Georgetown until the baby's born. I don't think she's going to graduate," she explained to Will, Garrett, and Kaimi.

Dan looked bereaved as well. "And Jeff is obviously a disaster."

Garrett and Will nodded their understanding. They both wondered what kind of burden that would be to bear. They'd certainly played when they were at the academy. Jeff had gotten caught doing what they'd all done, and to be the reason your wife didn't graduate would be really rough.

"Maybe her dad could arrange something," Garrett offered.

"With everything going on at Venton, Dad is sympathetic but afraid to let anything else slide. She was a good student until she had to start missing so many days of school. She only lacks two more credits."

"That sucks."

# CHAPTER 28
# SHIELD THE SECRETS

The ladies briefly discussed plans for Fionna's party. Garrett, Will, and Dan decided to take Lily Ana, Aida, and Halia to the farm to let them play while their significant others hosted a sex product party. They all would've loved to have at least overheard the party but knew they'd never be allowed to attend.

After that, Meredith came to pick up Aida, and Dan asked if she would mind watching Halia as well for a few hours so he and Fionna could have a nice dinner out.

Garrett knew he planned to capitalize on Fionna's exuberant mood, the fact that she'd been to a sex shop, and that she was obviously feeling amorous.

Meredith seemed delighted to keep the baby though Garrett wondered if he should have offered.

He and Kaimi took Duke out to the backyard before they loaded him up to take him back home.

"So far, I know you went to a sex shop and possibly got waxed. What else did you and Fi do on your excursion?" Garrett waggled his eyebrows as he pulled back onto the highway to head to the apartment.

Kaimi shook her head at him. "I'm marrying a detective, and that means I can have no secrets, apparently."

"I don't like secrets." He wasn't certain why the idea bothered him so much. He never wanted to stifle her. He just desperately wanted to know what she'd done.

"I don't either," she stated thoughtfully. "Okay, well, I was going to surprise you with the wax job because Maylea said you did prefer that, which I was so, so glad because if you dance every day for work before you go to the beach in a swimsuit, you wax. It's just sort of necessary."

Garrett grinned. "I'll show you how much I like it when I get you home." His heart hammered as he envisioned her completely bare and exposed all for him.

"Maylea kept trying to buy me stuff. She insisted on a few things, but I swear I only put two pairs of jeans and a few shirts on your card." Her face fell as she confessed this.

Garrett laced his fingers through hers. "As soon as Will gets to the office tomorrow morning, they'll be *our* cards, and you can buy whatever you want. We'll both be working soon. I rarely spent money on anything but beer and food. You have to have clothes. I don't want you getting sick again."

"I know," Kaimi agreed. Her smile returned a moment later. "Maylea is lingerie crazy. We went to several lingerie shops. I wouldn't buy anything, but she threatened to start picking out stuff for me and just giving it to you. So, I finally gave in. I figured for my engagement, I could probably move away from white cotton briefs to something a little more thrilling. When I finally told her that when I dance, I don't usually wear any underwear, and that I kind of preferred that, she said that seemed like something you would like. But then, she still ended up buying the pairs I picked out. Nana freaked out when she found out I'd decided to go panty-less when I was at Juilliard, so I started wearing them when I moved back."

Garrett's mouth went dry, and all he could manage was a nod. He finally figured out how to get his vocal cords to re-engage as he tried to steady his breath. "None at all is about the sexiest damn thing I can think of."

A sexy smirk formed on Kaimi's features, and God, he loved the confidence that he saw growing just a little each day she was with him. Suddenly, she giggled. "I met Lindley, and the fact that she's Dan's sister is just so funny to me. They couldn't be more different."

"You should've met Lindley several years ago." Garrett shook his head at just a few of Lindley Vindico's antics, many of which he would get called out for when she was arrested, since she was Gifted but often caught by the Non-Gifted police. "Did Lindley sell you anything, sweetheart?" He couldn't help himself. The fantasies were just too vivid in his mind.

"No, I could never buy anything like that with Maylea. Maybe with you, but that was just too much. I think that's why she decided to throw the party. I don't really have a lot of experience with that kind of thing." Her obvious discomfort touched the deepest wells of Garrett's soul and pricked his heart.

"You don't have to go to the party, and you don't have to buy anything like that ever if you don't want to. I'll tell Fi to back off. I don't want you doing anything that makes you uncomfortable."

She gave him a sweet grin. "No, it's okay. It sounds fun, and Maylea noticed that I was embarrassed in the store, so she didn't push or anything. I thought some of the stuff looked interesting. I just never really thought to buy stuff like that. Sex was so hard for me. I just did what I knew wouldn't hurt. Living with my grandmother, who occasionally still tried to clean my room for me until a week before she died, probably stunted my growth, I think." She wrinkled her nose, and Garrett chuckled. He lifted her hand to his mouth and brushed a tender kiss along her knuckles.

"If you'll tell me anything you ever want to do or to try, I'll make it happen. You can ask or tell me anything at all. I love you so much, and all I want is to make you happy. Just please don't be embarrassed with me, okay?"

CHAPTER 29

# A GOOD GOODNIGHT

~DAN VINDICO~

Dan grinned as Fionna sung along to one of her favorite songs blaring from the speaker in their bathroom as she got ready for their dinner out. He'd phoned several places trying to get a last-minute reservation and had finally lucked up on one at The Charis Inn. It was perfect. On the waterfront, quiet, dark, romantic. Dan had plans for his wife that evening.

"Hey, baby doll." He summoned and lowered the volume just a little.

"Yeah?"

"You know that gift I put in your stocking for Christmas?"

She shot him a mischievous smirk. "The one you told Aida was a remote control hair clip?"

Dan cracked up as he recalled his panic when Aida had shown a great deal of interest in Fionna's Christmas presents.

"That's the one." He brushed a kiss on her cheek. "Wear it for me tonight."

"I take it you would have the remote, Commander Vindico?"

He raised his left eyebrow in challenge. "That's how we both have fun at dinner."

"That sounds interesting. What happens if you drive me so crazy I want to take you on the table?"

"Then I'll pay and have you out of there in two seconds flat. The Ferrari is definitely an option, baby doll."

Fionna moved to her bedside table and pulled the slender black box that contained the remote control vibrator Dan had purchased just for such an occasion.


## Will Haydenshire

"Dayeee!!!" Rang from Lily Ana as she toddled into Will's arms at the door.

"Hey, baby girl." Will inhaled deeply of the soothing smells of Brooke's cooking, and of her, and of their home. It was his refuge from the world that always soothed his soul.

Brooke appeared, grinning at him. *God, she's so beautiful and perfect. How did I ever get so lucky?* Will pulled her close and kissed her heatedly until Lily Ana tried to join in the kiss.

He set Lily Ana back on the carpet, and she toddled toward her toy basket in the living room.

"What's wrong?" Brooke slipped her hand into Will's and guided him to the kitchen. It was her favorite room in their home. They'd made love on the counters, the table, and once, against the back door, which qualified it as one of Will's favorites as well.

"I just can't figure this thing out at Venton. It's getting to me." Will told a partial truth as he lifted the lid on the pot of coconut curry shrimp soup and helped himself to a bite. He fanned his tongue, but the burn was worth the bite.

She already had the makings of her spicy roast beef sandwiches going on the cutting board. He knew he should get down on his knees every night and thank God for her.

"And you are upset about Garrett, but you won't tell me that or tell him that."

Will saw no reason to lie. She knew him far too well anyway. "I don't get it. How is he a completely different person in a month's time? I know there's more to this, but he won't tell me. I used to know my brother like the back of my own hand. He's been my best friend since I was Lily Ana's age. He took Logan to go get the dog." Will knew he sounded like an overgrown child.

Brooke wrapped her arms around his waist. "I think somewhere in all of that is the fact that you're going to miss him, and you don't quite know how life will be without him being over here all the time," she soothed. "And my William likes numbers. Numbers don't change or lie. They are what they are, and this is hard to take."

Will nodded.

"I love you," she vowed.

"I love you too, my querida."

"Garrett will talk when he is ready to talk. You will always be his best friend, and what did you tell me when Mama moved to Paris?"

"That I'd take you to see her all the time."

"Hawaii is not such a bad place for vacation."

Will leaned back and lifted her chin before he devoured her mouth. "I have everything I need right here."

"I will make you feel better after we put Lily Ana to bed." Brooke leaned in for another kiss.


### Garrett Haydenshire

"You never told me you could cook." Kaimi watched Garrett work in the small kitchen in their apartment.

"I make do. My brother Levi is practically a freaking chef. He taught me some stuff. I'm way better on a grill."

"And did you have Levi teach you a few romantic dishes because you wanted girls to come back to your apartment?" Kaimi gave Garrett an eye roll.

"No comment, but the only girl who ever mattered is here in *our* apartment, so why don't you hush,"—he brushed a sweet kiss on her lips—"and let me make you a romantic dinner."


### Dan Vindico

Dan shrugged into his sport coat and helped Fionna with her wrap. She was wearing a tight sweater dress that clung to her luscious curves. Her hair was dripping in loose tendrilled curls down her back. Her eyes were dark, and she gave Dan looks that said they wouldn't be at the restaurant a terribly long time.

Dan nonchalantly stuck his hand in his pocket and touched the remote he'd stowed there. He eased the sliding dial up just slightly, and Fionna's body gave a twitch as her breath caught. She raised her eyebrow and gave him a sexy grin. He turned the wearable vibrator, held in place by a lacy black thong, back off.

"Just checking." Dan offered his wife his arm as his customary cocky smirk formed on his face.

### Will Haydenshire

Lily Ana wrapped her little arms around Will's neck. He'd stood her on the bathroom counter to dry her off after her bath and to put on her pajamas.

"I love you, baby girl."

She kissed his cheek, and he chuckled. He pulled the soft bristled brush from the drawer and awaited the customary response.

"I do eeet!!!!" she shrieked. Will handed Lily Ana her brush. He waited while she attempted to comb through her thin, wispy brown hair that had grown just to her neck line.

"Daddy's turn," Will informed her.

"No!" Lily Ana shook her head back and forth angrily. She sounded just like Brooke. Will knew he should get onto her, but he couldn't bring himself to scold her.

"Lily Ana, let your daddy comb your hair." Brooke joined them in the bathroom. Lily Ana scowled as she begrudgingly shoved the brush into Will's hand. He performed the task and then lifted her up off the counter. He handed her the toddler toothbrush and let her chew on it for a minute before he removed it from her grasp and carried her into her nursery.

She wiggled and leaned toward her bookshelf.

Will set her down and she quickly pulled the *Where is Baby's Belly Button* book off the shelf and waited on Will to sit in the rocking chair. She performed all of the moves the lift-the-flap book instructed her to do in order to locate the baby's hands, feet, nose, and belly button. Then she promptly showed Will her own belly button which always cracked him up.

When he closed the book, she turned and laid her head on his shoulder, cradling herself into his embrace. She'd discovered that if she snuggled with him, he would talk to her, and hug and kiss her, and that it would delay her inevitable bedtime. He couldn't argue though. He loved her sleepy snuggles each night. He'd been trying to teach her to count to ten. She not only favored her father, if he'd had the dark olive complexion she and her mother shared, but she'd also inherited his Predilect. They began counting her tiny fingers, and she giggled with delight.

"Five, six..." Will supplied.

"Seech," Lily Ana mimicked and then applauded herself.

"That's right. You're so smart."

All too soon, she was yawning and fighting to keep her eyes open.

Will laid her in her crib, told her how much he loved her, and kissed her good night.

# CHAPTER 30

# SCOTCH NEAT

## ~DAN VINDICO~

"Thank you. This is perfect." Dan guided Fionna into the chair the maître d' had pulled out for her. Dan had switched on the vibe as they'd approached the table.

"Wine this evening, folks?" A waiter asked, and Dan upped the sliding dial. Fionna's eyes goggled as she shot him a look that said for him to behave, but he had no intention of that.

"Shiraz, honey?" Dan quizzed with a heavy smirk.

She trembled slightly. "Yes…thank you," she managed in a slightly gasped breath.

"I'll take Talisker Eighteen if you have it? Neat." Dan eased the dial back to the off position.

"Yes, sir," the waiter supplied readily.

"Perfect. Thank you."

"Dan," Fionna huffed though she was trying not to laugh.

"What's wrong, baby?" Dan feigned confusion. "I thought you'd like this place."

Fionna rolled her eyes and shook her head at her husband. The darkened restaurant, with them tucked up at a tiny round table in the corner overlooking the river, was the perfect locale.

Garrett stirred the sautéed shrimp into the angel-hair noodles and gave himself a long moment to admire Kaimi's ass in the new jeans she'd purchased. She was tossing the salad. Her back was to him. She was shaking her hips to the song on the radio she'd turned on. He let himself fantasize again about her waxed bare for him.

As soon as dinner was over, he planned on bathing those sweet lips with his tongue. It had to hurt to have someone rip out that hair, and he was more than happy to soothe her pain and eventually to give her relief to the moves he planned on showing her that night.

As Garrett set the large dish of pasta on the table, he slapped Kaimi's ass as she leaned to set the salad beside the pasta. She spun with a delighted giggle.

"That hurt," she fussed as she stuck her bottom lip out deliciously. Garrett knew she was lying. He dragged her to him.

"Come here then, sweet girl. Let me make it feel better." He wrapped both of his hands over her lush backside and began groping her as he parted her lips with his tongue and consumed her mouth.

They broke apart, and Kaimi's curious hunger was back in full force.

"Let's eat," she whispered. He pulled her chair out and then seated himself. "This is really good." She sounded slightly shocked by that fact.

"I told you."

Her rhythms were rolling in their customary fluctuating patterns, and she turned introspective a moment later.

"I don't want to be one of those couples that talk bad about each other to their friends, and never have sex, and fight all the time." She was rapidly approaching panic.

"Me either." Garrett laced his fingers through hers, and her immediate draw had him groaning and panting for breath. She grinned at his reaction to their energies combining. He shook himself and drew a deep breath. "Sweetheart, I would never talk bad about you to anyone. If something is going on between us that I'm upset about, I need to be talking to you, not anyone else.

"Once we move, it will pretty much be me and Dan running the show. He's who I'll be with day in day out, not only at work but helping run the farm too. Dan doesn't complain about Fionna any more than I would ever complain about you. I may not have wanted to have anything to do with marriage for the last thirty years, but my dad was pretty adamant about how all of his kids were to treat their significant others. If I need advice, it's him I'd talk to, or Dan, or Will, but it would never be to bad-mouth you. Us not being together is not an option for me. How do you think my parents got eleven kids?" he pointed out wryly.

Kaimi laughed and seemed relieved that Garrett did have some idea how to make a lasting marriage. "How did that happen if you don't mind me asking? Do they not believe in the cast, or they just wanted that many kids always?" Her insatiable curiosity about life delighted his soul. He chuckled as he watched her spin more of the pasta on her fork and inhale it with a dramatic groan.

"They definitely believe in the cast, trust me. They beat that into us repeatedly growing up. Mom always wanted a big family. She liked being pregnant, never had any trouble with pregnancies until Abby." He shrugged. "I'm not sure what happened between Em and the twins. She miscarried one early on after Emily and then another one a few years later, but I don't actually know if they started using the cast then or if her body took a break. I came over for Sunday night dinner one night a little while after Cal had been killed and they announced they were pregnant with twins." He shook his head as he recalled his stunned reaction.

"Do you think maybe she wanted that because of Cal?" Kaimi shrank away from him as if she believed the question would upset him.

"You can ask me anything at all, remember. And yes, probably. She'd never admit that even to herself, but yeah, and Dad would've done anything at all to get her to smile again. It was really bad for that first year."

Kaimi reached this time and squeezed his hand.

"I love you."

"I love you too, sweetheart. Tell me about your day," he urged again. He knew she was thinking about whatever she'd seen at that sex shop, and he wanted her to talk to him. She was possibly the least experienced woman he'd ever been with, and if she needed something explained, he wanted to be the one to guide her.

She grinned. She knew perfectly well which parts of her day he was most curious about. "I asked Maylea about married life, and she was really, really sweet. She told me everything I wanted to know and then some."

Garrett chuckled. He was certain that was the case.

"She reminds me so much of Tutu. I asked her if she and Dan ever fought." Garrett tried to recall if Fionna had ever discussed an argument with Dan before. "She said they did sometimes, but they never let it get out of hand. She told me about when she was pregnant the first time and she sort of shut down. She said it scared them both so much they don't ever want to not talk like that again." Her grief for Dan and Fionna was evident in her tone.

"That was awful for both of them." Garrett swallowed down the heartbreak he'd gone through watching Fionna shatter as she lay in his arms sobbing and terrified to tell anyone but him. He couldn't fathom what Dan went through watching her like that day in and day out for weeks. "She didn't have any good options."

Kaimi nodded. "That's exactly what she said. She wanted the baby but couldn't keep challenging pregnant and then the whole mass murderer being after her. She said she never would've gotten through it if it hadn't been for you."

Garrett shook his head. "She's stronger than she's ever given herself credit for."

Kaimi studied him. "I think you're a huge part of her strength though. I think that's how it works for everyone. That was the worst part about Nana being sick. There was no one else but the two of us."

"I'm sorry, sweetheart." He served her more pasta, and a few minutes later she blushed. "Come on…just tell me. We are pretty good at this talking thing. I was in love with you before I ever got out to Lihue after you called me that morning. I really love how we talk about everything, so just tell me."

"Okay." Kaimi seemed to revel in Garrett's prodding. "Maylea is very sexually confident. Does that make sense?"

"Fionna had a great deal more experience than you did when she and Dan went from a one-night stand to married in a few months' time. Her dad was really rough on her when she was at the academy—really, really strict. She rebelled in a big way."

"She said that Tutu always taught her that sex was natural and wasn't something to be ashamed of and that you should kind of figure out what gets you going because it's good for your health and makes you whole."

Garrett nodded as he began to understand more of the pieces of the puzzle that made up one of his best friends. She rebelled against her father by using the beliefs of her mother and grandmother.

"Did she tell you what Dan put in her stocking for Christmas?!" Kaimi gasped with a broad mischievous grin. Garrett shook his head and forced himself not to laugh at her shock.

# CHAPTER 31

# RULES AND RECIPES

## ~DAN VINDICO~

Fionna let her eyes close for a split second as Dan slid the dial up and down while she tried to sip her wine.

"If you don't stop. We're not even going to get to order." She breathed as her entire body broadcast the insatiable need Dan was creating. Her voracious eyes held fire in their depths. Her breasts were swollen. Her nipples pressed against the thin sweater material, begging for Dan's touch. Her lips were raw in their need to be kissed and sucked. Her skin was flushed. He brushed a kiss just under her earlobe. She trembled from the hesitant caress.

"I know I'm making you wet, baby. I can tell without even touching you. I want you to drip for me. When I get you home, I'm gonna lay you out and drink you, and then, I'm gonna fuck you so hard the only thing you remember how to say is yes sir," he informed her in a breathy growl as he kept the vibrator shifting from a light caress to more forceful vibrations in rhythmic pulses. He knew the exact combination that would ultimately bring her, and he wouldn't give her that yet. The waiter appeared to take their order, and Fionna was trembling and gasping for breath.

"Ma'am?" the waiter prompted. Fionna shook her head and swallowed as she tried to catch her breath. Dan turned off the vibrator. He winked at her as she drew a deep breath and ordered the ahi salad.


### Garrett Haydenshire

Garrett was doubled over laughing at Kaimi's description of the remote control vibe Dan had given Fionna.

He shook his head. "I feel bad for whoever is eating in that restaurant near them tonight."

Kaimi had begun laughing as she'd told the story and was now giggling hysterically.

"But she thought it was the sweetest gift ever. He also got her, like, these gorgeous diamond earrings, and he had these really sweet pictures of the girls on the beach custom framed. He gave her this massive island wood bowl he had handcrafted by one of Papa's friends, and of course she loved those, but she was so excited about the vibrator thing. It cracked me up."

"Dan definitely has all of Fi's cards. They work on it, like I told you. And Dan is incapable of telling her no to pretty much anything, which I used to think was ridiculous until I met you. Now I get it."

Kaimi shook her head at him. "Maylea said Dan always puts her and the girls first, and that she always puts him first. They decided if anything was going to take away from their family then they weren't doing it. She's nervous about taking over the studio, but she says everything balances better for them on Kauai so she thinks they'll figure it out. But she said if it got to be too much that she would stop teaching the classes she wants to teach, so she would just be the owner and not really work there. I hope she doesn't do that. She's a really good dancer, and I think the studio suffers when the owners aren't on site."

"I think they'll make it work. Dan's pretty committed to her having the studio, and life is slower there. That much was obvious even to me."

Kaimi grinned as she glanced up at Garrett from under her eyelashes. "Maylea is not only into lingerie. She has this thing she calls a treasure chest only it's actually a drawer, and she said Dan gets her sex toys a lot and that they even kind of use them together some," Kaimi managed in a confused choke. "I thought vibrators and stuff were to use when you were alone and sort of, you know...." She blushed again, and Garrett couldn't quite halt his chuckle.

"Horny," he supplied for her as he stood, cleared their plates, refilled their wine glasses, and guided her to the couch. Duke hopped up with them, and they snuggled together under one of the large quilts Mrs. Haydenshire had left on the sofa when she'd come over to prepare Garrett's apartment for Kaimi while she was in the hospital. "Let's talk about all of that. Anything you think or I think or you want or I want, let's just talk. We're getting married, and I want to be married to you for the rest of my life, so let's talk about all of this."


## Will Haydenshire


Will groaned as Brooke's body arched back. He sucked her left nipple and dragged his fingers down her slit and up her backside.

"Will," she gasped his name deliciously.

"That's it, angel. Let me hear you beg."

"I want you. I want to have another baby. It took so long last time. Please," she pled.

He stopped short. That wasn't exactly the kind of begging he'd been intent on hearing.

"You're sure?" He wasn't doing anything until she was certain. It had taken them almost a year to get pregnant with Lily Ana, but that didn't mean it would take that long for the next one.

"Please," she begged.

"There is nothing more beautiful than you carrying my baby. I want that too," he assured her as he slipped his fingers deep inside her. He sought out her release before he penetrated her and made them one, before he allowed her to make everything wrong in his world fall away, as he clung to the only thing that he could never live without.

## Garrett Haydenshire

Kaimi's rhythms mellowed with the wine, and she seemed to want to connect just as much as Garrett did.

"I'm nervous about the party. I've never been to one. I don't want to come off completely naive. And, oh my gosh, she's gonna invite your mom? How am I supposed to act at a sex toy party with your mom there?" She shuddered slightly.

"Mom won't go," he assured her. "Not that she'd have any issue with her daughter or daughters-in-laws using anything they sell there, but she wouldn't go because she'd be afraid of what you just said. She's really good about not overstepping her bounds. She would feel like she was intruding with you being there and Brooke, and Emily, and Adeline.

"Also, Fionna is forgetting that my mom is the first lady of the American Realm now, and even though she should be able to attend parties like that and have a good time, there are a lot of people in this country who would be appalled. She wouldn't want my dad to catch the flak if someone found out." Garrett gave a rather lengthy explanation. "But, I'm gonna ask Fi not to invite her as that solves a myriad of problems."

Relief washed over Kaimi's entire body as she nodded.


## Dan Vindico

A slight, panted moan escaped Fionna's lips as she shuddered at the table.

"Shh, baby doll, just feel it," Dan whispered in her ear again.

"Dessert, sir?" the waiter requested as he made his reappearance.

"Not tonight. I'll take the check," Dan commanded. He was unable to take his eyes off of Fionna as she gripped his thigh and begged him with her eyes.


## Garrett Haydenshire

"Maylea said that Dan was just sort of amazing about everything. That he would talk to her about anything at all, and he was never offended or shocked. She said that between her pregnancies..."

Kaimi paused, so Garrett added, "Which wasn't that long so I'm assuming she meant between the time she got out of the hospital and then discovered she was pregnant again."

"Right." Kaimi seemed to melt before him when she realized that he would also talk with her about anything at all and wouldn't be offended or shocked either. "She said they'd talked about what they wanted their sex life to be like and what they wanted their whole life to look like. She said that she can tell that Dan keeps those conversations in his mind always, and he tries to make their life what they said they wanted. She even told him about other guys she'd slept with and stuff that she'd done only because she could feel how much the guy wanted that and how awful that made her feel. She said he wasn't mad at her or anything."

"Baby, I don't know if I'm offended about your opinion of guys in general or just offended for me and Dan."

"I'm sorry," she lamented and then stopped talking.

"Come on. You will not offend me. You will not embarrass me. If you want to know why Dan and Fionna have such a great marriage and why they're at a restaurant right now probably playing with a remote control vibe, driving each other wild, and having a ball, it's because they talk and she tells him everything.

"He's perfectly fine with the fact that he wasn't her first. She sure as hell knows she wasn't in the first fifty women for him. His deal after Amelia was murdered was to work incessantly for about a week and a half to two weeks, drive himself more insane, rarely sleep, then he'd go to a bar and find a woman who meant nothing to him. He'd try to not even remember her name." Garrett tried to get Kaimi to see that Dan and Fionna had come a long way by talking and accepting each other.

"He'd go back to her place, get a little relief, and then start it all over again. Even I didn't do that, but I agree. I do want what Dan and Fi have. I'm sitting here looking at the woman I want to be my wife, and who I want to have a phenomenal marriage with. The kind that makes other couples jealous, okay?" he teased just to get her to smile again. "I want to talk about stuff, try things out, see what you like, or what I might like. But I want that all within the confines of making each other happy and making damn sure that you always feel safe and content and that you always know how much I love you."

Kaimi nodded and gave him her sweet, sexy grin. "I do know you love me," she whispered. "And thank you for saying all of that. It means the world to me. This is just all so new for me, and I know we keep saying this, but it is crazy fast." She nuzzled the back of her head against Garrett's neck.

"I know," he soothed. "Crazy fast, but my God, I have never been happier. I sure as hell haven't ever been in love before now. So, let's just decide right now to do whatever it takes to make this work. And to talk about anything at all."

"Okay, but I want a few rules." She seemed to come into her own, and Garrett was overjoyed.

"Name them."

"No other women, and I don't mean like cheating on me, although obviously I mean that too."

"Never."

"I know, but I mean no other women in bed with us. I know you've done that. Maylea let that slip," she informed him, and he momentarily redacted Fionna's angel status in his mind.

"I have done that a few times, but I don't ever want to do that again. I want the girl sitting between my legs right now. I want her and nobody else. I'd never turn outside of our marriage for anything."

"I think that's my only rule right now, but there may be others later."

"Deal. No issue with that. But here are my rules. If you're curious about something, you'll ask, and we'll talk about it. If I do anything at all that upsets you or makes you doubt for a split second how much I love you, you'll speak up, and I get a chance to fix it. We talk every day no matter how tired we are or what's been going on. We reconnect at some point each and every day. If my job or anything at all makes you uncomfortable or makes you worry, you tell me right then, and we make the necessary changes."

Garrett laid out what he considered to be the recipe for a very happy marriage. He recalled numerous times growing up when he would come in from dates past his curfew and hear his parents up whispering and laughing in their bedroom. He'd often heard things far more carnal than talking.

His father was a Realm governor and occasionally worked endless hours. His mother ran a farm and a family with eleven children. She worked harder than his dad, but she knew his father would give up everything in an instant for her. That's how Garrett wanted Kaimi to feel always.

"Okay." Kaimi seemed overjoyed with his proclamation. "Maylea says she and Dan take baths together almost every night. They talk about their day, or the girls, or their night, or about sex, or whatever. She loves that, and she really loves taking them in Kauai. You know Tutu is big on baths, and all the houses there have those humongous soaker tubs."

"I noticed those. I thought it was a little odd to bathe outside, but that was before I fell madly in love with my own Hawaiian sweetheart. Now, taking a bath with you every night sounds pretty much like heaven to me."

Her rhythms trilled in delight as she nodded.

# CHAPTER 32

# AFTER GLOW AND LIES

## ~DAN VINDICO~

Fionna collapsed on Dan's chest, exhausted from her extended ride. A cocky smirk he couldn't seem to rid himself of was affixed to his features. "Did you like that, baby doll?"

A smirk of her own formed against his chest. "You sound a little like you'd like me to move so you can beat your own chest."

He laughed. "Guilty as charged."

His phone vibrated on the bedside table, and she pouted as she eased herself off of his cock.

"Let me make sure it's not Meredith calling about the girls, and we'll do it all over again," he promised.

It wasn't Meredith calling, but it was his father.

Fionna's brow furrowed. "Answer it," she demanded. "Something's wrong. I can feel it."

Dan answered before it went to his voicemail. "Everything okay, Dad?"

"Turn on the news. Now!"

**Will Haydenshire**

Will cradled Brooke to him.

She grinned as she traced her fingernails over the smattering of hair covering his chest. "Feeling better?"

"Much." He shifted slightly so that every part of her warm, luscious curves touched some part of him. "Do you think Garrett's okay?"

"I think Garrett hasn't been okay since Cal died. I don't think any of you have really been okay since then. You've all handled it in your own ways. You poured yourself into me and us and Lily Ana and into your work. You somehow gave even more, which I didn't know was possible."

"I could never have made it through that without you."

She brushed a tender kiss on his neck. "Garrett has been lost for so long. He's tried to find the thing that would heal him, just like you all did. Maybe Kaimi is that for him. She's who he needed all of this time to heal. Maybe he needs someone to pour all of his energy into," she smirked, "both physically and mentally."

Will laughed. "I do love your dirty sense of humor."

His cell phone rang from the kitchen. He debated but quickly decided that he'd much rather stay there in the cocoon he'd created for them with the heat and rhythms of their lovemaking than to answer his phone.

It went to voicemail and then immediately started ringing again. Brooke eased out of bed and pulled on a robe. "Get it before it wakes Lily Ana."

Will pulled on his boxer briefs. He and Brooke raced down the steps. "It's Mr. Buffett." He answered on the next ring.

"I'm sorry to call you at home, William, but we have a problem. Turn on the news. Channel 476."

"Yes, sir."

**Garrett Haydenshire**

"Can I ask you other things?" Kaimi laid her back against his chest and gazed up at him sweetly. Garrett repositioned his arms around her waist and allowed himself one quick moment to glide over her right breast with a slight caress.

192

"I really can't help myself."

"Mm-hmm." She rolled her eyes.

"You can ask me anything at all any time. I want you to ask me anything you want to know."

"What do you think about lingerie? Dan must love it, but Maylea is so much—" Garrett cupped his hand over her mouth.

"If you're about to say Maylea is so much prettier than you, you can stop talking now because that's a load of shit," he informed her. It drove Garrett insane that she couldn't see how stunningly gorgeous she was. Kaimi laughed and then promptly licked his hand.

"Not working. I like it when you lick me." He tightened his grip.

"Okay, okay," she mumbled against his hand, and he released her. "But she is," she defied and then broke out in a fit of giggles as Garrett reached down and pinched her backside.

"Okay, I'm sorry. So, on a scale of one to ten how much do you like lingerie."

"With one being?" Garrett probed.

"You don't like it at all."

"Honestly?" he hemmed.

"Obviously…"

With another nod, Garrett shrugged. "I don't know. Maybe a one and a half or a two."

"Really?" Kaimi seemed very pleased but shocked.

If Garrett wanted her to be completely honest with him, he needed to do the same, so he nodded.

"You're so beautiful, sweetheart. Your body and the tat and the belly ring. You drive me wild just the way you are, and truthfully, a nightie or some barely there thing is great if it makes you feel as beautiful as you are, but I just want you. Nothing does to me what seeing you naked does to me. I like you bare and raw and knowing you're mine and you're showing it all to me. I don't want you covered up. I want to see everything. Honestly, I prefer you without makeup. I love you unadulterated—just my sweet girl completely bare and ready for me." Garrett tried to explain to her what she did to him, but he wasn't certain he'd done all that good of a job.

"Wow." Kaimi shivered slightly in her whispered awe.

"That's really what I think, so if you like lingerie then I'm fine with it, but it's not what I really want."

Kaimi seemed deeply moved by his preferences. "I hardly ever wear makeup. I'd brought all of mine with me because I thought you would like me better like that, and then I saw Chloe all made up and perfect," she whispered her confusion as she held her hands out several inches over her breasts, indicating Chloe's rather large assets.

Garrett shook his head and rolled his eyes. "Those are fake, sweetheart, and if this isn't more than you want to hear, I preferred her the way she was when we were sleeping together at the academy before she became famed Angels' captain Chloe Sawyer, and her dad had a friend of his increase them several cup sizes, because she wanted them. But Chloe never cared what I thought. She wanted the designer clothes, makeup, shoes, and tits. I never cared enough to express my opinion."

"Can we go back to you like me without makeup and lingerie?"

Garrett chuckled as he continued to caress her body and try to reassure her.

"That's the honest-to-God truth. I just want you all for me."

In the middle of their conversation, Garrett's cell rang. He sighed and glanced at the screen. He leaned up, kept Kaimi tucked to his chest, and begrudgingly answered Will's call.

"Warren just called me. Turn on the news."

"Why?"

"Wilshire is giving a press conference!"

"What the fuck?" Garrett summoned on the television and casted it to reach the Gifted news networks.

Wilshire was in front of the Holiday Inn in downtown DC. He gestured to a man in a cheap suit who was recording the press conference on his phone.

The man cleared his throat. "Just to reiterate, you tried on three different occasions to make a two hundred and fifty thousand dollar contribution to Venton Academy and Governor Vindico denied the donation."

"That is correct." Wilshire nodded.

Garrett shook his head in disbelief. "Is that true?" he demanded of Will.

"We had the accounts locked for the audit. He may have tried to make a digital donation from his bank account to the online Venton account, but it would've been denied because of the audit. They're always locked over Christmas break. Wilshire knows that. Governor Vindico had nothing to do with it, but they're going to crucify him for this."

Garrett rubbed his temples. "What the hell is he thinking? Is this some kind of sick revenge because Dan caught him with his side piece?"

"I can't think of why else he'd do this." Will sounded every bit as disgusted as Garrett felt.

"Have you talked to Dan?"

"Not yet."

Garrett's phone beeped and he didn't even have to look to see who it was. "He's calling me."

"Let me know how he wants to handle this. Warren says he'll try to explain what happened to the press, but that would alert everyone to the missing money which isn't likely to help Governor Vindico's image."

"I'll call you back." Garrett switched the calls. "Will just called me."

"Find a replay of the press conference and watch it beginning to end," Dan commanded.

"O…kay." Garrett's brow furrowed as he searched through the news channels until he landed on one that was replaying the conference. "What am I looking for exactly?"

"I don't think this is revenge. Fi says his energy is frantic, not vicious and not smug, which is how revenge initially feels. The guilt comes later."

"Frantic about what? He's the idiot that called the press conference."

"I need you to help me figure out why."

"I'll call you back."

Garrett summoned and rewound the conference. He and Kaimi watched intently. Wilshire's eyes were slightly bloodshot. He constantly rubbed his palms against his khakis. "He's nervous," Garrett whispered.

Kaimi nodded her agreement. "Look at his energy bands. They're all jagged."

Wilshire was careful never to look into any of the available cameras. He constantly glanced to the side of the parking lot where he was standing. "That's because he's lying."

# CHAPTER 33
# MIDNIGHT CONFESSIONS
### ~DAN VINDICO~

Fionna came back through the door with Halia and Aida. "She decided she didn't want to spend the night after all," Fionna explained.

Dan tried to force a smile for his daughter's sake. "I just want to watch this again."

"It's fine. I'll get her to bed and get Halia's bottle."

Dan summoned and forced the feed to go back to the beginning of the press conference again. A few minutes into the fourth time he'd watched it, Fionna joined him.

Halia's hungry suckles on the bottle were the only sounds besides those of Wilshire's outright lies.

Wilshire glanced to the left again before he continued speaking.

"What does he keep looking at?" Fionna asked.

Dan paused the feed, summoned, and enlarged it. "There's no one over there. There's not even anyone in the parked cars. I can ask Landon to run the plates but I don't really see the point."

He started the feed again, and again Wilshire glanced to the left instead of looking at the reporters asking him questions.

"Dan!" Fionna gasped. "Could someone be making him do this? Maybe that's why he's so frantic."

"That gives credence to the idea that he's being blackmailed but still doesn't explain these extravagant donations he either has made or that he's claiming he tried to make." He gestured to the television.

Defeat plagued her features. She shook her head. "None of this makes any sense. I can't believe he's doing this to your dad."

~

At midnight, Dan eased farther down in the bed and cradled his Maylea tighter. She held their littlest girl in her arms. Halia was making steady draws on her bottle.

Dan hadn't yet slept. His mind churned on what he was seeing and far more importantly, what he was missing. "Do you want to go out tomorrow night for New Year's Eve or do you want to stay home?" He hoped she'd just want to stay home and celebrate the New Year on their sofa or in their bed. He desperately needed her distraction.

Fionna painted a tender kiss on his jawline. "I would love to stay home with you and with our baby girls, but we're taking Garrett and Kaimi over to your parents' house so that Garrett can sign that guest mentor contract. I kind of think we're supposed to stay for dinner, and then Thursday..."—she poked her lip out in a delicious pout— "you have to go back to work."

"As much as I'll miss you and our little coconut during the days, remember, me going back to work is the key to figuring out what the hell Wilshire is doing," Dan reminded her. "And I think I've been trying to block out the fact that I told Dad we'd bring Garrett and Kaimi by tomorrow."

Fionna shook her head at him. "We do need to go reassure your dad. He's so worried about all of this. Maybe Garrett and Kaimi would like to come over here afterward. I could make some snacks and we could watch the ball drop. Or is that lame, and I don't know anymore because I'm a mom now and a big night to me means both of my girls are asleep before I'm too exhausted to speak coherently?"

Dan chuckled as he kissed the top of her head. "Do you miss all the partying and late nights, baby doll? Because I sure as hell don't."

"No, not at all. I love every moment I have here with you and the girls. I have everything I could ever have wanted and so much more."

Peaceful serenity washed through Dan's veins as he inhaled deeply of her heavenly island coconut and musky vanilla scent. If they bottled that smell, he'd be a lush. He kissed her temple and then pulled the sheets and blankets up around them. He just couldn't think about Wilshire anymore.

"If you want to invite Garrett and Kaimi over, I think they'd come. Garrett seems to want the whole married life, settled down, only her kind of deal, as odd as that sounds." Dan explained everything he'd picked up on from Garrett that morning.

"Kaimi asked me tons of questions." She grinned. "It was so sweet. She seemed to think we have everything figured out when it comes to marriage, and she's always so excited to learn new things. I could tell they've been talking about how to have a great relationship. It's just more than I'd ever imagined possible for Garrett." Fionna's energy spun in euphoric joy. Dan chuckled as he cuddled her closer still. He was desperate to drink in her joy.

"I'd say we have a pretty damn good marriage, sweetheart. You taught me how to be the husband you need, and that's the most important thing to me."

"Thank you, and I think your dad taught you a lot about how to be an incredible husband and then just the fact that you're such an amazing man. But, I learned so much from Tutu and Papa and Malani and Kai. Kaimi's grandfather died when she was still in diapers, and her mother abandoned her after she was born. I couldn't ever get her to tell me what happened exactly." Fionna's rhythms spiraled down in her devastation for Kaimi.

"She never had anyone to teach her about relationships, and she told me that all of the guys she's ever been in a serious relationship with cheated on her." Her body spasmed from the dejected hurt she must have felt from Kaimi. "That's why this whole Chloe disaster had her running like that. She's so terrified, but she loves him so much. I just want to help them. I know Garrett better than just about anyone. He forgets that all of those years he was talking two girls into coming back to his apartment and banging Chloe one night and someone else the next, I could feel how miserable he was," she pointed out. Dan had never really considered that either.

"Duke helped," he realized suddenly.

"Tremendously." Fionna nodded. "Duke is a constant reminder to Kaimi that Garrett is committed to both of them. She feels like he helps her hold on to Garrett, even though he's head over heels no going back in love with her, with the puppy or without. I can feel that too."

"That's why she's so protective of Duke. She didn't want to leave him this morning." Dan's secondary Predilection had kicked in as Kaimi had leaned down to love Duke before Fionna had dragged her away.

"She feels like Duke bonds them more than she thinks she can." She seemed relieved that Dan had picked up on the same thing even if it was through a different path than the one she'd traveled to get there.

Dan shifted slightly as he considered everything he was learning. These late-night conversations with Fionna were becoming addictive. He did want Halia to start sleeping past her midnight feeding, but he would miss the whispered love they'd been sharing for the last few weeks after they returned their little coconut to her crib. "Kaimi may not have had any great examples of marriage and commitment, but Garrett has the Haydenshires. Honestly, I find myself patterning their marriage. If I can't decide on my own what Governor Haydenshire would've done in a situation, I ask him, which is huge for me.

"Garrett may not have ever had any intention of settling down and marrying, but he was raised by the two people that have a stronger marriage than anyone I've ever seen. If they have a question we can't help them figure out, his parents will help them. They're over the moon with Kaimi and Garrett finally really settling down.

"I don't know how, but I'm telling you Governor Haydenshire knows what Garrett did and what happened to him. He's the Crown Governor of the American Realm. If he wants to know something, people generally fall all over themselves to get him the information he wants. Somehow, he figured it all out. I don't think he'd confront Garrett outright, but he'll go out of his way to see to it that Garrett and Kaimi have every single thing they could ever need to have a strong, fulfilling marriage."

Fionna nodded her agreement as she processed everything. "I tried to tell her everything I could think of. She's kind of shy, and I could tell she was guarding with me because of Chloe. I wish she knew me well enough to know that I would never tell Chloe anything she said or asked.

"Honestly, that's why I took her out to Lindley's shop, and part of why I want to throw the party. I was hoping to loosen her up a little. Whatever she and Garrett are sharing in bed, she holds very close to her heart. It's not that I want her to tell me if she doesn't want to, but I could tell she wanted to ask me stuff and was afraid to. This is the only girl Garrett Haydenshire has taken to bed in the last fifteen years that I haven't heard about from him." Fionna wrinkled her nose. "I sort of just started talking, hoping she might jump in with her questions, but she never did." Dan chuckled as he envisioned what kinds of things Fionna had shared with Kaimi.

He tried to quell his embarrassment as he recalled Fionna and Emily whispering together on the Crown Governor's jet the morning after Dan and Fionna had slept together the first time. He'd begged her to come with him to Sydney and she'd agreed. Dan and Rainer had overheard part of one whispered conversation where Fionna was regaling Emily with her seemingly overwhelmed awe at how big Dan was. Fionna picked up on his slight unease instantly.

"Dan, you know I wouldn't tell her anything you would have minded me sharing. I want her to know that I love her because Garrett loves her. That's the only qualification I need. I want to be really good friends with her. We're going to live together on the farm, and work together, and she'll be with the girls all the time. I want her to trust me, and I want to help them."

"Fi, baby, how can I put this delicately?" He tried to phrase his knowledge without being crude. "It sounds to me like what you're saying is that Kaimi might not be quite as experienced as other women Garrett has dated long enough to bed until he got bored. But, she's the one, honey. She's the woman who turned it all around for him, and I bet her slight inexperience is part of what makes him so attentive and protective of her. Uh,"—Dan swallowed as he went ahead with the rest of his explanation—"I get the impression from how she acted with you today that she might want Garrett to be her sexual guide, and trust me, he wants to be that for her. He's not inexperienced at all, and I have no doubt he'll let her experiment with just about anything as long as it's with him."

"So, you're saying I should butt out," Fionna summed up for him.

Dan laughed and kissed her cheek. "Not in those terms per se."

"I'm not trying to butt in. I just want her to trust me if she had a girlie question or something."

"She told you when she wanted to go get waxed."

"Yeah, she got these adorable butterfly henna tats that they were doing at the salon today. They had this specialist in doing them, so I look over and Kaimi is drawing out what she wants. I was astonished. She had them do them right at the corners of her vag and out on her thighs. She just sketched it out and the girl did it and they looked amazing," Fionna gushed.

Dan shuddered slightly. "I really, really didn't need to know that."

Fionna giggled. "I started to get her to draw something for me, but my hibiscus tattoo is sort of my permanent decoration for you."

Dan gave her the shuddered growl she was after as he envisioned her perfection with the sexy vine of hibiscus flowers that led him right to the promised land.

"I bet Garrett goes nuts when he sees them, and it'll last awhile cause it's henna. She said if Garrett liked them as much as she thought he would, she might have them permanently tattooed on there." Fionna continued to supply Dan with vastly more information than he'd ever wanted to know.

"I…have no idea how I'm supposed to respond to any of this." He desperately wished for a subject change.

Fionna kissed his bare chest. "I'm sorry. I've lost two best friends in one week. I didn't mean to tell you more than you wanted to know."

Guilt replaced the discomfort Dan had been selfishly feeling. He strengthened his hold on his wife. "You haven't lost Garrett. You'll never lose him. He's just a little preoccupied right now."

In that moment, he knew Fionna had let Chloe go for him and the life they'd created together. He had to stop trying to push Garrett away as well. Dan hadn't consciously been doing it, but on occasion, his possessive jealousy reared its ugly head, and he needed to quell that monster. "You and Garrett will always be best friends. He'll always be a secondary Shield for you, and you will always be a Receiver for him. I'm sorry for the times I haven't really understood that. But you'll always be a part of him and he of you. You'll always have a side of him Kaimi won't have, just like he'll always hold a piece of your heart that I need to learn to share with him, because he will always be part of what makes you the phenomenal woman I get to share my life with."

Fionna clung to him fiercely. "I don't ever need anyone but you, but thank you for saying that. I still have Malani for all the girlie stuff and the mommy stuff. I guess I just wanted to get close to Kaimi. Garrett is also one of your closest friends too, and it would just be so cool if we were *all* really close, you know."

"Give her time. She's had it rough the last few years. Remember all that stuff Tutu told you. How she left Juilliard and then used all of her income from the studio to help pay for her grandmother's medical bills. Now the whole thing with Chloe, not to mention that she's fallen in love with a man who might not be able give her the life she might've been thinking about forever." Dan let his softer side show. The one she'd cultivated and nurtured. He'd been a willing pupil and he wanted her to know that.

"I don't think that's true. I think Tutu can help him. She can heal him. I just refuse to believe nothing can be done." It killed her for someone she loved to have suffered so much, and she wanted so desperately for Garrett and Kaimi to have what they had, so Dan simply nodded his lie.

"I hope so." He tried to hide his doubt. "But they don't have to have kids to be happy."

"I know. I just meant that Tutu can give them the option if they ever wanted to try." She paused for a moment and nuzzled her head on his chest. "Will is really upset with Garrett."

"Yeah, even I picked up on that."

"Do you think he should tell Will? He knows something more is going on besides Garrett abruptly falling in love and moving to Hawaii. Will feels really left out."

"I don't know, sweetheart. I think we have to let Garrett and Kaimi decide that."

Fionna nodded her begrudged agreement with a deep yawn.

"Go to sleep, my sweet Maylea. We'll figure out tomorrow in the morning, and then we'll start a whole new year. By summer, we'll be on Kauai. I can't wait to make it our home."

"Me, either." Fionna sighed contentedly. "And thank you for everything, but right here in your arms is where I'll always be home."

# CHAPTER 34

# ATTENTION

## ~GARRETT HAYDENSHIRE~

"You're sure he'll be all right?" Kaimi asked for the sixth time in a five-minute span.

"He'll be fine, sweetheart. We'll only be gone long enough to suffer through one of Mrs. Vindico's dinners and then for me to sign the agreement to be a guest mentor for the semester. It kills me that Wilshire is doing this to Governor Vindico. I have to try to save him. He's like a second father to me. We've got to get this all figured out so he can stop playing chancellor, and Dan can stop pretending to be a mentor when we all know he'll always be a cop."

Kaimi was seated on the hardwood floors with Duke playing tug-of-war. Duke would pull on the knotted sock for a few minutes and then leave it to give his mama kisses before he returned for more of the game.

He seemed to be concerned that if he took the sock from Kaimi, it might hurt her feelings, so he wanted to console her before they went back to playing. Kaimi was done for. Duke had firmly cemented himself in the spot of her most favorite guy, but Garrett decided being a close second was all right with him.

He finally pried Kaimi away from Duke and guided her into his car.

"Tell me about Dan's mom. You all act like she's nuts or something, even Dan and Maylea." Kaimi wore her inquisitiveness in her sweet grin and the light in her copper eyes. Garrett's heart skipped a beat as he laced his fingers through hers.

"Let's see here," he tried to determine where to begin. "You know how Dan doesn't ever give a shit what anyone thinks about him?"

"Except for Maylea."

"True," Garrett agreed. "But he got that way from living with a mother who obsesses over what everyone thinks all the time. She's fully of the opinion that her family is just a little bit better than everyone else's. She loves that her husband is a Realm governor, and she loved that her son ran National Iodex and the Elite Squadron." Garrett shook his head.

"But then Dan tumbled from grace, and Mrs. Vindico didn't handle that well. She was initially thrilled when Dan started dating Fionna because she was one of the most famous Arlington Angels ever to challenge. But then when the Realm found out about them, it was because she'd been shot and miscarried a baby they'd conceived out of wedlock, which was a big fucking deal to Marion Vindico.

"To rub salt in that wound, when it became apparent that Dan and Fi were going to run their lives the way they wanted instead of letting her run it for them, things disintegrated rapidly and they were bad to start with." He drew a deep breath, not certain how to explain the tenuous relationship between Dan and his mother. "For as long as I've known Danny, he and his mom have fought like cats and dogs. When we were kids, she'd draw a line in the sand, and he'd plow through it with bulldozers and dynamite." Garrett chuckled as he recalled just a few of the stunts he and Will and Dan had gotten into when they were in elementary and middle school.

"What about Lindley though? You said she was pretty wild, and she's the manager of the sex shop downtown. Her picture is up on the wall as, like, the best employee or whatever. If her mom was upset that Dan and Maylea got pregnant out of wedlock, did her mom disown her or something?"

"No, not officially. Lindley is more like Dan than you'd think. She just doesn't have his extreme sense of responsibility and thirst for justice. Everything that makes Dan a great guy, Lindley is the exact opposite, but when it comes to wanting to infuriate their mother and rebel, they share that desire. Dan can't stand Lindley either though."

"That's really sad."

"Yeah, I guess it is. I always took Dan's side, and then when Mrs. Vindico started being a bitch to Fionna, that just pissed me the hell off. I'll never forgive her for that." To his delight, his protective nature with Fionna didn't elicit any jealousy from his fiancée. She seemed pleased that Garrett and Fionna were so close.

"How would anyone not like Maylea? She's the sweetest, most sincere person on the planet. I've never met anyone like her."

Garrett considered the question thoughtfully. "Like I said, Mrs. Vindico was thrilled when Dan and Fi started dating because Fionna was so famous. Then Dan made it clear that she couldn't tell any of her cronies about it because Fionna would end up like Amelia. I stepped in to pretend to be Fi's boyfriend to keep her safe while she was around Dan. I ended up getting all of the attention Mrs. Vindico wanted and that pissed her off even more. Then Fionna ended up in the hospital, gunshot wound, and pregnant, and Dan carried her in. Mrs. Vindico begged me to take responsibility for the baby at least to the press. I don't think she cared whose it was as long as the press didn't think Dan was involved."

Kaimi rolled her eyes as she began to understand the shallow depths that consumed Marion Vindico.

"Fi made a full recovery. Dan stepped down from Iodex. They married in Kauai, and that was that. They cut Dan's parents out all together. They started living life the way that they'd wanted to the whole time they'd been together. They adopted Aida at a moment's notice, and Mrs. Vindico just never recovered her perceived command on their lives."

Kaimi timidly slid her hand closer to Garrett's. He chuckled as he laced his fingers through hers.

"You're gonna be my wife, sweetheart. If you want to hold my hand, just grab it. If you want to hold anything at all, just grab it, save maybe my nads."

She giggled, and Garrett reveled in the sound.

"Do you really like the butterflies?" she quizzed in an abrupt subject change that Garrett didn't think were so abrupt anymore. Her ever vacillating rhythms had cemented in his soul and taken up residence in his weary heart where she was healing him.

He let the image of her standing before him the night before form in his mind. He'd been seated on the floor up against the bed and had positioned her right in front of his mouth, which began to water from the memory alone.

"Baby, that was, my God, stunning," he finally vowed.

Kaimi had been overjoyed by Garrett's reaction to her waxed bare with two butterflies on either side of her mound.

"It was like they were bringing me the sexiest damn present I've ever seen." He continued his vows as he let his mind recall him assuring her that he could bring her with his tongue while she stood before him. He'd used his fingers to tease just along her opening as he lapped at her clit until it swelled and pulsed against his tongue. He'd slipped his fingers farther back and then massaged her ass until she'd tumbled out of control like a deck of cards. He held all of her aces. Her energy flooded his mouth and then he'd caught her as her legs had gone lax, and he'd cradled her long enough to stand and get her in their bed where he began building her again.

"The girl said it would last a couple of weeks. When I start working again, I think I'm gonna have something like that tattooed there."

Garrett fought back his initial reaction which was to tell her that she could get the tattoo as long as the artist was female and he was there. Recollections of Dan informing Fionna of the same guidelines was the only way Garrett kept quiet.

"I'm getting paid for this gig at Venton. If you want to get them done, there's a girl at the shop I've been going to for years. She's really good."

"No." Kaimi shook her head. "You are not spending any more money on me for something like that."

"If you change your mind, believe me, it would be just as much for me as for you."

"The henna ones will last a little longer if you don't lick them so much." She gave him an adorable, mischievous grin.

"Then you need to let me pay for the real deal, 'cause I'm gonna keep licking and sucking, and I believe my baby really likes it when I slide my teeth right along here." Garrett dropped Kaimi's hand long enough to lean and caress her mound through the jeans she was wearing. Her body tensed deliciously as a slight shiver overtook her.

Her own personal brand of intoxicating wildfire lit in her eyes, and Garrett forced himself not to pull off the road and beg her to join him in the back of the SUV.

"Do you think Maylea was upset when we told her we were just gonna spend New Year's alone?" Her mood shifted again, and Garrett had to shake himself from his erotic reverie.

He took a moment to consider how honest he should be. He didn't want to lie to her, but Fionna's feelings were hurt. But they'd wanted to return back to their apartment and revel in starting the New Year as an engaged couple instead of hanging out at the Vindicos'.

His lack of response seemed to be the only answer Kaimi needed. "I think Maylea and Will really, really miss you. I feel bad."

"I was planning on talking to Fi tonight, and not to sound like some kind of pompous prick or anything, but I know she's feeling a little left out. I'm sure Chloe shut her out completely, so she's probably feeling a little lacking in her usual friends department. I think that was part of her wanting to get to know you yesterday. It'll take some adjustment on everyone's part, but we'll figure it out. We'll find a balance."

"Not making me feel less guilty," Kaimi pointed out as she wrinkled her nose.

"You have nothing to feel guilty about."

She was so easy to talk to, and he wanted so desperately to tell her everything, that he was having a hard time discerning what he should and shouldn't say.

"Maybe we should go over there for a little while."

"Do you want to go over there, or are you just offering because you don't want Fi to be upset?" He knew Kaimi wanted to go home to Duke and to be with Garrett. Everyone really needed to back off.

They'd found each other, fallen madly in love, almost broken up, and gotten engaged in the matter of a few weeks. They needed some time to cocoon, to figure out their lives as a couple when both of them had been relatively independent.

Kaimi had spent all of her time teaching dance and taking care of her grandmother. She hadn't really figured herself out completely in the last few years, and now, she needed time to just be Kaimi and to let Garrett show her how much he loved her just the way she was. Whatever version of herself she wanted to be at any moment, he loved them all. His family and Dan and Fionna could just chill as far as he was concerned.

"Wow," Kaimi gasped as she stared up at the Vindicos' mansion. It was a solid, white brick affair set on the ninth hole of the private golf course. "I know your parents' house is even bigger than this, but it doesn't look so intimidating."

"If you think it's bad out here, wait 'til I get you inside."

Dan and Fionna's Mercedes was already in the driveway, so Garrett lifted Kaimi's hand to his mouth and brushed a kiss between her knuckles before he pulled her forward and brought her lips to his hungry mouth. She grinned against his lips.

"Aren't they waiting on us?"

"Yeah, yeah." Garrett exited the Highlander and opened Kaimi's door.

# CHAPTER 35
# HAMBURGER CASSEROLE

Governor Vindico met them at the door with a wry grin. "I hear the third musketeer has finally fallen." He shook Garrett's hand and then pulled him in for a hug.

Garrett laughed as he reached back for Kaimi's hand. "Governor Vindico, this is my fiancée, Kaimi Walyuo. Baby, this is Governor Vindico, Dan's dad."

"It's so nice to meet you, sir." Kaimi's nerves were evident in her tone. Governor Vindico chuckled as he closed the door behind them.

"The honor is all mine. Believe me, we thought Brooke and Fionna had conquered mighty beasts when they met Will and Dan at the end of the aisle, but Garrett…" Governor Vindico slapped Garrett on the back. "Let's just say how thrilled we are he finally met his match." Kaimi laughed and seemed to relax slightly.

Dan and Fionna greeted them, and Aida raced into Garrett and squeezed her arms around his waist. "Did you bring Duke?"

"No, baby girl, we left him at home, but Aunt Kaimi can bring him to your house this week, okay?" Garrett promised.

Fionna eased beside Kaimi. They both seemed anxious to bridge any gap they perceived in their new friendship.

"Before now, I'd obviously never been in any of the governors' mansions, and now I've been in two," Kaimi whispered as Fionna chuckled and nodded her understanding.

"Aida, dear, did you offer to take Mr. Haydenshire's coat?" Mrs. Vindico made her appearance wearing a cable-knit sweater over a button-down blouse that was tucked neatly in a pair of polyester pants. Her hair was in the same coif she'd been wearing for the last thirty years. A double strand of pearls lay on the sweater at the perfect height for her to clutch.

"He's not here, Grandma." Aida tucked her tiny hand in Garrett's, and her bottom lip went between her teeth. He leaned and lifted her up into his arms. His need to protect her pulsed in his shield though he couldn't understand why. She buried her face in his neck and held him tighter.

"I've got you," Garrett whispered.

"Marion." Governor Vindico rolled his eyes. "She thinks you're talking about Stephen. Garrett is her godfather. She calls him Garrett."

"Arthur, someone has to teach the child manners." Mrs. Vindico threw a hateful glare in Fionna's general direction, and Garrett ground his teeth.

"Can I get you a beer, son?" The governor ignored his wife completely.

"Sure, thank you. Do you want one, baby?" Garrett kept Aida cradled to his shoulder as he slipped out of his jacket and followed Dan into the living room.

"No, thank you. I'll just have water." Kaimi patted Aida's back. She seemed to want to console both Aida and Fionna over Mrs. Vindico's quip.

"I think Marion has dinner just about ready, so why don't we eat and then we can discuss what to do with this disaster at Venton that has me thinking I should just go ahead and take out stock in antacids. I can't believe Dean's stunt last night."

"We'll get this figured out, sir." Garrett seated Aida and then pulled Kaimi's chair out for her in the Vindicos' large dining room. It still held the Christmas tree adorned with Mrs. Vindico's crystal ornaments. Garrett would never have even noticed the ornaments except that Fionna had complained that Aida had crafted all of her grandparents clay ornaments at school for their Christmas presents, and though Mrs. Vindico had praised Aida's efforts, she'd refused to hang it on the tree.

"I certainly hope so, because I would like to serve another few years before I retire, but the price on my head grows exponentially with each passing day." Governor Vindico sighed.

Before anyone could reassure him that people did remember all of the time and effort he'd put into governing the Realm for the last thirty years and that Wilshire was to blame for Venton's dismantling, Mrs. Vindico lifted a sheet of what appeared to be reused tin foil off some horrendous looking dish with charred hamburger buns lining the top.

Dan's napkin hit his plate in furious acrimony. "Dammit, Mother, I told you yesterday, and Fionna called you this morning to make certain you understood that Kaimi is allergic to beef and pork. How freaking hard could that be to understand?"

Kaimi was horrified, not by the odd casserole, but by Dan's arguing with his mother over her.

"It's fine, Dan. I'll take her out after this. Chill, man," Garrett urged under his breath.

"Daniel, for your information, I checked in *Women of the Realm*, and I found several articles that explained that you cannot be allergic to beef or pork. She may have an intolerance to them, but she has to learn to tolerate them. If she never eats them, she'll never learn to like them. Now, it did say that intolerances can lead to indigestion and gas, so I took the liberty of fixing you a glass of the grapefruit juice that I make Arthur drink for his colon health. I mixed in two tablespoons of Metamucil for you." Mrs. Vindico explained the odd, swirling, salmon-colored drink at Kaimi's place.

Fionna's head fell into her hands. Kaimi appeared lost between bursting into tears and fleeing from the house and running for her life.

Garrett supplied his hand, well aware that drawing from him might be the only thing that kept her at the table.

"I remembered when Garrett and Dan were younger that you boys loved when Stephen grilled hamburgers on their back deck, so I found this four bean and beef casserole. I topped it with ketchup and mustard and then I cut up bags of hamburger buns in strips and covered it with them. I realized while it was baking that I forgot the chopped onion so I just shoved a few spears through the buns. It's supposed to be a summer dish, but I said why not?"

"So fucking many reasons I can't name them all," Dan growled under his breath.

Aida had picked up on Kaimi's horrific embarrassment. She grasped her other hand. "It's okay. Don't be sad, please, because a lot of times when what Grandma fixes for dinner makes Mommy's and my tummies hurt then Daddy will take us for a pizza party at Francetti's after here, so maybe Uncle Garrett will take you to Francetti's and he'll get you the pineappley up pizza. It's delicious!" she whispered to Kaimi though everyone at the table heard her.

"Drink up, Kaimi, then we'll pass the plates," Mrs. Vindico commanded.

"You do not have to drink that," Dan vaulted.

"Garrett," Kaimi pled under her breath. She seemed lost between being polite and the knowledge of what two tablespoons of Metamucil in grapefruit juice would do to a person that did not need that level of medication.

"Mrs. Vindico, thank you for making dinner. Kaimi is not going to drink that nor is she going to eat a hamburger casserole. Why don't I just sign the guest mentor contract and then we'll grab something on our way home?" Garrett huffed. He could not believe the audacity of Dan's mother.

Fionna leapt up from the table. "You all start eating. Kaimi and I will make a few grilled cheese sandwiches or peanut butter and jelly. I'm feeling queasy myself. I'm not certain beans would sit quite right." Before she could be reprimanded by her mother-in-law, Fionna dragged Kaimi into the kitchen, effectively rescuing her.

Dan was still shaking his head. "I'm so sorry," he vowed to Garrett.

Garrett glanced toward the kitchen. He wasn't certain what to do. He needed to sign the contract and go over the plan with Dan and the governor on how him aiding the entire Ioses teaching staff might help them gain the information they needed on all of the crimes being committed at Venton, but in that moment, the only logical thing to do seemed to be to get Kaimi as far away from Marion Vindico as he could manage.

Garrett helped himself to the smallest portion of the odd casserole he felt he could without being seen as extremely rude and then he stood.

"I'll be right back. Excuse me." He rushed into the kitchen. To his overwhelming relief, Fionna and Kaimi were tucked away in the far corner of the vast kitchen grasping each other's arms and laughing hysterically in whispered guffaws.

"Oh good." Fionna wiped away tears and tried to regain her composure. "Go get Aida and send her in here too."

"Oh, so just Dan and I have to suffer through that?" Garrett teased as Kaimi fell into his chest, still laughing.

"Yes," Fionna urged only making Kaimi laugh harder.

"Are you all right?" Garrett eased away from her so he could see her face. She nodded and tried to quell her laughter.

"Yes, but wow."

"Just stay in here. We'll get something to eat on the way home."

"We're making grilled cheese." Kaimi pointed to the beginnings of the sandwiches on the counter.

Garrett kissed the top of her head and begrudgingly returned to the dining room.

"I certainly hope Fionna isn't feeling queasy because she's expecting again," Mrs. Vindico sniped at Dan.

"And what would be wrong if she was, Mother?" Dan came right back. Garrett knew Fionna was not pregnant again, but Dan Vindico would never miss an opportunity to argue with his mom.

"Oh, yes, that's right. I forgot you and Fionna don't seem to mind the entire Realm discussing your relationship. You'd probably be perfectly fine with people talking about you the way they used to discuss Stephen and Lillian when she was pregnant every year without end." Garrett cleared his throat loudly and narrowed his eyes in on Mrs. Vindico.

Dan grimaced and rubbed his temples as the governor shot his wife an exasperated expression.

"Aida, baby, Mommy wants you to go in the kitchen with her and Aunt Kaimi," Garrett soothed. Aida raced into the kitchen. Dan's relief was written under his fury with his mother.

Garrett drew a deep breath and tried to be thankful his girls weren't having to eat the nastiest casserole he'd ever laid eyes on. The fact that he'd been served a larger helping in his absence made that task just a little bit difficult, however.

He followed Dan's lead and ate minute bites of the bun and a few beans.

"Dan told me about the additional assignment, and about Jeff casting those drives. What else needs to happen to get this figured out and to shut Dean up?" Governor Vindico seemed to understand Garrett's desperation to get on with the point of their visit.

"Actually, sir, I was going to ask Dan about this tonight, but I'm a little worried that you not only have corrupt students but mentors as well. We still don't have any evidence that leads us to believe Katherine Bryant isn't the mentor who's earning herself an extra paycheck. I wonder if we should only assign the extra paper to a few key mentors who we're certain aren't on the take, so to speak." Garrett stated the thing that had come to him that morning when he and Kaimi had lain in bed drinking coffee and discussing all of the many details of the Venton disaster.

Dan looked relieved to lay his fork beside his plate. "I did think about that. I'm just not certain how to go about selecting enough mentors to get all of the drives back, and if I'm taking the drives from other mentors, it's probably going to get around that we've figured out how they're stealing the tests."

"Why don't I make the assignment then?" Governor Vindico's gruff voice shook Garrett and Dan from their considerations.

"What do you mean?" Dan quizzed.

"I've come in and turned the whole academy over trying to figure out what's been going on. I'm the one that ordered in the Senate auditors. I don't think it would be too far-fetched to think I might suspect that the students' education has slipped in the past few years

216

as well. So, I'll set a paper for them to write. Something basic to prove their Gifted education has been worth something. The assignment isn't the important thing, right? Jeff just needs those drives back."

"Right." Dan seemed mildly shocked that his father had come up with what Garrett had to agree was a brilliant plan.

"I've been a governor of this Realm since you were two, Daniel. I didn't get here by not knowing my salt," Governor Vindico huffed. He was obviously hurt over his son's lack of faith in his abilities.

"No, Dad. I know how intelligent you are. I just guess I was surprised I didn't think of that."

Garrett chuckled as the governor shot his son a wry grin. "I'll send out an email ordering every mentor in for a meeting at eight o'clock Thursday morning. If you still feel the need to shower with my daughter-in-law before work, perhaps for this particular meeting, you could start the water running a little earlier." Governor Vindico rolled his eyes, and Garrett laughed. Dan nodded his begrudged agreement. "I'll spout off about Dean letting everything go to hell in a handbasket and require every student to…"—he paused thoughtfully, and his eyes lit a moment later—"write me a short paper explaining how their education at Venton will help them in their chosen career as it pertains to their Predilect. I'll have the drives turned in to me Friday, and we'll hand them over to Mr. Strenton. We'll see if we can't figure out who's been making my life miserable for the past four months."

"Bryant will have plenty to say about that, but it's ingenious, Dad, really." Pride filled Dan's tone.

"Maybe her estranged husband will defend her, since Thursday is his first day," Governor Vindico spat angrily. Garrett shuddered both over the information he'd shared and the way the governor was devouring the hamburger casserole.

"So, they hired him?" Dan shook his head.

"They did, as Governor Sherman is very anxious to reestablish Venton as a family-centered academy and chose the option that was, in her mind, certain to land us in the papers as rectifying the situation for now and deciding to bury her head about the forthcoming implosion that will inevitably be on the horizon."

"Great." Dan shook his head and Garrett began to see the visible strain that all of the unsolved cases at Venton had heaped on Dan and his father.

"Hey, we're gonna get this figured out," Garrett assured as quietly as he was able.

Dan offered him an appreciative nod as dinner dragged on.

"I really appreciate you helping Daniel and me with all of this, son, and I also thank you for agreeing to offer your expertise to the students. You really do have a great deal to teach them," Governor Vindico vowed.

"I'll do whatever needs to be done in both areas of this job." Garrett began to really think about what he needed to say and do for the teaching portion of the guest mentor position he was taking. He was going to need to work on some kind of lesson plans over the next few days.

Thus far, he'd been so focused on cementing his new relationship, rectifying his past, and trying to do anything in his power to get his fiancée back to Kauai so he could marry her and start a real life, he hadn't given much thought to anything at Venton beyond the crimes being committed.

Dan explained, "I came up with a few curriculum topic suggestions that are what the kids have been learning in all of their Ioses classes if you want to take them home and look over them. They'd work well under the guise of you being there to explain being a liaison between the Realms. That way you coming in will align with the curriculum, and no one will get too curious about the other reasons you're there."

"See, this is why we work so well together. If Fi and Kaimi decide to run off without us, I think we could make a go of it," Garrett harassed him.

Dan cracked up. "I don't know. How do you look in a G-string?"

"Are you kidding me? Have you seen my glutes? I rock a G-string."

Mrs. Vindico looked horrified as the governor rolled his eyes.

# CHAPTER 36
# POSSIBILITY

Garrett rushed through the process of signing the guest mentor contract and the forms to allow a background check. He dragged Kaimi out the front door, eager to get her some real food and out of the Vindicos' home.

"I cannot tell you how sorry I am. I didn't know what to do." He began apologizing before he'd cranked the Highlander. Thinking quickly, he casted the engine so the heater would warm the car instantly.

Kaimi began giggling much to Garrett's relief. "That was hysterical and awful, and Maylea totally saved me. I still can't believe she wants to be my friend so badly. I get how you two are best friends. She's so sweet and kind and it's like somehow she is loyal to Chloe and loyal to me. You know, like she's never ever talked about Chloe to me, but I know she would never talk about me to Chloe either."

Garrett lifted her hand to his lips, brushing a tender kiss along her knuckles. "I really am sorry about tonight, sweetheart. Just tell me where you want to go eat. I'll take you anywhere."

Kaimi grinned up at him. The peace and serenity that flooded through him at that moment had his breaths quickening as he reminded himself to keep his eyes on the road.

She turned and stared out at the darkening sky. Anticipation and hope permeated the air that evening. The brink of a new year and all the many options that it held. Possibility swam before them. Garrett squeezed Kaimi's hand again as he considered all he'd lost in the past few years and then all he'd gained in the woman sitting beside him waiting patiently to become his wife.

"What are you thinking about?" Garrett whispered. He was suddenly desperate for her to talk again. She turned back to him and blinked away tears. "Hey...what's wrong?"

She managed a broken smile. "I don't know. I was just thinking that I want some ice cream, and then I thought that I'm going to marry you and I don't even know your favorite kind of ice cream, and that seems like something I should know. I'm going to be your wife so I should know that. Why don't I know that?" She rapidly approached panic.

"Hey," Garrett soothed. He glanced in the rearview mirror and exited the interstate, not particularly caring where he parked. They just needed to talk. "Just because you don't know my favorite flavor of ice cream doesn't mean I don't want to spend the rest of my life with you. We're gonna grow and change together, and in fifty years, I'll still be just as fascinated to learn each and every thing about you." He began his vows as he pulled into an empty grocery store parking lot that had closed early for the holiday.

She managed a nod before she broke down completely. Garrett's heart fractured as he cradled her to him and let her tears fall onto his shirt.

"Shh, okay, it's okay, sweetheart."

She ran her hands over her face and pulled away with her chin still trembling.

"I'm sorry. I don't know why I freaked out. I was just so embarrassed about Dan yelling at his mom, and then you asked me what I wanted to eat, and then I thought I kind of wanted ice cream, and then I thought about how when I was a little girl Nana would say that I couldn't have any ice cream mochi until I ate all of my dinner, and then I thought about dinner again, and then I thought about all of the things that we don't know about each other. And then I thought about how Aida probably never even had ice cream until she came here, and about how mean Mrs. Vindico was to her. And then I thought about how much I miss Nana. And then I just cried." She tried to explain the bewildering journey her mind had taken her on in a matter of seconds.

Garrett wrapped his arms back around her and held her tight. He pushed his shield out from his pores.

"Sweetheart," he soothed. The words formed in his heart and he let them spill from his lips. "My favorite flavor of ice cream is rocky road with extra caramel, and your favorite kind of ice cream is either mocha toffee or lilikoi mochi depending on your mood, but you really like shave ice better. You told me on the phone before I ever went to Kauai, and will you please marry me?" She lifted her head as her brow furrowed.

"Didn't I already say I would do that?" Fear pulsed in her rhythms. Garrett couldn't help the grin that formed on his face as she went so far as to check the ring on her left hand, as if it might all have been a dream.

"Yeah, baby, you did." Garrett cradled her face in his hand and wiped away her tears. He stared into the flecks of gold in her copper-brown eyes. He'd never seen anything so beautiful. "But I want you to marry me right now, tonight. Please," he begged. "In a few hours, it's going to be a new year, and I've screwed up so many years of my life. I don't want to do that anymore. I want to start this year married to you. Please, we can have a ceremony or whatever you want in Kauai, but tonight, I want you to be my wife. Just please."

"But..." She shook her head. "You have to go to work Thursday, and I have to help Maylea and..." Hope and fear fought for dominance in her rhythms.

"I know it wouldn't be much of a honeymoon, but maybe when I'm done at Venton next Friday, we could use those two additional tickets I got you for Christmas and go back to Kauai for a few days. I know we need to deal with your apartment. If you want, we could camp on the beach for a long weekend. It's warm there, right? We could spend a few days alone together. We can talk about ice cream or anything you want. I know you need to go home. I can feel it when I hold you like this." He kept up his pleas and tried to reassure her that they knew more about each other than her fears would allow her to believe.

"You felt that?"

"I *feel* that."

She stared up at him with the fear that held her captive plaguing her eyes and gave a slight nod.

"Okay, but I don't know how to be a wife. I never even lived with a guy before you. What if we get married and I do it wrong and you hate it?"

"Neither of us has ever been married. I'm sure we have a lot to learn, but at the end of the day all that really matters is that you're my wife and I'm your husband, and that those are the most important roles in our life. Please, baby, I don't want you to be afraid anymore. It kills me for you to be afraid. I want the whole world to know I'm yours and you're mine. Just let it all go. Just do this with me. It feels so right."

A smile waged war against her tears, and Garrett was thrilled that for the moment it seemed to be winning.

"How do we do this?" Excitement began to pulse in her rhythms.

Garrett's brow furrowed as he began to consider. "Do you want to elope, or do you want my parents to know and Dad to do the ceremony?" He cranked the car and pulled out his cell phone simultaneously.

"I don't want to elope, elope. I want your family to be there," Kaimi decided as Garrett pulled back onto a small highway. "I was thinking maybe I could ask your dad to walk me down the aisle. I don't know. Can he do both?"

Garrett's mind began to go through everything that would need to be done in the next few hours.

"Governor Carrington or Governor Vindico could do the ceremony, and Dad could walk you down the aisle. Or Dan or Will could walk you down, and Dad could do the vows," he explained as he got back on the interstate though he was not entirely certain where he was heading.

"I want your dad to walk me down the aisle, but I don't want to ruin anyone's New Year's plans."

Garrett was fairly certain that Regis and Serena would be more than willing to forgo New Year's plans to see him actually settle down and finally really be happy.

"Let's see what I can do. I don't play the Crown Governor's son card ever, so I doubt anyone will mind too much. Are you okay staying at the apartment tonight or do you want to go to some swanky hotel downtown and let Duke stay on the farm?" He continued his inquisition as he touched his father's name on his contact list.

"Hey, Dad." Garrett tried to decide how to say what he needed to say. "Kaimi and I were just talking and sort of wondered if maybe you'd help us get married…tonight." He cleared his throat, not certain why he'd choked.

His father's delighted chuckle eased his nerves. "Most of your brothers are already here. Rainer and Emily are on their way over. Your sister seemed to feel like they should come. And I can't think of anything I'd rather do tonight, son," he vowed with emotion thick in his throat as well.

"I guess I never gave Em all the credit she deserved for being an awesome Receiver," Garrett allowed. "Kaimi was wondering if you'd walk her down the aisle, and I thought maybe Governor Carrington might step in if he's not busy. And I want Sam to come."

"Tell Kaimi I'd be honored. Your uncles are still here if you want to talk to Tad about a ring, and I'll give Regis and Sam a call. I can't imagine Regis would mind as long as he and Serena don't have any plans, and Sam would do absolutely anything for you, just like the rest of us. Can I make two requests?"

"I guess." Garrett wondered what the requests might be as they seemed to have made his father uneasy. Kaimi was chewing her lip as she stared up at Garrett.

"First, can your mother and I put you and Kaimi up at the Four Seasons tonight? I assume you're still planning on working at Venton this week, right?"

"Yeah, I know it's kind of rushed. And thanks, I guess our apartment doesn't make the best backdrop for our wedding night."

His father chuckled. "I think even if you're going to do this on the spur of the moment, the moment should be celebrated."

"Definitely." He wondered if Kaimi would be all right leaving Duke at the farm for the night. "What was the other thing?"

"I assume you'll be calling Dan and Fionna, so I was wondering if I could take you and Dan and Will out for a beer before we get you married?" His father's voice was pleading, and Garrett considered.

"I guess, but I want this done. We're going to go get ring tats first and then go get Duke. I want to be married before midnight." He wondered what his father was hearing in his voice.

"It's just after six. We can make this work. I'd just like a little time with you before I bring you your bride. Even if you are grown, I think we could at least have a beer."

"I'd like that. I just want to be married."

Tears swam in Kaimi's eyes as they pulled into the Gifted tattoo parlor that Garrett preferred.

"Let me tell your mother, and if you decide you also want wedding bands, Tad already has the cases out. We'll see you soon."

"Thanks, Dad." Garrett ended that call and phoned Dan. Garrett wasn't surprised that he was thrilled and was packing up Fionna and the girls to head over to the farm at a moment's notice. He called Will next, still trying to make certain he included his big brother in the decision-making.

"We're already here. Congrats, man," Will offered.

"Thanks. And you're still down for the best man gig, right?"

"Of course."

"See you soon," he promised. "Come on." He grabbed Kaimi's hand. There was no turning back. Impatience surged through his shield. He'd been waiting his whole life for her, and nothing made sense without her as his wife. He was shocked that he felt no fear in his own rhythms. He'd never been more certain of anything, but his patience was waning. She was his, and he wanted the world to know.

Kaimi raced behind him, clinging to his hand. Her curious, determined, wild glow lit her eyes.

"I love you," she vowed as Garrett flung open the door.

"I love you too, sweetheart, and I can't wait to marry you." He gave a nod and smile to the guy who had done most of his intricate tattoo work.

"Hey, man." Byron slapped Garrett's shoulder as he shook his hand. He offered Kaimi a kind smile.

"This is my fiancée, Kaimi. Kaimi, baby, this is Byron. He's done most of my ink. He's the best."

Byron scoffed as he shook Kaimi's hand.

"Who are we inking tonight, or are you just here for a touch-up?"

"Both of us. We're getting married tonight. She designed ring tats. Do you think you could do those quick?"

"Hell yeah, man. We're dead tonight. I was thinking about closing up. Kerri Ann's here. Do you mind if she does one?"

"That's fine." Truthfully, Garrett thought Kerri Ann was a little better than Byron. He preferred her to work on Kaimi as she was more precise and gentle. "Do you have the sketches, sweetheart?" he quizzed as he began to realize how unorganized this wedding was likely to be.

"Uh, yeah actually." Kaimi pulled the worn, folded piece of sketch paper from her handmade cloth bag that was slung in its customary place across her body. She handed it to Byron. He was impressed. Garrett could tell. Byron gestured his hand to two of the numerous empty tables in the well-equipped shop.

Kerri Ann smiled and introduced herself. "I was hoping I'd get to meet the girl that's gonna make Garrett her bitch."

Kaimi laughed. Heat began to climb up her neck and through her cheeks, turning her back into his peach. Garrett couldn't hide his beaming grin as he winked at her.

"Do you want a band mark in the center or is this the ring?" Byron quizzed as he began preparing the pens.

Garrett raised his eyebrows in question to Kaimi.

"If you want a band, I'd like that. I have my engagement ring."

"Go ahead and do the band mark," Garrett instructed.

Byron began sketching Kaimi's design on thermal paper. "You know what you ought to have him get you for a wedding present?" Kerri Ann shared a knowing grin with Byron.

"No." Garrett knew precisely where this was going as he laced his right hand through Kaimi's so he could soothe her pain when Kerri Ann brought out the needles.

"What?" Kaimi giggled.

"You get him to stand up and salute, Miss Thang, and I'll fit him for an ampallang."

"I said no." Garrett rolled his eyes and tried not to shudder.

"Girl, you should make him do it. It feels so damn good," Kerri Ann vowed with a highly unnecessary shiver of delight.

"Is that one of those bar things that goes through your…?" Kaimi wrinkled her nose adorably.

"Yeah, baby." Garrett was concerned Kerri Ann would harass her for being naive.

"I promise you'll love it." Byron continued to urge Kaimi on.

Kaimi shook her head. "I don't think I want you doing anything to that, especially on my wedding night." She blushed but seemed quite certain about her response.

Byron and Kerri Ann cracked up and nodded their agreement. Garrett was absolutely certain that anything that added to his girth would not be good for Kaimi. He winked at her and joined in the laughter.

"Okay, how's that?" Kerri Ann finished the penned guide of the intricate scrolling ring design on Kaimi's ring finger.

"Perfect." Kaimi nodded. She was holding her engagement ring tightly in her right hand. She considered for a minute before grinning up at Kerri Ann.

"How long would it take to do these right here?" She extracted another small notepad from her purse and handed it to Kerri Ann. Garrett's brow furrowed. After handing the notepad over, Kaimi pointed to either side of her mound where it met her legs.

"I'm fast, girl, and I'm good. If you want these done tonight, I'll let the ring be your wedding present. It won't take me long. We'll get you off to your wedding in time, and I'll get you all healed up too." Kaimi sketched often and was extremely talented, though she never believed Garrett's praise. He wasn't certain which sketch she might be having done.

True to their word, a couple of hours later Kaimi emerged from one of the back curtained rooms wearing a broad grin. She was walking gingerly, however. Garrett was concerned that Kerri Ann hadn't healed her skin completely.

He helped her climb back in the Highlander.

"Okay, let's go home and get Duke. Dad wants to put us up in the Four Seasons tonight as a wedding present. Is that okay with you?"

"I've never stayed somewhere like that." Excitement trilled in her rhythms. "I don't have any fancy dresses or anything," she confessed as if that might have Garrett turning and running away. He shook his head and wondered when she was going to finally believe he wasn't going anywhere ever.

"If you want a dress, I'm sure between Fi and Emily and Adeline and Olivia and Brooke, and God knows who else, we could come up with one, but I think you're gorgeous just like that." He gestured to the jeans and sweater she was wearing. Kaimi wrinkled her nose.

"I want a dress."

"Okay, let's go get Duke and then we'll head to the farm. I think Dad wants to go out for a little while with me and Will and Dan so you can get ready. I'll grab my suit when we get to the apartment."

"Oh, wait! I do have a dress," Kaimi gasped suddenly. "I bought it in New York on a complete whim. I've never ever worn it, but it's so pretty I couldn't give it away. I threw it in my suitcase because I packed all of my clothes because you know I knew I didn't have a job there anymore. It's not like a wedding dress though. It's just a fancy dress, dress."

"I don't care what you wear, sweetheart, as long as tomorrow morning when we wake up and start this new year, you're Mrs. Garrett Haydenshire." He let the sound of her new name reverberate through his soul.

Any other time he'd ever even allowed himself to consider settling down and marrying, he'd always felt sickened, like it would break him into irreparable pieces. Now, as he took in Kaimi's adoring smile, his soul mended. The plaguing restless murmurs of his mind went quiet and gave him peace. The beast that he swore lived in his chest, occasionally shredding him from the inside out, calmed and damn near purred. His heart pushed his life's blood through his veins as it longed to be timed to the only beat that would ever steady its frantic pace. His mind and his body needed to be one with hers forever.

"I can't wait," she whispered. "I can't believe we're doing this tonight, but I can't wait."

"Me either," Garrett vowed.

# CHAPTER 37

# POMP AND PREPARATIONS

"Duke," Garrett scolded several minutes later as they raced into the apartment to prepare for their rather rushed wedding.

"Don't fuss at him. He got scared. We were gone too long." Kaimi scooped him up in her arms. He was whimpering and cuddled into her. The remnants of one corner end of Garrett's leather sofa were scattered on the floor around him.

"We have to get on to him. He can't do this just because we aren't with him."

Kaimi nodded but she looked like she might cry. With a sigh, Garrett cleaned up the hardwood floor where Duke had used the bathroom and then swept up the shredded leather and cotton batting.

"I guess I'm glad he couldn't do more damage."

"Maybe we shouldn't leave him tonight?" She tried to cover the disappointment in her tone.

"Sweetheart, he'll be fine at the farm for one night. Mom and Dad and the twins will watch him. It's our wedding night, and Dad's right, it should be somewhere really special." Garrett wasn't going to let her put Duke's desires over her own. He was going to give her a proper wedding night where he spoiled her in a luxury honeymoon suite at the Four Seasons and worshipped her body for hours on end before he finally gave in and really made her his wife. They could spend the next few days together and then start preparing for their life as a married couple on her island.

Duke nudged Garrett's bicep with his cold nose. He knew Garrett was upset.

"Yeah, I still love you, but we do not eat couches." Garrett scratched under Duke's chin and down his neck.

"Are you only going to have Will or are you going to ask Dan to be a groomsman?" she asked as she laid a dry cleaning bag out on the bed.

"I'd like to ask Dan as well, but that's up to you."

"It's not just my wedding," she corrected him. "And I kind of thought I would see if Maylea would be my maid of honor and if Adeline would be a bridesmaid."

"I'm sure Adeline would be really happy to do that for you."

Garrett pulled into the barn where everyone else was already parked.

They were greeted enthusiastically by the entire household. Mrs. Haydenshire hugged Kaimi for a solid five minutes. Fionna and Aida were working at the kitchen table with dozens of bouquets of grocery store flowers spread around them.

"Oh, thank you for this." Tears swam in Kaimi's eyes again as she threw her arms around Fionna. Garrett understood a moment later that Fionna was creating Kaimi's all-white wedding lei, and Aida was crafting a more colorful floral crown for her as well.

"You're welcome. Who says you can't have an island wedding in December in Virginia?" Fionna teased as she continued making Kaimi an intricate lei.

"Can we make one for you too because I would really like you to be my maid of honor," Kaimi begged. Fionna was overjoyed as Emily and Adeline immediately offered to help in any way they could.

"Hey, baby, will you come here a minute?" Garrett grabbed Kaimi's hand. "Just give me a second, and we can go," he instructed his father and Will who were both waiting by the door. Garrett guided Kaimi up to his and Will's childhood bedroom.

"I need to help," she fussed.

"I want to make sure you're all healed up. Kerri Ann is a great artist, but she's not a great healer. I don't want you back in the hospital. I can't take you home for a while." His care had her beaming, but as he closed the bedroom door and reached for the snap on her jeans, she grabbed his hand and halted his progress.

"I want it to be a surprise. It doesn't hurt anymore, and maybe Adeline would heal it up for me. Most brides get special lingerie for their wedding night, but you don't really like lingerie, so I wanted it to be this special thing that you don't see until later."

Garrett pulled her into his chest and wrapped his arms around her. Worry, excitement, and overwhelming love all flooded through his rhythms.

"Baby, if you want to go get something to wear tonight, I'm sure Fionna could find some store that's open, or hell, they'd probably open just for her. I don't want you to feel like you're giving anything up because I'm so damn impatient."

"No, when you were holding me on the couch last night and you told me how you like me without makeup and without lingerie and stuff, you made me feel so beautiful and so loved and just like we really are perfect for each other. But, I wanted to do this for you, so please. If you really are worried it's okay. I understand. You can see them now." She tried to hide her disappointment, but Garrett felt it pulse in her rhythms.

"No." This time Garrett halted her progress. "And this will be the only time for the rest of our lives I'll stop you from taking off your jeans," he informed her just to hear her adorable giggle. He brushed a tender kiss across her forehead. "Get Adeline to do it. She'll be way better than me anyway. And Kaimi,"—he lifted her chin with his fingers and gazed down into her eyes—"I can't wait to get you in our hotel room. I can't wait to see what you had done for me, and baby, I cannot wait to make you my wife."

As a furtive moan spilled from her mouth, Garrett captured it with his lips as he began his intensive study of every curve of her beautiful mouth with his own. He dipped his tongue to hers and sucked gently before he pulled the energy from her and she panted for breath.

"I don't want you to leave."

"I won't go if you don't want me to." His dad would just have to get over it.

"No, I can tell your dad really wants you to, and maybe you could all talk. Maylea kind of hinted that Will is a little hurt that you didn't tell him more about us, even if it has all been really fast."

"Are you sure, because I can talk to Will and Dad later? You're all that matters to me."

Her rhythms trilled from his vows as she kissed his jawline. "I'll be fine, and when you get back, we're getting married!"

"Then I won't be long because I've never wanted anything as much as I want that," he assured her.

## CHAPTER 38

# THE PRIDE

Garrett begrudgingly climbed in Will's Volvo beside his father in the back seat. Dan had taken shotgun, which Garrett and the governor had allowed as Dan was several inches taller than they were.

"This is not really how I saw your bachelor party going," Will commented. He did look and sound disappointed.

"I know, man. I'm sorry. I need to stop fucking up my life, and I don't know, it just feels like it should be tonight." Garrett tried to be completely honest with the men in the car. He was well aware that his father and brother were both feeling a little lost when it came to their relationship.

Will guided the car through the clear, cold night to Lesco's, the Haydenshire family's favorite burger joint, that was only a few miles from the farm.

"Les is waiting. He stayed open for us," the governor commented.

"He didn't have to do that," Garrett scoffed.

"I know, son, but he feels like he had a hand in raising you as well. I think he'd like to at least congratulate you."

They entered the pub, and Les gave Garrett a kind smile that pulled the slight wrinkles around his eyes tight and made him look a decade younger. There was a wistful light that shone there as well as he slapped Garrett on the back. The sound of burgers hitting the hot grill sizzled in the air, and for a moment, Garrett was ten years old again, walking into Les's beside Will, Levi, and Cal. They were roughhousing, and the governor was trying to get them into a booth before they caused catastrophe to one of the waitresses' trays of food.

He shook himself and forced his mind back to the present. Les guided them to the governor's preferred table where he'd already placed pitchers of beer, wings, onion rings, hot dogs, and cheeseburgers.

Garrett immediately decided he wasn't eating much nor was he having more than two beers. He wanted to get back, and most importantly, he wanted to remember every single thing about this night of all nights. There were other things he planned to devour and drink, but they all resided inside the woman who was preparing to meet him at the end of what was sure to be a very short aisle.

"Regis and Serena are having dinner out, but they'll be over in a little while. Sam as well," Governor Haydenshire explained as everyone took a seat and thanked Les profusely for the food and beer.

"Okay, come on. You're getting married tonight. She's gotta be pregnant, right? Just tell us. Honestly, we're happy for you, and trust me, you can't hide it long," Will commanded as he threw an onion ring in his mouth and helped himself to a cheeseburger.

Garrett shook his head but slid his eyes to the side slightly. The look on his father's face was momentarily morose. He tried hard to hide it, but there was a reason Garrett was one of the best detectives in the force. *He knows,* the thought quaked through Garrett as he tried to determine how his father knew what had happened to him. *Dan would never have told him and neither would Fi or Kaimi.*

Garrett shook himself slightly. "She's not pregnant. I swear. I'd tell you if she was." He forced himself to eat something.

Dan did a much better job of feigning surprise. "Yeah, I figured that too," he lied in an effort to ease the strain on Garrett.

"Daniel, I don't really believe that," the governor stated with a slight air of challenge. He continued eating and took a small sip of the beer. He wasn't going to force it out of Garrett, but it seemed he was going to apply just a little pressure and see what happened.

"Is that why you wanted to come out?" Garrett narrowed his eyes in on his father.

"No, I wanted to come out to celebrate you getting married. If there's something you want to talk about, we can do that too, but this is your party and this is your night. I just want to be a part of your life again. I want you to understand how much this family loves you, and that you are always, always ours."

Guilt took up residence where Garrett's anger began to slip away. He shifted his eyes to Dan, and he offered him a sorrowful look. He gave a minute shrug but never dropped Garrett's gaze. He stood as a steadfast Shield, just as he always would be, right beside Garrett.

The table was silent. No one knew what to say, and Will was pouting.

Garrett tossed down a bite of the cheeseburger he'd been pulling apart.

"What do you want me to say, Dad? You clearly know something you want me to confirm. But you don't know the whole story, and you don't need to know any of this."

Will shook his head. "Garrett, what the hell is going on? You used to tell me everything, even shit I didn't want to know. I get it. You're getting married. She's the one, but I know there's more to this."

"Apparently, this is some kind of new tradition where we butt the hell in the groom's business instead of going out for beers and making crude comments about the honeymoon."

The governor shook his head. "No one here is trying to get you to say or do anything you don't want to. We do love you and care about you. That's it. Give us a little credit. If we didn't care, we wouldn't want to let you know that we want to be there for you and for Kaimi no matter what."

Garrett's cell chirped. Extremely thankful for the reprieve, he lifted it from his pocket and smiled automatically. He'd set his phone to show one of the shots of Kaimi blowing him a kiss whenever she called or texted.

> Are you okay? Maylea said you and Dan are upset. Where are you? I'll come.

Garrett swallowed. She was so damn sweet he'd never deserve her.



He sent that first.





Suddenly, his phone rang.

"I'm gonna take this. I'll be back." Garrett made a quick exit back out into the frigid night air.

"Hey, are you okay?" he managed as the emotions of his evening took chokehold of his vocal cords.

"I'm fine, but you're not fine, and I just wanted to hug you and tell you I love you and that I can't wait to marry you. You make everything so perfect. I'll never deserve you."

"That isn't true," he balked.

"I think it is true, and I'm sorry your dad found out. People probably don't keep things from the Crown Governor too often. But, your parents love you so much, and you don't even know how lucky you are to have a family like this. Tell them about both of us. Maybe telling them will help you see that what you did was this amazing thing instead of you trying to hold it all inside of you. And if you don't want to tell them what happened to you, I don't mind if you tell them about me if that helps."

"You help me do everything, baby. Absolutely everything. Let me go talk to them because I just want to marry you and then I want the rest of the world to fuck off for a little while." Garrett knew he sounded like an overgrown child, but the truth was tucked too close to the surface as he stood on the precipice of a new year and a new life, one finally worth living.

"Go talk and then come marry me, 'cause I miss you and everything works better when you're here."

"I love you so much." He continued to simply speak the truth without agenda or procedure.

"I love you too."

Garrett restowed his phone and drew a deep breath. He turned and marched back into the pub with determination armored in his shield.

"What you know has nothing to do with why I'm marrying her." He stared his father down as he sank back into the booth.

"I would never have assumed that." Governor Haydenshire sighed. "I'm sorry. I didn't mean to upset you. I just wanted to tell you how proud your mom and I are and how excited we are for you and Kaimi."

Garrett decided to accept that with a slight nod as he turned to Will. "Kaimi can't have kids, so if you'd drop the whole 'is she pregnant' thing that'd be great," he huffed as he ate a French fry just to have something to do. His opening statement shocked the entire table.

"What?" Governor Haydenshire gasped. "I thought…" he slipped.

"Yeah, I know."

"Are you okay with that?" Will asked. His voice took on a much kinder tone.

"I love every single thing about her. I'm fine with it."

Dan clearly didn't know what to say, so he kept quiet.

"Has she seen medios and stuff? What about Adeline?" was Will's next inquiry.

"Yeah, Will, she has, okay, and truthfully, that's only half the story. Trust me, no medio is going to get us kids, which again, is totally fine by me. I do not want kids." Garrett tried not to sound as irritated as he felt.

"Okay. I'm sorry. I've been an ass lately. You took off for Kauai and came back a different person. I'm sorry about Kaimi, and I know you love her. No one is doubting that," Will soothed. "I'm really happy for you. I just wish you'd talk to me like you used to. I…miss you."

"Will you tell us the other half of the story, Garrett? If you don't want to, we can eat and head back to the house, but if you'd like to lighten your load a little, everyone seated at this table would very much like to help you carry whatever burdens you might have." The governor was on the verge of begging.

Dan turned to Garrett. His eyes were pleading. "I swear I never said anything," he whispered.

"I know," Garrett assured him with an audible sigh. "I'm not saying any of this again so listen up," he ordered Will and his father. "First of all, know that what I'm about to tell you and what I just told you about Kaimi has nothing to do with our relationship or why I'm marrying her. I love her—end of story. She is the one that I never even believed existed, so whatever the hell happens next, she's it."

"Okay," Will agreed.

"I got into some shit in Brazil several years ago. I got shot and honestly, it's a miracle I'm sitting here talking to you. But I can't have kids either. Kaimi and I will not be procreating, and I just need everyone here to be okay with that. I am happier now than I have ever been. I do not need anything but her. Kids do not make a family. This was precisely why I didn't want to have this conversation. I don't need anyone deciding to play psychologist and conclude that me not being able to give her children and her inability to conceive was the foundation of our relationship because it wasn't. I love her. I fell in love with her before I even knew she couldn't have kids."

Will's mouth hung open, and Governor Haydenshire gave a slight nod.

"Wait, what shit in Brazil? When?" Will managed words a few seconds later. "Oh my God, Garrett!" He leaned in. His eyes goggled to the size of plates with the realization of what had happened. "The month you said you were in Cancun. You went after Pravus."

Dan leapt to Garrett's defense. "He saved Aida's life. They'd shot her parents and burned her house down. She was only four years old. He's taken care of her all these years."

"Why didn't you tell me? I would've helped you," Will demanded.

Garrett shook his head. "You wouldn't have helped me. That isn't you. You would have tried to talk me out of it, and I knew I couldn't be talked out of it. So I went, and what's done is done. But that's it. That's the story. That's the one thing I never told anyone. And somehow, I managed to find the girl that gets me and gets all of that and is fine with it, and honest to God, that's all I want."

Silence permeated the table once again as Garrett's confession settled harshly in the air.

Will finally nodded and swallowed before forcing a grin. "Seriously, Dad, this is the worst bachelor party I've ever been to. We're gonna have to get Les to strip or something."

Hesitant chuckles turned into hearty laughter as the governor slapped Garrett on the back and then shook his head at Will.

"As I recall, it was you who asked your mother if she knew how to get the permanent marker off your ass when your brothers and groomsmen got you so drunk the night before you married the mother of your child, they were all able to write special messages to Brooke via your can," the governor reminded Will, and everyone cracked up as Dan and Garrett recalled the messages they'd inscribed to Brooke.

# CHAPTER 39

# MAMA'S PRAYERS

An hour later, with his heart occasionally having difficulty finding a steady beat, Garrett's boots hit the worn grass pad where Will parked the Volvo.

"Officer Haydenshire, I have to say I never thought I would see this day." Governor Carrington was shaking his head as he sauntered out to the car.

Sam was with him. He gave Garrett his all-knowing grin. "Sometimes Mama's prayers work fast."

Garrett gave him a hug. "Hey…uh…thanks for being here tonight, and for always being there when I need you. I'm gonna miss you."

"There some reason you can't use one of these new, fancy phones, boy?"

Garrett chuckled. "No, and we'll be back to visit a lot."

"You just take care of yourself and of her. I'll be here when you need me."

"Thanks for doing this, Regis." Governor Haydenshire shook Governor Carrington's hand.

"Are you kidding me? If I didn't see this with my own eyes, I wouldn't believe it." Governor Carrington shook Garrett's hand and pulled him in for a hug.

Garrett echoed his father's thanks as he edged closer to the house.

He wanted Kaimi. He needed her beside him, to touch her silky skin and hear her sweet giggle at something stupid that he said. He hungered for the heat that spilled from her pores, the liquid satin between her legs, her lush lips on his as their tongues danced together. His fantasies about everything he planned on doing as soon as he'd promised his undying love and adoration to her had his breath quaking and his throat so dry he was unable to speak.

They entered the bustling kitchen.

"Fi, she doesn't want that." Emily was gently pleading with Fionna.

"I know…" Fionna sighed. "But it would have been so gorgeous."

Mrs. Haydenshire was shaking her head. Serena rushed toward Garrett.

"They were trying to attack her with makeup and lingerie. It's good you're back," she teased.

Garrett raised his eyebrow and shot Fionna a look that said for her to back off a little. "Do I need to go up there?"

"Yes, actually." Adeline looked concerned. "She wants to see you even though we keep trying to talk her out of it."

That was all Garrett needed to hear. He headed to the stairs and took them two at a time.

"She's in my room," Emily called from the kitchen.

His heart was pounding suddenly though Garrett couldn't quite discern why. He drew a deep breath and knocked as gently as he was able.

"Can I come in, baby?"

"Yes!" Kaimi's relief was evident in her tone as the door swung open. She fell into his arms, and Garrett cradled her closely. She was dressed in a short, sleeveless, emerald-green cocktail dress that framed her ass in stunning perfection. The back was sheer hunter-green lace from her shoulder blades to the dip in her back that always had Garrett eager to see the heart-shaped swell that formed at its base.

"You look beautiful, sweetheart." Garrett tried to see her while she attempted to burrow into his chest. After he squeezed her tight and let her hide in him for several long drawn moments, she eased back and let him take her hands so he could really study her. "Damn," he rasped as he shook his head. "What's under that?" he managed as a delighted grin formed on her face.

"Nothing." She giggled. A shuddering growl thundered from his chest as he closed the door.

He slid his hand under the skirt portion of the dress, but she wiggled away.

"I'm already not supposed to let you see me before I walk down the aisle, so I can't let you do that. What if this is really bad luck?"

"If I'm with you, it doesn't matter where or what's going on, that could never be bad luck. Are you sure you're okay with all of this?" Garrett gestured back to the world outside of his little sister's childhood bedroom.

"I'm really, really excited."

"Me too," he assured her.

Kaimi moved back to him. The magnetic pull of their bodies was just too much to deny. "I need to call Carlina and tell her, I think. She probably doesn't care. But I kept starting to and then I wanted you to be with me, and I decided I didn't care if you saw me. I wanted to see you and I was worried about you," she explained in her customary mass of confusing and oddly soothing thoughts. In all that intricate and complex puzzlement, in the mystifying delicate beauty of her, Garrett had found his saving grace.

"I gave an abbreviated version to Dad and Will, and they took it really well actually," Garrett sank down on Emily's bed and pulled Kaimi beside him.

"Good." She reclined her head on his shoulder, and he wrapped his arm around her bare shoulders.

"Let's call your mom, okay?" Garrett pulled her phone from her purse and handed it to Kaimi. "I'll talk to her if you want."

"No, I'll tell her. I just wanted you here with me."

"Right here, baby. Nowhere else I'll ever be."

Garrett braced as he listened to Kaimi greet her mother and explain that she'd moved temporarily to DC to be with him.

"So, anyway, we kind of decided, spur-of-the-moment, to get married, like, now, so I was just gonna let you know that in a few minutes I'll be Kaimi Haydenshire." Her delighted grin turned dour in an instant. "Because I love him, and I want to only be with him," she huffed a moment later. After her dramatic eye roll, a scowl etched her face. Garrett leaned and kissed her temple, willing calm into her. "I don't feel that way," she spat. "Yes, he knows that. No, he's fine with it."

Garrett debated taking the phone. He could feel the pain and fury as it swam in her rhythms. "No, he will not cheat on me because of that or because of anything at all," she vowed, but the fear crept inside and began its constricting coil around her heart. Garrett understood immediately where her self-doubt had been seeded and who'd been tending that crop her whole life.

"It hasn't been so much of a problem lately." Kaimi shuddered, and Garrett reached the end of his rope. He removed the phone from her hands, and his shield set firmly over her.

"Carlina, this is Garrett," he snarled as Kaimi's mother abruptly stopped talking. "I find it rude to the point of abusive for you to suggest that I would do something like that just a few minutes before your daughter and I get married. Since you don't really know me, let's get a few things straight. I'll never cheat on Kaimi. I don't think there is anything at all wrong with her. But that being said, when I vow to love her in sickness and in health, that will be precisely what I mean. This whole making her feel like she's not good enough or whatever the hell it is that you do when she calls you, that will not be happening anymore. Not on my watch. So, I'm going to thank you for the congratulations I'm certain you meant to give, and then I'm going to end this call and go marry your phenomenal daughter." With that, Garrett ended the call. Kaimi was staring up at him in complete bewilderment. He tossed her phone on the bed and tucked her into his embrace.

"Wow," she whispered. She laced her fingers through his and drew from him deeply.

"That's incredible, baby, but if you don't stop, we're gonna get to the honeymoon portion of our evening before the wedding portion. I'm not gonna be able to help myself."

"Thank you for loving me like that and for talking to her and for saying all of that," she managed as her breaths stuttered.

"Hey, Kaimi." Garrett kissed her forehead and let his hand trace over her cleavage that was just barely exposed in the dress. She trembled, and he clenched his jaw in an effort not to rip the dress from her and pull her underneath him long before the ceremony.

"Yeah."

"Let's go get married."

# CHAPTER 40

# THE TANGLE OF MAGIC

Aida rubbed her eyes as she tried to remain awake for the quick ceremony though it was well after ten.

"Are we ready, son?" Governor Haydenshire offered Kaimi a kind, fatherly smile. Garrett nodded as he guided Kaimi down the last few steps on his arm.

"Yeah, let's do this."

"You look beautiful, sweetheart." Mrs. Haydenshire was on the verge of tears that Garrett was certain would become her victor before he got to kiss his bride.

"Thank you." Kaimi was clinging to Garrett with all of her might. He leaned and brushed a tender kiss on her head.

"Okay, I'm gonna go stand in there, and then you walk in there, and then we'll get this show on the road." He was trying to get her to relax and enjoy the moment. Kaimi nodded and glanced down at her feet.

"I'm kind of better in pointe shoes than heels." She cringed.

Garrett assumed she was worried she might fall in the rather high heels she'd borrowed from Fionna. "Dad will not let you fall, and neither will I." He continued to calm her fears and soothe her soul. Kaimi nodded, and Garrett brushed another quick kiss on her cheek before he handed her off to his father.

He joined Will in the kitchen as his uncles arranged his siblings and goddaughters on the sectional sofa. Music began playing softly, and Garrett smiled as Levi walked his mother in and then sat beside Olivia.

"Are you ready?" Will grinned.

Garrett nodded though he noted that he could no longer feel his feet. He assumed the problem would rectify itself as soon as he had her in his arms again. "I really am sorry, Garrett. I was being a prick. I couldn't see how good she is for you. I got mad that you're moving, and I just stayed pissed. That was easier than being depressed," Will offered a whispered apology.

"S'ok," Garrett assured his big brother as he watched Dan walk Adeline through the living room and then shake Governor Carrington's hand. "I've always known you're a prick," he teased. "We'll be back a lot, and you can come out there whenever you want. We'd love that. I'm not ducking out on you, man. I'm just trying to live. Besides, Dad's the Crown Governor. He has a jet."

Will laughed. "Yeah, I'm gonna take you up on that, and I want you to live. You've been drowning for a long time." He shoved Garrett forward and they took their place by Dan. Fionna carried Kaimi's all-white lei in her arms. As she started down the makeshift aisle, a broad, delighted grin formed rapidly on Dan's face.

"Hawaiian girls," he whispered to Garrett.

"Nothin' like 'em," Garrett concluded with a slight whispered chuckle.

"Damn straight." Dan nodded his head back toward the entry hall. The music shifted under Uncle Nate's casting, and Garrett swallowed harshly.

"Wow," echoed from the hollow spaces in his heart that filled with each step she gained on his father's arm.

Governor Haydenshire handed Kaimi's hand back to Garrett and offered him that smile that said he was so proud, something Garrett never felt he deserved. "Sometimes somebody else holds the missing pieces to the puzzle, and I'm so thankful you found the woman that had yours."

Garrett nodded but couldn't take his eyes off Kaimi. She was staring up at him with tears cascading down her face. He gazed into her eyes and the tangle of magic they held in their copper depths. The keys to heaven were right there when he'd been certain for so long that he was damned to hell.

"I believe, Deputy Haydenshire, you're supposed to put that lei on your beautiful bride first," Governor Carrington urged.

Garrett took the lei from Fionna. She was crying as well.

Kaimi bowed her head, and Garrett placed the lei around her neck. She was beaming through her steadily flowing tears as they began their vows.

Just as Garrett slipped Kaimi's engagement ring back over the ring tattoo, he heard Lucy gasp slightly. Everyone turned. She was clutching her very swollen midsection.

"Sorry." She shook her head and waved them off. Panic set firmly in Patrick's features. "Go on," Lucy commanded.

With a nod, Kaimi slid the black tungsten and ceramic wedding band that Garrett had selected from his uncle's vast collection over his finger. They continued their promises to love and adore each other for the rest of their lives.

"I'd say you can kiss your lovely bride," Governor Carrington allowed. Just as Garrett's lips sought Kaimi's, he heard a gasped, "Oh my gosh," echo from Lucy. They broke the kiss, and Garrett's mouth hung open as the maternity dress Lucy was wearing began to look as though she'd sat in a tub of water.

"Well, this is quite a night." Mrs. Haydenshire moved in at once.

"You said this wouldn't happen for two more weeks," Patrick shouted at Adeline.

"Hey!" Logan's shield pulsed violently as he leapt up to defend his wife. He shoved Patrick back.

Adeline shook her head. "I didn't say that, Patrick. I said anytime between yesterday and the next two weeks."

"This is a lot closer to yesterday than two weeks," Patrick panicked.

Garrett rolled his eyes. He kept Kaimi's hand in his own and moved to Patrick.

"Hey, why don't you go find the jar you keep your acorns in, slip those suckers back in your sac, man up, and take your wife to the hospital."

"Wait, what? Talk slower." Patrick grasped Garrett's forearms.

Kaimi covered her mouth to keep from cracking up over Garrett's terse command.

Mrs. Haydenshire shot Garrett an expression that said she agreed but couldn't say that out loud.

"You two go on to the hotel. Your dad booked you the honeymoon suite. This is her first, so it will be a while. We'll talk to you tomorrow." She urged Garrett and Kaimi on.

"Are you sure we shouldn't go to the hospital?" Kaimi quizzed. Garrett grinned as he heard the disappointment in her tone. She didn't want to go wait on Lucy and Patrick's baby to be born. She wanted her wedding night, and he couldn't agree more.

"Nah, trust me, there will be lots and lots of Haydenshire nieces and nephews over the next few years. I don't think Lucy needs us there. She does, however, need her husband to pry his head out of his ass, but he'll figure that out. You, Mrs. Haydenshire, I have plans for this evening." He made certain only Kaimi heard him. She looked delighted with his plans.

Patrick was a disaster as he tried to determine how to get back to their house to get Lucy's bags and get her to Georgetown, while Lucy was doubled over, cringing in horrific pain with Fionna and Emily trying to cast her through it. He continued to mumble something about annuity investments and academy funds.

Adeline was already on the phone calling in a delivery room and directing Patrick who'd begun pacing and shaking his head in the living room as sweat poured down his neck.

The governor was not impressed. "My God, get it together, son. What is wrong with you? You got her this way. Now take care of her!" he shouted.

"And with that, I think we'll just be leaving," Garrett announced. Everyone moved away from Lucy just long enough to congratulate Garrett and Kaimi and wave to them before they returned to the living room.

# CHAPTER 41
# THE SEEKER'S MATE

Garrett helped Kaimi up into the Highlander just as everyone began heading toward their cars to drive to the hospital.

"Just shut up, Patrick. Your voice is so stupid!" shrieked furiously from Lucy as Patrick attempted to help her to the car.

"My voice is not stupid," he whined.

Garrett shook his head as Kaimi doubled over laughing. He climbed in the driver's side door in time to hear his father ordering Patrick not to talk anymore.

"Oh my gosh. Poor thing. That looked horrible. I feel so bad I'm laughing," Kaimi confessed as Garrett drove toward the Four Seasons in the heart of Georgetown. She was still giggling hysterically over Patrick's idiotic behavior.

"She'll be fine. Patrick will either get it together or she'll scalp him. Either way, they will probably both survive. And I love it when you laugh."

"We're married," she squealed.

"Yeah, we are. I'm sorry Lucy stole your thunder there."

"Oh, I was kind of glad. I was tired of getting so much attention."

"Well, I'm sorry about that, Mrs. Haydenshire, but I was planning on paying you a whole lot of attention for the next several hours."

"I want you to pay me attention, just not everyone else. And I have to get used to that being my name. I keep thinking you're talking about your mom."

Garrett shuddered. "Could you get used to that quickly? I really don't want to think about my mother when I'm thinking about our wedding night."

"Sorry." She was still laughing as Garrett pulled up to the valet parking at the Four Seasons hotel.

An attendant was at his window as soon as Garrett had shifted into park.

"Mr. Haydenshire, welcome to the Four Seasons. Your father phoned, and we'll be happy to take care of you and your bride this evening," he drawled nobly.

"Thanks," Garrett bristled. He wasn't comfortable being treated like royalty because of his father's job. Kaimi noticed his slight disdain and laced her fingers through his. She gave him her sweet smile, pushed her soothing energy to him, and Garrett's entire body eased at once.

They were whisked quickly to the royal honeymoon suite on the top floor. Two maids followed them inside.

"Can we unpack for you, Mrs. Haydenshire?" a round woman with a turned-up nose and wind-pricked cheeks offered Kaimi. Garrett noted that she didn't look particularly thrilled with her own suggestion.

"Uh, no, thank you. That's okay." Kaimi shook her head.

"We'll take it from here. Thank you." Garrett wasn't certain whom to tip or how to tip two women discreetly, so he laid two twenties on the massive glass-top table that sat in the entryway of their suite.

"Shall I turn down the bed then?" The other woman, who had her graying black hair pulled up in a tight bun, proceeded to fluff all eight pillows on the large king-sized bed like the pillows had greatly offended her and she was seeking revenge. She flipped the sheets and down comforter into a crisp fold with a quick flick of her wrist and then smoothed her work.

"Shall I light the fire, sir?" she quizzed as soon as the bed met her satisfaction.

"Yeah, that'd be good. Thank you." Garrett decided to let them do that much. If he lit it with his hand and left it burning most of the night, they might wonder how he'd started the fire as there didn't appear to be any matches other than in the attendants' aprons. They weren't Gifted.

"We'll be in twice for housekeeping unless you turn the privacy lock here." The reddish woman pointed to a turn knob that would block entry from outside even with a key. "If you'd like us to draw your wife a bath before we go, I'd be happy to take care of that." She gestured toward the grand bathroom that took up a quarter of the four thousand square foot suite. Kaimi blushed automatically, and Garrett's mouth watered as he watched the luscious heat her body created creep up her neck and flood through her cheeks.

"I'll take care of my wife's bath, but thank you. If you could just leave us alone for the evening, we won't be requiring any further assistance," Garrett ordered using his best deputy commander tone.

"Yes, sir, certainly." The women did offer kind smiles as they closed the double doors, finally leaving them blissfully alone.

Kaimi was still blushing as she moved to Garrett and wrapped her arms around his chest.

"She said your wife and that's me," she trilled. He was unable to halt his laughter as he squeezed her to him. She was the cutest thing he'd ever seen.

"I know. I'm the luckiest guy around." He fought the ardent desire to unzip her dress. Her heart picked up pace in her rhythms and reverberated through his soul. Garrett glanced at his watch with a grin before he stared down into the most beautiful eyes he'd ever seen. The windows to her soul and the windows to his entire world swirled with copper fire lit in their depths.

"So, Mrs. Kaimi Haydenshire." Garrett tilted her chin upward. Her breaths quickened, and he groaned as his ability to fight his own desires bled from his body. He grabbed a handful of her ass and began groping her. "I want my New Year's kiss and then, sweet girl, I want a whole lot more." As fireworks began going off all over the city, Garrett consumed her lips with his own.

He pulled away, gasping for breath as he watched her own brand of fireworks blaze in her eyes. They were dark and hungry and the curiosity that drove him wild was penned in every curve of her luscious body. He let his eyes close for half a second. He couldn't look at her like that, aching for him and starved for his fullness and draw this out as long as he wanted it to last. *Get it together, Haydenshire. It's your wedding night. She's your wife and she deserves more than you losing it all as soon as you get that dress off her,* he ordered himself fiercely.

"How about that bath?" His heart reverberated against his rib cage.

"We don't have to do that. I mean…that doesn't seem like what you want to do right now." She swallowed down what Garrett was finally able to discern was disappointment.

"I want to take care of you tonight. I want to spoil you and take hours celebrating the fact that I found you and somehow got lucky enough to marry you. Let me give you a bath. I've never done that for anyone else. I would love to do that for you. I'm gonna take good care of my sweet girl for the rest of my life." His voice was low and reverent in his desperation for her.

A breathy moan escaped her as she trembled against him.

"Turn around for me," he began his whispered requests. She gave him a slight nod. She spun, and Garrett eased the tiny zipper down the dress. He watched the fabric separate slowly and reveal his wife to his hungry eyes. The dress slipped from her silky skin into a pile of satin on the floor, and a growl Garrett couldn't halt thundered from his lungs.

She was stunning and on full display. He leaned and began kissing from the nape of her neck down her spine. Her back arched with every inch he slowly gained. He grasped her backside and began massaging with fire and need surging through his veins. He pulled her apart slightly, and another low guttural groan echoed from him. She spun suddenly with an eager inquisitiveness that played in her rhythms.

Garrett's eyes traced down her body, and his heart flew as he took in the new tattoos. They were butterflies that started at the luscious spot where her pussy met each of her legs. They were much larger than the ones she'd had done in henna earlier. Kerri Ann had removed the henna altogether. The new butterflies were line drawn without color and extended their wings to the tops of her thighs and up her waist. Garrett traced his fingers over them softly as he read the GAH of his initials interwoven beautifully with the four of hers. They all centered in the butterflies' wings that were formed from the Haydenshire H's.

"It's a new beginning," she whispered as she stared down at her tattoos as well. "I feel like you pulled me out of my cocoon, and now I can fly with you." Her voice caught in her confession, and she blushed again.

"I love you. God, just…so fucking much." He drew her body back into his protective embrace before he lifted her up into his arms. She fit against him gracefully as he carried her into the enormous white marble bathroom.

Garrett summoned and lit the lights in the chandelier over the tub then pulled the light back so that the room glowed romantically. He set her gently on the cool floor and began to fill the deep claw-foot bathtub.

He couldn't take his eyes off of her beautiful body that tempted him with every curving swell and every depth that he longed to fill. Garrett dispensed with his shirt after he jerked the tie from his neck. He summoned and set the water to the perfect temperature and then lifted Kaimi back into his arms.

He eased her into the water and knelt beside her as he watched the water lap at her breasts and conceal a few of the places made all for him.

Garrett debated momentarily. He'd never bathed a woman before. He thought that odd. Of all the things he had done, of all of the women he'd bedded, he'd never really cared enough to nurture any of them, until Kaimi.

Her bottom lip slid through her teeth as she stared up at him. His slacks tugged sharply. He wanted to own her so badly he could taste it. Reminding himself that they had all night and that you only got one wedding night, Garrett grabbed a bottle from the side of the tub. He lathered his hands. He didn't want anything, not even a washcloth, between his fingers and her skin. The tub was in the center of the large room so he was able to move all around her. He began at her neck and used his strength from years of law enforcement to massage away any nervous apprehension or stress that she'd locked away inside of her muscles.

She was nervous. He realized as soon as he'd locked on to her rhythms. Something about this night had her rhythms tensing slightly.

"Close your eyes and relax for me, sweetheart. Just let me touch you. Let me take it all away tonight. I've got you."

A soft moan slipped from her beautiful lips as she settled back in the tub and let her legs fall open for him. Her eyes lowered while Garrett stared ardently at what she'd just revealed.

He rubbed soft circles over her collar bone before allowing his hands to glide over her breasts. They were swollen, and her nipples were pulled into taut pebbled beads that beckoned him like a siren's song. He was unable to look away.

Her breath caught as his fingers circled the throbbing brown tips of her that ached to be touched and sucked and nibbled.

"You're so damn beautiful," Garrett confessed in a choked whisper as he forced his hands to move down her abdomen. She tensed in anticipation as he neared the heart of her.

She grinned and blushed slightly though the water already had her body glowing from its heat. His hands slid easily over her skin from the lather, and he was unable to keep them from her new tattoos and her mound. The energy in that tempting rise of nerve endings pulsed as he traced it with his hands. She moaned, and Garrett had to close his eyes to keep his concentration.

He moved his massage to her inner thighs. She tensed and sought his eyes with her own. Her needy looks had Garrett panting for breath. Working with tender care, he washed her lips and what portion of her backside he could reach without getting drenched. Her breath caught as he cared for the parts of her that no one else would ever touch. The parts of her all for him that he would tend and care for constantly.

He forced himself onward. He moved to the other end of the tub and kneaded her calves and feet. The sheer amount of muscle there astonished him. She was his dancer through and through. She groaned from having him care for the muscles she worked the hardest.

He pushed his hands back up her legs and then slid his fingers up the center of her backside as he held her right leg away from her left. She gasped from the sensation. It startled her and she shivered slightly.

"Does that feel good, baby?" He let his fingertips slowly caress her puckered opening again. She moaned. Her eyes closed as she allowed her body to feel the heady sensation.

Fear pulsed in her rhythms, and her breath caught again. She eased her calves back in the heated water. Garrett stood and grabbed a bath sheet from the marble shelves. He heated it for her and then did the same with one of the plush white robes that was folded near the towels.

"Come here to me." He helped her step out of the water and wrapped the warm towel around her. He dried her tenderly. He stared at her as he slid the towel to her svelte legs. The butterfly tattoos framed her abdomen and pussy to perfection. He let the towel fall to the floor and traced his index fingers from her hip bones down to the perfection of her along the butterfly wings. She shuddered from the sensation, and her body pitched toward him.

Garrett wrapped his fingers around her hips and pulled her close enough to feel what she was causing. She panted as she felt him throb against her stomach. He leaned and devoured her mouth with tender greed.

He drew from her, sucking her heady erotic rhythms into his mouth and letting them flood through his own strains. Hungry, covetous need pulsed there, but her nerves were still quaking as well.

"What's wrong, baby? Why are you nervous?" He kept her cradled to his chest.

"I don't know what you're going to do," she confessed in a whispered pant.

"I would never do anything you didn't want me to do, sweetheart. You know that." Garrett slid his hand tenderly up her back to cosset her head to his shoulder.

"I know," she whispered. Her left hand groped and pulled at his pecs. Then she swallowed harshly and lifted her head. Her eyes were at the same moment pleading and terrified. "I'm scared of what I want you to do."

Garrett's entire body tensed as he gazed down at her, unable to believe how astoundingly perfect she was.

"We have all night, sweetheart." He managed to formulate a reassuring phrase though his mind was full of the imagery of every inch of her body being his to possess. "I'll do anything you want. Just come to bed with me and let's see where you want to go from there. Okay?"

Kaimi seemed to will courage from Garrett's embrace. She turned and padded softly toward the massive bed in the bedroom portion of their suite. Garrett's heart timed itself to the pace of her glide. He stared after her for a moment, allowing himself to take her all in as she moved.

He followed after her, dispensing with his clothes as he moved. She crawled up on all fours to get in the high bed mounted on risers.

Garrett grasped her hips firmly and leaned low to lick from one opening to the other.

She arched her back with a heady moan. She wanted more, and Garrett groaned against her as he continued his torturous moves.

He gave her reprieve after several long minutes of bathing her with his tongue, and she fell onto the soft mattress covered in silk linens and down coverings. Garrett retrieved the lube from their bag and returned to her.

She shivered again as she felt the mattress lower under his weight. *She's scared.* The thought broke Garrett's heart as he set the lube on the table and then wrapped his arms and his body around her.

"Listen to me, sweetheart. Please don't be afraid, especially of me. Please. We don't have to do anything at all. I will hold you right here in this bed and turn on that gigantic television over there, and we can sleep or watch vastly overpriced movies all night long. Or we can do that for a little while and then turn it off and see if I can't get you turned back on."

"Is that what you want to do?" she asked in a choked whisper.

"No." He wasn't going to lie to her. "It's not. I want to run my hands all over your body. I want to lay you out. I want to touch you places no one else has ever touched. I want to share this night of all nights with you, inside and out. But mostly, baby, I want to make you my wife. But what I want more than all of those things, is for you to be comfortable and for you to know that I would never do any of that unless I knew it's what you want as well."

"I want that too. I just don't want to think anymore. I want to be with you. I want to do everything with you." Her voice broke over the fervency of her vow.

Garrett understood. Her thoughts, so often jumbled and confusing, had simply become too much for her to handle alone. The hunger she was afraid to feel and terrified to admit to having, the need to be his and to know that she was everything important in his world, and desperation to be his wife when she wasn't entirely certain yet how to be that had her crippled and bound.

*Whenever you tell me what you can't do, I'm going to kiss you like that and then show you what you can.* The vow he'd made to himself when he first took her to bed seared through his mind. He rolled slightly and eased her body under his.

"Look at me, sweet girl," he urged. "I'm right here. You are everything to me, and I know what you want and what you need. I'm going to give you everything. All I need is for you to relax for me and just feel. Just feel my hands on you, and my tongue on you, feel me inside of you. Feel everything I do that makes you all mine. I'm gonna kiss my wife now, you ready?" he commanded her in a low pleading growl. Her breasts prodded rapidly at his chest as she tried to draw full breaths, but the task appeared too much for her.

"Please," she gave in. Her body gave a convulsive shudder of imminent relent. She knew what was coming and she wanted it desperately, but she had to quiet her mind and let him own her soul.

Once he'd pushed past her fears of not being enough, she tapped into his all-encompassing love and found that to him, she was everything.

Garrett leaned and brushed a kiss across her swollen lips. She parted them as his tongue sought hers. He groaned in her mouth as he pulled back slightly and sucked her tongue before he began grinding against her mound. He eased her legs farther apart with his thigh, and her body rolled in eager anticipation.

"There's my sweet, needy girl. Relax and let me have you." He continued to guide her, to force her body's desires and his will over the restless worries of her mind.

He began groping her breasts, kneading them in his hands, feeling her nipples pebble and beg his palms as he slipped them between his fingers. He moved quickly down her body and lapped his tongue over the swollen tips that beckoned his tongue. He laved them in his mouth, sucking and pulling, nipping and biting gently, unable to help himself. He listened to her fervent moans as her back arched and she urged him onward. He flicked his tongue over her left nipple rapidly in a rough caress, and she cried out for him.

"That's it, sweet girl. It feels good, doesn't it? Feels better when you just let me have you. I know how to make my sweet girl come for me." Echoed voracious moans seemed the only sound she was capable of making as Garrett continued his build.

She bucked under him impatiently, and Garrett watched her body rise in need and beg for his relief. He eased himself back and dragged his index finger from her throbbing mound down her slit. He lightly teased and caressed just below her, the heaven between the valleys that would have her flying in moments.

Her eyes flashed open as she tensed and panted from the gentle caress. Her body contorted deliciously, and her moans began to echo around them as she slowly surrendered to the love between them.

"I know that feels good, doesn't it, baby? I don't even have to be inside of you to know it makes you clench. It makes you ache because you need to let it go for me. It's supposed to feel good, sweet girl. Everywhere I touch you tonight, I'm gonna make feel so damn good, but you have to relax for me. Just feel how that makes you swell and ache. Feel how wet you're getting for me. I can see it. I can see how wet and needy you're getting for me." He urged her onward as he kept his gentle strokes timed to her climbing rhythms. He watched her beautiful pussy glisten in the moonlight.

She trembled as her head shook back and forth on the pillow. She was afraid of the power of the orgasm he was building and afraid to admit to the heavenly sensations he brought her.

Garrett leaned in, closing the distance between them and protecting her from any distraction, allowing her to exist only in the ecstasy of them.

"Tell me how good it feels," he urged.

"It's incredible," she admitted with pent-up desire thrumming out of her on every strain of her rhythms.

"That's right, and it wouldn't feel so good if you weren't supposed to let me touch you here. But it does feel good, doesn't it? Now let it go for me like my sweet girl," he soothed, and she was done for. Her body lifted off the bed. Her back arched deeply as she tensed around his fingers and cried out for him as she lost it all.

She continued to convulse as she reached out for him. Garrett pulled his hand away and cradled her inside of his powerful embrace. His shield spilled from his pores as he held her tight, allowing nothing to exist but the two of them inside of that moment.

"I'm right here. I've got you." He brushed tender kisses in her hair and held her in his muscled embrace.

She trembled in his arms as she began to let him truly own her deepest desires. It wasn't something she ever would have done before he married her. Garrett realized this as he was overcome with the emotion of all she was willing to give up for him and for all she was willing to let him see and have.

The heady floral scent of her mixed with his own musk, and the flames of the heat from the fire flooded his nostrils with the distinct fragrance of sex and the two of them together.

"You're so beautiful," he vowed. He was simply unable not to tell her. "I love you so much. You are so perfect."

Garrett saw her lips turn up in her abashed grin in the firelight. He was overwhelmed by her wild spirit so tender and seeking. The need to protect her and to fill her full fought for dominance in his shield.

Deciding he could do both, Garrett eased away and began another round of soft, lush kisses as he drank in her energy and replaced it with his own. His tongue made deep exploration of her mouth as he memorized every intimate detail of his wife. His right hand slipped back to her breasts, and he groped and prodded before pulling the erotic energy from the storehouse where it was so desperate to be taken.

She trembled and writhed as his shield filled with their erotic energy so desperate to be joined.

"Let me taste you. God, I need all of you." He propped her calves over his shoulders and used the expanse of his chest to reveal all of her to his starving eyes just before he leaned and devoured her. "So damn sweet." He spun his tongue over her clit, coaxing it to bloom all for him. As it swelled, he gave gentle sucks that had her begging for more.

"God, that's good," she grunted.

He kept us his work until she relented and the energy of her orgasm flooded his mouth. He gasped for breath as he lowered his shield and reached for the lube.

"I'm gonna touch you now, sweetheart. Just relax and feel me," he soothed as he began coating her inner lips with the healing salve. A low, throaty moan spilled from her as her body pitched and tensed from his caress.

He slipped his fingers slowly inside of his wife. She began to give way under the gentle prod of his touch. He continued his methodical work with a great deal of finesse as he lubed the index finger on his left hand while keeping his right working her over slowly. Dipping it between her cheeks ever so slightly, he began to brush the tight rosebud opening of her backside delicately as he watched her entire body seize and writhe.

"Oh, god, yes," she gasped. Garrett couldn't halt the grin that formed on his face. He kept up his fervent strokes over her G-spot until her breath washed from her lungs and her temperature spiked.

He leaned and ordered himself to barely move his fingers.

"Relax for me, baby. Just relax." It took her a moment, but she managed to ease her body's tense grip and he dipped his finger inside of her. She groaned in ecstasy from the sensation of being completely full as he began to stroke and then with a few continued caresses of her G-spot from both sides, she lost it all. He eased his strokes until she stopped writhing and had regained the ability to breathe.

He pulled both hands away from her openings and crawled over her. The ability to drag it out any longer was gone in an instant.

He handed her the lube and watched as she slid her hands up and down his shaft. She licked his head and sucked away the salty need that was dripping from him.

"Does it taste good, sweet girl? I'm gonna fill you so full of it, so fucking full it drips out of you for days." A breathy moan lashed at his head as she rubbed the lube there as well. Garrett's entire body was hot-wired and starving to be inside of hers.

He eased her back on the soft sheets and covered her body with his own. In that moment as he prodded and then dipped low to penetrate his wife, he felt her open and take him in inch by delicious inch. He wanted nothing more than to stand between her and the world.

It was different. Her eyes flew open as the love and adoration between them spilled out around them in their rhythms. Her body shook from the recognition that marriage had indeed changed things all for the better.

"I feel it too, baby," he assured her, trying to wash the shock and fear from her body. "Now feel me," he urged as he began to grind and rock his body in time to hers. He dipped his cock inside of the hot, wet perfection of her, watching her body swell and pulse for more.

He pulled away and then pushed back farther with each pass until he was claiming every inch of her all for himself. No one else would ever exist in that space again. She was his, and with a low, guttural growl of delight, he began pounding into her as she begged him for more force. Her body cinched tight around him, and Garrett's jaw locked as he denied the explosion that throbbed in his groin.

"All mine. You're all fucking mine," he groaned in the ecstasy of that knowledge.

"Yes," gasped from her.

Her body heated and tensed around him tighter still. She begged for breath that eluded her as she began to writhe and claw at his back. He reared up on his hands and fucked her hard and fast.

"Yes, yes!"

"I feel it, baby. It's coming, isn't it? You just can't stop it, can you? I make it feel too good. It's okay, sweet girl. Let it go and then I'm gonna fill you full of me." He guided her, desperate for release.

That was it. She exploded in his arms. Her moans reverberated off the air, so thick with their rhythms it swam and coiled in syncopated desire all around them. Her body began to tremble beyond her control, and Garrett gave one final, ragged thrust and buried himself deep inside of the woman that was his other half, the missing piece to his impossible puzzle, his soul's mate.

When he regained the ability to breathe and move, he eased out of her as gently as he was able. He turned on his side, knowing that she wanted to hide away in him after all of that. He cradled her closely as she tucked herself to his chest. With an adoring grin, he kissed the top of her head as she buried her face in him.

"Wow," he whispered her quoted phrase from a few of the times they'd been together. Her giggle soothed his soul of his worry that he might've pushed her farther than she was quite ready to go.

"That was amazing." She nuzzled her head against him.

"Yeah, it definitely was." He strengthened his hold.

"Shield, please," she begged timidly. He could feel the heat from her cheeks against his chest. Certain she was the cutest thing in the entire world, Garrett grinned as his powerful shield formed around her instantly.

His own rhythms weren't quite as fierce after his explosive release, but they quieted her mind and soothed her soul and were always filled with his adoring love of her.

"I love you," he vowed.

"I love you too, and that was really, really amazing." She shivered in her own delight, and Garrett couldn't quite halt his chuckle.

"It was amazing. You're amazing, and Kaimi, I've never been happier in my entire life than I am right now, lying with my wife in this bed."

"Me either," she whispered.

Kaimi tried to stifle a yawn as her blinks grew heavy. It was nearing two in the morning, so Garrett was exhausted as well.

"Go to sleep, sweetheart," he soothed. "I've got you."

"Being your wife is really awesome," she informed him through another deep yawn.

"Oh yeah?" Garrett chuckled. "Well, I just have to keep you thinking like that."

She tucked closer into his embrace as he pulled the covers over them. He watched over her as she drifted off to sleep.

# CHAPTER 42

# THE CROWN GOVERNOR'S SON

A low, guttural moan shuddered from Garrett's lungs at ten the next morning. Kaimi was lying on her side with her back tucked to his chest, the position they'd made love in three hours before. She'd reached her hand back and was caressing him, though she hadn't yet opened her eyes. An adorable, mischievous grin played on her features. Garrett leaned up slightly to kiss her cheek.

"You already need that again, baby?" he harassed. He was fairly certain she was just playing, but if she was up for it three times in one night, he was all about it.

"No." She giggled.

Garrett wrapped his hands around her sides right at her rib cage and tickled her. She shrieked and tried to wiggle away. "What are you laughing about, Mrs. Haydenshire?"

"I just like that I can make it hard," she confessed before she hid under her pillow trying to stop giggling.

Her confession had Garrett doubled over laughing.

"My God, I love you," he vowed. He pulled the pillow away from her face.

"I love the way your cheeks get all pink and your hair looks kinda wild in the mornings. The way you look after I've fucked you hard. Don't cover that up. I want to see it," he explained in complete honesty as he recalled the fact that she'd shared a part of herself so tender and intimate it could never be explained.

She stared at him speculatively as she sat up and ran her fingers through her dark hair. The red streaks were starting to fade slightly, and Garrett kind of missed them.

She examined the red as well. "Maybe Zizi can re-streak it when we're in Lihue next weekend."

"I really like the red."

She grinned. "I know."

"Can I get my beautiful bride some coffee?" Garrett reached for the room service menu.

"Is that expensive?"

"Honey, we got married last night, and the only thing I paid for were those tremendously sexy tats you had done all for me. We didn't even have to pay for the license, since my dad is the one who signed and casted it, so I'm pretty sure I can get you coffee and breakfast."

"I'm starving."

Garrett lamented the fact that she'd only had a grilled cheese sandwich for dinner and then nothing else with their whirlwind wedding just a few hours later. He'd gone out with his dad and Dan and Will but had forgotten she hadn't eaten. They washed up, and he phoned in a large breakfast order.

He'd just hung up the phone when a knock sounded on their suite door. Perhaps, occasionally, it was a good thing to be the Crown Governor's son. Garrett waited until Kaimi had pulled on one of his T-shirts and crawled back under the covers before he opened the door. He tipped the man who delivered their elaborate breakfast.

"I've got it." He halted his progress inside the suite.

"Yes sir, certainly. Your complimentary copy of the paper is there under the fruit tray," the attendant offered. "Please let me know if I can get anything else for you and Mrs. Haydenshire."

"Thanks." Garrett couldn't hide his own broad grin over how good her new name sounded.

He arranged the tray on the bed and placed the large carafe of coffee on the table beside her before he poured her a cup.

"Mm," she purred as he handed her a mug of her favorite beverage.

"I like it better when you do that when I'm in your mouth." He laughed as she swatted his chest with the back of her hand.

"Shh, I'm drinking coffee," she sassed.

"And that means I can't talk?" He feigned confusion.

"Yes. Obviously."

Shaking his head at her, Garrett lifted a pastry off one of the plates and unfolded the newspaper.

"The Crown Governor Heralds Another Haydenshire Boy," was the headline.

"I'm thinking Patrick heralded this one, not Dad," he huffed with an eye roll as he glanced down the paper.

Kaimi laid her head on his shoulder as she began eating grapes off the plate of fruit. She studied the paper as well.

Garrett's mouth fell open as he read the line. *Patrick Haydenshire, the fifth in the long line of Haydenshire men, and his wife, Lucy, proudly announced the birth of their son, Garrett Alexander, at three forty-seven this morning.*

"Oh, Garrett!" Kaimi swooned as she pointed to the name.

"Wow." Garrett was stunned.

*Patrick did greet the press early this morning. When asked about giving his son his older brother Garrett's name, he said this, "My brother, Garrett, was always there for us growing up and even now. I can't tell you how much stuff he got me out of or helped me out with. How much he's taught me. He's one of the greatest men I've ever known, and we wanted Alex to have that legacy."*

"I feel bad I wasn't there." Garrett wondered if he'd upset Patrick by his absence.

"We can go now," Kaimi immediately volunteered. Garrett nodded, but something else caught his eye.

*Noticeably absent in the customary crowd of aunts and uncles at Georgetown last evening was our new little Prince Alex's namesake, his uncle Garrett. Realm Times supposes Alex will give his uncle a pass as we've learned that late last evening, Garrett wed his girlfriend, Miss Kaimi Walyuo of Koloa, Hawaii. We assume Garrett and his new bride have been dating longer than when they debuted as a couple in the press and that must be what prompted Garrett to accept the deputy commander of Hawaii Iodex position*

"Oh no." Panic seared through Garrett's chest. His gut clenched tight as he turned the page.

Kaimi's hands flew to her face as Garrett took in a black and white shot of her from many years before sitting with a group of friends among several dime bags. There was a blunt in her hand.

"I swear I only did it once when I was at Juilliard. I just tried it and I hated it. It made me so sick. How did they get that picture? Oh my god! Your parents are gonna see that." Tears sprang to her eyes and spilled down her face.

"Baby, please don't worry about it. Believe me, my brothers and I have pulled some stupid shit in our time. They won't care." Garrett wrapped his arm around her. He was sick. Kaimi had told him weeks ago on the phone during a conversation about the wildest things they'd done that she'd smoked pot once and hated it. He hadn't thought much about it since then. It was a common practice to try it. Pot was far more dangerous to Gifted people than it was to the Non-Gifted because it affected rhythm strands, but it was over and done with and she was fine. Garrett was certain the papers had been looking for sources about Kaimi ever since he'd taken her home from Georgetown and announced to the Realm that she was his fiancée. Someone had been paid very well for the shot they'd sold the papers.

"What else does it say?" She tried to wipe away her tears and look back at the paper.

Garrett forced himself to read the report.



270

"Ugh, no!" Kaimi shook her head. "I didn't drop out until I'd been accepted at Juilliard. I had to. That's how you do that."

"Don't you see? This is what they do. They paint the worst possible picture they can. Remember the shit I told you about with Emily's honeymoon."

*But as it turns out after experimenting with recreational drugs, Kaimi dropped out of Juilliard as well in her senior year.*

"Of course, they don't say why you dropped out." Garrett shook his head.

*Two years ago, Kaimi moved to Koloa, Kauai and began dancing again full time. This reporter can only assume from the newly crowned Mrs. Haydenshire's very questionable past, perhaps Garrett has gotten himself in over his head. Was the wedding rushed because the Crown Governor and First Lady might be expecting yet another grandchild? Perhaps this time the baby carriage came before the marriage.*

"I'm so, so sorry." Garrett knew Kaimi was crushed over the article, and it was entirely his fault.

"Your parents must hate me."

"They adore you. They do not care what the paper says or what anyone but I say, and you are it for me. None of that was even true. They can paint a great picture that shows absolutely nothing at all about who you are or what you mean to me."

Kaimi nodded, but she seemed woefully unable to stop her chin from trembling and the tears from pouring out of her eyes. Garrett tossed the paper aside and wrapped his arms around her. She was so sweet and her life had been hard enough. He was furious that the press was being so cruel though he certainly wasn't surprised.

Garrett's phone chirped on the dresser. "That's gonna be Fionna texting to make sure you're all right," he explained softly. Kaimi continued to rub her hands over her face.

Garrett's phone began chirping in rapid succession.

"And that's everyone in my family. They're afraid to call because we may not have seen the paper or we might be making the most of the morning after our wedding, but they're all worried about you and they all love you." He eased himself from the bed and retrieved his phone. He handed it to her after scrolling through the dozens of texts.

Kaimi shuddered as she read over the texts from Fionna, Emily, Logan, Will, Brooke, both of Garrett's parents, Levi, Olivia, Rainer, Adeline, Connor, Reid, and Dan. Her brow furrowed as she opened Dan's text. Garrett had only glanced at them, so he leaned in to read it as well.

"Hey, tell Kaimi the papers are full of shit. Let's hope Kalakona doesn't freak over it, and we'll be fine."

"Oh my gosh! You're the deputy commander of Iodex. I've ruined your career because of some idiotic thing I did seven years ago."

Garrett fought the desire to whimper himself as he cradled her back in his arms. "You did nothing that the average twenty-year-old academy kid doesn't do. It was seven years ago, just like you said. Kalakona will be fine. Dan is my boss. I may get called in to assure her that you're not using, and I may even get the canned reputation shit speech. Big deal. Please, please stop crying. I swear to you this is nothing."

"Garrett, it is not nothing!" she fumed. He was shocked by her vehemence. "What if that gets back to Kauai? What if people don't want me teaching their kids to dance because I was a moron once in my life? What if what I did all those years ago affects Maylea and the studio?"

"Kaimi." Garrett grasped her shoulders and forced her out of her own terror. "First of all, most of the people whose kids you teach to dance did that too. Maylea and Dan included. Please, honey, just for me, take a deep breath and we'll deal with this."

Garrett's phone chirped yet again. He read Patrick's text.

> Hey, man, tell Kaimi we're sorry about the papers and that we've all been there. Alex would really like to meet you when you get your head out of her crotch.

Garrett couldn't help but chuckle. He was happy Patrick seemed to have stopped his freak-out and was able to joke around and be a good dad and a good husband.

"We need to go see him." Kaimi continued to blink away tears.

"We do, but the press is going to be all over the hospital. Are you up to that?"

"Maybe I could get a T-shirt that says, 'I swear I only used once and it was horrible,'" she fussed pitifully. Garrett was certain she was thinking that being his wife at that moment wasn't all that awesome. "Let's just go. It's my fault you weren't there last night." She jerked his T-shirt off and stomped to their suitcase. Garrett let his eyes close in defeat as he stood and began to get dressed. He wasn't certain what else to do.

**CHAPTER 43**

# A THOUSAND WORDS

"Just don't say anything to them. It only makes it worse. They twist everything," Garrett explained as he wrapped his arm over Kaimi, and they raced toward the entrance doors of Georgetown Hospital. A thousand flash bulbs went off in their face.

"Garrett, Garrett, when's the next addition due?"

"Can we get a picture of the rings?"

"Kaimi, what do you have to say about your recreational drug use?"

"Have you and Garrett ever used drugs together?"

Abject defeat colored Kaimi's face as she tucked her head and ran faster.

Three reporters and two cameramen leapt in front of the door. Kaimi shrank back into Garrett with fear surging through her rhythms.

"Move!" Garrett snarled.

"Can we get a statement?" the reporter pressed.

"Yeah." Garrett nodded as fury lit through his shield. "Here's the statement—stay the fuck away from my wife, stay the fuck out of our business, and get the fuck out of our way." He shoved a cameraman out of Kaimi's path and jerked the entrance door open.

His diatribe had done nothing to soothe his wife, but it was high time he said something.

"I'm so sorry," Kaimi began as soon as they stepped on the elevator.

"You didn't do anything wrong." His heart fissured and his shield whirred, as she nodded and then shrank away from him. She edged away from him physically just a few inches, but the emotional strain and gap he'd just created felt miles long.

She walked with two feet of space between them as they exited on the obstetrics floor.

Mrs. Haydenshire had Kaimi in her embrace as soon as she laid eyes on her. "You didn't ask for all of this, did you."

Kaimi began crying again on his mother's shoulder. "I'm so sorry. I had no idea what I was doing. I swear, I only did that once, and it was so long ago. I'm so sorry," she managed in convulsive sobs.

The governor moved to her instantly. "Sweetheart, I cannot tell you the number of times one of our own made that same speech to us including your husband more times than I can count." He shot Garrett a look that said he wasn't pleased, but Garrett had no idea why.

Levi, who was sitting in the waiting room with Rainer and Logan, gestured to the television. There was a live feed running of Garrett cussing out the cameramen who had jumped in front of Kaimi on the way in. Garrett rolled his eyes and regretted ever opening the paper that morning.

"I will say that I do wish you hadn't done that, only because I don't want any of my kids using, but the fact that the papers got ahold of that photo was entirely my fault, not yours. So please don't cry. It'll blow over, and I'm not concerned about it in any way." He patted her back. Garrett's mother was still holding Kaimi to her chest and consoling her.

"Son, let's take a walk. Now." The governor marched toward Garrett and pointed down the long corridor that led to the snack machines.

With another distinct eye roll, Garrett knew he didn't really have a choice. "I'll be right back."

She gave him a slight nod, and the harrowed terror in her eyes crushed him.

276

"Pretty sure I'm going to yell, so why don't we take the quick jaunt to my office," Governor Haydenshire ordered.

"Dad, what the hell is it? I came to see the baby, and then I need to figure out how to get my wife of less than twenty-four hours to stop crying and actually believe this is not a big deal."

"Since that's what I want to discuss with you, I think I'm going to insist. Walk." The governor half guided and half shoved Garrett back on the opening elevator.

He followed his father back to the Metro, and then to the Pentagon, and up to his plush office on the top floor.

"Have a seat," the governor ordered tersely.

With an audible huff, Garrett threw a chair back and glared at his dad.

"I do understand that you've done quite a bit of changing recently, so don't start shouting until I've said my piece," the governor commanded.

Garrett threw his arms out to his dad. "Go for it," he sniped.

"Let's start with what I know, and we'll work from there." His father narrowed his eyes, and Garrett bit his tongue to keep from making another retort.

"I know that you and Kaimi a couple of weeks before you flew out there to be with her when her grandmother passed, so let's start there. You told us last night that you'd fallen for your newly crowned wife before she called you in tears because the only person in her entire world who had ever cared about her was going on and leaving her here to deal with life alone. Correct?" The governor began what Garrett discerned was going to be a lengthy lecture.

"Yeah," he agreed mostly to move this along.

"I'm thrilled you found who I really do believe is the only woman you would ever have married and settled down for, but let's go back there for a moment." Governor Haydenshire left no room for rebuttal. "You quit your job and rushed to her side, all very admirable things, son. Again, no issue, but if I may just broach a warning, I'd appreciate it if you'd think about this for a moment. From what little I know about my newest daughter-in-law from my interactions with her, and from the press, and from brief conversations with Daniel and Fionna,

I'd have to say that she's..." He considered his words carefully, and Garrett narrowed his eyes. "Let's go with not particularly secure in herself."

As Garrett couldn't argue that, he swallowed down the irritation that had bubbled in his gut.

"Again, no issue, but I don't think I'd be walking too far out on a limb to suggest that you are going to have to be her security, son. And that works out well because you are her Shield. But you can't only be her Shield in the storm. You're also going to have to be her anchor because she didn't have to ability or the foundation to do that growing up.

"As gallant and courageous as I'm certain you quitting your job and racing to her side might've seemed at the time—and I'm not saying that it wasn't either of those things—I wonder if maybe when the dust settled and she began to ride that roller-coaster ride downward after her grandmother's death, if that didn't give her a slight sense of insecurity.

"But you forged onward, so let's do the same. I also know beyond a shadow of a doubt that you hadn't been on the island of Kauai for more than a few hours before you had her in bed with you." His father's tone was knowing but didn't seem to hold a great deal of judgment, so Garrett continued to listen. "Again, you're two consenting adults, and you certainly didn't ask my opinion on that, but I can tell you this, as much fun and love as you shared that night and however much that cemented your relationship, it might've left Kaimi feeling even more insecure.

"Her grandmother had just passed, and although I'm certain you offered her a very nice change of pace from all of that, she was left wondering what might happen when you left and where this was going. I doubt any amount of your verbal reassurances quite soothed over the inevitable question in her mind as to whether or not she could really hold on to you," Governor Haydenshire pointed out.

"So, fast forward a little. You uprooted her and dragged her to Brazil. You brought her up here, and honestly, I don't think she's had any time at all to deal with the devastating loss she's gone through."

Garrett hated that his father was right, but he was, so Garrett gave a begrudged nod.

"I also happened to have overheard a conversation between your mother and Fionna about the fact that Kaimi surprised you when you returned home from London with the news that she'd lost her job and stumbled upon Chloe Sawyer in your apartment. Now,"—Governor Haydenshire held up his hands, halting Garrett's leap to rebuke him—"I know you were trying to end things with Chloe. Again, you didn't do anything wrong, but try, just for a moment, to think about what you have asked this woman to do in the past few weeks, what she's given up to be with you. And I'm sorry, son, for as much as you love her, for as much as we all love her, she really is just blowing in the wind, Garrett.

"She needs you to think before you act, because I'm not sure she's capable of that right now. In the past few weeks alone, she's gotten her chest pierced, received several tattoos, and has shared a bed with you in what I feel certain has expanded her horizons. She's looking for something, son. She's trying on a lot of different brands to find one that might fit who she is right now, an entirely different woman than who she was when her life revolved around being a caretaker just a few weeks ago.

"She's looking for some kind of stabilizing force, and you have her heart in your hands and your ring on her finger and everything that she's shared with you, every intimate thing she's given up for you, you have that knowledge and that trust, and you have got to make damn sure that she knows you will be the rock she can cling to. That you will not allow her to drift endlessly at sea. That you will get up off your ass and be the man she needs you to be." The governor was shouting, but Garrett was unable to argue. His father was absolutely right.

"We all woke up this morning to a photograph of her that certainly wasn't the image she wanted to give your mother and me or any of your family. That rocked her already very unpredictable world. Think about it. Someone she knew, and probably assumed was her friend, sold that picture to the *Times*. She got sold out by someone she'd counted on in the past, someone she'd shared something with. This came the morning after your marriage, after just a few weeks of dating. You quit your job. You had her under you, naked and willing, hours after the only person in this entire world who'd ever really cared about her had gone on without her.

"You jerked her out of her home, dragged her out here, dragged her to Brazil, left her to go to London, came back, and she thought she'd lost you to a former flame. You got engaged, purchased a dog that is going to require the both of you to take on a tremendous responsibility, and then dragged her down the aisle. You took her off to a honeymoon suite last night, and I know you better than you'd ever like to admit, and I know you shared things last night that left her feeling both loved and extremely exposed.

"Then you wake up and see what the papers brought out this morning, and did you ever think that maybe, just maybe, instead of cussing out the press and convincing her that you were mad at her too, you should try to convince her that you're not going to let her down? Did it ever occur to you that what she needed was reassurance that you will hold every single thing she has so freely given you close to your heart, and never let anyone else take anything away from her ever again? Did you do that, or did you just get angry over her reaction and leave her wondering, yet again, if she'd finally done the thing that would have you abandoning her as well?" Governor Haydenshire roared.

"No," Garrett choked as he swallowed harshly and shook his head.

His father gave a slight nod. "Her mother abandoned her, and she has no idea who her father is. You don't get over something like that. You don't leave that in the past because that's a trauma she'll be forced to carry her entire life. It shaped who she was and who she is. So, you've got to show her that her trauma can have a place in your marriage where it can exist and it can be healed.

"So, welcome to married life. It's not always sex and joking around and laughing and playing, although there is definitely that as well, but right now your wife is walking a very dangerous bridge, one that isn't going to leave her anywhere good. So, your days of being the wild, irresponsible life of the party are gone, son. I know you don't mind that, but there's another piece of this life you've flown into without a great deal of thought. She can't settle herself right now. Her life has been too unpredictable and chaotic for far too long, so you have to be the way she comes back to earth. Try, son, *try* to make her landing easy and in your arms rather than on the cold concrete all alone."

Garrett tried to swallow down the expanding knot of regret that burned in his throat as he nodded.

"She has to be able to deal with her grandmother's death. And you need to understand that it's not just the death that must be mourned, but Kaimi's role as her caretaker is also gone. The person she's been for seven long years disappeared in that hospital as well. First and foremost, she has to deal with those devastating losses so she can figure out who she wants to be now. And whether that means you holding her fully clothed in your bed and letting her cry without you trying to use sex to take her mind off of it, or you two talking about who her grandmother was and what she meant to Kaimi, or some other way, but you've got to teach her that when she's sad or hurt or angry or scared, that you will be there and you will deal with whatever life brings your way together. You've got to prove to her that you love her no matter who she is at any given moment, even if she's not sure who that might be."

"She needs to go back to Kauai," Garrett pled as he let the harsh reality of his father's words settle on him.

"Then it's your job to get her there or anywhere else she needs to be," Governor Haydenshire challenged.

"I just signed a contract to teach at Venton." Garrett decided to just do whatever his father suggested. He wasn't screwing up on Kaimi's account ever again.

The governor's voice returned to its customary, soothing thrum. "Maybe try to bring a little of her island to her here and then plan a trip there soon to really get to know her and what that island means to her and what she wants out of this life with you. Let her heal, Garrett, before you try to make her whole."

"Yeah, okay." Garrett hated that he felt like a child and hated that he hadn't been able to see what his wife was going through. He hated that their romance was tied so heavily in time to the loss of her grandmother.

His father was right. He hadn't given her any time to heal, and Kaimi had gladly taken his offered reprieve. He'd shielded her from every negative emotion, and neither of them had understood she was slowly coming apart from the inside out. Every time she'd started to cry, Garrett had stupidly sought only to wipe away the tears instead of helping her deal with the pain that had caused them.

"Build the foundation. Build the ship and make certain it's seaworthy before you ever put it in the water. You need to spend the next few months doing little else but being with her and dating her and really learning this woman that you've fallen for and married. Go to work when you have to, but the rest of your day needs to be with her, and for the most part, her and her alone. Not with Dan, or the girls, or even your mother and me, while you're still living here. As much as I want to see you and as much as I'll miss you when you move, your marriage is the most important thing in your world now. Treat it as such."

"I will. I swear."

"Good. Guard it with your life. Nurture it constantly. Whatever makes her feel safe and loved, do. Listen closely when she talks and even harder when she's silent. Bring her out to the farm. She feels safe there. I could tell. So, don't come out there alone, and when you're there, take a long while to be with just her whether out on the dock or up in your bedroom. Let her see the way you grew up and tell her just a few of the asinine things you did. Make damn sure she knows you adore every single thing about her, even whoever she was at that moment of defiant rebellion when she decided to disconnect from her grandmother's ways, all the way back on their island, and to pretend that she was something she never was to gain approval she really didn't even want.

"She needs to know that you love her now and that you love who she was then because that moment when someone rolled a blunt and handed it to her, and she decided to let everything go, that moment will be cemented in the Realm's mind for a long time. But that moment is also when she felt more disconnected than she ever has before. And your anger at the press only left her feeling more ashamed. You rebuked the people judging her instead of lifting her up and telling her that you love her no matter what someone has a photo of her doing."

Garrett tried desperately to listen to his father's wisdom and soak in deeply into his soul and his mind.

"Don't take her anywhere she doesn't feel safe and secure. For heaven's sake, don't take her back over to Arthur and Marion's." The governor rolled his eyes. A slight chuckle finally escaped Garrett.

"If she wants to go off and do something with Fionna or any of her sisters-in-law, make certain she knows you'll be right there waiting on her to come back home, and that you want to know each and every thing she experienced without you. Don't ever judge her, just listen to her. She needs to feel safe and free inside of your love and your relationship. Take care of her, Garrett, and teach her that you will always take care of her. Whether by choice or by death, every tie she ever had has come undone."

"I will always take care of her," Garrett vowed to his father.

The governor nodded and gave Garrett his kindest smile. "I know that, but I'm not the one that you have to convince." His father laid out his decree softly and with a great deal of concern.

"I will, Dad. I swear." Garrett stood, desperate to put action to his words.

"Go meet your namesake, and then go by the farm and rescue Duke from your little brothers. Then go build a home for her, son. She's never had that before. Not really, but if anyone can do that for her, you can. I have no doubt." Garrett was certain that wasn't true, but he appreciated his father bolstering his badly bruised ego.

Garrett raced past cameramen and reporters and sprinted back onto the elevator. He casted it and had it flying to the obstetrics floor.

Kaimi was seated between Garrett's mother and Emily who was sweetly casting her. Garrett reached for her hand. Her brow furrowed, and a remnant of hope glistened in her tear-stained eyes as he guided her up and then wrapped his arms around her tightly. His mother swooned as he began to sway her in his arms.

"I love you and I was never, ever mad at you. You could never disappoint me, baby, okay? I swear. I was an ass, but just please know that I was never upset with you, and that I will get all of this figured out so I can be the husband you need me to be," he whispered in her ear, not caring who might overhear him. There was one heart in the room that needed his reassurance, and that was all that would ever matter.

# CHAPTER 44
# MOMENTS AND MEMORIES

Garrett and Kaimi both held little Alex. Lucy continually asked whom they thought Alex looked like. They both assured her that he looked like Patrick, but truthfully, Garrett thought he looked more like some kind of overly ripe tomato. He was very red and cried more times than not.

Guilt continued to pump through Garrett's veins as he replayed his father's harrowing lecture and then attempted to show his appreciation that Patrick had named his son after him. Truthfully, Garrett felt so undeserving he wasn't certain he'd managed more than an offhanded, "Thanks."

Apparently, Patrick had asked Will, after Lucy had been casted and was no longer in pain, if Garrett would mind them giving Alex his name. He'd wondered if Garrett might like to name his own son after himself. Will had assured Patrick that Garrett would be honored and that he would never have wanted a junior.

"So, are you ever going to talk to me or be like we used to be again?" Kaimi's terrified plea cut Garrett's weary soul. He hadn't said much since they'd left the hospital, picked up Duke, and headed back to the apartment. He'd been too busy mentally lambasting himself, but his silence had only served to frighten her more.

"Baby, I swear I'm not mad at you or upset with you. I feel terrible they went after you because of whose kid I am. I feel like I've really screwed up on your account for a long time, and I'm trying to figure out how to stop screwing up."

"That isn't true. You didn't screw anything up. I screwed up again. I always screw up. Just ask anybody."

"Stop it," Garrett commanded. "That isn't true. You are an amazing, wonderful woman who gave up everything to take care of the people you love—me included. You came out here to live because I begged you to. You have forever put your life on hold for other people because that's the kind of woman you are. I'm so damn stubborn and was so hell-bent on helping Dan clean up Venton, that I took you away from your home right after your grandmother died." His father wasn't there, so he could lecture himself. "Don't you see? I don't want you to have to give up anything for me. You shouldn't have to give up anything else ever. If I hadn't signed that damn contract at Venton, I'd pack everything today and take you home tomorrow. That's where you need to be. See, I screwed up again. I haven't been taking care of you at all. I've been the same selfish prick I've always been." His tone gained intensity with his fervor.

"That isn't true." Kaimi's voice shook. Duke leapt up in her lap and tried to lick away her tears. "No one has ever taken care of me the way you do. I love you so much, and I'm so sorry for whatever I did that made you so angry. I didn't mean to. I just want it to go back to the way it was last night. I wish we'd never gotten out of bed this morning. I just want to go back." She managed the last words before her tears overwhelmed her, and she collapsed under the weight of all that life had been.

Garrett eased beside her on the couch so he could wrap her up inside his arms.

"I was never angry with you, sweetheart." He cradled her head between his shoulder and his stubbled chin. He ran his hands up and down her back as she sobbed. She certainly had a lot of tears he'd never given her time to cry. "We don't have to go back anywhere. Nothing between us has changed except the fact that I need to learn to be a better husband. I don't care what you did in the past that you're ashamed of. I will never ever be ashamed of anything about you. I love each and every part of you, and my God, baby, believe me, I wish if someone were going to take a picture of the worst mistakes I made in my life that it would only be that I'd smoked pot once.

"But there are so many moments that you accepted and decided to forgive me for when that was the last thing I deserved. I think we have a lot to figure out about marriage and who we're going to be now that it's *us* instead of you and me individually. But I want to figure it out. I want you to know how much I love you and that I don't give a damn what you did at Juilliard or any other time. I'm not upset with you at all. I'm upset with me."

Kaimi clung fiercely to him. Her fingers dug into his soul as if she thought if she eased her grip that he would take the opportunity to slip away.

"But I don't want you to be mad at you. It hurts me when you're mad. Because you're so good. You do all of this amazing stuff. You take care of everyone. You shouldn't ever be upset with yourself. I'm the one that's always screwing up. You just married me before you figured that out."

"Stop saying that. I know that you are the most important person in the world to me and that you are the person I want to spend the rest of my life with, and that is all I will ever need to know."

That did it. Whatever he'd said, she buried her face in his chest and sobbed in heaving, gushing waves of unending tears. He handed her tissue after tissue and let her cry.

He forced himself not to try and stop her or to tell a stupid joke or kiss her pain away. He couldn't slap a bandage on the gaping wounds anymore. She had to be healed, and he couldn't just be her Shield. He had to be her healer. He held her, promised that he would always love her and would always be there for her, while her tears soaked through his shirt and burned like hot iron against his skin.

Duke was panicked and heartbroken. He paced the length of the couch, whimpering and barking insistently at Garrett. He was desperate for Garrett to do something to make his mommy stop crying. Eventually Kaimi did sit up and scrub her eyes and face with her hands.

Garrett was too worried and ashamed to feel hope. He handed her another tissue and kept his hands on her. She'd been drawing from him steadily for the last several minutes, and he would never have broken the connection.

"I'm sorry." She shuddered as she pulled her hand away to stop her draw.

"Why are you sorry?" Garrett willed her to believe how much he loved her.

"I don't know. I just thought I should be." She held up her hand to indicate her draws on his energy.

"Baby, I wish you understood what you mean to me. Everything I have, every ounce of this energy I have, it's all for you. I'm your Shield. Drain me dry. Take it all. It's all for you," he vowed which only elicited more tears.

She gave a hesitant nod as she blew her adorable nose and pulled herself up into a ball in the corner of the couch. Garrett set Duke back beside her, hoping he might be able to do a better job of easing her tears.

Kaimi cradled Duke close and let him lick away the remnants of her tears. Garrett had never been more lost in all his life. He wanted to be everything for her, but he wasn't certain he knew how.

"I don't want to be sad," she fussed. "Yesterday was the best day of my whole life. This is stupid. You're this amazing man, and I get to be married to you. I shouldn't ever be sad." Her criticism of her own emotions overwhelmed him.

He shook his head. "I know we keep saying this, but seriously, it has been crazy fast. A lot of shit has happened since the day I landed in Kauai, and we haven't dealt with any of it. And believe me, as honored as I am that you think of me like that, it's just not how life works. If anyone never has the right to be upset because of the amazing person they get to be married to, it's me."

A timid smile played on her lips. Garrett was so thrilled to see it appear he pulled her close again and kissed the side of her head.

"Why don't I make us something to eat and then we can talk about everything that's happened lately? Maybe we could talk about that shit with your mom on the phone last night. I get the impression there's a lot of history there besides her just not being involved in your life. Or…we could talk about Nana," he suggested cautiously.

Kaimi gave a slight nod and tucked Duke farther into her embrace. He seemed to be the security she needed at the moment.

Garrett raced into the tiny kitchen. He pulled off his soaked T-shirt on the way and tossed it down the hallway toward the bedroom. As he entered the kitchen, he began considering. He'd never really eaten there much before Kaimi had moved in. He usually stocked cereal for breakfast and then ate out or at his parents' the rest of the time. He heard Duke's paws click as he moved through the breakfast area and into the kitchen. Kaimi padded softly behind him.

"I can help," she offered though it sounded more like a pitiful plea.

"Okay." He didn't ever want her to think he didn't want her with him whatever he was doing. "We don't have much."

She opened the fridge and considered. "We could have that yummy leftover pasta from two nights ago and some Fruit Loops." She wrinkled her nose. The bashful hope in her eye had Garrett's heart swelling at a moment's notice.

He drew her back to him and cradled her to his chest once again.

"Are you sure that's all right with you? I can order us something." He was perfectly content to hold her to his chest and sway her in their kitchen while he awaited her answer.

"Nana used to yell at me all the time about how I was going to get sick again when I would teach classes all day long and never ate lunch and then came home and ate cereal for dinner. That's when I started making sandwiches all the time. It made her happy, and bread is pretty cheap. She liked the ones I made for her. I never told her that the medications she was taking cost so much money I couldn't afford much more than off-brand cereal."

Garrett's heart ached as he nodded his acceptance of her life before him. "Yeah, see, that woman, the one who gave up everything including food to take care of someone she loved, that's the girl I fell in love with. That's the woman I married, and that's the story that should be in every fucking paper in this Realm."

"That doesn't mean I didn't screw up a bunch of things."

Garrett scoffed as he opened the cabinet and got out two bowls.

After grabbing the Fruit Loops, he set them on the table and returned for the container of pasta and silverware for their bizarrely perfect meal.

"Oh yeah, well then I know you're perfect for me, because I've screwed so much shit up it's not even funny."

They sat down at Garrett's secondhand kitchen table. It had belonged to Will and Brooke when they'd first married. Brooke had wanted something bigger when they'd bought the house out in Great Falls.

"So, you think it's okay to be screwed up together?" she begged hopefully.

"Yeah, baby. I think everybody's screwed up somehow. And with you is the only way I ever want to be. We just have to figure out how to deal with life here and then on Kauai, how we're gonna make everything work."

"I don't really understand how I'm supposed to feel about Nana. I miss her so much. I miss taking care of her. It's like I don't know how to do life without constantly thinking about how to take care of her. I'm so confused. If I don't think about her and only think about you, then it doesn't hurt so much." Her voice shook again as she tried to explain the pain of losing the only person who had ever really loved her.

Garrett forced himself to tell her his story. She'd heard a few, but they hadn't yet shared so many moments in time that had made them who they were. The ones that had woven them together through tears and bloodshed and had led them to their kitchen table the day after their wedding, sharing pasta and Fruit Loops and finally really digging in and peeling back layers until they revealed the wounds that had bound them together.

"I've never told anyone this. I didn't even tell Dan and Fionna about this part of the story. But...you have to understand that Cal basically told me that he was on a suicide mission. He'd fallen for this woman. She told him she was a spy too. I didn't believe what she was telling him. I was certain she was working for Nic, and that *she* was going to be the reason he got killed. So, I was just fucking furious. I did everything I could think of to get him out of Russia. But he made certain I couldn't. Every day I was more and more angry, more and more volatile. It was so easy for me to be mad at her, even though I'd never even met her. Then we got the call that I'd known was coming. And we found out that she was killed right beside him. So, I couldn't be angry with her anymore. Nic wouldn't have killed her if she'd been providing him information. So, that left only myself to be furious with.

"The afternoon the call came in, Rainer had gone out to check on his Uncle Stan. He'd just moved down to Norfolk trying to get away from some guys he owed money to." Garrett choked over this harrowing confession, but he drew a breath and forged onward. "Anyway, Emily freaked out. She just started screaming, and no one could calm her down. Not me. Not Dad. She could feel all of that terror and sickness and devastation that we all felt in that moment. She had to feel my rage, but she didn't understand it. She just kept staring at me and I could see how confused I was making her. God, I'll never forgive myself for what that did to her. She couldn't even process her own terror through my fury. She was a disaster, and her Shield wasn't there. It was pouring down rain, and she ran out into this horrible storm and got in her car and left. She'd barely been driving three weeks.

"Two hours later, we got another call. Emily was being life-flighted to Georgetown under constant casting. She couldn't breathe on her own. I remember standing in the hospital and watching through that window while they worked on her, and Rainer sitting there and it was like he couldn't even see anyone there. And I was so angry that I couldn't contain it anymore, so I got mad at Cal that he'd signed up for Elite when I'd told him not to, and he was so damn determined to prove himself to me and to whomever." Garrett tried to swallow down the rock-like enclosure in his throat. "I was so angry he wasn't there and that it was my fault he wasn't there and my fault Emily was dying before my eyes. And I felt so guilty that I was so angry, but I couldn't help it."

Slow tears were leaking down Kaimi's eyes as she nodded her understanding and then slid her hands in his.

"Anyway." Garrett blinked back tears of his own with a shrug. "I guess the point of telling you all of that is I don't think there's any one way you're supposed to feel about someone you love dying. For a little while, you walk on the edge of insanity because you don't have any idea how to go on, and nothing at all makes sense. Everything's wrong and not the way it's supposed to be, and you know it won't ever be the same way again. And that scares the shit out of you because you don't know any other way for it to be. There's this hole in your life, and you can't go into it and you can't stay outside of it."

"I did feel like that but then you were there." She managed to speak through her tears. "But earlier, when I put her to bed that night, remember, I told you she had a fever?"

Garrett nodded. He remembered every detail of that night.

"It was like I could feel it coming, but I kept telling myself I didn't feel that and that she would be okay. And then I took her to the hospital and medios and nurses kept talking to me like I should have known she wasn't going to get better. I was so scared and so mad, and I just didn't understand why they couldn't make her better. I needed them to make her better. And that's when I called you and then you couldn't make her better, but you did make me better. I would never have gotten through that without you. You ran in the hospital and you told me to kiss you, and I remembered that night that you were fixing my car." She was smiling slightly through her cascading tears, and Garrett was certain he'd never seen anything more devastating or more beautiful. "And you asked me to go get a drink with you and I wanted to so, so bad, but I had to go take care of Nana. I remembered feeling guilty because when you asked me to go out with you, I wished, just for a second, that I didn't have to take care of her anymore. But I didn't really want that. It was just for that second, you know. But I still feel really bad about it." Her confession seemed to weight her head. It dropped with every word she uttered. Her eyes flitted upward in hope but then cast down as she deemed herself unworthy.

Garrett touched her chin and guided it up until their eyes met. "Sweetheart, I know you never meant you didn't want to have to take care of her. And she knows you never meant that, just like Cal knew I wasn't mad at him and that I didn't hate him. She loved you so much," he vowed without having any evidence of his statement other than the woman he'd made his wife.

"I wish you could have met her or even just talked to her." Kaimi shrugged and picked at the cold pasta. "It just feels like the two most important people in my life should've at least talked to each other."

"I wish I could have asked her for your hand." The words fell from Garrett's mouth without thought or warning, but they seemed to soothe Kaimi's soul.

She smiled his smile—the first one he'd seen all day. His heart sped as he winked at her in an effort to keep it on her face.

"Yeah, me too. Only she wouldn't have liked our wedding probably."

Garrett finally allowed himself to believe that maybe, just maybe, he could be everything she needed someday, if she'd just give him time to learn.

"Why?"

She shrugged and began eating with more fervor. "She would've wanted it to be on Kauai, the traditional ceremony, white dress, don't see the groom for a day or two before the wedding, stuff like that." She wrinkled her nose at the thought. Garrett chuckled.

"I would've hated that part, but we can still do a Hawaiian wedding on Kauai if you want. Maybe none of my sisters-in-law will go into labor, but I could never guarantee you that."

She laughed and the sound eased the terror Garrett had felt for the last several hours.

"No, I liked our wedding. I like that it was just us, and I thought last night was perfect. I mean until we got up this morning."

Garrett drew a deep breath and decided to go on with his statement. "I don't want you to regret anything about our wedding or our wedding night. I was serious when I said that I don't care what you did at Juilliard. You are an amazing person, and I hate that you did that only because you won't forgive yourself for doing it. I love you and I'm always, always so proud of you."

Kaimi looked astonished. She studied him in shock.

"No one's ever been proud of me before. I mean, maybe Nana

sometimes, but not usually," she admitted with a slight head shake. His pride seemed to make her uncomfortable.

Garrett had been raised in a home where his parents told him they were proud of him constantly. They were always quick to correct him as well, but Mrs. Haydenshire would kiss each of her kids on the way out the door in the mornings as the long line of them left for school and tell each of them how much they were loved, how proud they were of them, and then to beg them to behave.

Guilt washed through him in heavy waves. He'd pushed his parents away for so long. He'd been so certain they would never understand why he'd done what he'd done, but his father had known for some time it appeared, and all he really wanted was for Garrett to know that he still loved him and was still proud of him.

"I am truly proud to be your husband, and I don't care what anyone else thinks of you, because I know how amazing you are."

"Thank you," Kaimi managed.

CHAPTER 45

# THE DANCE

"I'm sorry, baby, I wish we could just hang out and keep talking, but I really should go over all of this stuff Dan gave me for Venton." Garrett grabbed the binders on the defense classes he would be teaching. "I couldn't wait to get out when I was there, and now, I have to go back." He reminded himself that it was his job to build her a firm foundation, one where he proved that he'd take responsibility for their lives. He had to show her that he was more than willing to work.

"I figured you were a really good student." Her tone rang of hopeless defeat. She did smile and lift Duke up on the couch beside her.

"I did well in my defense classes and in my energy sciences and humanities classes. I got A's in my math classes, 'cause I cheated off Will," he informed her and was pleased that he got a giggle. "Fionna got me through my emotional energies classes, but I sucked at my writing classes." Garrett had never understood how being able to write creatively would aid him in being an Iodex officer, and that was all he'd ever wanted to be.

"I did terribly in all of my classes. All I wanted to do was dance. I used to skip classes to go take dance classes because I needed to be better to get into Juilliard. Nana thought I was skipping to go off and be with guys just like my mom. It wasn't a good time."

Garrett laced his fingers through Kaimi's. He lifted her hand to his mouth and brushed a tender kiss between her knuckles.

"That was a long time ago, and right now, I just want to get through this stuff so I can take my wife to bed."

He had no expectations after their day that she would want to have sex. He just wanted to hold her on his chest and try to right the wrongs he'd made. Keeping his father's words of wisdom planted firmly in his mind, Garrett set to work. He couldn't be the freewheeling playboy anymore. Determination set in his jaw as he opened the binders and resolved to do the job he'd agreed to do and then to get her back to Kauai and build a home for them.

Kaimi switched on the television and immediately turned the volume down.

"You don't have to do that, baby. I can go in the bedroom."

"No, it's okay. I'm fine." She sounded panicked at the thought of being left alone in the living room. She wasn't even comfortable in their apartment yet, and he'd just married her.

With defeat tugging at his shield, Garrett began reading over the coursework for the new semester and tried to determine ways to engage the students enough to get them to chat around him or Dan.

Students who were fascinated with the material being shown would generally ask questions. If a mentor answered appropriately, they could begin to gain a little rapport with the kids. Almost an hour in, Garrett was rolling his eyes at the banality of what he was reading. This wasn't going to get anyone talking. The curriculum was set by the school governors, and Dan had improved it dramatically, but it was still pretty dull.

Kaimi stood and stretched. A hungry grin formed on Garrett's face as her leg extended up until her calf was beside her face.

"Yum stay just like that, sweetheart." He waggled his eyebrows. She giggled and switched legs.

"I need to stretch and dance. I'm getting a little crazy." Her adorable, wrinkled nose and slight bite of her lip had Garrett's mouth watering.

"You can dance for me anytime."

He was shocked at her next move. Her rapidly changing moods kept him never quite knowing what might be coming next, and that was extremely appealing.

She laughed and moved to stand right in front of him. She turned with a delighted light in her eyes as she shook her ass right in his face.

He gave her a loud, hungry growl.

"Shake it right here, sweet girl." He lifted the binder from his lap. She was still giggling which made the act all the more enticing. She slid to the side smoothly and then leaned to gyrate over his crotch.

"Fuck Venton, let's break in the couch." He groaned as he shoved the binders away all together.

Kaimi doubled over laughing but shook her head.

"No, I'm stretching and you're working. I shouldn't interrupt you. I'm supposed to be good and let you work."

"I'd much prefer you be bad for me," Garrett informed her. The broad, delicious grin he received had his breath catching rapidly in his lungs.

"Work," she ordered.

Kaimi continued to stretch. She spread her feet wide apart on the floor and then leaned and reached her body back far enough that her hands were behind her and resting on the floor.

*You've got to prove to her that you love her no matter who she is at any given moment, even if she's not sure who that might be.*

Another round of deep regret filled Garrett's shield. He closed the binder, stood, and made his way to his wife. When she stood from her stretch, she gave him a timid grin.

He took her hand. "Dance with me," he choked out in a heartfelt plea.

"What?"

"If anyone should've had a dance at their wedding, it should've been you. It should've been us. So, will you please dance with me?" He forced a slight grin. "I'm no good. It's okay if you don't want to."

A harsh swallow tensed her neck. "I want to."

With a nod, he summoned on the speaker system in his living room. He grabbed his phone and turned on *Dance With You* by Live.

The lyrics to that song had always spoken to some part of Garrett, and as he stared down into her eyes, he finally really understood them.

"I love this song," she whispered.

"Me too."

He cradled her in his arms and swayed with her back and forth in their living room.

As the final verse began to play, he paused and guided her lips to his own. "I swear I'll figure this out."

"We'll figure it out together."

And with those words, there in the streams of moonlight that glowed on the floor and lit the bands of energy their bodies created, a peace he hadn't been able to access for so damn long finally settled him.

That voice that constantly reinforced that he wasn't worth the trouble was silenced. With the sway of her hips in his hands, he understood that the horrifying past no longer held him in a chokehold. She'd set him free. She'd danced with his demons and she'd found him worthy.

# CHAPTER 46

# HUNGER

Wednesday night they went out to the farm for dinner and then returned home. Constantly trying to keep is father's advice in the forefront of his mind, Garrett settled on the couch and pulled Kaimi beside him. He forced himself to return to the binders, but nothing held his attention. He just wanted her. "Can I kiss you?" he asked. His tone was rough and desperate.

She grinned. "You don't even have to ask."

Garrett caught her hand and pulled her body toward his. She fell gracefully onto his chest and between his legs.

Her eyes flashed in fevered need, and Garrett was done for. He reached and popped the snap on her jeans in a second flat. His right hand sought her mound.

"Have I mentioned how fucking sexy it is that my sweet girl doesn't wear panties?" He groaned as he reached farther. "You drive me wild." His declarations had her writhing and moaning for him.

"Get up on your knees," he commanded as he kicked the binders off the couch. Duke stalked to the kitchen. He apparently didn't want to watch the show. Kaimi looked thrilled to be taking direction. She sprung up on her knees, staring at him with that ardent, excited curiosity that he was completely addicted to. She was a delicious drug he'd never give up.

"Right here, sweetheart." Garrett took her hand and spun her to the side. He pinned her waist to the back cushions with his body and put her ass on full display. He jerked her jeans down and away from her.

"I want you naked, baby. I want to see my sweet girl needy and wet for me." Her gasping moan had him throbbing as she hoisted her shirt off and flung it away. He grasped both of her breasts and began massaging.

"Yes," hissed from her as her head fell back on his shoulder, and she allowed herself to do nothing but feel his need. He guided his right hand down her stomach and cupped her mound. He strummed just over her clit with his thumb, and her deep, needy moan spoke directly to his cock.

He kissed the nape of her neck. She trembled against him as his cock bounced and left a trail of ownership that ran down her ass. "Do you feel what you do to me? Do you like me marking you, honey?"

Suddenly, she twisted at her waist, and pushed him back. Garrett's head fell back as she turned completely and managed to lick him clean. She sucked out everything his body made in preparation for her.

"You like that, sweet girl? You like what you do to me? It's all for you, and baby, I'm gonna fill you full of it. I'm gonna explode in that tight, wet hole that's all mine. Be a sweet girl for me and shake that ass like you were earlier. Shake it for me and then watch what I do when my sweet girl wants to go wild."

"Oh, god yes!" She was on fire. Her body writhed as she arched her back and let her cheeks brush back and forth over his strain. With another feral growl, Garrett stroked from her clit over her swollen lips, spreading the liquid heat her body slowly made for him.

She tensed in an effort to pull his fingers inside of her.

"You want me to touch you, don't you, sweet girl? That little pussy is clenching for me, isn't it?" He continued to torture her. She whimpered in frustrated need.

"All right, baby, I'm gonna make it better." With that, he slid two fingers between her lips rapidly. She groaned her adamant approval. "That's what my sweet girl wanted. I know. You need it, don't you?

You need to be taken. Need me to fuck you hard. You need to be full of me."

Her body consumed his fingers, pulled them deeper, so desperate for release. "I'm not gonna take you until you're soaking wet for me, sweetheart. Relax and let it drip for me. I want you so wet you drown my cock in that sweet cum," he commanded and she lost it instantly. "Such a sweet girl. Now more," he ordered, unable to stop himself. She was so sweet and innocent and so willing to let him have all of her. It drove him wild.

"God, you are perfect." His patience evaporated in the heat between them. He grasped her hips and jerked her back over his strain. He filled the tight space completely. He still didn't know how she managed him in all of that delicious, virgin tightness that just never seemed to stretch no matter how many times he pounded into her.

"I'm so deep, baby. Feel how far inside of you I own. It's all mine." He gasped in her ear as she inhaled him. He reached around her waist. "I'm gonna touch your clit, sweet girl." He had no intention of asking permission this time. "It's throbbing for me, isn't it? Oh yeah, so nice and swollen. Such a sweet girl." Her entire body began to shake as he circled the heavenly spot where her energy pulsed and begged for his attention.

He tenderly touched her with his finger and pounded into her from behind. He worked fervently for the blended orgasm that built explosively inside of her. "There it is. You're gonna lose control for me because you're my sweet, sweet girl." She screamed out for him, and Garrett sank his teeth into that heavenly spot where her slender shoulder met her neck, and she melted in ecstasy as her body spasmed around him. He exploded right after she'd given it up.

He begrudgingly withdrew and then cradled her in his lap.

"Are you okay?" he managed. The slightly concerned look on her face was not what he'd been expecting. She nodded and forced a smile.

"What's wrong?" he asked.

"Just a little sore," she confessed.

"What? Why?" Garrett instantly panicked. "I'm so sorry."

"No, I mean, that was amazing. I just think I need the lube," she explained hesitantly. Garrett nodded. He lifted her folded form off of him and eased her naked body to the couch, then raced into their bedroom to find one of the many jars of the lube that would heal her. He sprinted back to the living room and began trying to undo the damage he'd caused.

He began rubbing her down in copious amounts of the salve that Fionna's grandmother made from coconut oils and a few other things he couldn't yet identify.

"I'm sorry. I had no idea. I didn't mean to be too rough."

"That was amazing. I wish I knew how to explain it to you. Even if I'm a little sore later, it feels so good when I'm with you like that, when I feel like us together when we're...one, I guess. It's just amazing. I don't know how to make you understand."

He finished rubbing her down and wiped his hands on his jeans that he grabbed from the floor. He lifted her chin tenderly with his hand. "I do understand, baby, believe me." She grinned and tucked her head back under his chin. "Come here to me," he soothed as he lifted her back into his lap. He grabbed the blanket his mother had left on their couch and swathed her inside of it.

"Any better?" He prayed that she'd say yes. She gave a slight nod.

"You need to work." She gasped suddenly as she attempted to climb out of his lap.

"Nope." Garrett held her tighter. He wasn't letting her go. "I've done enough. I can wing it tomorrow. Right now, I'm taking my wife to bed where I'm gonna cast her until she's feeling better."

"You don't have to do that. I don't want you to get in trouble or anything."

"Honey, I'll be fine. I'm working for Dan. He's bigger than I am, but I throw a harder punch," he teased. She laughed and shook her head at him. "I'm serious, taking care of you is all that matters to me." Kaimi was biting her lip nervously while she tugged on the ends of her hair.

"Are you hurting worse? Do you want to take a bath?" Garrett was consumed with guilt. He eased her legs apart and began casting her mound and lips.

She shook her head and squeezed her eyes closed tightly for a split second.

"It's not that. I think I need to go to the drugstore." She was on the verge of panic. Garrett dropped his cast. "Is there one nearby?"

"Yeah, but what's wrong?" He pulled his shirt back over his head.

"I may not be right, but I think I am right. I don't have them very often. Just every once in a while. I never think to buy anything because I hardly ever need them." She tugged her own jeans back on.

"I need you to talk to me. What is going on?" Garrett tried to get her to focus.

"Sorry." She wrinkled her nose. "I kind of feel like my period is going to start. Maybe, but I'm not sure. I only have them like two or three times a year. That's part of everything that's wrong with me. Sometimes, I get really weak and sick when I have them. I'm sorry."

"Why are you sorry?" Garrett pulled his underwear back on and ran to the bedroom to locate clean jeans.

"It only lasts a couple of days, but I usually sleep a lot. I haven't had one in almost a year." She continued to fret.

Thoughts ricocheted through Garrett's mind. Since they were never having children, the fact that his wife didn't have periods often seemed like a good thing. Not really a point in being miserable and in pain and bitchy.

"Baby, I can go get whatever you need. You stay here and rest. Just give me very, very detailed instructions. Text them to me. A picture would be good."

Kaimi laughed at him outright. "I'll be okay. I couldn't make you do that."

As Garrett had most certainly never purchased feminine care products, he was a little nervous going without her. He didn't want to buy the wrong thing.

She grabbed the coat she'd purchased with Fionna a few days before and headed to the door, eager to leave.

He made sure Duke had water and then followed her out. There was a drugstore just a few blocks from the apartment.

"Are you okay to walk? Parking down there is a bitch, and it will take longer than it would take to walk."

"I think so. Let's walk fast just in case."

"Did I do something that caused this?" He tried to fathom how that would've happened but thought he should at least ask.

She grinned and laid her head against his bicep as they walked in the chilly night air. "No, I was wondering a couple of days ago if I was going to have one. I never know when they're coming. That was totally amazing couch sex, but even you are not amazing enough to make a girl start."

Garrett shook his head. "That would be the worst superpower ever in the history of superpowers, but I thought it was pretty damn hot myself." He leaned and kissed the side of her head. Garrett guided her inside the drugstore, keeping her wrapped tightly in his embrace.

# CHAPTER 47

# MENSTRUATION INTERROGATION

He followed her to the feminine care aisle. He was pleased marriage seemed to have removed the awkward discomfort over menstruation he'd had most of his life. It seemed to be replaced with concern that she was going to be in pain and about her warning that it made her sick.

"Do you have any money, babe? I'm sorry I'm flat broke." They heard a guilt-ridden plea a few feet away. Garrett discreetly took in two Gifted college-aged kids standing near the condoms. Both of their rhythms were pulling toward each other.

"Josh," the girl huffed. "I didn't like that cast. It felt weird. I don't think I learned to do it right. I can't just go in the nurses' station and make them cast me again. I have to get somebody to teach me. Pem said she would, but she hasn't yet. I want to be with you again. Those three times weren't enough. What do you mean you don't have any money?"

Kaimi shot a concerned glance at Garrett.

"I'm sorry. I told you I had to pay those guys. They were gonna tell my parents about the tests. I had to give them two hundred and fifty dollars. I don't get paid until next Friday," Josh begged her to understand. Garrett's mind began moving frantically. "You can only get pregnant, like, a couple of days a month, right? I really need you." Josh continued to apply pressure, and Garrett fought not to deck him.

"I don't know. I think so. I don't really remember how to tell when though."

"Garrett!" Kaimi panicked for them.

"Here." Garrett pulled his wallet from his back pocket as he moved toward Josh. He slapped a twenty on the guy's chest. "How about I give you that, and you tell me where you said all of your money went."

"Uh, thanks," Josh stammered as his eyes flitted from his girlfriend to Garrett. "I really appreciate this."

"Good." Garrett narrowed his eyes as he slipped into interrogation mode.

"Some kids at school were making up some shit to tell my folks. I didn't want to get into trouble, so I just gave them the money." Josh both confessed and lied easily.

"What were they going to tell your parents?"

"There's…uh…some rumors going around school. About getting copies of tests or something." He stared at the ground. "I don't know."

"That sucks, man. You know, I'm gonna be up at Venton tomorrow. Maybe you could point them out to me."

"Oh, no, sir." Josh shook his head. "I don't know who they are. I had to leave the money in this car in the senior parking lot. It was a black Silverado. Custom wheels and everything, but I'd never seen it before."

Garrett was shocked. He'd expected Josh to back down and claim that he didn't know whom he'd paid. He hadn't expected so much detail.

"Take that and get a box or two of those. And thanks for your help." Garrett pointed to the vast array of condoms on the shelves.

"No problem." Josh swallowed uncomfortably.

"Josh, why did Garrett Haydenshire just give you money, and why is he going to be at school? Do you know him?" Josh's girlfriend hissed as Garrett walked away.

Garrett grabbed Kaimi's hand as she silently picked up a box of slim tampons and some extra long pads.

"I'm gonna go get his tags, baby. Are you okay in here for a second?" Garrett whispered as Josh and his girl made their way to the cash registers. Kaimi nodded. She glanced around. An excited smile played on her lips.

Garrett didn't have time to think about how adorable she was as he discreetly slipped back outside and hid in the shadows. Josh looped his arm over his girlfriend's shoulders, and they walked west toward Canterfield Court. They either hadn't driven or they'd parked far away. Garrett returned inside with his mind still processing everything Josh had said.

"Garrett, I don't have any money," Kaimi fussed. This shook him from his reverie.

"Use the debit card Will gave you that belongs to our bank account. I'd give you cash, but now I only have a ten on me."

She begrudgingly swiped the card as the woman behind the counter bagged her feminine care products.

"Uh, would this be a time when I should stock up on chocolate or that caramel ice cream Fi used to make me bring her or anything?" he asked though his mind was still full of everything he'd learned on their impromptu drugstore run.

"Aww, that's so sweet. You took care of her." Kaimi took the bag from the attendant and thanked her sweetly.

"She's one of my best friends, and she has them pretty rough. But Danny's taking care of Fionna, so why don't you let me take care of my beautiful bride?" He held up a Snickers, a pack of Reese's, and 3 Musketeers. "A, B, C, or D all of the above."

She leaned up on her tiptoes to kiss his jawline and then tugged his hand in an effort to leave the store. "You're not buying me anything else, and mine makes me nauseous so chocolate would be particularly bad."

It wasn't lost on Garrett that they walked with a great deal more speed back to the apartment. She ran into the bathroom as soon as they entered. When she returned, she'd traded her jeans for a pair of yoga pants and pulled on one of Garrett's Iodex sweatshirts.

"Is it okay if I borrow this?" she asked hesitantly.

"Of course, baby. You don't have to ask." He was increasingly more uncomfortable with how insecure she seemed. "Hey, Mrs.

Haydenshire, come here to me." He settled on the couch beside her. He lifted her feet into his lap and began massaging.

"Oh wow, you're the best husband ever."

Garrett chuckled and went on with his question. "Is there anything else I can do to make this easier on you? I'll do anything."

"I can set the cast as soon as I start. I almost always do this in the middle of the night. It's horrible but it should be over with soon. How are you going to figure out that stuff with Josh and his horny cheeky mama?"

Garrett laughed and shook his head at her. "I can tell you exactly what's going on with Josh. Right about now, he's blowing his wad before his horny cheeky mama even gets her shirt off." Kaimi laughed as she nodded her agreement. "Did you hear them? I'm surprised he didn't take her over the condom display." He shook his head.

They settled down, and Kaimi turned to lay her head in his lap. Garrett began easing his fingers through her silky hair. Her eyes closed in contentment.

"That feels almost as good as when those are inside of me," she informed him in a relaxed whisper.

Garrett chuckled. "I guess I'll take that as a compliment?"

"You definitely should." She sighed. "Okay, tell me what we learned tonight?"

She was so intrigued it lit Garrett's soul. He continued to drag his fingers through her hair as he began explaining. "We know for sure Josh is buying tests. I guarantee you he's purchased more than one or whoever is selling them wouldn't have seen him as a potential bribe. Josh was fairly forthcoming with information about these pricks who are running this kiddie gang, which tells me he's ready to come clean just to relieve himself of his guilt and probably so he'll have cash with which to bang Miss Horny Cheeky Mama. You can only push a target so far. Eventually they'll cave and ask for legal help. These morons haven't figured that out yet."

# CHAPTER 48

# IN SICKNESS AND IN HEALTH

The alarm on Garrett's phone went off, and he jerked it off the bedside table. He managed to pull himself into a seated position through a deep yawn. Kaimi had indeed started in the middle of the night. At midnight, Garrett had sprinted into the bathroom to find her hunched over the toilet. According to his bride, she only got sick with them when she was off her islands. She'd hoped it wouldn't be that way anymore, but apparently, she'd been sick every time she'd had one while she'd lived in New York.

She'd managed to keep some pain killers down, and Garrett had casted her for several hours. She'd gotten back up every hour or so to head back to the bathroom because of the sheer amount of blood flowing from her. She'd finally fallen asleep heavily after Garrett had insisted she take a bath. Tutu had recommended them and had sent some salts and oils for her to use when she menstruated. When Kaimi had recalled this, Garrett had located the pack Fionna's grandmother had mailed, and he'd insisted that she at least try the remedy. It had worked to some degree. She'd been sleeping for the past two hours without waking.

He eased silently from the bed and prayed she'd remain asleep. His fervent desire to get her back home to her island drove everything he did. *I sure as hell wouldn't leave her to go to work if I didn't have to,* he thought vengefully.

There wasn't a shower in the bathroom in the hall, so Garrett tried to quietly turn on the water and wash away the remnants of salt and oils from Kaimi's bath so that he could shower off. He thought of every possible scenario of how he could solve the cases at Venton with Dan and then get his wife to their home. *She needs to be there, and she's only here because of me.* The guilt mocked his shield.

He shut down the shower and grabbed a towel from the cabinet. He reminded himself to do laundry when he got home from work as he dragged it through his hair and lathered his face with shaving cream.

He eased from the bathroom and tried to dress silently until he noted that the bed was empty. With his polo shirt hanging unbuttoned off him, he buttoned and zipped his slacks as he searched for Kaimi in the apartment.

"Baby, what are you doing? Go back to bed," he commanded when he found her in the kitchen perking coffee and pouring a bowl of cereal. "I'll bring this to you. Are you sure you can stomach coffee and Fruit Loops?"

She was pale and drawn. Dark circles plagued her exhausted eyes.

"I was making this for you." She managed a weak explanation.

"Sweetheart." Garrett shook his head in disbelief. "Thank you, but I can make my own cereal. Please go get back in the bed. I wish I could stay home and take care of you. The faster I help Dan get this shit cleaned up, the faster we can get you home. You need to sleep, not to make me breakfast."

"I know, but I don't have to go to work, and you do, so I thought I should." She yawned.

"Baby, you don't have to make me breakfast ever. You're sick, and you don't need to do that even if you aren't sick."

"I just thought you'd like it." Her disappointment was evident even through her exhaustion.

Garrett drew a deep breath and moved to her. He wrapped his arms around her tightly.

"We're gonna have to figure out who gets to take care of whom I guess, but how about if one of us is sick, the other gets to call the shots. Deal?"

"I'm not really sick, sick."

"Okay, rule change then. If one of us is up puking in the middle of the night, the other one is in charge of breakfast."

"At some point you're going to get sick of taking care of me, because I'm sick all the time. Then you'll see how much trouble I am." She pouted dejectedly as she leaned down to pet Duke. He'd been worried about her all night.

"Kaimi, stop it." He wasn't going to let her mother's insistence that she wasn't worth the trouble haunt her soul anymore. He didn't care how many times he had to combat the thoughts that were coiled so deeply in her heart.

"Thank you for this and for you. I hate that I have to go to work this morning, but I want to get this finished so that we can get you home and start our life there."

Kaimi managed a smile as she laid her weary head on Garrett's chest.

"I'm gonna be lonely."

"I'm sorry, sweetheart. I'd take you to Dan and Fi's, but I don't really think you're up for dancing and playing with babies. Just chill out here with Duke. Watch movies or do whatever. I'll bring lunch home and then I have to go back for two more classes, but at least I can check on you," Garrett explained his plans for the day.

"You don't have to do that," she continued to argue.

"Woman,"—Garrett lifted her chin in his hand—"you're making me nuts. I don't have to do anything. I want to take care of you. You are *my* baby. Now pipe down and go lie on the couch. Duke is going to call me if you try to do anything but chill today."

Kaimi gave him a weak grin. "I can't make you stay at work if you're so determined to bring me lunch and take care of me. You're so stubborn."

"You are the second Mrs. Haydenshire to tell me that," Garrett harassed as he kissed the tip of her nose.

He couldn't quite wipe the smile off of his face as he shut down the Harley. *Not selling it. Definitely taking it with me to Kauai,* he decided as he allowed himself a few minutes to envision his beautiful bride, back to full health and clinging tightly to his chest as he found all of the island hideaways of their new home. He climbed off his bike and headed toward the admin building. It was distinctly odd to be back at Venton.

Dan caught up with him. "Hey, how's Kaimi?"

"Not great actually." Garrett decided marriage might be a little tougher than he'd originally planned, and it might be nice to be able to talk to Dan and Fi about everything going on.

"I took care of Kalakona. She wanted to make certain that I understood that you and Kaimi are now a representation of the state of Hawaii." Dan sneered with a vengeful eye roll.

"I'd nearly forgotten that. Thanks. I'm sorry. It was almost eight years ago. People need to move on."

"I pointed out that she was barely twenty when that picture was taken and that no one would have gone after a photo if it hadn't been for your dad. She backed down pretty quickly. Wait, what's wrong with Kaimi if it isn't the press?" Dan's detective skills kicked in.

"She's not feeling all that well. Actually, we went to the drugstore last night, and I stumbled upon something pretty interesting."

"Do you need to go home?"

"I'm gonna head home for lunch and check on her. I think she'll be okay. You know how Fi gets about once a month?" He didn't want to make Dan uncomfortable.

"Yeah. Does she get better in Kauai as well?" Dan didn't seem uncomfortable. He seemed genuinely intrigued.

"Apparently, she only gets sick like that when she's here." Garrett shrugged his confusion.

"The Kauaian rhythms are really strong. They're very healing. I think it affects Fi just as much when she can't feel them as when she can."

They made their way in the building. The meeting was in ten

minutes. Garrett followed Dan into the mentor's lounge and explained everything he'd learned the night before at the drugstore.

At the meeting, Governor Vindico made quick work of royally pissing off Katherine Bryant with the announcement of the mandatory paper.

# CHAPTER 49

# UNLIKELY SOURCES

Dan and Garrett filed back out into the sea of students in the corridor.

"Now, let's go find Pendergrath's little shit. I want to have a chat about him redecorating my house," Dan growled.

"You know, I can really tell this whole letting go of the vengeance thing and changing for Fionna has made a world of difference in you."

"Are you going to keep running your trap or are you gonna help me?"

"I'm there for you, honey." As they turned the corner, they were both shocked to find none other than Clarence Pendergrath waiting outside of Dan's office.

"Got more guts than his old man ever did," Garrett pointed out.

"Just the prick I was looking for," Dan bellowed ominously. Garrett wondered what the reprimand for calling one of the students a prick might be, but he refocused on Clarence.

"I didn't do that to your house, I swear. You have to believe me. I knew that's what you'd think," Clarence vowed adamantly.

"Then who did if it wasn't you?" Garrett challenged.

"I don't know, but it wasn't me. Probably one of those kids that are blackmailing everybody or something. There are a bunch of kids who pretty much hate you here, so..." Clarence shrugged.

"I'm wounded." Dan rolled his eyes.

"Just believe me. Look, I can help you," Clarence began negotiating. This struck Garrett as odd since they had no evidence with which to convict Clarence, and yet he was offering to help.

"You...want to help me?" Dan sounded shocked to the point of stupefaction.

"Maybe."

"Why?" Garrett edged in.

"Because..." Clarence glanced nervously up and down the hallway. "Look, could I just talk to you somewhere else?"

Dan flung open his office door. He seemed shocked he was even entertaining the idea that Pendergrath's kid could help them, but Garrett saw this as a way to get Kaimi to Kauai faster.

"Okay, so look, there is a bunch of shit going on here. I can't believe you haven't been shooting people or at least arresting people every freaking day. I mean, you're you."

"People tend to get a little upset if I start arresting their children," Dan sniped.

"Yeah, well, you need to do something."

Dan's eyes flashed in fury, and Garrett leapt between Clarence and Dan.

"Why don't you either say something to help us or shut your mouth before I have to wedge Dan's fist out of your face?" Garrett strongly suggested.

Clarence spared them an eye roll. "All I know is that last year kids were stealing tests out of the exam vault or whatever, and now, they're on some website, and the kids who were buying the tests are getting blackmailed, and somebody is getting rich, but none of that is me."

"Where did you spend Christmas, Clarence?" Dan leveled a glare as he asked what in Garrett's opinion was a very bizarre question. But when you'd been working with someone as long as Garrett and Dan had worked together, you knew you were about to get a major break.

Clarence bristled, and Garrett couldn't halt his slight grin. Dan Vindico was the best detective in the Realm. There was no doubt.

"What does that have to do with anything?"

"If you want me to listen to you, answer me." Dan never dropped Clarence's gaze.

"A friend's."

"A girlfriend's?" Dan leaned in.

"Yeah… so…"

"Are you in trouble, or is she?"

"I don't need you. I just thought I'd help." Clarence balked, and Garrett knew Dan had struck a vein.

"Okay." Dan shrugged. He gestured his hand toward the door. The challenge was implicit. Dan didn't need Clarence, or at least that was the firm image he was projecting.

"Fine." Clarence rolled his eyes. "I know what being in trouble is like. She hasn't done anything that bad, but her parents are going to flip if these people tell them stuff." He stumbled through his explanation of the problem.

Dan nodded. "I'll go ahead and assume your father, at the very least, taught you to be vague, so I take it you're not going to give me the goods on your girl. Why don't you tell me what you are willing to give up?"

"I only know this one kid who's doing the blackmail thing, but I think he's working for a bigger organization or something. Maybe his older brother, I don't know. But he's making a shit ton of money. He just bought a new Vette." Clarence threw his hand out toward the student parking lot. The disdain and jealousy in his voice gave Garrett and Dan a little more information.

Garrett pulled the blinds in Dan's office to the side to view a brand-new navy blue Corvette.

"Can I get a name?" Dan asked.

"Brodie Quentin."

Garrett's head turned to the side. Dan's shield pulsed, and Garrett was close enough to feel it.

"He was talking about your house, and he's definitely on the take. I mean, I should know that, right?" Clarence admitted wryly.

"Okay, I'll look into Mr. Quentin, and maybe we can get this all figured out before your girl gets herself into serious trouble, but if I were you, I'd encourage her to stop buying tests or using, whichever it is she's doing."

"She has stopped. But you'll figure this out soon, right?"

"Took me ten damn years to catch you and your old man, so that depends on how much help I get."

Garrett glanced discreetly at Clarence to see how that information might go over.

"If I find out other stuff, I'll tell you."

Dan shook his head in stunned disbelief. "Thank you, I guess. Why are you doing this?"

"I don't know." Clarence shrugged. "I got sent to see your dad before we got out for Christmas, and he was kinda nice. He said if I needed help, he thought you would help me, and Governor Haydenshire told me that you were the guy that had to sign the papers to get me out of that hellhole in New Mexico. I guess I owed you. And you know, that day, what your wife said…" he choked suddenly.

"What did Fionna say?" Dan demanded.

Garrett leaned in. He didn't like the idea that Fionna and Clarence had ever had a conversation any more than Dan did. This information was far more pressing than the fact that Garrett's father had lied to Clarence about who got him out of the work camp. He wanted Clarence to look up to Dan instead of his old man if that would ever be possible.

Clarence clammed up before their eyes. "I don't know. You're married to her. Ask her." He flung open the office door and joined the other students in the hallway.

# CHAPTER 50

# ARIAL'S TALE

Dan shook his head as the door closed. "Who the hell thought I should work with teenagers?!"

Garrett had to laugh at that. "How do we figure out who Pendergrath Jr. is boning?"

"Like this." Dan grabbed his laptop bag, a few papers, and stalked into the corridor. Garrett followed.

"Hey, Mentor Vindico," rang from a young lady who had her hand wrapped up in a guy's. They both looked pleased to be together.

"Hey Arial, could you help me out with something?" Dan asked with an overly kind smile.

"Oh, of course." Arial was eager. She halted in her tracks.

"Can you tell me who Clarence Pendergrath is dating?"

"Yes! He went out with Libby Ellington once right after he moved here, but lately he's gotten serious with Kristen Cinders. I think he spent the holidays with her. She and Libby are like good friends, but I don't think there's any bad blood between them. You know like sometimes there is if you date a guy and then your friend dates him. I mean not with Chancey and me because we're never ever ever breaking up. Have you seen our heart tattoo? It's so sweet and it's like we can never be broken.

"I don't know Kristen that well. She just moved here last year when her parents split up. Her mom remarried. I think she was cheating." Arial whispered the last sentence but still didn't draw a breath. "Anyway, I heard Meira Chenowith tell Vivian that Kristen is really like liking loving but more loving than liking Clarence. I think his name is kinda geeky, but he has that bad boy vibe going on so I guess it balances out kinda. Anyway, Vivian told Cynthia Rycroft and Cynthia told Kimberly Masters that Clarence really likes Kristen too, and they're making out in the hallways like all the time. Chancey and I used to do that too until I got one too many detentions, and my dad said we had to stop. But do you know who his dad was? I mean I guess you obviously know who he was, but he was like a really bad guy, so like how does Kristin know if Clarence is gonna be like a bad good guy or a bad bad guy, you know?"

Garrett's eyes goggled as he stared bewilderedly at Arial.

She turned on him. "Oh, you're Garrett, right? I was like such amazing good friends with Logan and Emily. You and Logan kind of look alike. They were so cute together. I really couldn't believe she forgot to invite me to their wedding."

"Uh, Logan is my brother, and Emily is married to Rainer Lawson."

"Oh right, right, right, well you know, they were like always together. Anyway, I totally kind of think that Clarence is gonna ask Kristen to go to the Snowdrop ball, and a bunch of people are gonna rent chalets down in Chesley Creek, and I heard that they might go if Kristen's dad will let her. I don't really think she's dated a lot since she moved here, so he might be her first. Do you think he's her first? I wonder if he is. That might be sweet. Chesley Creek is so romantic. Chancey and I went there after the Valentine ball last year, and it was so romantic. We were in one of the hot tubs and it was like so hot, and there were like only ten maybe more other people in there." Arial swooned.

Dan was rubbing his temples. "Thank you for telling me *all* of that."

"Oh, no problem. I love telling people stuff."

"No joke," Garrett coughed over his own words.

Dan tried not to laugh. "Hey, show Deputy Haydenshire the tats you got. He'd like that."

"Okay," Arial squealed. Chance supplied his inner arm, and Arial placed her arm beside his to complete the stupidest tattoo Garrett had ever seen. He managed a nod as he tried to bite back his smirk.

"Nice."

"Thanks, we're just like, so one, we had to do it. You know?"

"Of course."

"We gotta get to class my Ari-angel," Chance cooed, and Garrett thought he was going to vomit.

"Awww," Arial swooned and kissed Chance's nose before they headed down the hall.

"Are we certain she's not high?" Garrett gasped. "Please, please tell me she is not in any of the classes I'm teaching."

"Arial is in the 3rd period History of Defense and Chancey," Dan rolled his eyes, "is in my Senior Defense class on Wednesdays and Fridays."

"Is Chance allowed to speak in class or does she tag along and talk for him there as well? Maybe my first lesson as a guest mentor should be how to tell your girlfriend to shut the fuck up."

Dan was still laughing as he pointed to his first period classroom. "I'm sure you tell Kaimi to shut up all the time."

"My wife hasn't said that many words in her entire life."

"Just wait until Arial starts telling people Logan and Emily are married."

# CHAPTER 51

# PUZZLE PIECES

Dan released his third period class ten minutes before the bell rang.

"You know, I'm still incredibly pissed about what that little prick did to my children's home. And I'm sick to death of this job, so let's have a little fun." He headed toward the gym.

Garrett had just spent three class periods trying to make his lesson plans last longer than five minutes since no one would talk, so he was eager to see what Dan had in mind.

Dan extracted a metal baseball bat from one of the equipment rooms.

"Uh man, I get that you're ready to get this done and get our lives going in Kauai, but I'm pretty sure you can't smash his skull in."

"Trust me, Haydenshire," was his only response as he headed down the corridor. They moved through the cafeteria as most everyone was finding a seat for lunch.

"He wants to fuck up my house then I will happily teach him a lesson about other people's property. He just acquired himself a new Corvette." Dan sneered loudly as they passed by a table of guys. Garrett assumed one of them was Brodie Quentin.

Dan shoved the exit doors on the other side of the large room open. They shuddered against the brick of the building. Dan spun and headed to the student parking lot.

Garrett chuckled as he followed Dan in his infuriated march. "Five, four, three, two..."

"Mentor Vindico," rang frantically from behind them.

Dan narrowed his eyes as he turned on Brodie Quentin.

It was like playing cops and robbers quite literally with children. Children that knew just enough to get themselves in more trouble than they could see their way out of. They didn't seem to understand all of the intricate pieces to the puzzle. They only understood the parts they were participating in.

Garrett crossed his arms and showed off his massive biceps as the polo shirt he'd worn edged upward.

"Uh...uh, where are you going?" Brodie was on the brink of panic.

Dan shrugged. "It was my understanding that you and a few of your friends decided you might like to vandalize my home, the home where I live with my wife and my daughters. My sweet, innocent little girls. So, my grandpa used to say, let the punishment fit the crime." Dan spun the bat and then slammed it against his other hand.

"I didn't do that. I was just talking. That's my brother's car."

"Then who did?" Dan demanded.

"I'm not sure," Brodie lied. "I mean that Pendergrath kid hates you, right? You killed his old man or whatever?"

"Wasn't Clarence. Try again," Dan stated confidently.

"All I know is it wasn't me."

Dan tossed the bat to the side. It clattered ominously to the concrete as he jerked Brodie forward by the scruff of his collar.

"Let me tell you something. I know you had something to do with what happened to my home, so beware. I don't know when or where, but I will eventually have my say, and when that day comes, you will be going to jail for felony vandalism. So, if someone else helped you do this or if there are other things you might like to come clean about, now would be the time," he snarled in his face.

He almost had him. Fear flashed in Brodie's eyes but resolve and defiance took over.

"You can't arrest me. You aren't even a cop anymore." He

began wiggling, and Dan released his collar. "Just leave me alone," he demanded as he turned and sprinted back into the school.

Dan grinned. "We're at least rounding first now. We might even be heading to second."

"Yeah, I prefer to slide quickly into third and then take it on home," Garrett huffed as he watched Brodie disappear back into the lunchroom.

Garrett's heart pricked as he opened the apartment door that afternoon and stepped inside. He set the Chinese takeout on the table and moved to the couch.

"Hey baby, how are you feeling?" He knelt down and kissed Kaimi's head. She grinned up at him.

"A little better. Duke needs to go out," she remembered suddenly.

"Come on boy," Garrett urged.

When they returned, Garrett handed Kaimi her requested meal and settled beside her.

"Are you sure your stomach is up to Chinese?"

Her sweet giggle lit his soul as she nodded. "I feel better. I promise. I'm just really tired."

"Then how about we inhale some fried rice and then I'll put you to bed."

"First, tell me how your day went? Did students flirt with you to get you to give them a better grade? Or did you just walk around being macho all day?" She broke out in a fit of giggles.

"Excuse me, Mrs. Haydenshire, when have I ever been macho?" Garrett scoffed just to hear more of her laughter.

"Um, all day every day."

"Dan did go after a kid's car with a bat."

"What?!" Kaimi gasped.

"Yeah, to say Dan's done with Venton would be a serious understatement. However, I've worked up there one day and I couldn't agree more."

Kaimi leaned up to kiss Garrett's cheek. "I missed you," she confessed.

"I missed you too." Garrett wrapped his arm over her and continued to eat. "You do look like you're feeling better."

"I promise I am. I slept a lot today, and by tomorrow night, it should be gone," she urged hopefully.

# CHAPTER 52

# AN EQUAL AND OPPOSITE REACTION

## ~DAN VINDICO~

Dan raced inside the house and apologized. "I'm sorry."

Fionna was smiling politely, but irritation pulsed in her rhythms. He was supposed to have been home an hour earlier to help get the girls ready to go out for the evening.

It was Tuesday night, and Patrick was hosting an open house from four until seven for them. He'd lined up several potential buyers. The market was down and they were expecting it to take months to sell. If somehow it sold quickly, they'd decided to rent an Airbnb until summer.

Fionna wanted Dan home early so she could keep the house looking immaculate. Dan had gotten caught up digging through Brodie Quentin's permanent files. After that, he'd leapt into Libby Ellington's and then Kristen Cinders's. He would have been thirty minutes earlier, but his father had needed help with yet another Venton financial issue. It seemed that some of the tracers that were being tagged on the upcoming paychecks weren't working properly.

"We have to get out of here," Fionna spoke through her teeth.

"I'm sorry." Dan scooped Halia out of her mother's arms and gathered the contents for her diaper bag off the kitchen table and stowed them in the bag in one quick move.

"My room is very beautiful," Aida announced as she raced down the steps. "I cleaned it up and Halia's."

"Thank you, baby." Dan kissed the top of her head as he moved to answer the front door to let Patrick inside.

Patrick looked confused as he stood before Dan right beside Fred and Betty Scheckles. "I guess these would be your first potential customers?"

"No, these would be our neighbors. Why on earth would you need to see our home, Fred?"

"Well, you know…property values, and we were thinking maybe of selling ours and moving across the street." Fred seemed to come up with his excuse as he spoke.

Patrick gave Dan a discreet eye roll. "We'll take a very abbreviated glance," he assured.

"I think if any of our neighbors feel the need to look in our home, they can stay on the ground floor here. Our bedrooms will only be shown to people with pre-approved loans," Dan commanded.

"I'll do my best." Patrick looked almost as relieved as Fionna.

Fionna grabbed Aida's backpack and took her hand.

"How's Lucy and little Alex?" she asked before they headed out the door.

"Oh Lucy's doing pretty well. She's exhausted. Does Halia sleep…ever?"

"When all of the planets align," Dan offered with a slight chuckle.

"It does get better," Fionna assured. Her demeanor softened. Patrick nodded though he still looked disheartened and exhausted himself.

"Mom was going to come over and help, but Henry came down with a stomach virus and Keaton was drinking after him, so she's just waiting on him to get sick and hoping Abby doesn't get it. She's scared to be around Alex," Patrick lamented.

"I'm sorry," Fionna fretted. Dan knew she was trying to come up with a way to help.

"Thanks. I'm heading back home as soon as I finish here. I think I'm going to take off for a couple of weeks. We'll get it figured out. He has to sleep eventually, right?"

"Sure. Go with that," Dan agreed.

Before anyone could stop them, the Scheckles were poking around the kitchen. Fionna clenched her jaw and stomped out the front door, dragging Aida in her wake.

They took the girls to a special hands-on event at the National Museum that promised to have interactive displays for infants and elementary-aged children. After two hours of that, Dan drove his family to Big Buns for dinner, and Fionna was smiling by the time she was stealing a sip of his mocha milkshake.

"And then Mrs. Powell said I get to go to the kindergarten room tomorrow and read them a story. And I said that maybe I could read *The Paper Bag Princess,* and then Mrs. Powell said that I could!" Aida's delight filled Dan's heart.

"Wow, baby. I'm so proud of you," Dan gushed.

"Thank you!" She wiggled in her seat, unable to contain her excitement. "And then Mrs. Powell sent a note to Mommy, that Mommy let me read after I asked permission, that said that maybe Mommy could bring Halia to my class on Friday. I hope she doesn't smell bad."

Dan and Fionna both bit their lips to keep from chuckling.

"I'll bring her lots of clean diapers and clothes," Fionna assured her.

Halia certainly never smelled bad for any length of time, but Aida had been appalled when Halia's diaper had leaked all over her car seat. She hadn't quite recovered from the experience.

Dan glanced at his watch and smiled. He was ready to head home, and he wanted to discuss everything he and Garrett had learned in the last week at Venton with Fionna.

He snapped Halia's car seat in the Mercedes, and after Aida was buckled, he drove home slowly. It was still a few minutes before seven.

Fionna laced her fingers through Dan's as he drove. Fear timed in her rhythms. They came in rapid successions of panic. Dan's brow furrowed. "What's wrong?" he mouthed to keep Aida from worrying.

Fionna shook her head. "I don't know," she whispered. "But it's bad."

He released her hand as his cell phone buzzed in his pocket. His brow furrowed as he glanced at the screen and read Blocked. "Vindico…"

"Mentor Vindico. You need to check your email. Send the money to the address I'll text to your phone in five minutes."

"Who the hell is this?" Dan demanded but the call ended as abruptly as it had begun.

"Daddy, remember you're not supposed to say that word," Aida fussed.

Dan threw the car into park and forced himself to remember to get Halia out of the car instead of leaving both girls for Fionna to manage before he raced into the house.

"Dan, who was that?" Fionna was on the verge of panic as they rushed into the house.

"You had quite a few potential buyers come through. Took me an hour to get rid of your neighbors, but we got several leads." Patrick glanced nervously at Dan who'd not yet spoken.

"Thanks, Patrick. Do you need anything else from us?" Fionna asked kindly though her eyes were trained on Dan. He'd opened his laptop case and was turning it on while rocking Halia's car seat with his foot. He was hoping to pacify her just long enough to figure out what was going on before she wanted another bottle.

"No, I'll get back to you when we have a showing." Patrick waved. "See you later, Dan.

"Yeah, thanks," Dan managed as he loaded his email program.

His eyes goggled as his blood ran ice-cold. There, in an encrypted message, were several photographs and a video. His head shook defiantly as he willed the photographs to be anyone or anything else. They'd been on his phone. He'd forgotten. There were photos of Fionna blowing him kisses, flashing him, of her ample cleavage and her luscious ass, pictures of her in nothing but heels, numerous shots of her in lingerie that she'd sent him from lingerie stores in Paris, and a video they'd made in Kauai of her on all fours while Dan was thrusting inside of her. Unless someone could identify his dick, Fionna was the only one recognizable in those shots, since Dan had

330

been the one holding the phone. Frenzied rage surged through his shield. It set inside his muscles of its own accord.

Aida moved toward him. He was certain she felt his fury and wanted to soothe him. Dan slammed the laptop shut as his cell phone gave an ominous chirp from his pocket.

> Send $250,000 to P.O. Box 4027 M St. SW Washington DC, 20003 by January 31 or these go viral.

# ABOUT THE AUTHOR

J.E. Neal (aka Jillian) vastly prefers coffee to tea, guac to salsa, the beach over anywhere else, and the world inside her head over the one outside her front door. She also loves not having to choose.

Driven by the question 'what if,' J.E. Neal's world began to manifest. What if there were people with powers the rest of us couldn't see? What if the energy of our world could be summoned and used at their will? Characters with these amazing abilities took shape in her mind. She created—and continues to create—an endless number of stories full of delicious escape from our reality where emotions are visible, desire is palpable, and danger is universal.

Learn more about J.E. Neal at JillianNeal.com

facebook.com/jilliannealauthor
twitter.com/JillianNeal_
instagram.com/jilliannealauthor

# ALSO BY J.E. NEAL

## TANGLE OF MAGIC

Tangle of Magic Boxed Set (Books 1-6)

Tangle of Lies (Book 1)

Tangle of Chaos (Book 2)

Tangle of Desires (Book 3)

Tangle of Fates (Book 4)

Tangle of Trust (Book 5)

Tangle of Ruin (Book 6)

## ENERGY OF MAGIC

Shield and Shattered Cages (Book 1)

Shield and Faltered Steps (Book 2)

Shield and Splintered Oaths (Book 3)

Shield and Humbled Crown (Book 4)

Shield and Vile Serpents (Book 5)

Shield and Coveted Splendor (Book 6)

Shield and Guarded Shadow (Book 7)

Shield and Worthy Sinner (Book 8)

Shield and Sacrificial Heirs (Book 9)

www.ingramcontent.com/pod-product-compliance
Lightning Source LLC
Chambersburg PA
CBHW060747190726
48285CB00002B/328